This Day

Also by Blanka Lipińska

365 Days

An Imprint of Simon & Schuster, Inc.
1230 Avenue of the Americas
New York, NY 10020

This book is a work of fiction. Any references to historical events, real people, or real places are used fictitiously. Other names, characters, places, and events are products of the author's imagination, and any resemblance to actual events or places or persons, living or dead, is entirely coincidental.

Originally published in Poland in 2018 by Wydawnictwo Edipresse Polska as *Ten dzień*

First Emily Bestler Books/Atria Paperback edition December 2021

EMILY BESTLER BOOKS / ATRIA PAPERBACKS and colophon are trademarks of Simon & Schuster, Inc.

For information about special discounts for bulk purchases, please contact Simon & Schuster Special Sales at 1-866-506-1949 or business@simonandschuster.com.

The Simon & Schuster Speakers Bureau can bring authors to your live event. For more information or to book an event, contact the Simon & Schuster Speakers Bureau at 1-866-248-3049 or visit our website at www.simonspeakers.com.

Interior design by Erika R. Genova

Manufactured in the United States of America

1 3 5 7 9 10 8 6 4 2

ISBN 978-1-9821-7438-5
ISBN 978-1-9821-7439-2 (ebook)

This Day

A NOVEL

By Blanka Lipińska
Translated by Filip Sporczyk

EMILY BESTLER BOOKS

ATRIA

New York • London • Toronto • Sydney • New Delhi

This Day

PROLOGUE

The yacht moored in the port of Fiumicino. My lady's body double was still on deck. The woman's task was simple—she was supposed to stick around.

"Get Laura in a car and send her my way," I said as soon as Domenico picked up the phone. He was in Rome.

"Thank God," he sighed. "She was starting to get on my nerves." I heard him closing a door. "She's been asking about you."

"Don't come with her," I said, ignoring his words.

"We'll meet in Venice. Get some rest."

"You won't even ask what she said?" Domenico wasn't about to let it go. I could hear the amusement in his voice.

"Am I supposed to?" I asked sternly, though deep inside I was dying to learn what they'd been talking about.

"She misses you." My stomach knotted. "At least, that's what I think."

"Make sure she's on her way."

I hung up and looked out to the sea.

That woman was making me panic. Again. The feeling was too alien to figure out its root. I couldn't keep it in check.

◇◇◇◇◇◇◇◇◇◇◇

I dismissed the girl who was supposed to stand in for Laura, ordering her to keep close by. There was no telling if I'd need her again. If Matos's information was accurate, after having his hands shot through, Flavio returned to the island. So far all was quiet. As if the Nostro debacle hadn't happened. The fragmentary intel I was getting was not enough, so I sent my men to scrounge up more data. They confirmed Matos's version.

During lunch, I had a conference call with people from the US. I wanted to make sure they'd be there at the Venice film festival. What I needed was to meet them eye to eye. There were firearms to buy if I was to continue my dealings in the Middle East, and that required my presence.

"Don Torricelli?" It was Fabio, sticking his head in through the door. I raised a hand before hanging up. "Miss Biel is on board."

"Let's take off, then," I said, getting to my feet.

I took the stairs to the top deck and glanced about. There she was. My woman, dressed like a teenager. My fists clenched. So did my jaw. Revealing shorts and a skimpy blouse were no clothes for a Sicilian mob boss's girlfriend.

"What the hell are you wearing this time? You look like . . ." I stopped, noticing the half-empty bottle of champagne.

She spun around and slammed into me, bouncing off my torso and falling to the couch. *Drunk again*, I thought.

"I look however I want. It's none of your business," she spluttered, waving an arm. The clumsy gesture elicited a smile from me. "You left me without a word, and you keep treating me like a doll you play with whenever you feel like it." She shot out her hand and aimed a finger at me, simultaneously trying to get up again. "Well, the doll's playing solo today."

She lurched forward, stumbled, and lost a shoe.

"Laura!" I said with a laugh, unable to keep the mirth away anymore. "Goddamn it, Laura!" My laughter quickly turned into a growl as I saw her veering dangerously close to the deck of the yacht. I launched myself after her with a shout.

"Stop!"

Either she couldn't hear me, or she chose not to listen. Suddenly, she slipped. The bottle fell from her hand and a moment later, Laura bumped into the railing and tumbled down into the sea.

"Oh, fuck no . . ." I started running. I kicked my shoes off and threw myself after her, diving into the water. We were lucky the *Titan* was at its lowest speed, and Laura fell to the starboard instead of back where the engines were. A moment later, she was in my arms.

Fortunately, Fabio saw the entire thing and immediately stopped the boat. He threw me a lifeline and yanked us both back to the yacht. Laura wasn't breathing.

Frantically, I started giving her CPR. All the pressing and breathing into her mouth wasn't doing any good.

"Breathe, goddamn you!"

I was losing her. I kept pressing her chest harder and breathing the air into her lungs faster and faster.

"Breathe!" I called out in English, irrationally thinking that maybe she'd do as I asked if she heard a language she understood. Suddenly, she gasped for air and threw up.

I stroked her cheek, staring into her half-conscious eyes as they tried to focus on my face. I took Laura in my arms, picked her up, and headed toward our cabin.

"Should I call a doctor?" Fabio asked.

"Yes, send a helicopter."

I had to take Laura below deck and make sure she was all right. I put her down on the bed, keeping my eyes fixed on her face, searching for something that would tell me she was okay.

"What happened?" she whispered.

I nearly fainted. My head throbbed, and my heart was pounding like crazy. I knelt by the bed, trying to calm my nerves down.

"You fell from the deck. Thank God we weren't going faster and that you fell to the side of the boat. Still, you nearly drowned. Goddamn it, Laura, I feel like killing you myself now. At the same time, I'm so happy you're alive."

I dropped my head, clenching my jaw. That overwhelming headache was making it impossible to think clearly.

Laura's delicate fingers touched my cheek, lifting my face so I had to look her in the eyes.

"You saved me?"

"You were lucky I was close. I don't even want to think what would have happened otherwise. Why are you being so stubborn? Why don't you listen to me?" The fear I experienced as I said this was something completely new to me. I had never felt this way before about anyone.

"I'd like to take a shower now," she said.

I nearly burst out laughing then. She had nearly died, and the only thing she could think of was the salt water on her skin. I couldn't believe it. I was drained and didn't feel like fighting. The only thing that counted was her being close by, so I could smother her with kisses and protect her from the entire world. I couldn't conceive what would have happened if the boat had been sailing at a higher speed . . .

Automatically, I offered to wash her, and she didn't protest, so I went to the bathroom to turn the tap on, before walking back to the room to help her undress. I was focused and wasn't really thinking about what I was about to see. It was only after a longer while that I realized there she was, naked, lying on the bed. With a jolt of surprise I learned that it wasn't making me feel like I had thought it would. The only thing that counted was that she was alive.

I picked up Laura, and went to the shower. The water was hot. As Laura's back rested against my chest, I pressed my face into her hair. I was angry, scared . . . and more than a little grateful. There was no need to talk, and I definitely didn't want to fight now. I just basked in her presence. Unaware of my thoughts, she put her cheek against my skin. Laura had no idea that everything that had happened over the last few days, happened because of her. And meanwhile, it dawned on me that everything was about to change now. Business would grow difficult because my enemies had already learned about my weak spot—the petite woman I was holding now. I wasn't ready and nothing could make me ready for what the future had in store.

Slowly, silently, I washed her body. I didn't get an erection, which seemed to surprise her. I didn't even try to touch her in any way that she might have interpreted as erotic.

Then I dried her with a towel and laid her on the bed, planting a delicate kiss on her forehead. Before my lips parted with her skin, Laura was already asleep. I checked her pulse, suddenly afraid she had fallen unconscious again. Luckily, it was steady. For a while, I just stood there, watching her. Then I heard the sound of a helicopter approaching. For an instant, I was puzzled, but then remembered we were still relatively close to the shoreline.

◇◇◇◇◇◇◇◇◇◇◇

Having read Laura's medical files, the doctor said her life wasn't in any immediate danger. I thanked him and returned to my cabin.

The night was warm and quiet. And quiet was what I needed the most right now. I snorted a line and helped myself to a glass of my favorite liquor before stepping into a steaming-hot Jacuzzi. Then, I sent away all staff, ordering them to stay out of sight, and relaxed, delighting in my solitude. I didn't think about anything in particular. Anything apart from the calm around me and, at least seemingly, inside me. A couple of minutes must have passed before I saw something in the darkness. It was Laura, standing still in her white bathrobe, glancing around the deck. That was pleasing. If she was awake, she must be feeling better.

"Sleep well?" I asked. The sound of my voice made her startle. "I can see you're feeling better. Care to join me?"

She took a moment to think, keeping her eyes fixed on me. It didn't look like she was trying to decide what to do. She knew the bathrobe would slip and hit the floor.

Naked, she sat across from me. I drank in the view, taking a sip of my cocktail. For a while, I said nothing, just staring at her beautiful—if a bit tired—face. Her hair was in disarray, and her lips were slightly swollen. Suddenly, she moved, surprising me. She sat on my knees and wrapped her arms around me. My prick reacted instantaneously.

As her teeth bit into my lower lip, I lost it. She started moving, rubbing her clit against me, pressing against my skin. I had no idea where this was going, but I wasn't in the mood for her games. Not today. Not after I had nearly lost her.

Her tongue slid into my mouth, and on instinct, I grabbed her ass, squeezing tight.

"I've missed you," she whispered.

That short utterance staggered me. My whole body went rigid. I had no idea why I was reacting this way. I pulled away to look at her face. She was serious. I couldn't let her sense my weakness. I wasn't ready to open up to her yet, especially about the fact that I didn't know what was happening to me.

"Is that how you display your longing? Because if this is your way of saying thank you for saving your life, baby girl, I can't accept it. I won't do it with you until you're absolutely sure you want it."

I wanted her to pull away. I needed the feeling of discomfort to vanish. She sent me a look full of reproach, but the feeling inside me didn't dissipate. It was only getting stronger. *What the fuck is happening?* I thought, as she jumped out of the Jacuzzi and ran across the deck, grabbing the bathrobe on her way.

"The hell are you doing, you fuckwit?" I growled at myself, getting up. "You're getting what you wanted from the start, and you push her away?" I kept muttering in my mother tongue, following Laura's wet tracks.

My heart was pounding, because deep down I knew what would happen when I found her. I noticed her slipping into my cabin and smiled. This was no accident. I went inside and saw her standing with her back turned to me, trying to find the light switch. Suddenly, the lights went on and I saw her spin around, startled. I slammed the door, paralyzing her with the loud *bang*. She knew it was me. I killed the light and approached her, untying her bathrobe with one swift pull, letting it slip to the floor. I waited patiently. I needed to be sure of what I was doing, even though for the first time in my life, I had no idea. I started to kiss her, and she kissed me back. Passionately.

I took her in my arms, and carried her to bed. She lay in front of me, the pale light of the lamp illuminating her perfect body. I was waiting for a sign.

And then, there it was: she lifted her arms, crossing them behind her head, and smiled at me, as if inviting me to get inside her.

"If we do it now, I won't be able to stop. You know that, right? If we cross this line, I'll fuck you whether you like it or not."

"So fuck me."

She sat up, her big eyes pinning me in place.

"You're mine now, and I'll keep you forever," I growled in Italian, looming a few inches above her.

Her eyes darkened. Lust was about to rip this lithe body apart. Her hands clasped my buttocks, and she pulled me closer.

I smiled. She couldn't wait to taste me.

"Put your hands on my head. And punish me."

Her words took my breath away. The woman who was supposed to become the mother of my children was acting like a whore. I couldn't believe she wanted to give herself to me like that. I was gleeful, but at the same time I felt fear. It was terrifying just how perfect she was.

"Are you asking me to treat you like a whore? Is this what you want?"

"Yes, don Massimo."

Her quiet words and her submissiveness woke the demon in me. I felt all the muscles in my body tense. I was calm, though. In control. When she asked me to just be myself, all the unnecessary emotions just went away. Slowly but surely I pushed myself into her mouth and came nearly at the same instant as her eyes found mine. I felt my cock pressing against the wall of her throat, but I went even deeper, feeling that pressure I loved so much. I was ecstatic. And as Laura dealt with the entire length of my prick, I felt proud of her. My hips started thrusting slightly, just to see how much she'd take. She was incredible. She took it all.

"If at any point you stop enjoying it, tell me. Just make sure I know you're not teasing me," I said.

There was no resistance on her part. She was giving herself to me entirely.

"Same goes for you," she replied, pulling away for a second.

As her lips closed around my cock again, she picked up the pace. I knew she was playing with me and enjoying it. She was lascivious, trying to prove something to me. I fucked her throat, and she wanted more. The thought brought me to the very edge of ecstasy. I did my best to slow her down, but to no avail.

The orgasm crashed like a wave all over me. I didn't want it. Not now, not so fast. I pushed her away, heaving and trying to stem the tide of cum. Laura smiled triumphantly. That was it. I slammed her into the bed and rolled her to her belly. I couldn't watch. Not during our first time. I didn't want to come again so quickly, and I knew that was what was going to happen if I saw the rapture on her face.

I slipped two fingers inside her and realized with satisfaction that she was dripping wet. Laura moaned and writhed beneath me, and I went out of my mind again. I grabbed my cock and slowly slid it into her tight snatch. She was hot, wet, and all mine. I could feel each inch of her sex-starved pussy. I pushed myself all the way in and clung to her, freezing in place. I wanted to savor the moment. I pulled out and then pushed myself inside again, harder. My Lady moaned louder, growing impatient. She wanted me to fuck her. She needed to feel it hard and fast. My hips stroked and started pounding. I fucked her as hard as I was able, and still she wanted more. She screamed, only to lose her breath an instant later. I slowed down to lift her hips, intending to see my trophy in all its glory. As her back arched, I saw the dark hole and couldn't help myself. I licked my thumb and started trailing it around her back entrance.

"Don Massimo?" she moaned, suddenly afraid, but didn't move an inch away.

I laughed.

"Don't be afraid, baby girl. We're going to get there, but not tonight."

She didn't resist, and I felt glad she couldn't see the wide grin on my face. My Lady liked anal. She really was perfect.

I took a deep breath and grabbed her hips, shoving my cock deep inside her cunt. And then again, and again. I fucked her hard and without mercy. Leaning down, I started to fondle her clit, and after a moment I felt her clamp around my dick. She pushed her face into the pillow, screaming something I didn't understand, and I charged in even harder, feeling her climax. I couldn't stand not seeing her face after all. I needed to see her orgasm. I wanted to see the relief in her eyes. I turned her over and clung to her, wrapping my arms around her body, fucking her like a whore again. Then I felt her spasm rhythmically. Her eyes glazed over. Her lips parted, but no sound came out. She climaxed for a long while, nearly crushing my dick with her pussy. Suddenly, her body went limp, and she fell onto the mattress. I slowed down, allowing my hips to keep gently stroking. I reached for her wrists. She was exhausted. I pinned her arms above her head. She was going to resist what I was going to do now.

"Come on my belly. I want to see it," she rasped, half-conscious.

"No," I replied with a smile and started to fuck her again.

I exploded.

I could feel the waves of cum flood into her.

This was the perfect day to conceive a baby. It was as if the whole universe wanted her to get pregnant. She fought me, trying to push me away, but was too weak to overcome my strength. A while later I collapsed on her, sweaty and hot.

"Massimo, what the hell are you doing?" she cried. "You know I don't use pills!"

She kept trying to free herself from my clutches, and I couldn't hide my satisfaction.

"You're right—you can't trust those pills. But you have a contraceptive implant. See?" I aimed a finger at her arm.

The tracker I had ordered implanted inside her was very similar in size to the contraceptive implant like the one Anna had. That's why I knew she'd fall for it.

"When you were asleep that first night, I ordered it implanted. I didn't want to risk anything. It'll work for three years, but you can remove it after the first one." I couldn't stop smiling at the thought that my son might start growing inside her after that night.

"Will you get off me?" she sputtered angrily.

I chose to ignore her.

"Unfortunately, I won't be able to do it for a while yet. It would be hard to fuck you from a distance." I flicked a strand of hair from her forehead.

"When I saw your face for the first time, I didn't desire you. I was terrified by that vision. With time, when your portraits were all around my house, I began to notice the details of your soul.

"You have no idea how perfectly they reflect the real you. You and I are so alike, Laura."

If I was even able to love, this was the moment I fell in love with the woman lying beneath me on the bed. I looked at her, feeling something changing inside me.

"That first night I stayed beside you and watched you until morning. I could feel your scent, the heat of your body. You were alive. Real. And you were right there, next to me. Later that day, I couldn't leave you. I felt an irrational fear that you wouldn't be there when I returned."

I had no idea why I was saying all that, but I just felt the need for her to know everything about me. There was fear in my voice.

On the one hand I wanted her to fear me, but on the other, I needed her to know the truth.

CHAPTER
one

It grew quiet, and I closed my eyes, realizing what I'd just said. It was another one of those times my mind only wanted to think something, but mistakenly ordered my mouth to voice the thought.

"Say that again," he said calmly, raising my chin.

I looked at him and felt my eyes welling with tears.

"I'm pregnant, Massimo. We're going to have a baby."

The Man in Black fixed me with a wide-eyed stare before collapsing to the ground and kneeling before me. He lifted my shirt and planted a soft kiss on my belly, muttering something in Italian. I had no idea what was happening, but as I took his face in my hands, I felt tears running down his cheeks. That strong, imperious, dangerous man was kneeling before me and crying. I couldn't stop myself and felt tears streaking down my face, too. We froze for a long while, allowing ourselves to take in the new circumstances.

The Man in Black rose from his knees and kissed me passionately on the lips.

"I'll buy you a tank," he said. "And if that's not enough, I'll dig a bunker myself. I promise you I'll protect the two of you, even if I'll have to pay with my own life."

He said "you two," I thought, and broke down again.

"Hey, baby girl, it's all right." I wiped away the tears with the hem of my sleeve.

"Those are tears of joy," I said, making my way to the bathroom. "I'll just be a minute."

When I returned, Massimo was sitting on the bed with nothing but his boxers on. Then he got up and crossed the distance between us to plant a kiss on my forehead.

"I'll take a shower. Don't go anywhere."

I lay down, snuggling against the pillow and analyzing what had happened. I hadn't been aware the Man in Black was even capable of crying, least of all out of joy. A few minutes later, the door to the bathroom opened and he appeared in the doorway, naked and dripping with water. Slowly, he made his way to the bed, allowing me to drink in the sight of him before lying down next to me.

"When did you find out?" he asked.

"On Monday, when I got my blood tested."

"Why didn't you tell me before?"

"I didn't want to tell you before your trip. Besides, I needed to come to terms with it myself."

"Does Olga know?"

"Yes. And your brother, too."

Massimo frowned and rolled to his back.

"Why didn't you tell me Domenico and you were family?" I asked.

He took a moment to think, biting on his lip.

"I wanted you to have a friend. Someone close, who you'd

trust. If you knew he was my brother, you would have acted differently. Domenico knows how valuable you are to me. I wouldn't have anyone else taking care of you when I was gone."

It made sense, I thought. I wasn't mad and didn't hold anything against him.

"So . . . are we calling off the wedding?" I asked, looking him in the eyes.

Massimo rolled to his side and stuck to me with the entire length of his body.

"You're joking, right? The child needs to have a full family. And a family is three people. Remember?" He started to kiss me. Gently. "What did the doctor say? Did you ask him if we can . . ."

I laughed and slid my tongue into his mouth. He moaned and crushed my lips in a passionate kiss.

"Yeah . . . I'll take it as a yes," he rasped, pulling away from me. "I'll be gentle. I promise."

He reached out to the nightstand and turned off the TV, plunging the room into complete darkness. His hand shot out and snatched the sheets from me, tossing them to the ground, before it slid beneath my blouse and pulled it off. Massimo's hands explored my body, gently touching my face before trailing down and clamping onto my breasts and squeezing. His head followed his hands, as he pinched my nipple between his teeth and sucked. A strange feeling overcame me—a kind of pure ecstasy that I'd never felt before when someone did that. Massimo didn't rush it. He took his time, savoring the different areas of my body. His lips flew from one nipple to the other, only to venture back to my face, kissing me passionately on the mouth. I could feel his cock swelling slowly as it rubbed against me with each motion of his body. A while later I started growing impatient. Horny and starved of his attentions, I took over the initiative. I wanted to have him.

Right now. I lifted myself a fraction, but the Man in Black predicted my movement and pinned my shoulders to the bed.

"Come to me," I whispered, squirming beneath him.

I felt, rather than saw, his triumphant smirk. He knew how much I wanted him.

"I'm only just beginning, baby girl."

Massimo's lips trailed slowly down my skin, starting with the neck, passing my breasts and my tummy to finally end up where they should have been from the very beginning. He kissed and licked me through the thin lace of my thong, teasing my throbbing clit, before slowly pulling the underwear down my legs and tossing it aside.

I spread my legs, knowing what was coming. My hips started to undulate in the silk sheets, delicately and steadily. I felt his breath between my legs, and a wave of lust crashed over me. Massimo slowly slid his tongue inside me and moaned.

"You're so wet, Laura . . ." he breathed. "I don't know if it's the pregnancy or if you've just missed me."

"Shut up, Massimo," I replied, pressing his head against my wet snatch. "Make me come."

My commanding tone brought out the animal in him. He clasped his hands on my thighs and pulled me rapidly down the bed, pushing a pillow under my back and kneeling on the cover he had thrown off the bed earlier. My breathing quickened. I knew whatever he was about to do, he wouldn't take much time doing it.

The Man in Black slid two fingers inside me while his thumb trailed soft circles around my clitoris. My muscles tensed, and I let out a loud moan. That's when he turned his palm around and his thumb gave way to his tongue.

"Help me out a bit, baby girl."

I knew what he was asking for. With one hand I spread my

pussy, giving him better access to the most sensitive spots. As his tongue started to rhythmically flick against my clit, I knew I wasn't going to last long. His fingers picked up the pace inside me, and their pressure became harder. I couldn't keep the orgasm at bay anymore. It had been looming over me like a great cloud since Massimo had first touched me. I came with a long, piercing scream, before collapsing on the pillow.

"I'll have another go," he whispered, keeping his lips clamped around my clit. "I've neglected you lately, babe."

I thought he was joking but I was wrong. His fingers began to move faster, and the thumb that had been playing with my clitoris earlier now moved to my back entrance. My buttocks tensed involuntarily. Oh no, he wasn't joking at all.

"Relax, my love."

I did as he told me. I was in for more ecstasy. When his finger finally slipped delicately inside, I could already feel another orgasm coming. Massimo knew perfectly how to make my body react the way he wanted it to. His fingers pistoned into both my holes, his tongue and lips pushing against my sweet spot. Another wave of orgasm washed over me, and then one more. When I reached the point at which the ecstasy was physically painful, I clawed at his neck. I was out of breath. I collapsed on the pillow, breathing heavily.

The Man in Black turned me over, yanking me up the bed and lifting my legs so that my knees nearly touched my shoulders. He knelt with his cock fully erect.

"If it hurts, just say so," he breathed, pushing himself inside me before I could react.

His thick, bulging prick slid deeper into me, pushing its way forward. As he reached the end, Massimo's hips stopped, as if waiting for me to say something.

"Fuck me, don Massimo," I said, my arms wrapping around his neck.

I didn't have to say it twice. His body burst into motion, pumping like a machine gun. He fucked me fast and hard—just the way we both liked it.

After a while, the Man in Black stopped, put his hands around me, and rolled me over before sliding his dick back in and going back to his wild ride.

I could feel him getting close, but he couldn't decide how and when he wanted to come.

Another instant later, he slid out and rolled me back to my initial position. His hand groped around the nightstand. He found the remote and turned the lights on, bathing the bedroom in a delicate light. With his knees, he spread my thighs and slowly slid back into my wet pussy, his gaze never leaving my face. He leaned over and lowered himself, clinging to me, his lips hovering just a few inches above mine. I could see his eyes glazing over, as a powerful shiver of ecstasy shook the Man in Black. His hips pumped even harder, slamming into me, and his back ran with sweat. Massimo orgasmed for a long time, but his eyes never wavered. I had never seen anything as sexy in my entire life.

"I don't want to pull it out," he said, rasping.

I laughed and ran my fingers through his hair.

"You're crushing our daughter."

Massimo closed me in a viselike grip and rolled us both over. Now I was on top. With one hand, he picked up the bedcover, pulling it over my back.

"A girl?" he asked, stroking my hair.

"I'd like it to be a girl, but knowing my luck, it'll be a boy. And I'll never stop worrying if he follows in your steps."

The Man in Black laughed out loud and nestled his head in the crook of my neck.

"He'll do whatever he likes. I'll make sure to get him everything he'd ever dream of."

"We'll have to talk this over one day, but let's leave it for now."

Massimo said nothing for a while, only tightening his embrace. Finally, he ordered, "Go to sleep now."

I'm not sure how long I slept. When I opened my eyes, the first thing I did was grab my phone.

Goddamn it! It was noon. *Who sleeps this late?* I turned my head, searching for the Man in Black, but the space beside me on the bed was empty. Why wasn't I surprised . . . For a while, I stayed in bed, slowly shaking off the sleep, before I got up and went to the bathroom. If Massimo was back, I needed to look my best. Better than I had for the last couple of days. But, of course, without actually revealing that I had done anything to make myself up. I wanted him to believe I woke up this pretty. I accented my eyes and brushed my newly cut hair. Then I rummaged through the wardrobe and found a pair of denim shorts, a bright sweater leaving one shoulder bare, and a pair of beige Emus. As long as I could show off my body, and it was still warm outside, I would dress however I liked.

I met Domenico in the corridor.

"Oh, hi! Have you seen Olga?"

"She woke up a moment ago. I just ordered breakfast. Or lunch, more like."

"And Massimo?"

"He left early in the morning, but he should be back any time now. How are you feeling?"

I leaned against a door frame and smiled playfully.

"Oh, just perfect . . . wonderful." Domenico raised his hand and waved me off.

"Yadda-yadda. My brother was just as bubbly. I'm asking if anything hurts. I've booked you another visit to the cardiologist. And a gynecologist. You should be at the clinic by three."

"Thanks, Domenico," I said, leaving him on my way to the garden.

The day was warm, and the sun shone through the cloud cover. Olga was sitting by the table, reading a newspaper. Passing her by, I planted a kiss on the top of her head before taking a seat in an armchair.

"What's up, bitch?" she greeted me, sending me a glance through her shades. "What's with the smug face? They give you the same pills I had? I totally blacked out. Only just got up. Think that doc has more of those?"

"I got something way better," I replied, raising my brows with a meaningful smirk.

Olga took her sunglasses off and put the paper down, staring at something behind me.

"All right, tits up! Massimo's back." I turned in my chair and saw the Man in Black appearing through the door, making his way toward us. I felt hot all of a sudden. He wore gray pants and a graphite sweater with the collar of a white shirt sticking out from underneath. He had one hand in his pocket, while the other held a cell phone to his ear. He was breathtaking. Godly. And most important—mine.

Olga watched Massimo closely as he stopped near the edge of the garden, talking over the phone and staring out to the sea.

"I bet he fucks like a god," she mused, shaking her head.

I raised a cup of tea to my lips, keeping my eyes on the Man in Black.

"Want me to tell you just how good he is?"

"No need. The look on your face alone tells me all I need to know. Besides, a guy like that pretty much guarantees satisfaction, eh?"

I felt glad her humor was back and that she'd decided not to talk about what had happened yesterday. I needed to keep it out of my head, too. Otherwise, I might have gone mad. Massimo ended the call and approached the table with a stony expression.

"Good to see you, Olga."

"Thanks for inviting me, don Massimo. It's very kind of you to let me accompany Laura during her big day."

Massimo grimaced, while I kicked Olga in the shin under the table.

"What's with the kick?" she asked, genuinely baffled. "It *is* an honor. Not even your parents are here, are they?"

She took a breath, apparently intending to continue, but suddenly reminded herself that I was supposed to keep my nerves under control.

"How are my girls?" The Man in Black changed the subject, bending over me and planting a kiss on my tummy and then my lips.

That only disconcerted Olga.

"You told him?!" she burst out in Polish. "I thought he just got back."

"I did. He returned last night."

"Well, then. Now I know why you're in such a good mood. Nothing like a good fuck. Especially after popping a bunch of tranquilizers." She nodded her head knowingly and got back to skimming through her paper.

Massimo took his place at the head of the table and turned his head to me.

"When are we going to see the doctor?"

"What do you mean, 'we'?"

"I'm going with you."

"I'm not sure I'd like that." I grimaced at the image of him accompanying me to the gynecologist. "The doctor is a man. I'd like him to stay alive a bit longer. Do you even know what an obgyn exam looks like?"

Olga spat out her coffee.

"If Domenico chose him, he's the best at what he does. Besides, I can wait outside if you prefer."

"No way, Massimo. There's a special screen," Olga chimed in, putting her newspaper down. "You'll have the time of your life."

"Want another kick? Just say a word," I hissed at her in Polish.

"Can you two speak English?" the Man in Black growled. "When you speak Polish, I get the feeling you're laughing at me."

Domenico appeared out of the blue to defuse the situation. He sat down in the last free chair.

"I need your help, Olga," he said. "Would you come with me, please?"

I raised an eyebrow, turning to the young Italian.

"Keeping secrets from me?"

"Nope," Olga replied and then turned to Domenico, saying, "Sure I would. When our little lovebirds go to the doctor. Not as if I have anything better to do anyway."

"Brother"—Domenico's eyes moved to Massimo—"can I officially congratulate you now?"

Massimo's stare grew less hostile, and a slight smile illuminated his face.

Domenico got up and walked over to his brother, saying something in Italian. The two men embraced, patting each other's backs. It was a new and heartwarming sight for me. The Man in Black sat back down and took a sip of his coffee.

"I have something for you, baby girl," he said, placing a small black box on the table. "I hope this one will be luckier."

I sent him a quizzical look but took the little box and opened it. Immediately, I slumped back in my seat, shocked. Olga took a look above my shoulder and whistled in appreciation.

"A Bentley. Pretty cool. Have any more of those little boxes?"

My eyes darted from the car key to Massimo.

"At first I didn't want you to have a car of your own. But I can't let you go paranoid. Besides, I've learned everything there is to learn about this whole situation, and I don't think you're in any more danger."

"Excuse me? What do you mean?"

"I saw my inside man at the police station in the morning and took a look at the CCTV recordings from the highway. There was only one person in the car that hit you. We couldn't identify them from the recording, but we also got ourselves a copy of the recordings from the spa. Same story there—the driver wore a baseball cap and a hoodie. Nevertheless, I was able to exclude some people from the circle of suspects. The driver acted very chaotic, you see. And the person who wanted to ram you had no idea how to do it properly. If it had been a professional, you would have been dead by now. So, either it was a coincidence, or the situation was unrelated to the family business."

"Sure, we're the luckiest girls in the world." Olga snickered, rolling her eyes.

"That doesn't make me any happier," she continued. "One day, I'll have to leave her here with you. I hope nothing happens to her while I'm away. Otherwise, even your horde of goons won't protect you from me."

Massimo couldn't hide his amusement at that. Domenico,

on the other hand, looked utterly dumbfounded, staring at my personal protector.

"That temperament must be a Polish thing, Massimo," he said.

I gave Olga a smooch on the cheek and stroked her hair, laughing.

The table was piled with all kinds of delicacies. The four of us got to eating. Uncharacteristically, I had a great appetite and wasn't feeling nauseous today.

"All right, boys," I said, putting my fork down, "how about you two tell us something about your brotherly relationship? Did you have fun pretending to be boss and underling?"

The brothers exchanged glances, unsure of who should begin.

"It wasn't exactly pretending," Domenico said finally. "As the head of the family, Massimo is actually my boss. Though of course, first and foremost, he's my brother. Family comes first, you know. But he's the don, so I owe him a kind of respect that goes beyond what you feel toward relatives." He propped his elbows on the tabletop and leaned forward. "Besides, we only found out we're brothers a couple years ago. When our father died."

"When I was shot, I needed blood," the Man in Black cut in, "and when our blood tests came in, it turned out we were genetically related. Then, after I recuperated, we decided to get to the bottom of this and found out that we were half brothers. Domenico's mother is my mum's sister. And we have the same father."

"Wait a minute," Olga chimed in, "doesn't that mean your old man banged both sisters?"

The men frowned, adopting similar expressions.

"If you put it as colloquially as you did," Massimo said flatly, "then yes. That's what happened."

An awkward silence fell over us all.

"Anything else you'd like to know, Laura?" the Man in Black asked, keeping his eyes on Olga.

"Since we're among family," I said, "let's pick a name for the baby to defuse the tension a bit."

"Henryk!" Olga called out. "A beautiful name! A king's name!"

Domenico frowned as he and Massimo tried pronouncing the Polish name.

"Nah, I don't like it." I shook my head. "And I'm still convinced it's going to be a girl."

Three seconds later, an argument was already raging, and I started to regret trying to change the subject in the first place. Olga was yelling, and Massimo calmly rebuffed her arguments. They didn't need me, it seemed. Observing the exchange, I realized that until Olga accepted I was happy and safe, her war with the Man in Black wouldn't end. She'd just keep whipping him up and gauging his reactions.

I got up and planted another kiss on her head.

"I love you."

Olga trailed off at that, growing silent again. I crossed the patio and kissed Massimo—long and passionate.

"*We* love you," I said. "Now. I'm off to the clinic. Don't want to be late." I snatched the black box from the table and left.

Massimo excused himself and stood up, launching himself after me and catching up in no time. He wrapped his arm around my shoulders.

"Do you even know where I parked the car, baby? Or were you planning to go on a treasure hunt?"

I jabbed an elbow into his gut with a laugh, and he led me to a part of the garden that I'd never visited before. It sat behind the house. It was covered in deep shade and had no view of the sea, so I had never even thought about going there.

When we reached the place, I saw a large, single-floor building set into the mountainside. The gate lifted and I realized the garage—or rather the hangar—was indeed carved into the mountain. There were dozens of cars inside. I froze, shocked. *Who needs that many cars?*

"You drive them all?"

"I've driven all of them at least once, yes. They were a hobby of my father's. He collected them."

My eyes focused on the line of motorcycles by the wall, and I edged closer.

"Oh, I love this one," I said, running a hand along the curves of a Suzuki Hayabusa. "Four cylinders, six gears, and crazy torque!" I squealed with delight. "'Hayabusa' means 'peregrine falcon' in Japanese. It's the fastest animal in the world. It's wonderful."

Massimo kept a step behind, listening to me with a look of surprise.

"Forget it," he barked as I finished, pulling me toward the exit. "You'll never—and I mean ever—ride a bike. I'm being serious."

I snatched my hand away and sent him a furious glare.

"Who are you to tell me what to do?"

The Man in Black turned to face me and clasped his hands around my cheeks.

"You're pregnant with my child. When it's born, you'll be my baby's mother." He stressed the word "my," keeping his eyes fixed on mine.

"I will not risk losing you or the two of you. So forgive me, but I *will* tell you what to do."

His finger pointed at the bikes.

"I will get rid of those. This isn't about your skills or your care or the lack of it. You just can't be entirely safe on the road. Things happen."

I had to agree with that. I didn't like it, but he was right. I wasn't only responsible for myself anymore.

Looking into his cold, angry eyes, I put my hands on my belly and gently stroked it. The gesture seemed to calm him down. He put his palms over mine and leaned his brow against my own. I didn't have to say anything. I understood. And he knew what I felt and what I thought.

"Please don't be stubborn, Laura. At least not without a good cause. And let me take care of both of you. Now come with me."

There was a black Bentley Continental parked by one of the gates. The muscular coupe had nothing in common with the bulky Porsche that I had driven last time.

"You told me I wouldn't get a sports car."

"I changed my mind. Besides, I'm going to strap it with a speed limiter."

I paused, confused, sending him a wary glance.

"You're joking, right?"

Massimo grinned at that. "Of course I am. The Bentley doesn't offer anything like that." He raised his brows, amused. "But it's very safe and very fast. I've chosen it for you after some . . . consultations. It's simpler than the Porsche and much more elegant. And it has a lot of interior space, so your belly will fit without any issue. Do you like it?"

"I like the Hayabusa," I grumbled, pouting.

Massimo shot me a warning glare and opened the driver's door. Surprised that he was allowing me to drive, I got inside. The cockpit was a beautiful honey-and-almond color. It was elegant, simple, and refined.

The seats and parts of the door were covered in quilted leather, and the rest was wood.

With a start, I discovered that it wasn't really a typical coupe inside—it was a large four-seat car. Still looking around, dazzled by the luxury of the interior, I heard Massimo getting comfy in the passenger seat.

"You like it?" he asked.

"Well, I guess I can live with it," I replied sarcastically.

On the way to the clinic, Massimo gave me a crash course in using the various functions of the car, and after twenty minutes or so, I became a Bentley driving expert.

Massimo was calm and disciplined at the doctor's office. He listened to the gynecologist and asked questions, all of them rational and insightful. During the examination, he left the room, explaining that he wanted me to feel as comfortable as possible. Just as I thought, yesterday's accident hadn't impacted my health in any way, nor had it hurt the child inside me. The cardiologist confirmed that I was okay, and that my heart was as good as it got, considering the circumstances. He prescribed me some drugs I was supposed to take whenever I felt under the weather.

Two hours later, we were on our way back home. This time I asked the Man in Black to drive. Those visits at the clinic were a bit taxing on my nerves, and I didn't want to take any unnecessary risks.

"Luca," Massimo said suddenly, keeping his eyes on the road.

"I'd like our son to have my grandfather's name. He was a great and wise Sicilian. You would have liked him. A charming and intelligent man. Truly ahead of his time. It was his idea to send me to university instead of allowing me to play around with guns."

I mulled the name over for a while, finally deciding I liked it. The only thing that counted for me was for the baby to be healthy and have a chance at a normal childhood.

"It's going to be a girl. You'll see."

Massimo's lips spread in a shy smile, and his hand landed on my knee.

"So we're going to name her Eleonore Claire. Like our mothers."

"Do I have a say in this at all?" I asked.

"Nope. I'll get the birth certificate sorted out while you're recovering."

I shot him a stormy glare and punched him on the shoulder.

"What?" He laughed. "It's tradition! The head of the family decides about everything. And I've made up my mind."

"Oh yeah? How about I tell you some Polish traditions? First of all, we castrate the husband after the first son is born, so he doesn't cheat on his wife."

"That would mean I'd keep my privates for some time yet, since you're saying our first child is going to be a girl."

"You're unbearable," I said, shaking my head.

We drove down the highway at a leisurely pace. I delighted in the beautiful view of Mount Etna, crowned with a tall plume of smoke. Suddenly, Massimo's cell chimed, trying to connect to the car's speaker. The Man in Black shot me a look and said, "I need to take this. It's Mario."

The consigliere had a habit of interrupting our more intimate moments, but I knew how important he was for the family business, so I had nothing against it. I waved a hand dismissively.

Listening to Massimo talk in Italian was a pleasure. He sounded very sexy, and it always turned me on. A couple of minutes into the conversation, I was beginning to feel bored. That's when an idea came to my head.

I placed a hand on Massimo's thigh and moved it slowly toward his crotch. My fingers stroked him delicately through the fabric of his pants. The Man in Black didn't react in any way to my attentions, so I decided to go a step further. I unzipped his pants and discovered he wasn't wearing any underwear. I purred and licked my lips, pulling his manhood out through the opening.

Massimo shot a glance down, then at me, but didn't stop talking. The mock indifference was a challenge. I unbuckled the seat belt and slid the clasp into the socket behind me until it clicked into place. I didn't want the car's beeping alarm to distract my man from his conversation. Massimo changed lanes and slowed down. He grabbed the steering wheel with his left hand, while his right wrapped around the passenger seat. He was making space for me. I bent down and took his cock in my mouth, sucking. The Man in Black inhaled sharply. I lifted my head and whispered in his ear, "I'll be quiet, but you don't have to. Please don't interrupt on my account."

I planted a kiss on his cheek and went back to playing with his dick. Each moment it was growing harder in my mouth, I noticed my attentions were making it difficult for him to keep a neutral tone of voice. I picked up the pace, my hand joining in the fun. A moment later, I felt Massimo's hand landing on top of my head and pressing down, pushing my mouth over his cock. I wanted him to come. It was one of the best blow jobs I had ever given—period. Massimo's hips trembled, and I heard his breath quickening. I didn't care if we were seen. I was turned on and wanted to satisfy him. Nothing else counted. An instant later, Massimo said ciao and hung up. The car drove off the road abruptly and stopped, tires screeching. The Man in Black unbuckled his seat belt and grabbed me by the hair with full force. He pushed his prick into my throat, groaning loudly, his hips pumping.

"You're acting like a whore," he hissed. "But you're *my* whore."

It aroused me when he was so vulgar. I loved his dark side. In bed, it was an undeniable asset. I moaned, clamping my lips over his penis and allowing him to treat my mouth like a plaything. As he felt the pressure of my lips, his moans became even louder. A moment later, a wave of semen flooded my throat. I swallowed each and every drop of the spurting cum. When he was done, I licked him clean before putting it back into his pants and zipping them up. I leaned back in the passenger seat and wiped my mouth with a sleeve.

"Are we going or what?" I asked, keeping my expression neutral.

For a while, Massimo sat silently with his eyes closed, head leaned back. Then he turned to me, fixing me with a lustful gaze.

"Was that a punishment or a reward?" he asked.

"Only a whim. I was bored and decided to give you a blow job."

He smiled, lifting his eyebrows and shaking his head in disbelief, and stepped on the accelerator.

"You're the perfect woman," he said, speeding down the highway. "Sometimes you make me furious, but I couldn't imagine being with anyone else."

"Good for you, then. We're in for at least half a century together."

CHAPTER
two

When we reached the mansion, Domenico's car parked right next to us. Olga stepped out, beaming and visibly excited about something. Massimo opened the door for me and the four of us met on the driveway.

"You got something on your pants," Olga said, pointing at Massimo's crotch.

I glanced at the spot.

There was a small stain there.

"We had ice cream," I explained with a silly grin.

Olga chuckled, passing me on the way to the house.

"Or at least you did," she said.

I lifted my brows, nodding, and followed her. After a while, we reached the bedroom and collapsed on the gigantic bed.

"I could really use a good fuck right now," said Olga, disarmingly honest. "And watching Domenico doesn't help. He's so charming and . . ." She broke off, looking for the right word, "Italian. I think he's into pussy licking. And that slim butt of his . . . I like butts like that."

For a short while I thought about her words, finally concluding that I'd never seen Domenico like that.

"I don't know . . . He doesn't really look like someone who'd like it. But if being brothers makes them comparable in bed, you wouldn't regret it."

I nodded confidently, while Olga fidgeted about, unable to find a comfy position.

"You're not helping!" she cried out, jumping to her feet and bouncing on the mattress with girly glee. "It's not fun to watch you so . . . satisfied! I need some of that, too. I need attention."

"A vibrator is a girl's best friend, you know."

Olga settled down on the bed again.

"You think I brought one with me? Fucking hell! I thought they were going to chop your head off here! A rubber cock wasn't on my list of things that'd help me fight for your life!"

"Tough luck, then. No dildo and no murder," I said.

Olga went silent, desperately trying to think about a solution to her problem. Suddenly, her face brightened up in a big smile. Curious as to her newest dirty idea, I lifted my head from the pillow and rested it against the headboard.

"Guess what?"

"I'm listening."

"Theoretically, it's your bachelorette party today. So . . ." She paused. "Maybe we should go out? You know . . . Have some fun, dance a bit. How about that?"

"Yeah, right. And tomorrow I'll be a sober, exhausted, puffed-up, pregnant bride. Thanks, but no thanks."

Resigned, Olga slumped down next to me.

"And here I was, thinking I'd score."

The door swung open suddenly. It was the Man in Black.

"You changed your pants," Olga noticed with a smirk. "Bad memories, right? A spoiled ice cream is no laughing matter."

I jabbed her in the gut and got up, making my way to Massimo, while Olga stayed in bed, staring at him defiantly. She was only waiting for an opportunity to argue with him again. Massimo knew it wouldn't get them anywhere, so he ignored her. I kissed him on the cheek, silently thanking him for his wisdom and composure. Keeping his eyes on Olga, the Man in Black said, "I like you. You have a weird sense of humor . . ." He trailed off and his eyes met mine.

"Now, pack your things. We're setting off in an hour. See you at the quay." He kissed me on the forehead and disappeared into the corridor.

"We're taking a boat?" Olga asked.

"Don't look at me. I'm as surprised as you are."

"What boat are we talking about? Like, a rowing boat? What do I wear? A wet suit?"

I picked up the phone and dialed Domenico, but he told me nothing besides confirming that we wouldn't be having dinner at home. He danced around the issue for a while, before finally telling me he was about to have a meeting. He hung up.

Rude, I thought and went back to Olga. We decided that since we knew nothing of the plans for the night, and since it was supposed to be my bachelorette party, we'd dress up.

Twenty minutes later in the dressing room, we picked our best outfits. I knew that Massimo liked it when I looked classy, so I opted for a Chanel. The gray dress had more in common with a messy bundle of material than an actual piece of attire, but it looked delicate and sensuous on me. It covered what needed to be covered, while showing off my assets. I knew we'd be taking the boat, but it didn't dissuade me from grabbing black, lacquered, pointed-toe stilettos. I threw in a wide black Hermès bracelet and concluded that I looked astonishing. A beautiful future mother. Still thin and good-looking.

Olga went with her standard high-end escort look, choosing a colorful Dolce & Gabbana tunic that barely covered her ass. *You really should wear shorts with that, but whatever*, I thought. We wore the same size shoes, so rummaging through my wardrobe was a blast for my friend.

Ten minutes in, she finally found a pair of ridiculously high heels and a matching purse.

"Holy shit!" she cried, glancing at her watch. "Only fifteen minutes left." There was a moment of panic, but then she settled down, coming to a calming conclusion. "Why should I listen to him, though? No man tells me how to live my life. We'll come down when we're ready."

I burst out in laughter and pulled her with me to the bathroom. The makeup and hairdressing took us a bit more time than we had been given, but we managed to get ourselves in order in the end. Red lip balm and eyes richly accented in black perfectly rounded up my dutiful, elegant wife look.

I left the bathroom and started, seeing Domenico waiting by the bed. He was dressed up, too, even more dapper and glam than usual. In a black suit and a dark shirt, he did resemble his older brother. His dark, swept-back hair emphasized the boyishness of his face and the fullness of his lips.

I felt Olga stopping right behind me. She leaned to my ear and whispered in Polish, "Can you fucking see him? I swear I'm just gonna kneel right in front of him."

The young Italian observed us with amusement, and when we did nothing to break the silence, he grinned and said, "I just wanted to check up on you two. Will we be leaving before the wedding day?"

I grabbed Olga by the hand (she was barely standing now, shaking nervously), and pretending indifference, I headed to the stairs. We took our shoes off in the garden, making our way to the quay.

Seeing the *Titan*'s silhouette in the distance made me recall my first night with Massimo. A wave of heat washed over me. I stopped, and Olga walked straight into me, failing to notice my change of pace.

"What's up?" she asked, eyes wide and anxious.

"There it is," I replied, pointing to the yacht.

"That's where it all started."

I felt all kinds of emotions. My heart was beating like crazy, and the only thing I could think of was to find the Man in Black. Right away.

"Ladies first," Domenico said, gesturing to the motorboat and offering me a hand.

We sat in the comfortable white leather seats, and a while later the boat was zooming through the water, heading to the monumental yacht. Domenico and Olga kept stealing glances at each other, both feigning disinterest while I thought about that night. Without my even noticing, my finger flew to my mouth, and a moment later I felt another wave of heat. I wanted him. I couldn't see him or smell him or touch him, but I was getting horny all the same. The memory of him alone was making me crazy. I felt like I was going to explode.

"Quit it, Laura," Olga chided. "I can see what you're doing with that finger. I don't even have to ask what you're thinking of."

I smiled, shrugging, and willed my hands down onto the white leather of the seat. The motorboat slowly moored to the enormous yacht, and I couldn't help thinking that going with the high heels had been a stupid idea. If not for those shoes, I could have jumped on deck and run to Massimo.

Domenico stepped out first and helped us get off the boat. I raised my eyes and saw Massimo standing at the top of the stairs. He looked breathtaking in his gray, single-breasted suit and a white shirt with the top unbuttoned. I wanted him so much that even if he had been standing there in a clown's outfit, I would have been left breathless. I decided to play my role, though, and edged closer to him slowly, in a steady, practiced gait. My eyes never left him. As I closed the distance between us, he offered me a hand and silently led me to a table. Olga and Domenico joined us shortly.

The waiter served us wine, and a few minutes later we were all deep in conversation. Still, all I could think of was sex. I tried reining in my stubborn brain, but to no avail. *What's happening to me?* I thought, trying to get to the bottom of my strange mood. After fifteen more minutes, I started growing impatient and irritable. I stared at whoever was speaking, making a face that, in my mind, suggested I was listening intently, but I probably wasn't going to fool anyone for long.

My head swarmed with ideas on how to make the Man in Black leave the table with me. I could pretend to feel nauseous, but then he'd just panic and there wouldn't be any sex involved. I also thought about just leaving, pretending to be offended by something, but then Olga would have gone after me first, so that plan was also out of the question. That left only one option.

"Can we talk, Massimo?" I asked suddenly, pushing myself up and heading to the stairs to the lower deck.

The Man in Black slowly rose from his seat and followed me. I took a wrong turn, of course, and quickly got lost in the maze of corridors.

"I think I know what you're looking for," Massimo said with a smirk.

He passed me by and opened a door, letting me through and closing the latch behind me. I took a deep breath, recalling a similar scene from a couple of weeks ago.

"What do you want, Laura? Because I'm pretty sure it's not a conversation."

I went to the living room and leaned over a table, pulling my short dress up and sending Massimo a lust-filled gaze. He walked up to me slowly, watching my movements.

"I want you to fuck me. Now! Quick and hard. I need to feel you inside me!"

The Man in Black approached me, suddenly gripping the back of my neck and pressing me into the tabletop. He slid his hand down my neck and squeezed.

"Open your mouth," he commanded and then slipped two fingers past my lips.

When they were wet, he pulled them out and pushed them beneath the lace of my panties, rubbing at my pussy. *Oh, God, this feels good.* I needed his touch. I had wanted it since first seeing the *Titan* earlier. I arched my back down, raising my ass and waiting for him to enter.

"Give me your hand," he said, his fingers gently moving inside me.

I did as he had asked and heard him unzipping his pants. A while later, my fingers wrapped around his cock. It was growing by the second, demanding more of my touch. The Man in Black was just waiting for it to be ready.

"That's enough," he barked, pulling my panties to the side.

I could feel his prick sliding into me, and my body tensed. He grabbed me by the hips and started fucking, his hips pumping in a frenzied rush. He drilled me like a machine, breathing loudly and whispering in Italian.

Two, maybe three minutes. I came. And then two more times. When he decided I'd had enough, and my body slumped to the table, he slid out.

"Kneel," he breathed, grabbing his dick with one hand.

Slowly sliding off the table, I fell to my knees. He pushed his cock into my mouth and started pumping again, rushing at my throat. He climaxed in a furious wave, without a sound, and propped his hands on the edge of the table, spent.

"Satisfied?" he asked as I wiped my mouth, sitting on the floor.

Not even trying to hide my glee, I nodded vigorously and closed my eyes. Would this last forever? Would he still have this magical effect on me years from now? Would I always want him like I wanted him now?

Massimo composed himself and zipped up his pants, reclining in an armchair a few feet away. I turned to him and smiled.

"Do you know this is the place you got me pregnant?" I asked.

For a while, he kept silent, his eyes pinning me in place.

"I think so. At least this is where I wanted it to happen."

I rolled over, looking at the ceiling. Of course it was. Everything was always as he wanted it to be. It shouldn't be surprising that this had been no exception.

I got up and smoothed down my dress. The Man in Black stayed in his place, watching me.

"Shall we go?" I asked, and he got up and went to the door without another word.

The sun was setting. Olga and Domenico were having a great time without us.

"Hot damn!" I heard Olga's exclamation. "Laura, look! Dolphins!"

The yacht was slowly making its way across the sea, flanked by pods of those majestic mammals. I took my shoes off and edged closer to the railing. At least a dozen dolphins frolicked in the water, leaping above the surface. Massimo wrapped his arms around me, kissing me on the back of my neck. I felt like a little girl watching a magic show.

"I know you probably counted on a striptease and a night of heavy drinking with your girlfriends, but I hope this might make it up to you at least in part."

I spun around and shot him a puzzled look.

"What's there to make up? I'm on a cruise on a three-hundred-foot yacht with valets, delicious food, and you! This is perfect."

I kept staring at Massimo in disbelief, and when I saw my words failed to move him, I planted a long kiss on his lips.

"Besides, nobody else could make me feel like you did ten minutes ago. Booze, friends, and strippers can't compare with that."

He looked at me amusedly, as if waiting for me to continue heaping the praise. I decided it was enough, though, seeing as his ego was already as bloated as it got. I turned to look at the water and watched as the dolphins raced the *Titan*. My attention was quickly diverted by something else, though.

Olga and Domenico were clearly growing fond of each other by now. With growing concern, I turned back to Massimo.

"What's the deal with Emi and Domenico, darling? They're a couple, aren't they?" I asked.

The Man in Black leaned back against the railing, allowing a wide smile to cross his face.

"A couple?" He ran a hand through his hair. "Not the word I'd use. They aren't exactly in a relationship, unless you really want to call it that. But I get it you conservative Poles might want to put old-fashioned labels on such things."

I frowned, quietly trying to get his words straight, at a loss as to what he really meant. Finally, I chose the direct approach.

"What are they to each other?"

"You really don't get it? It's pretty obvious if you ask me. They're fuck-buddies. The only thing that keeps them together is sex." He chuckled and wrapped his arm around me. "Did you think it was love?"

I struggled to come to grips with his words, feeling dread rising inside me. If they had been a genuine couple, Olga would be safe. It wasn't the case, though. I observed my friend doing her mating dance, wrapping Domenico around her finger. Olga was a natural. The Italian reacted just like she needed him to. She wanted him, and when she had her eyes on something, she got it. In this, she and don Torricelli were very much alike. My thoughts trailed back to our last conversation before setting off on the *Titan*. I had an inkling as to how the evening was going to end for those two.

"Massimo," I said, "is there a chance that they're not going to end up in bed together?"

"If my brother has his sights on her, I can't see it going any other way," he replied. "But they're both consenting adults and can decide for themselves. Not our business, if you ask me."

Not our business. You don't know what it's like when Olga wants something.

Olga's voice broke me out of my reverie.

"Let's go for a swim!"

"Are you out of your mind?" I barked in Polish.

"What are you even doing? You want to get stuck in the same shit I'm in?"

That stopped her in her tracks. She looked puzzled.

"I can see what you're doing. Wanting to fuck him is one thing, but treating it as a challenge? That's another story."

Olga kept quiet for an instant, before bursting out in laughter and squeezing me in a tight hug.

"Laurie, dear, I'm going to fuck him whether you like it or not. Now stop worrying about everything."

I shook my head and sent her a probing look. She knew what she was doing. All her actions were practiced. *Well*, I thought, *I let her do stupid shit all the time.* This wasn't her first rodeo, but she was going to regret it all the same. Olga wasn't one to suffer from a broken heart, however she often cried when she lost something she hadn't had the time to fully appreciate.

"Dessert?" Domenico derailed my train of thought, motioning us to the table.

"Pretty lame party," Olga muttered, heading his way.

"That's what you get for partying with parents," I retorted and stuck out my tongue.

We all sat down, and I started devouring the freshly served fluffy raspberry dessert. Three portions in, I felt full and wholly satisfied.

Domenico fished out a small plastic bag from a pocket in his trousers and tossed it to the middle of the table.

"I'm not offering any to you, Laura, of course, but it is stag night, so . . ." He trailed off.

I glanced at the bag filled with white powder and then at Massimo. It wasn't hard to figure out what it was, and I still remembered what happened the last time the Man in Black had taken cocaine. Snatching it away wouldn't change anything, though. He would have his way in the end.

Domenico pushed himself up and left, only to reappear a moment later with a small mirror. He spilled the contents of the bag over it and occupied himself by dividing the powder into lines. I leaned to Massimo's ear.

"Remember that if you take even a little, I won't allow you to have sex with me. And I'm not saying that to shake you down. The drugs would make their way inside me with your cum. And you wouldn't like that for your child, would you?"

Having said that, I straightened up again and took another sip of my alcohol-free wine. It was delicious and tasted just like the real thing.

The Man in Black took a moment to consider his reaction, and when Domenico offered him the mirror, he just waved it away. The younger man couldn't hide his surprise. They exchanged a few words in Italian. I watched Massimo's impassive face. As soon as they finished speaking, they both burst out in laughter. I had no idea what they found so funny, but what counted was that Massimo refused the coke. Olga wasn't as assertive, and leaned over the table, crying out, "Fire in the hole!" Then she snorted two full lines in quick succession before snapping her head back and rubbing at her nose with appreciation. I suddenly lost all interest in partying. I didn't want to watch the events unfold.

"I'm exhausted," I said, sending Massimo a glance. "Are we staying the night here or should we go back home?"

He stroked my cheek and kissed me on the forehead.

"Come. I'll put you to bed."

Olga grimaced and waved at the waiter, signaling she needed a refill of champagne.

"You're so boring, bitch," she muttered at me, pouting.

I turned my head to look at her and gave her the finger.

"I'm pregnant," I muttered in response.

Massimo led me to our cabin and locked the door. I wasn't in the mood for sex, but the sight of the room and the sound of the lock made a shiver run down my spine. The Man in Black threw his blazer over a hanger and unzipped my dress. He allowed it to slowly slide down, got on his knees, and delicately pulled off my shoes. Then he grabbed a soft, dark bathrobe from the bathroom and wrapped me in it. I knew we weren't going to have sex. This was his way of showing me his love and respect.

We both took a shower and, thirty minutes later, we were snuggling in bed.

"Aren't you getting bored with me?" I asked him, my hand moving in circles over his chest. "Before I showed up, your life must have been so much more interesting."

Massimo said nothing. I raised my head to look at him. It was completely dark, but I knew he was smiling.

"Well . . . I wouldn't call it boring. Besides, I did what I did freely. Have you forgotten you've been kidnapped?"

He planted a kiss on the top of my head and ran his fingers through my hair, pulling me closer. "If you're asking if I'd like to go back to my life before I met you, the answer is no."

"Just one woman for the rest of your life . . . Are you sure?"

The Man in Black rolled to the side and hugged me even tighter.

"You think I'd prefer fucking two girls at a time only to wake up alone in the morning? Making money stopped being a challenge a long time ago, too. The only thing I'm left with is strengthening the family." He sighed. "But, you see, I've been starting everything over each day. I didn't have anyone to do things for. I had different girls each night. Drugs, booze, parties, and hangovers. That might sound fun, but for how long? And when you start thinking if it's time to stop that, you ask yourself 'why'? You can't be sure if it's worth it if you don't have anyone to try for." He sighed again. "I changed after I was shot. Suddenly, I had another goal in my life."

"I don't understand your world," I whispered, kissing his ear.

"I'd be seriously surprised if you did, baby girl," he replied.

"Whether you want it or not, everything changes. That will, too. You'll start learning about what I do and how I do it. You'll never know enough for it to threaten you in any way, though." His fingers stroked my back. "Besides, you'll never have anyone to talk to about some things. I'll tell you what I mean, just to be sure. There is such a thing as *omertà.* It's an informal law of the Sicilian Mafia. We aren't allowed to talk about our business and the people working for us. As long as we stick to that simple rule, the family will stay strong."

"Who's Domenico in all this?"

Massimo laughed and rolled over.

"You seriously want to talk about this the night before our wedding?"

"See anything better to do?" I barked, suddenly annoyed.

"All right, darling." He wrapped his arm around my shoulders again. "Junior is a capo. How to explain this . . ." He trailed off, thinking about how to best put it into words. "He commands a group of people tasked with . . . things."

"Such as rescuing me?"

"For example. They also have some less chivalrous duties, but you don't need to know about that. To summarize, he earns me money and keeps tabs on my clubs and restaurants."

I kept still, thinking about how very different the Domenico I knew was from how Massimo was describing him. To me, he was a friend, a confidant. Someone who supported me . . . and picked my clothes. For a while I had thought he was gay. I could definitely believe he was gay more than I could believe he was a dangerous mobster.

"So, is Domenico a baddie?"

Massimo snorted with laughter and couldn't stop shaking with it for a long while.

"A what? A baddie?" he managed finally. "Baby, we're the Sicilian Mafia! We're all baddies." He chuckled.

"If you're asking if he's dangerous—yes, he is. My brother is a very dangerous and very unpredictable man. He can be ruthless and determined. That's why he's so far up in the hierarchy. I've entrusted my life to him multiple times. Now I've also entrusted him with yours. I know he always does his job with utter conviction and diligence."

"And here I had been thinking he's gay."

Massimo burst out in uncontrolled laughter again. He switched the lights on.

"You're outdoing yourself today, honey. I adore you, but if I don't stop laughing, I'll never go to sleep." He fell to the pillow and hid his face in his hands. "Jesus Christ! Domenico's gay! He must have gone too far with the pretending. Sure, he loves fashion and knows more about it than almost anyone, but show me an Italian who doesn't. What a ridiculous idea."

I frowned and pouted.

"Not many guys in Poland take any interest in fashion. At least not many straight guys." I rolled over and climbed on top of Massimo, looking him in the eyes. "But . . . he won't do anything to Olga, will he?"

The Man in Black swallowed loudly and focused his eyes on me, knitting his brows.

"Babe, he's dangerous to people who threaten the family. When it comes to women, as you've probably managed to notice already, he treasures you. Protects you." Massimo's eyes probed mine, searching for understanding. "Worst-case scenario, he'll fuck her brains out. Now go to sleep."

He kissed my forehead and flicked the lights out.

◇◇◇◇◇◇◇◇◇◇

I don't know how long I was asleep, but as soon as I woke up, I was filled with concern. I felt around the covers and found Massimo, sleeping soundly.

It was still dark. I slipped out of bed and pulled on a bathrobe. The Man in Black didn't move. I felt excitement and fear in equal measure, but it was dawning on me that it was just the anxiousness before today's big moment—simple stage fright. I grabbed the door handle and left the bedroom. There was no chance of getting back to sleep. I needed to get out and calm my nerves. Barefoot, wearing only the bathrobe, I headed toward the stairs. There was a sound coming from the top deck. Moaning. Was the party still on? I took a few steps up and froze, quickly hiding behind a corner with my back to the wall.

"Fuck me. I don't believe it," I whispered to myself, shaking my head.

I peeked around the corner to make sure I wasn't seeing things. There was Olga, splayed on the tabletop, and Domenico, fucking her vigorously. They were both completely naked, coked out of their minds, and horny. The sight was unbearable, but I kept looking out of sheer shock. The young Italian was tireless. Despite my distaste, I knew Olga would wake up happy as a clam tomorrow.

Suddenly, a hand clasped around my mouth.

"Shh . . ." It was Massimo, looming right behind me. He lowered his hand. "Like what you see, Laura?"

I was scared at first, but shame quickly trumped my fear. I hid again behind the corner and stood face-to-face with the Man in Black.

"I just . . . ," I stammered. "I wanted to look out to the sea. I couldn't sleep. And instead . . . this!" I spread my arms.

"And you decided to just stand here and have a good look? Does this turn you on?"

My eyes widened. I desperately tried catching a breath, but Massimo rapidly pinned me to the wall and kissed me, keeping me quiet. His hands slid under the bathrobe, exploring my skin. The moans were getting louder on the upper deck. I wasn't sure if the whole situation was turning me on or just making me nervous. I pushed Massimo away.

"Stop it!" I hissed, taking the stairs down.

He laughed and followed me. A moment later I was back in bed.

"I ordered you some hot milk," he said, placing a cup on the nightstand. "What's up, babe? How are you feeling?"

"I'm just stressed about the wedding," I replied, taking a sip.

"And now this." I raised a finger, pointing to the upper deck. "Isn't that enough to make me nervous?"

The Man in Black glanced at me and frowned. He wanted to say something but decided to keep quiet for now.

"Massimo?" I asked hesitantly. "What's wrong?"

He didn't reply, only running his fingers through his hair and edging closer to me. He slipped under the covers and stuck his head between my legs, pulling at my thin lace panties. His tongue touched my clit and started dancing, but I was so disoriented that I couldn't focus on his attentions.

"Stop that!" I cried. "Tell me what's wrong first!"

I kicked the covers away and jerked backward, crossing my arms and sending Massimo a stormy stare. He didn't interrupt what he was doing but met my eyes. Suddenly, he pulled my panties down and spread my legs wide, grabbing me by the ankles and pulling me toward himself. I gave in. It wasn't easy to resist the pleasure he was giving. I delighted in each movement of his tongue.

"We're going to have a wedding party," he said quietly, breaking contact for an instant. At first, I didn't even register the words, so it took me a couple of seconds to realize their meaning. I tried jumping to my feet, but Massimo held me down by the thighs and pushed me into the mattress, his tongue picking up the pace. When his fingers joined in the fun, I surrendered to his caress. After I came, he climbed atop me, and his cock rammed up my pussy. His hands held me tightly by the wrists.

"Two hundred people," he whispered as his hips began pumping. "Olga was supposed to tell you tomorrow so you didn't occupy your mind with it during the night. And it's going to be more of a business meeting than a party, but it can't be avoided."

I didn't pay too much heed to his words. His manhood sliding in and out of me wasn't doing anything to help me focus.

"It's going to be beautiful," Massimo continued. "Olga picked most things with Domenico. She told me you'll like it."

He finished the sentence and froze, looking at me quizzically. It wasn't a good moment to have a conversation. I clasped my hands on his buttocks and pulled him closer.

"I'm glad you don't have anything against it." He smiled, delicately biting my lower lip. "Now, enough talk. Let me fuck you properly."

CHAPTER *three*

I woke up to the sight of the sun shining through the blinds into the room. I reached for my phone and let out an involuntary groan. It was ten in the morning. The wedding was supposed to start at four in the afternoon. There was still time to get ready. Massimo had disappeared as usual, so I sprang up, wrapped myself in the bathrobe, and went to the upper deck.

The dining table was heaped with food. Olga sat in her chair, scrolling on her phone. I took a seat next to her and reached for a cup of tea.

"I think I'm going to puke," I said, taking a sip.

"Feeling sick again, poor thing?"

"A bit. Especially thinking about the fact that I'm about to eat off the table you got laid on last night."

Olga snorted with laughter and put her smartphone down.

"Well, then you should probably keep away from the Jacuzzi and the couch in the living room, too."

"You're unbearable," I grumbled, shaking my head.

"That I am," she replied, beaming. "And, by the way, you were right. They're both naturals. I've never been fucked this good in my life. He just doesn't stop. I think it might be something in the air. And the size of his cock!"

"All right, enough, or I swear I'll be sick." A moment later, Domenico joined us. He was dressed casually—joggers and a black T-shirt. His hair cascaded down his face. He looked as if he had just woken up. He poured himself a cup of tea and hid behind a pair of sunglasses.

"I've booked you a hairstylist at noon. Then it's time for makeup. After that, I'm picking you up from the villa. The dress has already been prepared. It's in your room. Emi will be there at quarter to three. She'll give you a hand. Meanwhile, I'm going to do something about this massive hangover."

He pulled out a small plastic bag from his pocket, poured some white powder on his plate, quickly formed two lines, and snorted them loudly. Then he leaned back in his chair, wrapping his arms behind his head, and said, "I feel better already."

I watched all this, wondering how they could just sit there, ignoring each other like nothing had happened last night. Olga was looking at the screen of her phone again, while Domenico enjoyed the morning, slowly regaining strength.

"When were you going to tell me about the wedding party?" I asked suddenly.

Olga rolled her eyes and shrugged, glancing at the young Italian.

He spread his arms and pointed in her direction, deflecting the question.

"Olga was supposed to tell you. It's not my fault she waited this long."

"How long have you known?" I snapped at him.

"Since the day you agreed to marry Massimo, but . . ."

I gestured for him to shut up before hiding my face in my hands.

"It'll be fun, honey, you'll see," Olga chimed in, running a hand through my hair. "It's going to be perfect. Flowers, white doves, colorful lanterns . . . Just like you wanted."

"Yeah, and mobsters, and guns, and the Mafia, and cocaine! Just perfect!"

Domenico raised his plate in a toast and sucked in another line.

"Don't you worry," he said, rubbing at his nose. "Not everyone's going to attend the ceremony at the church. There's only going to be a couple people. Heads of the families and their closest lieutenants. Besides, the Madonna Della Rocca is a small church. So don't worry about the crowd. Now go ahead and eat something."

I looked at the table and grimaced. I was too tense to eat. My stomach knotted.

"Where's Massimo?" I asked.

"You'll meet him at church. He has some things to take care of first," Domenico replied. "Just between us"—he winked—"I think he's a bundle of nerves now." He lifted his eyebrows and smiled. "He woke up at six. We had a little chat, and then he took the boat back home."

An hour later I was in my room in the mansion, staring at the large box housing my wedding dress. *I'm going to get married today*, I thought. I picked up my phone and called Mom. My eyes teared up. Everything was wrong! A few seconds later, I heard Mom's voice through the speaker. She asked me how I was doing and how work was, and instead of just telling her the truth, I lied. The only truthful answer she got was when she asked me how things were going with Massimo. I told her everything was wonderful. Then I listened to her prattling on about things at home and how Dad was always at work. I didn't learn anything new, but I really needed that short talk. When I hung up, it was nearly noon. Olga barged into the room.

"What?!" she cried. "You haven't even showered yet!"

The phone still in my hands, I collapsed to my knees and burst out in tears.

"I don't want any of that, Olga!" I sobbed. "Mom should be here. Dad was supposed to lead me to the altar! And my brother was going to be the best man. It's all wrong!" I wailed, my arms wrapping closely around Olga's legs. "Let's run away! Let's take the car and run away. Just for a while."

My panic didn't seem to move Olga at all. She raised an eyebrow and sent me a disapproving look.

"Stop fucking around and get up," she snapped. "You're having a panic attack. Just breathe. And go take a shower. Everyone is going to be here any moment."

I didn't react, instead clinging tightly to her legs.

"Laura," she said gently and lowered herself to the floor to sit next to me.

"You love him, and he loves you. Isn't that right? This wedding is going to take place. Besides, it's only a formality. You wake up tomorrow and nothing is going to change. And I'm here for you. Normally, I'd take you somewhere to get piss drunk, but we can't do that now, can we? So just take heart in the knowledge that I'm going to drink to your health."

Her words didn't have the intended effect. I crumpled to the floor, wracked by sobs, repeating over and over again that I would just pack my things and leave.

"You're getting on my fucking nerves, Laura!" Olga barked suddenly, grabbing my ankle. She sprang up and started dragging me to the bathroom. I tried to jerk away, but she was a lot stronger than me. She hauled me to the shower and turned the water on. I was fully clothed, and it was ice-cold. I jumped to my feet, fully intending to kill my friend.

"Well, now. Since you're already standing, take a while to wash yourself. Meanwhile, I'll get you some of that alcohol-free shit you keep drinking." Olga spun around and left.

I took a shower, dried myself, wrapped my head with a towel, and put on a bathrobe. I felt better. My fears were gone. When I returned to the bedroom, the view made me freeze in my tracks. As I was showering, the room had been transformed into a hair salon. There were two professional seats, one next to the other, and two large mirrors in front of them. Lights, tons of cosmetics, hundreds of hairbrushes, several dryers and curling irons, and about ten people standing at attention and waiting for me.

"Come on. Sit down and have a drink," Olga said, pointing to the seat next to her own.

When I got up again, it was way past two. I'd never felt so exhausted by just sitting around. My shortish hair had been tied into an impressive and elaborate bun formed using bundles of fake hair. To keep faithful to my style, the bun rested on the back of my head in a large, graceful ball, while the rest of my hair was slicked back, kept out of my eyes and face. It was very elegant and stylish, but also unpretentious. Perfect for the occasion. Domenico had brought in the best stylists. They'd done a great job. My eyes were heavily accented with chocolate-hued mascara and my lips delicately rouged. I looked fresh and gleaming.

The effect was topped off by a set of thick, long, fake lashes. My face got a perfect makeover and was now covered in a camouflage layer of foundation, powder, and blush, making me look like someone else, or at least not like the everyday me. It was glorious.

I was enchanted. I couldn't stop looking at myself in the mirror. I had never looked this pretty. Even the makeup I had worn during the film festival in Venice couldn't compare.

As I marveled at my reflection in the mirror, Emi suddenly entered the room. Olga froze, pretending to scroll on her smartphone.

Emi greeted me with a kiss on the cheek and unwrapped my wedding dress.

"Let's get to work, girls. Shall we?" She grabbed the garment.

Battling with the zipper on my back, I realized that one of two things had happened—either the dress had shrunk, or I had grown bigger. Somehow, between the three of us, we managed to zip it up, and Emi went to work on the veil.

A couple of minutes before three, we were ready. My heart was racing.

Olga stopped by my side and squeezed my hand. It was obvious she was close to tears, and only her beautiful makeup kept her from crying.

"I packed some things for your wedding night. The bag is by the bathroom door. There's some makeup stuff inside, and lingerie."

"Could you toss in that pink toiletry bag from the dresser by the bed, too?"

Olga went to grab the small bag.

"Why the fuck would you need a vibrator for your wedding night?" she asked, bemused. "Having problems?"

I turned to her and raised my brows.

"Not at all. I'm just planning a little surprise for my husband."

"You are so fucked up. And kinky as hell. And that's why

we're such good friends," she said. "I forgot my lip balm. Be back in a sec."

She disappeared through the door, and I heard a shriek from downstairs.

"Get out! It's bad luck for you to see her before the ceremony!"

I spun on my heel and saw it was my breathtaking fiancée. He looked at me and went perfectly still. I was doing my best to keep calm. We faced each other. Finally, Massimo made the first step and closed the distance between us.

"I don't give a flying fuck about your superstition," he said, lifting my veil. "I couldn't wait any longer. I just had to see you."

The only times Massimo cussed were in bed or when he was really angry about something.

"I'm scared," I breathed, looking him in the eyes. He took my face in his hands and planted a delicate kiss on my lips before pulling away and looking at me.

"I'm here for you, baby girl," he said gently. "You're so beautiful . . . You look like an angel." He closed his eyes and touched his forehead to mine. "I want to have you just for myself. I love you, Laura."

I adored it when he said that. A wave of incredible happiness washed over me then. It was difficult to describe. That hard, inhuman, ruthless man was showing me affection. I wanted this moment to last forever, so that we didn't have to go anywhere or see anyone. So that all that counted was the two of us.

Domenico's and Olga's voices reached us from downstairs, but the two didn't have the courage to interrupt us. The Man in Black opened his eyes again and kissed me on the lips. "It's time, baby girl. I'll be waiting for you. Hurry."

He turned away and headed toward the stairs. I looked on, mesmerized, as he disappeared. He was wearing a stylish dark blue tuxedo, a white shirt and a bow tie the color of the tux. A delicate flower matching the color of my dress decorated his lapel. He looked like a model from an Armani show.

I heard Olga climbing the steps. My friend joined me to adjust the veil on my head.

"This damned dress is too fucking overcomplicated," she grumbled, fussing about her own outfit, trying to straighten it down on both sides. "Can't really walk in it, not to mention taking the stairs. You ready?"

I nodded and grabbed her hand.

The Madonna Della Rocca church was perched on the slope at the very top of Taormina. It was an impressive building from the twelfth century, restored in 1640, overlooking the town. A few dozen feet below, there was an old castle. Farther down the slope, the sea shimmered in blue.

I stepped out of the car and saw a white carpet leading to the entrance, lined by elaborate floral decorations. The only things that distorted that perfect view were the burly men in black suits standing guard over the gate.

The church was one of the town's main tourist sites—the last stop for the most determined visitors, undaunted by the thousands of steps they had to climb to get there.

"I'll wait for you inside. I love you," Olga whispered and gave me one last hug.

I stopped, disoriented, and looked around. I couldn't breathe. Domenico appeared out of nowhere, and we locked arms.

"I know I'm not the one who should be standing at your side now, but it is nevertheless a great honor for me, Laura."

My legs were shaking, and I couldn't stop wobbling back and forth like an abandoned child.

"What are we waiting for?" I asked impatiently. Suddenly,

music blared from somewhere, and a woman's beautiful, sonorous voice intoned "'Ave Maria.'"

"This." He raised his brows and smiled gently. "Now, come with me."

Domenico prodded me forward and we started walking to the entrance. My impossibly long train snaked behind our backs. The stairs were guarded by security guards, who made sure none of the dozens of tourists broke through. The onlookers applauded as I approached the building. I was nervous and strangely calm at the same time. Panicked, but also euphoric. The closer we were getting to the great doors, the faster my heart was pounding. Finally, we crossed the threshold, and the sound of singing became louder. The voice surrounded me, wrapped itself around me, and tore into me. The people lining the way to the altar all went silent. I kept my eyes fixed ahead of me. By the altar, with a gleaming smile, watching my approach, was my breathtaking future husband. Domenico led me all the way to him before taking his place next to Olga.

As I stopped by the altar, Massimo took my hand in his, placing a gentle kiss on my palm and squeezing it tightly. The priest began the ceremony, and I tried tearing my eyes away from Massimo. He was mine! In a couple of minutes we were about to seal our fates, intertwining our lives forever.

The ceremony only took a little time, and it was all in English. To be honest, I can't really remember any of it. I was too nervous. I recall silently praying for it to be over.

When it was done, we went to the chapel to sign the documents. On our way there, I finally took the opportunity to take a look around. The guests were squeezed into the pews with barely any space between them. If I had to imagine a Mafia wedding before, this is how I would have pictured it in my mind. The men were watching us stern-faced, whispering among themselves, and their women, dressed up to the nines and evidently bored out of their minds, were rolling their eyes, stealing glances at their phones.

The formalities took more time than I had imagined, so when we finally left the sacristy, I was surprised to see that everybody had left.

I stopped in front of the building and looked over the city and the sea while tourists tried snapping photos. The security guards made it all but impossible, of course. I couldn't have cared less.

My fingers fiddled with the platinum wedding ring around my finger, perfectly matching the engagement ring right next to it.

"Does it chafe, Mrs. Torricelli?" Massimo asked, wrapping his arm around me.

I smiled, looking at him.

"I just can't believe it."

The Man in Black leaned closer and kissed me. It was a long, deep, and very passionate kiss. The sight made the onlookers cheer loudly. They whistled and applauded us, but we paid them no mind. Finally, we tore away from each other. Massimo took my hand and led me along the white carpet to the car that was already waiting. I waved at the tourists as we walked away, allowing them to finally enter the church.

Getting into the car wasn't easy in my wedding dress, but I managed. The car wasn't a limousine, but a white Mercedes SLS AMG—a vehicle as gaudy and ostentatious as they got.

Massimo took his seat behind the wheel and gunned the engine.

"Now the hardest part," he said, putting the machine in motion. "I need you to be courteous and do as I say. Please do not act out or speak against me in any way. Can you do this for me until the end of the party?"

I sent him a surprised look, completely baffled.

"Are you telling me to behave?" I asked irritably.

"I'm simply saying that you don't know how to behave in the company I'm introducing you to. And I had no time to give you any pointers before. This is about business and the family image, baby. It has nothing to do with us. Many family heads are hard-line mobsters. They have pretty conservative views on what roles women should play in life. They're easy to offend, and they might feel disrespected without you knowing what you did wrong. That would undermine my authority," Massimo explained, placing a hand on my knee. "The upside is that most of them don't know English. That said, they're all very observant. So just watch your manners, I guess."

"We've been married for twenty minutes, and you're already ordering me around," I complained.

Massimo sighed and slammed the steering wheel with both hands.

"This is what I'm talking about!" he thundered. "Don't talk back to me!"

I froze, bewildered and angry, glaring through the window, mulling over his words. I'd already had enough of this farce, and the party hadn't even started yet.

"I'll play the trophy wife under one condition."

"Trophy wife?" He grimaced.

"Yes, don Massimo, trophy wife. An insignificant thing you just show off to everybody. Someone you show up with everywhere to prove just how much of an alpha male you are. I'll be your trophy if you submit to me fully for one whole day after that."

The Man in Black leaned his head back, and for a while, he stared ahead impassively.

"If you weren't pregnant, I'd stop the car right away and spank you. And then I'd do that thing I've already done to that pretty round butt of yours." He turned his head and sent me an angry stare. "But your current status makes you untouchable, so I'll negotiate instead. I'll give you one hour of power."

"A whole day." I wasn't about to budge.

"Don't overstep your bounds, girl. An hour. At night. I won't take any risks."

I brooded, a cunning plan already taking shape in my head.

"All right, Massimo. One hour during the night, but you can't say no."

He knew I'd make the best of those sixty minutes, and it was evident that giving me even that short while in the saddle wasn't something he relished, but it was too late to back out.

"Well, then, trophy wife," he said, "you behave today and do as I say."

A couple of minutes later, we stopped at a historical hotel. The driveway was blocked by two black SUVs and a dozen muscled men in black suits.

"What's that all about?" I asked, looking around.

Massimo laughed, before knitting his brows and becoming serious.

"Our wedding party."

Light-headed with the view, I felt my stomach knotting—I was among dozens of armed men and cars that looked like tanks. I rested my head against the seat and closed my eyes, trying to calm my breath.

"It's okay," Massimo said, grabbing my wrist to check my pulse and glancing at his watch. "Your heart is racing, baby girl.

What's wrong? You need your pills? Is your heart condition acting up?"

I shook my head and turned to look at him.

"Do we need all this?"

His face didn't lose its stern expression. He stared at his watch, counting the beats of my heart.

"The heads of practically all the Sicilian families are present, not to mention my partners from the continent and America. A lot of people would give away everything they have to be let inside and snap some photos. Not to mention the police. I thought you were used to the security detail by now anyway."

I was doing my best to keep calm, but I just couldn't help feeling overwhelmed with the sheer number of armed guards. I was paralyzed. My head swam with thoughts of an attack—an attempt on my life. Or Massimo's.

"Yeah, I am, but why so many?"

"Each family brings their own security team. That's why." He patted my hand. "You're perfectly safe, if that's what's bothering you. Nobody's going to hurt you. Not here and not with me around."

He lifted my hand, pressing it to his lips. He watched me the whole time.

"Ready?"

I wasn't. I didn't want to step out of the car. I was afraid and close to tears. I knew this wouldn't go away, though. There was no way of escaping it. I nodded reluctantly.

The Man in Black opened the door and helped me out of the car. We headed to the entrance. I wanted to disappear, or at least pull the veil over my face, so that nobody saw me.

As we entered the great hall, we were flooded with applause and merry cheering. Massimo stopped and greeted everyone with a simple gesture. His face was absolutely impassive. He stood rigidly, his legs slightly spread and one of his arms around my waist. The other, he kept in his pocket. A man brought him a microphone, and Massimo began his speech. In Italian. It didn't worry me that I couldn't understand a word. The sound of him speaking, nonchalant and self-assured, made my knees wobble. He finished in a couple of minutes and returned the mic, before leading me to the opposite end of the hall toward a table. I felt relieved, seeing Olga was already there.

I sat down in my place of honor, and before long, Domenico appeared, leaning to my ear and whispering: "Your alcohol-free wine is on the right. The waiter knows you'll only be drinking that, so you don't have to worry."

"I'll stop worrying when I get in bed and this whole shitshow is just an unpleasant memory."

Olga edged closer to me, grinning, and said, "Can you fucking see all this? That's got to be the biggest crowd of mobsters and hookers I've ever seen. I haven't seen a single normal-looking guy! The dude on the right has to be at least ninety, and the bitch he's groping is probably younger than us." Olga squinted funnily. "That's gross. Even for me. And that guy in black two tables away . . ."

I loved it when Olga acted that way. She was the only person in the world who could make me smile in any situation. I couldn't rein myself in and snorted with laughter. Massimo slowly turned his head to me and stared me down. I offered him my fakest smile and turned away to look at Olga.

"Can you see that slut over there," she prattled on, "the one looking like a Victoria's Secret Angel? I like her."

Suddenly, I felt strangely anxious. I shot a glance at the table Olga was talking about. At the opposite end of the room, wearing a beautiful black lace dress, sat the woman who had tried to take Massimo away from me. Anna.

"What's that bitch doing here?" I growled, balling my fists. "I told you about her. Remember when Massimo disappeared when we were on Lido?"

Olga nodded.

"Well, this is the whore that nearly killed him." I spat out the words, feeling tremors of fury. I rose, lifted the elaborate dress a bit, so I could move faster, and started heading her way. There was no way in hell I'd allow this slut to attend my wedding party. I didn't care who'd invited her. If I had a gun, I'd have shot her then and there. All the days I'd spent crying and all the moments I'd doubted Massimo's true feelings for me were her doing.

I felt everyone's eyes on me, but I didn't care. It was *my* day and *my* party. As I approached the table, need for vengeance threatening to boil over into full-blown hostility, I felt a hand clasping around my arm and pulling me past my target. I snapped my head back and saw my husband, leading me to the dance floor.

"Waltz," he whispered and nodded to the orchestra, as we were applauded.

I was in no mood for dancing. There was murder on my mind, but Massimo held me in a strong grip, and I wasn't able to escape. The first notes of the waltz reverberated, and I found that my feet just moved on their own.

"What the hell were you thinking?" Massimo hissed, gracefully gliding across the dance floor, leading me along.

I plastered a smile on my face and adjusted my position.

"What was *I* thinking?" I growled. "Better tell me what that whore's doing here!"

The air between us grew deathly cold. We were glaring at

each other with barely restrained fury. We should be dancing a *paso doble* or a tango instead of the waltz.

"It's business, Laura. I told you. There's a truce between our families. We need it for you to stay safe. And we need the family to keep functioning as usual. Believe me, I'm not happy seeing her here, either. But do I need to remind you what you promised me back in the car?" he finished and bent me backward so far that my head nearly scraped the floor. A deafening wall of applause crashed over us. Massimo's lips gently touched the skin of my neck, as he turned me around, finally pulling me toward himself.

"I'm pregnant and I'm pissed off," I hissed. "Don't expect me to keep my emotions in check."

"If you need a moment alone to calm down, I'm happy to oblige."

"A gun to shoot that bitch is what I need."

Massimo's face brightened in a wide smile. He finished the dance with a long, passionate kiss.

"I knew you had that Sicilian temperament," he said, proud of me. "Our son is going to be a great man."

"It's going to be a girl!" I countered.

A couple of bows later, we headed back to our table, ignoring Anna's acidic glare. I sat down next to Olga and downed my wine in one gulp, as if the alcohol-free beverage would do anything to help.

"I can punch out her teeth, if you want me to," my friend offered innocently. "Or maybe gouge out an eye?"

I laughed and pinned a piece of meat on my plate with a knife.

"It's all right. I'll take care of her. Just not today. I promised Massimo."

I chewed on the morsel, immediately feeling nauseous. I made myself swallow, fighting the wave of sickness.

"What's wrong?" Olga asked with a worried expression, grabbing my hand.

"I'm going to throw up," I said, matter-of-factly, and pushed myself to my feet.

Massimo jumped up as soon as I left the table, but Olga pushed him down and followed me instead.

I hate being pregnant, I thought, wiping spittle off my lips and flushing the toilet. I'd had enough of the constant puking and the feeling of vertigo. Besides, I had thought that should only happen in the mornings. I grabbed the door handle and left the stall.

Olga was standing with her back to the wall, observing me with a smirk.

"Was the meat not to your liking?" she asked mockingly as I washed my hands.

"Fuck off. It's not funny." I raised my eyes and took a look at my reflection. I was pale, and my makeup was smudged. "Got any mascara on you?"

"In my bag. Wait here. I'll fetch it," she replied and left.

There was a nice, white leather armchair standing in the corner of the large restroom. I took a seat, waiting for Olga. A short while later, the door opened. I lifted my head and saw her. Anna.

"You have a lot of nerve to show yourself here," I snarled, sending her a murderous glare. She stopped by the mirror, ignoring me. "First you try to intimidate me, then you try to kill my husband, and now you've somehow weaseled yourself into my wedding party. Why don't you stop embarrassing yourself?"

I rose and headed her way. Anna didn't make a move. Her eyes trailed my reflection in the mirror.

I was calm now. Composed. Just as Massimo would have liked. I reined myself in, though deep down I wanted to grab her by the hair and smash her face on the marble sink.

"You think you've won?" she asked.

I laughed roughly, noticing that Olga was back.

"There was no competition. I hope you've had your fill already, because you're leaving."

Olga opened the door and gestured for Anna to leave.

"We'll see each other again," the woman hissed, throwing her handbag over her shoulder and disappearing into the corridor.

"Not before your funeral, bitch!" I called after her, lifting my chin defiantly.

She snapped back, glaring at me, and left.

When we were alone again, I collapsed on the armchair and hid my face in my hands. Olga walked over and patted me on the back.

"I can see you're already acting like a real gangster. I liked that part with the funeral."

"She's scary, Olga. I know she's planning something," I sighed. "Just you wait."

Suddenly, the door swung open, and Domenico stormed in, followed by a security guard. We looked at them, confused.

"You got the wrong fucking door, dude," Olga said, raising her brows.

The two men were clearly agitated. They were panting. They must have been running. Both men shot quick glances around, but having found nothing worrying, they nodded apologetically and left.

I crossed my arms and dropped my head.

"Maybe there's a camera installed somewhere on me, too. As if a transmitter wasn't enough . . ."

I shook my head, wondering at the scope of control Massimo was exerting over me. Were they here to save me or Anna? And how had they known the situation might have warranted an armed intervention? I couldn't find a logical explanation. I got up, went to the mirror, and touched up my makeup. I needed to look beautiful and fresh again.

Then we returned to the main hall and I sat down next to my husband.

"Everything all right, baby girl?"

"The child doesn't like alcohol-free wine, it seems," I replied.

"If you're feeling better now, I'd like to introduce you to some people. Come."

We slalomed between tables, greeting what seemed like dozens of gloomy goons. That's what Olga and I called guys who looked too grim not to be mobsters. They were betrayed by their scars, and sometimes simply by their empty, cold stares. Besides, it wasn't hard to tell. They all had one or two bodyguards standing behind their backs. I did my best to be charming and sweet, just as Massimo had told me. Meanwhile, the mobsters ostentatiously ignored me.

I hated it. I knew I was smarter than most of them. I could have easily blown them all away with my knowledge and wit. With growing admiration, I looked at Massimo, who clearly stood out in this crowd. For starters, he was a lot younger than the other men. He also surpassed them in strength and intellect. I could see they respected him, listened to him, and craved his attention.

At some point, I felt someone's touch on my back. Then a hand slid around my hips and turned me around, and then someone planted an unexpected kiss on my lips. I pushed the man away, and raised my hand to slap him in the face. As he pulled away, I froze, my arm still raised.

"Hello there, sister-in-law! You're as beautiful as they say." The man looked like Massimo. I took a step back, walking into the Man in Black.

"What the fuck?" I blurted, shocked.

My husband's clone wasn't disappearing. What's worse, his face was really the same as Massimo's. So was his stature. Even their hair was the same. Totally disoriented, I stood dumbfounded, mouth agape.

"Laura, meet my brother Adriano," Massimo said.

The man offered me a hand, and I retreated, pushing my back into my husband's torso.

"A twin. Fuck me . . ." I breathed.

Adriano burst out in laughter and took my hand, bowing to kiss it.

"That's me."

I turned to Massimo and stared him in the eyes, shocked out of my mind. I tried comparing his face to Adriano's. They were practically identical. And when Adriano spoke, the sound of his voice was indistinguishable from Massimo's.

"I think I'm going to faint," I whispered, staggering. Massimo said two sentences in Italian to his brother and led me to the door at the end of the hall. We passed through to a room with an adjoining balcony. It looked like an office. The walls were covered with bookshelves, but the two most prominent pieces of furniture were an old wooden desk and a massive couch. I sat on the soft cushions of the latter, while Massimo knelt next to me.

"It's just scary," I said. "It's really fucking scary, Massimo. When were you going to tell me you had a twin brother?"

The Man in Black grimaced, running a hand through his hair.

"I didn't think he'd show up. He hadn't been home for a long time. He lives in England."

"You didn't answer my question. I just married you. I'm your goddamned wife now!"

I cried out, jumping to my feet. "I'm having your baby, for fuck's sake, and still you can't do me the courtesy of being honest!"

I heard the door click shut behind me.

"A child?" a familiar voice said. "My brother is going to be a father. Good for you!"

Adriano entered and walked over to us with a self-assured smirk on his face. I nearly blacked out again. He looked and moved like my Man in Black. His gait was calm and confident as he made his way to us. He stopped by his brother, who had risen to his feet by that time, and placed a kiss on his forehead.

"So, Massimo," he said, pouring himself a glass of whisky from a carafe standing on a little table by the couch, "everything you ever wished for has come true. You got your girl and are going to have an heir. Father must be turning in his grave."

The Man in Black spun to face his brother and spewed out a tirade that I couldn't understand.

"Brother dearest," Adriano replied calmly, "Laura can't understand you. Why don't you speak English for her comfort, eh?"

Massimo was fuming. His jaw worked rhythmically.

"You see, Laura, in our culture, marrying an outsider is considered inappropriate. Our father's plans for his favorite son did not involve such a marriage."

"Enough!" Massimo bellowed, staring Adriano down. "Have some respect for my wife."

Adriano lifted his hands, capitulating, and withdrew to the door, sending me an innocent smile.

"My apologies, don Massimo," he said ironically, bowing his head. "See you around, Laura." He nodded at me and left.

As soon as we were alone, I went out to the balcony and propped my hands on the railing. Massimo joined me shortly, still enraged.

"When we were kids, Adriano got it stuck in his head that I was Father's favorite. He competed with me for everything, trying to prove Dad wrong. The difference between me and my brother was that I never wanted to be the head of the family. Adriano did. It was his greatest dream. So when Father died and I was chosen to be the next don, he didn't take it well. Mario, my consigliere, was Father's right hand. It was he who decided I was the better pick. When he learned of the decision, Adriano left and told us he'd never come back. We haven't seen him in years. That's why I didn't tell you."

"So what's he doing here right now?" I asked.

"I'm as curious as you are."

It wouldn't be fair to take my anger out on Massimo. This conversation was over.

"Come on, let's join the others," I said, taking his hand.

The Man in Black raised it and kissed my fingers before leading me to the door.

We went back to our table, and I took a seat. Massimo leaned to my ear.

"I have to talk to a couple people now. I'm leaving you with Olga. If something goes awry, tell Domenico."

He straightened up and walked out of the hall. Several men rose from their seats and followed suit.

I felt another pang of anxiousness. I couldn't stop thinking about Adriano, Massimo, the baby, and Anna, scheming with the guests.

Olga's voice broke my reverie.

"I was a tad horny, so I took Domenico upstairs," she said, taking a seat next to me. "We did two, maybe three lines of coke, but the Italians must have mixed it with some shit, 'cause when I was on my way back, I had the weirdest hallucination. I thought I was seeing Massimo, but then I bumped into Massimo. Another Massimo, I mean. The first one wore a suit and the other a tuxedo." She leaned back in her chair and gulped down a glass of wine. "I think I've had enough drugs for today."

"It wasn't a hallucination," I said somberly.

"There's two of them."

Olga frowned and moved closer, as if she misheard me.

"What?"

"They're twins," I explained, staring at Adriano, who was making his way toward us. "The one coming our way isn't Massimo. It's his brother."

Olga couldn't hide her shock. She gaped at the handsome Italian.

"Holy crap . . ." she managed.

"Who is your lovely friend with the unusual expression?" Adriano asked, sitting down next to us and offering Olga a hand. "If all Poles are as beautiful as you two, I've chosen the wrong country to immigrate to."

"You got to be fucking kidding," Olga muttered in Polish, taking the man's hand.

Exhausted with all that had happened, I leaned back in my chair, observing as Adriano stroked my friend's hand with a satisfied half smile.

"Unfortunately, that isn't the case. And I really hope you're not thinking what I guess you're thinking right now."

"Holy crap," Olga repeated, touching Adriano's cheek. "They're fucking clones."

Adriano laughed at her reaction. He couldn't understand a word, but he knew what we were talking about.

"This is serious, Laura. He's real . . ."

"Of course he's fucking real. I'm telling you, they're twins."

Stunned, Olga pulled away from Adriano and straightened up, squinting at him.

"Can I fuck him?" she asked disarmingly and sent me a sly smirk.

I couldn't believe it, but I supposed I shouldn't be surprised. I rose and snatched the hem of my dress, lifting the long fabric a few inches above the floor. I was done with this.

"I swear I'm going to go crazy. I need a moment alone," I said, leaving them.

I passed the exit door and took a right turn. There was a small gate ahead. I passed it and found myself in a beautiful garden with a breathtaking view of the sea. The evening was warm, and the sun shone on Sicily with the remainder of its golden brilliance. I sat down on a little bench, enjoying the moment of solitude and thinking of all the things I still knew nothing about and of all the shock and pain they would cause me when I finally did learn about them. I wanted to call my mom, or—even better—to have her with me. She would have protected me from all those people and the whole world. My eyes teared up. What would my parents think about this? I kept still, watching the sea until it went completely dark and dozens of small lanterns flashed with warm light. I was reminded of the evening when I had been kidnapped. *God, it was just a few months ago,* I thought, *and so much has changed.*

"You'll catch a cold," Domenico said, appearing out of

nowhere and covering me with his jacket. He sat next to me. "What's up?"

I sighed, turning to look at him.

"Why didn't you tell me you two had a brother? His twin, to be precise."

Domenico just shrugged and pulled out his bag of coke. He poured some into his palm and snorted two doses.

"I told you already—there are things that you two must tell each other directly. Me? I don't want to get mixed up in this." He got back up and licked a speck of cocaine from his skin. "Massimo told me to get you."

I watched him with revulsion. I couldn't hide my disdain for his addiction.

"You're fucking my friend," I said, getting up. "And I won't butt into whatever is between the two of you, but I won't let her lead you to a point of no return."

Domenico dropped his eyes, his foot playing with a pebble.

"I wasn't planning on that," he said quietly. "I can't help it. I just like her."

I burst out in laughter and patted him on the back.

"You're not the only one, but I'm not talking about sex. I'm talking about the coke. Please be careful. She's easily tempted."

Domenico led me through a series of corridors all the way to the top floor, closed off from the party guests. He stopped by a double wing door and pushed it open. The heavy wooden door opened and I saw a massive table with rounded corners and Massimo sitting at the head. The celebration inside didn't pause as I entered. Only the Man in Black pinned me with his cold, dead eyes. I took a look around. Several men were groping half-naked women, and the rest were occupying themselves with forming lines and snorting coke off the tabletop. I passed them, my back straight and my pace measured and confident, as I made my way toward my husband. The train stretched out behind me, making me look even more aloof than I felt. I rounded the whole group and stopped behind Massimo, placing my hands on his shoulders. My man straightened and raised a hand to touch my ring finger.

"Signora Torricelli," one of the men addressed me. "Care to join in?"

He pointed to the surface of the table with neat, long, parallel lines formed across it. I took a moment to think about the right answer.

"Don Massimo doesn't allow me those kinds of diversions, and I respect his wishes."

The hand on my palm squeezed. I felt satisfied, knowing that my answer was the right one.

"But I hope you're having a pleasant evening, gentlemen." I nodded and smiled my most charming smile.

A security guard offered me a chair. I took a seat and observed. I kept a stoic demeanor, but inside I was shaking with shock and anger. Old, ugly bastards groping those women, snorting like wild hogs, inhaling the white powder and talking about things I wasn't privy to. Why did Massimo want me here? I couldn't shake the thought that something was wrong. Maybe he wanted to display me for his peers to see, showing me off as the dutiful wife. Or maybe he wanted me to learn a thing or two about his world? This had nothing to do with what I had seen in *The Godfather.*

In the movie, the mobsters had rules they lived by. A code. Or, at least, a bit of class. There was nothing of the sort here.

A couple of minutes later, a waiter brought me a glass of wine. Massimo motioned him over and asked him something that I couldn't hear. Only then did he allow me to take a sip. I really did feel like a trophy wife then. Useful only as a decoration.

"I'd like to leave now," I whispered to Massimo's ear. "I'm tired and those men make me want to throw up."

I pulled away and made myself smile again. The Man in Black swallowed loudly and gestured to his consigliere. The man pulled out a cell phone and dialed a number. Domenico appeared in the door a moment later. I got up and was just about to say goodbye, when I heard a familiar voice. "Best wishes, dear! Sorry we're late. Congratulations to the young couple!"

I spun and saw Monika and Karol. They were nodding at everyone in greeting, walking in my direction. I hugged and kissed them both, genuinely happy to see them.

"Massimo didn't tell me you were coming."

Monika took a long look at me and hugged me again.

"You look gorgeous, Laura. Life's been treating you well, I see. Even with the baby on its way," she said in Polish, winking.

I had no idea who had told her, but I was glad that Massimo hadn't kept my pregnancy a secret from everyone. Monika grabbed me by the hand and pulled me aside, to the exit.

"This is no place for you," she said sternly, leading me out.

We stopped in the corridor, waiting for Domenico, who joined us shortly and gave me a key.

"Your apartment is the one at the end of the corridor." He pointed to a door in the distance. "Your bag and your things are by the table. I ordered another wine for you. If you'd like anything to eat, just call me."

I patted him on the back and planted a grateful kiss on his cheek. Then I pulled Monika with me and went to my room.

"Tell Olga where I am!" I called out when Domenico turned to leave.

We entered the apartment. I kicked off my shoes. Monika took the bottle of wine Domenico had left us, opened and poured it.

"It's alcohol-free," I said, shrugging.

She sent me a surprised look and took a sip.

"Pretty good, though I think I prefer the real thing. I'll order something for myself."

Olga joined us twenty minutes later. She was tipsy. The three of us started talking about this and that. Monika told us about her long life among the Mafia, about the rules and the taboos. She talked about the customs during parties such as this one, and I learned just how much my opinions about a woman's place in the world and the family would have to change. Olga disputed her every word, but in the end she had to capitulate, too. There was little we could do to change the Sicilians' honored traditions. Two hours passed, and we were still sitting on the floor, chatting.

Suddenly, the door opened. It was Massimo. He didn't have his jacket and his shirt collar was unbuttoned. In the light of the candles we had placed all around the room, he looked magical.

"Can I excuse you ladies for a second?" he asked, motioning my friends outside.

A bit disoriented, they both got to their feet and left, grimacing behind his back. The Man in Black shut the door as they left and walked over to me, sitting down on the floor. He reached out and gently touched my lips. His fingers slid to my cheek and then fell, landing on the lace of my dress. I watched his face as his hand roamed my body.

"What the hell are you thinking, Adriano?" I asked furiously, suddenly realizing it wasn't my husband. I scrambled away until my back hit the wall.

"How did you know it was me?"

"Your brother's face is different when he touches me."

"Ah yes. I forgot that lace turns him on. But aside from that little slip, I was pretty convincing, wasn't I?"

I heard the door opening and closing again. I glanced up and saw my husband. He switched the lights on and froze, seeing the two of us. Immediately, his eyes flared with anger. His eyes darted from me to Adriano and back again. His fists clenched. I rose and crossed my arms.

"Gentlemen. I have something to ask of you," I said, desperately trying to sound confident. "Stop playing 'spot the impostor' with me right now. I can only see the difference between you when you stand next to each other. I can't help it, but I'm just not that observant." Secretly livid, I started walking to the door, but Massimo deftly wrapped his arms around my waist, stopping me.

"Stay," he said, letting me go. "We will have words, Adriano. In the morning. For now, allow me some time with my wife."

The handsome clone headed to the door, but before he left, he planted a kiss on my forehead. I glared at Massimo, wondering if I'd ever learn how to distinguish the two brothers.

The Man in Black walked to the table and poured himself a glass of liquor from a carafe. He took a sip and shook his jacket off. "You'll learn to see the differences. Don't worry."

"What if I mix you up? Your brother evidently counts on that. He's checking how well I know you."

He took another sip, keeping his eyes trained on me.

"It would definitely be like him to do that," he said, nodding. "But no. I don't think he'd do anything beyond what I allow. If it makes you feel better, you're not the only one with the same problem. The only person who always knew how to spot who was who, was our mother. When we're in the same room, it's easier, but we are different in some ways. You'll get it, sooner or later."

"I'm afraid I'd only be able to tell you apart if you were naked. I know each scar on your skin."

I closed the distance between us, putting a hand on his chest and sliding it down, allowing it to stop on the zipper of his pants. I'd counted on a reaction, but didn't get one. Irritated, I pressed my hand against his crotch, but Massimo only bit his lip, his expression otherwise impassive. His eyes drilled holes in me. On the one hand, his reaction was frustrating, but on the other, I knew it was just a game. He was provoking me to be more active.

Well, then. You got it. I pulled the glass out of his hand and placed it on the table. Then I softly pushed him until his back touched the wall. I knelt, keeping my eyes locked on his, and started to unzip his pants.

"Was I a good girl, don Massimo?"

"You were," he replied, and finally his stony face changed, showing the lust underneath his icy mask.

"So I can get a reward?"

He nodded with a half smile, his fingers stroking my cheek.

I pulled up his sleeve and glanced at his watch. It was half past one.

"Off we go, then. You'll be a free man in an hour," I whispered, jerking his pants down.

His smile vanished, replaced by curiosity and something I could only identify as fear, even though he was doing his best to mask it.

"We have to wake up early tomorrow. We're leaving. You're sure you want to take your hour right now?"

I laughed grimly and pulled off his boxers, revealing his gorgeous cock. I took a lick and then nudged it with the tip of my nose.

"I've never been so sure about anything. Before we start, let's set out some ground rules," I said, smooching his rising manhood. "I can do whatever I want for an hour, right? As long as it doesn't endanger my or your life, everything's fair play?"

He tensed, observing me with narrowed eyes.

"Should I be worried, Laura?"

"You can, if you'd like. So. The rules."

"Do anything you want, but remember—your time will be up in sixty minutes, but you'll have to live with the consequences forever."

I smiled, raised one eyebrow, and got to sucking his prick. Rough and fast. It wasn't my intention to get him to come, so when a couple of minutes later I felt he was feeling too comfortable, I stopped.

I stood up and faced him. My hands wrapped themselves around his chin and I kissed him. Deep. My tongue pushed its way into his mouth. His hands clasped around my buttocks, but I shook them off.

"Do not touch me," I snapped. "Unless I tell you to."

I knew he'd hate having to stay passive, unable to do anything. To have no say in what was going to happen would be difficult for him. Slowly, I untied his bow tie and undid the buttons of his shirt. I slid it off his shoulders, allowing it to fall to the floor. He stood before me, naked, hands hanging loosely down his sides. His eyes were burning with desire. I grabbed his hand and led him to an antique armchair in the opposite corner of the room.

"Slide it next to the table," I said, pointing to the spot. "And then sit down in it."

As he was setting up his seat, I grabbed the bag Olga had packed for me and took out the toiletry bag before returning to Massimo and placing my rubber friend on the table.

"Untie my dress," I ordered, turning my back on my husband. "How much do you want me, don Massimo?"

"Very much," he whispered, sliding the fabric off my shoulders and revealing my lace underwear.

The dress landed softly on the floor, and I turned around, slowly taking off my stockings—one after the other. I went to my knees again and took Massimo's cock in my mouth. I could feel it growing with each movement of my tongue, its taste becoming more pronounced. I didn't keep sucking him off. Instead, I pulled away and grabbed the thin stockings I had thrown away a moment before, wrapping them around Massimo's wrists and tying them to the armrests of the chair he was in. Then, I rose and sat on the edge of the table, keeping my eyes on him. On the exterior, he was calm, but I knew he was boiling with passion inside.

"Watch the time," I said, nodding at his watch and tossing a pillow from the couch to the table.

I took my panties off and sat facing the Man in Black, spreading my legs wide. I grabbed my vibrator and pressed its button. It started to buzz and turn. With my feet propped on the edge of the table, I reclined, resting my head on the pillow. All this so I could keep watching Massimo's face. He was burning with desire and his jaw clenched.

"I'll have my revenge as soon as you untie me," he hissed.

I ignored the threat and slid the pink trident inside me. I knew my body and knew it wouldn't take me long to come. The vibrator pushed deeper inside, and I moaned, squirming. Massimo couldn't take his eyes off me, only breathing a couple of words in Italian every now and then.

My first orgasm came after only twenty seconds. Then the second and the third. I moaned and screamed, pushing with my legs, my body arching until I felt the tension leave me. For a moment, I didn't move, eventually pulling the vibrator out and letting my legs dangle from the table.

Staring Massimo in the eyes, I licked my own juices from the toy lasciviously and put it down.

"Untie me."

I took a step closer and glanced at the watch.

"In thirty-two minutes, darling."

"Right now, Laura!"

I sent him a mocking look and scoffed, ignoring his anger.

Massimo jerked his hand so hard that the armrest of his seat creaked, close to breaking.

His reaction scared me. I quickly untied him. When both his hands were free, he jumped to his feet. His arm shot out and his hand wrapped around my throat, pushing me back to the table.

"Don't ever tease me like that again," he growled and rammed his cock inside me. He pulled me to the very edge of the tabletop and spread my legs before his hands clenched my hips, and he started to fuck me. I could see he was seriously angry, and I'd be lying if I said that didn't turn me on. I lifted a hand and slapped him. That's when another orgasm pierced my body. My back arched, and my fingers dug into the wood of the table.

"Harder!" I shouted, coming.

A few seconds later he came, too, with a loud roar, before collapsing on me. With his head between my breasts, he gently sucked on my nipples as his cock pulsated in my pussy.

I tried calming my breath.

"If you think that's it, you're wrong," the Man in Black whispered and bit my nipple hard.

I yelped in pain and pushed his head away. He grabbed me by the wrists and pressed my arms to the table. He was now hovering above me, his eyes insane with lust. Now I wasn't scared. I liked provoking him. He wouldn't hurt me.

"I'm finished, so don't think I'll come again." I smirked. As soon as the words left my mouth and I saw the change in his eyes, I knew that had been a mistake.

With one swift movement, he pulled me off the table, rolled me over, and pressed me back into the wood. He had both my wrists in a viselike grip behind my back, and I couldn't move.

A thick white fluid trickled lazily down my thigh, and he slowly rubbed it into my clit. It was swollen and very, very sensitive. Each touch of Massimo's fingers felt more intense than it really was. A moment later, I was ready for more. I allowed the tension to fade away from my body and stopped resisting. He didn't let go. Instead, he picked up the stockings and wrapped them around my wrists, keeping in control. Then he knelt down, spread my butt cheeks, and started to lick my anus.

"I don't want that," I breathed, my face pressed to the table. I tried breaking free, but it was only a game. I *did* want him to slam his dick up my ass.

"Trust me, baby girl," he said without interrupting, before standing up and snatching my pink vibrator off the table. It buzzed to life.

Massimo slowly inserted it in my wet pussy, wiggling it gently every now and then, simultaneously rubbing his finger on my anus, preparing it for his thick prick. With each passing second, my need to feel him inside me rose.

When his thumb finally penetrated my ass, I moaned and spread my legs wider in a silent invitation. Massimo knew every inch of my body and could easily gauge its reactions, quickly interpreting the signs. He read it like an open book, knowing when I wanted something and when to take a step back. His finger slid out, only to be replaced by his lubricated cock. It went in delicately but quickly.

I swore loudly, surprised by the intensity of what it made me feel. I've never done something like that before. It wasn't painful, but intensely and deeply arousing—both mentally and physically. Massimo's hips began to stroke, slowly picking up the pace. The only thing I regretted was not seeing his face.

"I love your tight little butt," the Man in Black breathed in my ear. "And I love it when you act like a dirty whore for me."

His words were turning me on. He only ever allowed himself to be this vulgar in bed. That's when his emotions were unleashed. I felt I was about to come. My body tensed, and I gritted my teeth. With a swift motion, Massimo pulled out the vibrator. His hand started to dance in circles around my clit.

I came so hard, for a moment I was afraid I'd end up blacking out.

◇◇◇◇◇◇◇◇◇◇

"Where are we going?" I asked him, exhausted, cuddled under his arm in a massive bed piled with dozens of pillows.

Massimo played with my hair, kissing my head once in a while.

"What is it with your hair? It's short, then it gets long, only to get shorter again the next day . . . I don't get it why you women feel the need to do that."

I grabbed his hand and raised my eyes to look him in the eyes.

"Don't change the subject, Massimo."

He laughed and smooched me on the top of the nose, rolling over so that he was on top.

"I could fuck you all night long, baby girl. You just turn me on so much."

No answer forthcoming, I tried pushing him off me, but he was too heavy. I resigned, sighing deeply and pouting.

"I feel absolutely satisfied right now," I said. "After what you did on that table, and then in the bathroom and on the terrace, I think I'll be good for the next few months."

He chuckled and freed me, rolling over to his back again. I loved it when he was so happy. It was a rare occurrence when we were alone, and he never allowed himself to express such joviality with anyone else present.

At the same time, I adored his moderation and nonchalance, always impressed by his calmness and self-discipline. There were two souls inside Massimo. The first was the one only I knew—the caring, loving guardian angel. The second, feared by everyone—the cold, ruthless mafioso who could kill as if it didn't mean a thing. Cuddling with him in bed now, I recalled all that had happened throughout the last three months. Now, from a distance, the whole story sounded like something incredibly exciting, an adventure to remember and explore, always discovering new and fascinating facets. I already forgot how I'd felt when he had first taken me prisoner—how scared I had been of this incredible man. Typical Stockholm syndrome, I realized.

Semiconscious, already halfway to sleep, I felt my body lifted and covered with a blanket. I was so sleepy that I couldn't keep my eyes open. A quiet moan emerged from my throat, and soft lips planted a kiss on my forehead.

"Sleep, baby. It's me." I heard the familiar, gentle voice and plummeted into a deep slumber.

When I opened my eyes, the Man in Black was next to me. His legs and arms were wrapped around me. I couldn't move. There was a strange noise. Droning steadily. Like an engine. Slowly, I shook off the sleep. Suddenly, I realized what was happening and jumped out of bed. My reaction woke Massimo, who launched himself out of bed at least as abruptly as me.

"We're in the air!" I cried, feeling my heart starting to gallop.

Massimo quickly closed the distance between us and wrapped his arms around me.

He stroked my back and my head, pressing me against him in a protective embrace.

"I'm here, baby girl. I can get you your pills if you'd like. You'll sleep through the entire flight."

I thought about it and decided that would probably be my best option.

CHAPTER *four*

The next two weeks were the most beautiful time in my life. The Caribbean was breathtaking. We swam with dolphins, ate delicious food, sailed a catamaran across the whole archipelago, and above all, we were inseparable. At first, I was a bit afraid of having to spend the entire time with Massimo. We had never spent so much time together before. Normally, I'd try to avoid that. Usually, I tended to grow impatient and irritated by my partner's constant presence. It always felt like too much pressure. This time, I yearned for more. Each minute I spent with Massimo made me want to experience even more.

When our honeymoon came to an end, I couldn't help feeling sad, but the news that Olga was still on Sicily cheered me up a bit. Come to think about it, I must have felt surprised, too. What had she been doing there all that time? Paolo the security guard picked us up at the airport and drove us to the residence. On the driveway, I was surprised to discover just how much I missed this place. We stepped out of the car, and Massimo asked something of a security guard, before leading me to the garden. We passed the threshold and froze. Sitting in one of the armchairs was Domenico, and on his knees was Olga. Kissing him passionately. They didn't even register our arrival. He had his arms around her and stroked her back, touching his nose to hers, while Olga was making a cute and innocent expression. For a while, I couldn't wrap my head around what I was seeing. I had to get their attention to sort this mess out. My hand squeezed Massimo's, and we headed deeper into the garden. The patter of my heels brought the two lovebirds back to Earth. They finally noticed we were there.

"Laura!" Olga exclaimed, jumping to her feet. She took me in her arms and gave me a great hug. I pulled away and took her face in my hands, giving her a scrutinizing look.

"What's this, Olga?" I asked in Polish in a conspiratorial whisper. "What are you doing?"

She shrugged, smiling awkwardly, but said nothing. Massimo walked over and gave her a kiss on the cheek before continuing to walk toward his brother. I kept staring at my friend, searching for an answer.

"I'm totally in love, Laura," Olga said, sitting in the grass. "I can't help it. Domenico just turns me on so fucking much!"

I tossed my handbag to the grass and took a seat next to her. Summer had ended some time before, and though it was still warm, it definitely wasn't hot anymore.

The grass was still damp and the earth still had some residual heat to it, but the truly scorching weather was a thing of the past. I moved my hand through the blades of green, wondering what to say, when Massimo's shadow obstructed the sun.

"Don't sit on the grass," he said, pushing a pillow under my butt and throwing another to Olga.

"I need to work for a couple of hours. I'm taking Domenico with me."

I sent him a look from behind smoky shades, still fascinated by the way he could change so much in such a short time. Now he was my brilliant, haughty husband. The mob boss—cold and lordly. But if we found some time only for the two of us, he would instantly transform into his gentle and loving true self. For a while longer, Massimo stood there, as if giving me a chance to burn his image in my mind, and then he kissed me on the brow and left, taking his younger brother with him. Domenico only waved at us briefly before vanishing behind the house.

"Why are we sitting on the grass anyway?"

I grimaced, puzzled.

"I'm not sure anymore. Let's go to the table and I'll tell you what happened. I swear you're going to die!"

I was finishing my third croissant, and my friend was nodding approvingly.

"I can see your puking days are behind you," she said.

"Yeah, yeah, quit fucking around and tell me the story." My eyes didn't leave her as I took a sip of hot milk from a cup.

Olga propped her head on her hands, hiding her face in her palms. She spread her fingers, sending me a strange look. It spelled nothing good.

"When we left your room back at the wedding, I ran into Massimo. He looked pretty fucked off when I told him I saw his clone on my way out. He probably realized it was his twin. So, anyway, he went red with fury and sprinted your way. I had enough of your weird shit, so I went in search of Domenico. Before I found him, though, I found another apartment filled with guys with the best coke I've ever had."

She paused. Suddenly, her head smacked against the table.

"I'm so sorry, Laura!" She raised her eyes again with a guilty expression, sending me a look so full of shame, I nearly shed a tear or two.

I waited for her to continue, but she only stared at me. I leaned back and took another sip of milk.

"There's not much that can still surprise me when it comes to your adventures, so you can just spill the beans."

My friend touched her forehead to the table again with a heavy sigh.

"You're going to kill me, but someone's going to tell you sooner or later, so it might as well be me. I sat there and snorted lines with two Mafia guys who picked me off the corridor. They were Dutch, I think. That's when Adriano arrived.

"I knew it was him. He and Massimo wore different suits, so I could tell them apart. He said something to the two men, and they left and shut the door. So he got closer and lifted me up and set me on the table. He was so fucking strong!"

Olga cried, hitting her head on the table again. "So he set me on that table, and I was getting pretty nervous. If he wanted something from me, I wouldn't be able to do anything."

"Stop right there," I cut in. "You're sure you want to tell me the rest?"

She froze in utter stillness, taking a moment to think, before her forehead resumed slamming the table.

"He fucked me, Laura. But I was drunk and doped. Don't look at me like that," she groaned, seeing my disapproving look. "You married his clone within three months of first meeting him. And you did it sober!"

I shook my head and put the cup down.

"What has this got to do with your sudden adoration for Domenico?"

"The next day, when you left, I came to and sobered up. I wanted to run from that room but couldn't. The doors were locked. That motherfucker Adriano doped me with some shit and fucked me like a whore. The guys I'd partied with were his men, it turned out.

"The drugs were his, too. And me being there was no coincidence, either. So anyway, as I sat there, Adriano came back and wanted some more. I was so completely furious, I fucking punched him in his stupid face. I think I might have loosened up some of his teeth. And that was a mistake. He's just like your Massimo, and took a shot at me, too."

I launched myself up, eyes bulging with outrage.

"What the fuck are you saying?" I snapped, grabbing Olga by the shoulders and shaking her violently.

She pulled down her sweater from one shoulder, revealing the bruises. I lifted the hem of the fabric and started looking for other signs on her skin.

"What the fuck is all this?"

"Stop," she said quietly, pulling the sweater back on. "It doesn't hurt anymore. I wouldn't have told you, but I figured someone else would eventually do that. No use lying. He roughed me up, the piece of shit, but I gave as good as I got. I smacked him on the head with a lamp and a bottle. Anyway, here's the answer to your question: Domenico was trying to find me the whole night. It was him who finally ended that nightmare when he barged into the apartment. The two started fighting, and the fucking clone lost. Pretty surprising, eh?" She smiled with satisfaction. "Turns out Domenico knows martial arts. Adriano should be happy he's alive. When he finished beating the shit out of the mutt, Domenico took me in his arms and got me to a doctor. He cared for me. That's when I stopped seeing him as a talking prick." Olga shrugged and dropped her eyes.

I couldn't believe it. How could my husband's brother do that? A disconcerting thought occurred to me then: Had Massimo known what was happening back on Sicily? And if yes, why didn't he tell me? I rose and headed toward the mansion, fuming with hatred for Adriano. I wanted to kill the bastard and wondered if the Man in Black would allow me to do it. I felt my heart racing and knew I had to rein in my emotions for the sake of my child, but I just couldn't.

"Wait here," I said, passing Olga on my way.

I crossed the main hall and took the corridor opposite, knowing Massimo would be in his study. He always worked from there. It was the best-protected room in the whole villa. I opened the door and stormed inside. I was about to inhale to start screaming, when my brain finally processed what I was seeing. By the massive fireplace in the opposite end of the room, there was Massimo. Standing next to Adriano. Blinded by hate and fury and unable to discern which man was my enemy, I shot toward them. I passed heavy, book-laden shelves with murder in my eyes.

"Massimo!" I cried, my eyes tracking the reactions of both men.

"Yes, baby girl?" replied the man standing closer to the wall.

That was enough for me. I knew my target. Without another thought, I launched myself at Adriano and cannoned a fist into his face before preparing another attack.

"Punch away. I deserve it," he said quietly, wiping blood from his lip.

His words took me aback. My arms dropped to my sides. What the hell was happening?

"You're fucking trash!" I yelled.

Massimo's arms wrapped around me, and I hugged him back. I felt the need to keep shouting, but he turned me to him and stifled my scream with a kiss. He was so warm. I submitted to him fully. The calming rhythm of his tongue on mine calmed me down. I shrugged him off only when I heard the sound of the door closing.

"Don't worry, baby girl. I have this under control," he said. That stoked my rage all over again.

"Were you in control when this fucker was beating the shit out of my friend?" I cried. "What the hell is he even doing here after that?" I was beyond calming down now. "She's still here and I am here! Your child is here! Inside me! Where did that bastard go?"

"Listen to me, Laura! My brother has anger management problems," Massimo said matter-of-factly, taking a seat on the couch. "When he's on coke, he can be a bit unpredictable. I had him under surveillance during the party. My people can't be there all the time, though. What happens in the bedroom is off-limits, so they waited outside. Nobody could have known what was happening."

"Domenico could and did," I retorted, crossing my arms.

"Adriano is harmless as long as he's sober. I talked to Olga directly after it happened. I asked for her forgiveness. I know it won't count for much, but I'll keep asking. I know that she sees him in me." He paused. "Adriano isn't staying in the mansion. I moved him to an apartment in Palermo. I don't want you to feel in danger, honey. He'll leave the island later today. I've booked him a plane already."

Massimo stood up and wrapped his arms around me again, planting a kiss on my forehead. I lifted my eyes and sent him a sad and pained look.

"How could you keep this from me? My friend was in danger."

The Man in Black sighed deeply and pressed my head to his chest.

"It would have changed nothing, and our vacation would have been ruined," he said simply. "I knew you'd worry, and I was afraid you'd panic. I decided this was the best way to deal with this. And Olga agreed."

He was right. The feeling of helplessness would have overcome me. It would have been too much of a burden.

I went back to Olga.

"Hey," I said gently, sitting next to her on a white sunbed. "How are you feeling?"

She turned her head my way and sent me a quizzical look.

"Good. Why would I feel bad?"

"Goddamn it, I don't know! How does someone who's been raped feel?"

Olga burst out in laughter and rolled to her tummy.

"Been what? Raped? He didn't rape me! He only . . . how to phrase it . . . made me more susceptible to his charms with some drugs. And it wasn't a roofie, only some MDMA, so I can remember everything. And besides, I didn't exactly try to resist. I wanted it a bit more than I would have if I was sober, but I wouldn't call a good fuck rape!"

Now I was completely dumbfounded. Apparently, I wasn't keeping track of the whole situation, and it must have showed on my face.

"Think of it this way. Massimo looks identical. Would you have thrown him out of bed? We're talking about the strictly physical thing, right? He's hot stuff.

"He has a great body and a godly cock. His brother is the same. If he wasn't such a fucking bastard, and you weren't with his twin, I would have taken him for myself. Get it now?" I just sat there, staring at the trees. They were neatly trimmed. Perfect. Everything around me seemed perfect and harmonious. The house, the cars, the garden . . . my life at the side of an incredible man. And still, I found problems. Was something wrong with me?

"What about Domenico?"

Olga groaned and turned to her back, kicking out with her feet like a little girl.

"Oh, well, he's my Prince Charming. And each time he gets off his white stallion, he fucks me like an animal," she paused. "Just kidding. I'm in love with him."

She shrugged. "I didn't think I'd say that about anyone, but the way he cared about me, and how gallant he was . . . and he knows so much! Did you know he studied art history? Did you see his paintings? He can paint so well, I couldn't believe he hadn't just printed those things out! They're beautiful. So imagine this. For the last two weeks I have been going to sleep and waking up next to this man. In the evenings, we took the boat, walked along the beach, and then we went back and I watched him paint. Laura!" She knelt before me and put her head on my knees. "You got the adventure of your lifetime and I accidentally got mine, too. I know that what I'm saying may sound irrational and, you know, chaotic, but I think I really do love him!"

I stared at her, mouth agape, unable to wrap my head around her words. Olga and I, we've known each other for years. She had a propensity for the irrational. But her words sounded so unlike her, I had difficulty believing her.

"I'm happy for you, darling," I said hesitantly. "But please, please don't get so excited about all this. You've never loved anyone, and trust me, there's nothing worse than disappointment. Better to keep a healthy perspective and be positively surprised in the end than to get your heart broken."

She pulled away with a grimace.

"Okay, fuck it." I gave up. "Let's just go with the flow. Now come on. It's getting cold."

Retreating into the house, I noticed Domenico passing through a door. He stopped, seeing me, and took a step back into the corridor. Olga kissed him on the cheek and continued walking, but I took a while to look him straight in his chestnut eyes.

"Thank you, Domenico," I whispered, pressing myself against his chest.

He hugged me and patted my back.

"It was nothing, Laura," he said. "Now, Massimo wants to see you. Come with me."

Before Domenico pulled me inside, I called out to Olga, assuring her I'd join her shortly.

The Man in Black was sitting behind a massive wooden desk, working on his laptop. When the door closed behind me, he raised his cold eyes and leaned back in his chair.

"We got a problem, babe," he said coolly. "We've been away for too long, and things have gotten a bit out of hand. There's going to be a meeting. It's going to be difficult. And I *don't* want you to be there. I know you missed Olga, so I thought you two should get away for a day or two. There's this hotel a couple dozen miles from here. I'm the co-owner of it. I booked you an apartment there. They have a spa, a beauty salon, great cuisine, and—most important—peace and quiet. You'll be going today. I'll join you as soon as possible. Then we're going to Paris. See you in three days."

I stood still, stupefied. Where was my loving husband? Where was the man I had been with for the last two weeks?

"Do I have anything to say about it?" I asked, propping my hands on the desktop.

Massimo observed me impassively, playing with a pen.

"Of course. You can choose your security detail."

"That's no choice at all," I grumbled, turning and heading back to the door.

Before I reached it, I felt hot breath on the back of my neck and strong hands on my hips. The Man in Black spun me around and pushed me against the wooden door, slamming my back into the handle painfully. His palm hovered inches above my skin. For an instant, it touched my most sensitive spot. His lips closed with mine.

"Before you go, Laura," he breathed, pulling away for a second, "I'll take you right there on that desk. Quick and hard, just as you like." He took me in his arms and carried me back to the desk. "You know, I've been strangely attracted to wood since our wedding night."

He did as he said. It was hard and violent, but wasn't quick and didn't end with the first orgasm.

Massimo adored sex. His body was made for it. He was unsatiable—the perfect lover. But what I loved most about him was that he didn't only take. He gave back just as much. With every iota of his being, he gave me the confidence that I was the best in bed. That I made him lose his mind with lust. That each of my movements was perfect. That I was perfect. I couldn't be sure if that was entirely true, of course, but with him that was what I felt. With Massimo, I was a porn superstar. I lost all my inhibitions, allowing him to do with me whatever he pleased. And I only wanted more. It's strange how different men can be, and how differently they affect women. I had never been especially easy to get. My mom had raised me to make sure I didn't always fit in with the current trends and customs. I might have done a lot with my men, but I had never been as open with anyone before. Massimo's nonchalance, as well as the fact that he was always able to keep me at a distance, made me feel crazy about him. And that imperious tone he adopted at times made me do his bidding without question. Even when his bidding was weirder than I could have anticipated. I loved him, but I also adored the kind of man he was.

"Pack up, Olga," I called, entering my friend's room. I didn't knock first. My bad.

What I saw made me stop in my tracks. It wasn't anything I hadn't seen before, though. Olga was naked and leaning against a wall, while Domenico—with his pants down—was fucking her from behind. As soon as he noticed I'd opened the door, he hid his face in Olga's hair and waited for me to leave. My friend slowly turned her head to me and laughed.

"I'll do that as soon as Domenico is finished here," she said. "Now stop gaping and fuck off."

I waved at her awkwardly and turned around to leave, calling out to the young Italian before I left, "Nice ass, Domenico!"

I sat in the armchair back in my dressing room and shot a glance at the still-packed suitcases that had flown in from the Carribbean with us. I sighed. We hadn't even managed to settle in yet, and Massimo was already making me leave again. I went to my bedroom and sprawled across the fluffy white carpet, crossing my arms behind my head. I realized how much I missed all the little things I had lost. Staying in bed late on the weekends, watching the morning shows on TV. Lazing around in my sweatpants, covered in blankets, with a book to read and some music on. I remembered I used to keep my hair unbrushed for days at a time, living like a troll under a bridge, not caring about a thing. This wouldn't stand with Massimo. For starters, I couldn't allow him to see me in such a state—an unwashed ogre with a bird's-nest mess on my head. Besides, he always kept me on the move. I was never sure where I'd wake up the next day or who I'd meet. Being with a man like that was a full-time job. I had to do my best to look my best. I sighed again and reluctantly plodded back to the suitcases.

An hour later, my things were repacked. I took a shower and put on sexy brown leggings. My pregnancy still wasn't showing. Its only visible sign was my rapidly growing breasts. I had to say, larger tits nicely complemented my body—it was still slim and toned. I simply adored this new look.

I grabbed a pair of my beloved Givenchy boots, snatched a Prada handbag, and threw on a thick sweater that left one of my shoulders bare.

As I went down the corridor, pulling the heavy suitcase behind me, Olga joined me. She looked exhausted.

"You just came back, for fuck's sake! Where are you going now?" she asked, plopping down on the stairs. "My ass hurts, and I'm all sweaty."

"Charming, as always. Did you pack your things?"

"I was a bit too occupied for that. Where are we going, if I may ask? I don't know what to take."

"A hotel on the other side of Etna. Just you and me. We're going to go to the spa, overeat, and do yoga. We can pop out to a gallery or two, too. If Domenico's paintings brought out a passion for the spiritual in you, let's see how you like a volcano explosion. Anything else you'd need on a trip?"

Olga sat still, frowning.

"The fuck are you looking at?" I barked angrily. "Massimo told me to get lost. What? Was I supposed to tell him no?"

"Domenico is a bit off too lately. You know what? Fuck them. Give me ten minutes."

Some time later, we left the house. The Bentley was parked on the driveway, ready to go. A large, black SUV was waiting right behind it. Paolo and two more security guards stepped out, noticing us. I waved at them, and we got in to the car. I liked Paolo—he must have been the smartest and most discreet security guy there ever was. I really felt safe with him around. I gunned the engine and programmed the navi, setting the address. Fifteen minutes later, we were speeding down the highway.

Massimo had been right, saying that the hotel wasn't far away. We reached it within the hour. Having unpacked our things, we went to dinner, then Olga downed a bottle of champagne while I had alcohol-free bubbly juice. Three hours of chatting later, we went to sleep. The next day started with a trip to Etna. The mountain was breathtaking, reminding me of the childhood stories that Massimo used to tell me. It was a pity he wasn't there with us, but at least I had Olga.

We returned to the hotel in the afternoon, tired and hungry, and ordered lunch.

"I'd love a massage now," Olga said dreamingly, stretching in her chair. "A long, hard massage by a naked, muscular stud."

I chewed on a bread stick, looking at Olga with interest.

"I think that can be arranged," I replied, swallowing. "I just don't know if the stud would agree to strip for you."

My cell vibrated. I immediately snatched it from the table and read the text.

It made shivers of excitement run down my spine. I grinned.

"Let me guess," Olga said, "Massimo wrote that he loves you and the kid, and is generally barfing rainbows with glee right now."

"Something like that. Texted me that he missed me. To be precise: 'I miss you, baby girl.'"

"A real poet!" She snorted.

"He *did* text me, though. Maybe the third time since I've known him, so, you know . . ."

I stared into my phone, rereading the short text, and felt my heart starting to race. If another guy expressed his love to a normal woman by hanging out an enormous banner on the highest skyscraper in town, she'd feel the way I felt now.

"You know what? I have an idea." I put down my phone. "I'm going to surprise him. I'll go back home in the evening. I'll sneak him away from that meeting of his, blow him quickly, and come back to the hotel."

"The security guys will follow you, and your surprise will be ruined, genius."

"That's where you come in. You'll distract Paolo, and I'll sneak out. The car is in the garage, and the security stays outside. Besides, when we go to sleep, so do they. It's not a prison. Their room is next to ours. So I'll pretend to go to sleep. I'll say I'm not feeling too well. Meanwhile, you'll stay out and cover me."

Olga grimaced, watching me with incredulity.

"To sum up: I am to go to Paolo and tell him you went to sleep because you were feeling under the weather, and that I'm going to sleep, too, and that we want to go shopping in the morning, so I'd like them to go to sleep, too?"

"Yeah, something like that." I clapped my hands. My secret plan got me all excited, and not even a relaxing trip to the spa could change that. I picked the most fragrant stuff from the spa menu, happily imagining how surprised and horny my husband would be when he saw me. And smelled me. We finished with the massages late in the evening. It was showtime.

I put on my red lace underwear, covering it with only a loose, long sweater, which I tied with a sash. The look was inconspicuous, but all it took was to loosen up the belt a little, and it became intriguing.

"Do I look okay?" I asked Olga as the expert, pulling apart the sweater like an exhibitionist by a girls' school.

"If you ask me, it's one hell of a shitty idea, but you look like a hooker, so I guess you got what you wanted," she replied, lying on the couch, skipping channels on the TV. "Call me as soon as you're done. I won't be able to sleep until you come back."

Our plan worked pretty well. Twenty minutes later, I was driving back home.

Before I went inside, I checked my location app, tracking where Massimo was. I could be sure he was home now. It wasn't a Batman gadget, but I had an idea where I might find him. Each time he had an official meeting, he hosted his guests in the library—the same room where I saw him that night after he had abducted me. I loved that room. It was a symbol of the new, the unknown, and the titillating.

I pressed the button on the gate remote. The driveway was clear. Another car parked by the house wasn't suspicious. Not everyone had been informed I'd gone away, so the coast was clear. I snuck into the mansion.

It was covered in darkness. I could hear someone talking in the garden, but my way lay elsewhere. I crept down the hallway, feeling my heart racing, and planned ahead. I knew Massimo wouldn't be alone in there, so I couldn't just barge in, pull apart the sweater, and let him fuck me on the desk or the sofa. That might have disoriented his guests. First, I needed to peek inside and make sure he really was there. Then, I would sent him a text or call him—I wasn't sure which one yet.

That would get him out of the library. And I'd wait for him outside, half-naked, horny, and totally unexpected. I could already imagine throwing myself at him, wrapping my legs around him. He would carry me to my old room and fuck my brains out on the soft carpet or in the dressing room.

I grabbed the handle and slowly, delicately turned it, opening the door just a tiny fraction. Only the fireplace illuminated the interior. I couldn't hear anyone talking. The door moved a few inches further, widening the gap. And that's when my world collapsed. My husband was fucking his ex-lover, Anna, on the heavy desk. He was pounding her just like he had done with me not even a full day before. I froze, unable to breathe. My heart nearly exploded. I don't know how much time passed. It might have been seconds or minutes. My stomach cramped, and I regained my wits. As I was turning away to run as far as my legs would carry me, Anna's head swung to the side. She looked straight at me, smirked, and pulled the Man in Black toward herself. I ran.

CHAPTER *five*

I sprinted out of the house, needing to put as much distance between me and that place as I could. I jumped into the car and revved the engine. Tears were cascading down my cheeks. Tires screeching, I drove away. Some distance away, when I felt safe, I stopped the car and fished out my heart pills from the handbag. I'd never needed them so much in my life. My breathing was quick and heavy. I waited for the drugs to start working. What would I do now? I was having his baby! And he had lied to me and cheated on me! He had tricked me into leaving the mansion so he could fuck this bitch. I slammed the steering wheel with both hands. I should have gone back there and killed both of them. The only thing I needed now was to kill myself, though. If not for the baby inside me, I would have done it, too. The thought of the innocent child gave me strength. I needed to be brave for my daughter. I started the engine again and joined the traffic.

It dawned on me that I had to leave. Right away. But how would I arrange that? I was totally, utterly deprived of any freedom. I had allowed that man to control me! He knew where I was and what I was doing. His eyes were on me all the time. I pulled out my phone and called Olga.

"So soon?" I heard her bored voice in the receiver.

"Listen to me and don't ask anything. We need to leave the island right now. Take your laptop and find us the first plane to Warsaw. I don't care about the price. Pack only the most important things. Take a sweat suit for me. I'll be at the hotel in an hour. Sneak out so that nobody sees you. Get it?"

She was silent. I didn't know what she was thinking.

"Do you understand what I'm saying?"

"I do."

I hung up and stepped on the accelerator. The tears weren't stopping, and I did nothing to stem their flow. They were soothing. I had never hated anyone in my life as much as I hated Massimo now. To see him suffer, to know he felt the same despair I did . . . I wanted to cause him as much pain as I could. After all those talks about loyalty, all the confessions of love, and the vows taken before God himself, he'd taken the first opportunity he'd gotten to cheat on me. It didn't matter why he had done it. It didn't mean a thing to me. My Sicilian dream had been too beautiful to last, but I hadn't thought it would end this fast, quickly morphing into a nightmare.

I stopped the car in the parking lot by the hotel, having earlier called Olga. She was standing in the shadows, signaling to me with a lit cigarette.

"What's going on, Laura?" she asked, getting into the car.

"The flight. When?" I barked incoherently.

"In two hours from Catania. First, we fly to Rome. Then, at six in the morning, we go to Warsaw. Now, would you tell me what happened?"

"You were right," I replied. "That surprise was a lousy idea."

Olga was sitting in the passenger seat, half turned toward me, eyeing me in silence.

"He cheated on me," I breathed and burst out in tears again.

"Stop the car. I'll drive."

I was in no state to argue, so I just did as she said.

"Fucking prick," she growled, buckling up. "What a motherfucker. I told you not to go. What now? He's going to find you."

"I've been thinking about it on the way," I said, feeling numb, staring out the window. "I'll cash out in Poland as his wife. He gave me access to an account. I'll take just enough to stay afloat for a while. We'll go to Warsaw and I'll rip this fucking implant out. If we're fast, he's not going to realize I'm gone until the morning. Before he locates me, I'll be rid of the tracker. And then I'll go somewhere far away. He won't find me. Don't ask what then. I don't have a clue."

Olga was tapping the steering wheel nervously. She was thinking about my plan.

"We'll do this: first, we lose the phones. They won't be able to track us without them. We'll take my car. Yours has a GPS tracker. You can't go to your family or anyplace Massimo might know. You have to disappear." She paused for a moment, before continuing. "I have an idea. We'll go to Hungary."

"What do you mean, 'we'? You've done enough for me."

"You're right about that. Can't do anything about that now, can I? So I might as well see this through." She smiled. "Now, shut up and listen. I got an ex in Budapest. Name's István. I used to tell you about him."

"Yeah, about five years ago. Did I miss something?"

"Is it five already? He's still hopelessly in love with me. Calls me at least once a week. Wants me to come over. Pathetic, right?

Anyway, now's his chance. Besides, he's not exactly poor. He owns a car factory so our expenses won't hurt him. We're friends. He'll be glad to help. I'll call him as soon as we get new phones."

"Shit, Hungary is pretty close to Poland," I said doubtfully. "Let's go to the Canary Islands. I have a friend there who works at a hotel on Lanzarote."

Olga sent me a disdainful look.

"The Canary Islands? Think, Laura! We can't use our IDs. Wherever we go, we need to go by car. That's the only way to keep Massimo in the dark. And to think you wanted to do this alone . . ." She shook her head. She was right, of course. I wasn't thinking rationally. I couldn't believe what he had done and wasn't able to imagine what would happen now.

"Just remember, Laura: if you get too much cash from the bank—twenty grand or something like that—you have to notify the bank in advance. You know, let them know you'll be taking out a large sum. They need time to prepare. So go ahead and call them right now. Tell them how much you need and where you're going to cash out."

I took her cell and searched for the number on the Internet. I felt like a kid—Olga was like my mother, thinking for me, remembering about all the important details so I didn't have to.

When we reached the airport, I changed into the tracksuit she had brought for me. A glance at the red lace of my underwear made me want to retch. I drove the Bentley to one of the parking lots and left the keys inside before going straight to the terminal.

◇◇◇◇◇◇◇◇◇◇

The flight was short, and we passed the time by copying all the numbers in our phones to a piece of paper. This was the only way. Transferring contacts to another phone was out of the question.

At nine in the morning, we left the Chopin Airport in Warsaw, got a cab, and went to my place in Mokotów. The security guard downstairs had an extra key, as Domenico had hired a cleaning lady after we left.

I needed to change from that pink tracksuit. If I was to go get a large sum of money from the bank, I didn't want to look like an exhausted, pregnant idiot whose husband had cheated on her. The problem was, I didn't really have anything good for the occasion. At the cab, I presented my newest plan. "Let's go to the doctor," I told Olga. "We'll drop by a mall on our way back and buy ourselves something more appropriate. Then we'll go to the bank . . ." I trailed off, seeing Olga's expression. "Okay, no. Let's go home first. You'll pack our things, and I'll pick you up when I'm finished with everything."

She nodded and a minute later, we were riding the elevator upstairs. I left Olga at the apartment and went to the hospital in Wilanów.

Was Dr. Ome at the clinic at all? I needed to call first.

"Hello, Laura. How are you?" I heard the man's voice in the receiver.

"Hi there, Paweł. I'm great, more or less. Are you at work?"

"Sure, for another hour or so. What's up?"

"I need to see you right away. I'll be there in fifteen minutes."

"All right, then. See you soon."

The formalities at the reception took only a short while this time. There was no handsome Italian to distract the receptionists. They pointed me to the ward, and I entered the doctor's office.

"What's going on?" Paweł asked, sitting behind his desk.

"I'm pregnant," I said.

"Congratulations, but that's not my specialty."

"I know, but the thing I'm going to ask of you is. I just didn't know if pregnancy changed anything, so I told you just in case."

I rolled up my sleeve. "I have an implant in my arm and need to get rid of it right away. As my doctor and friend, I'm asking you to keep any questions to yourself."

Paweł took a close look at my arm, touched the short tube implanted under my skin, and said, "You didn't ask any questions when I partied at your hotels, so I'll offer you the same courtesy. Go sit in the treatment chair over there. The implant seems to be pretty shallow. You won't even feel me taking it out."

In another fifteen minutes, I was already back in the car, driving to the mall. I felt . . . free. I might have lost everything, but losing that leash made me feel an inner peace and hope like I hadn't felt in a long time. As I was parking the car on the top floor of the parking garage, my phone chimed. It was Massimo. My stomach knotted painfully, and my heart skipped a beat. What was I to do? It was late morning. The security detail must have noticed we weren't in the hotel. On the one hand, I wanted to hear his voice, but on the other I still wanted to kill the man. I declined the call and got out of the car.

First, I went to a cell phone store and bought two smartphones and two SIM cards. I paid in cash. Any card transactions could be tracked. Then I went upstairs and headed to the Versace boutique.

The sales assistants watched me with open contempt as I rummaged through the expensive clothes wearing a pink Victoria's Secret sweat suit. I dug through all the hangers, feeling the phone vibrating in my handbag, and finally found a gorgeous matching skirt and cream-colored shirt. I picked up a black leather jacket and a pair of black pumps. That should do it. I looked sufficiently rich now. I put the clothes on the counter, and relished the surprised look of the store clerk as I pulled out a credit card and offered it to her. Paying for clothes by card shouldn't be a problem.

Massimo probably already knew I was in Poland, but he couldn't do much with that knowledge. The large amount that displayed on the cash register screen didn't impress me in the least.

It was Massimo's penance. He owed me that much. Not that he'd notice this couple grand missing from his account. The clerk's eyes bulged in the funniest way. I wished I could save her photo on my phone so it could make me smile whenever I was down.

"Thanks," I said with a smug expression and left.

I changed in the bathroom, applied some lip balm I had fished out of my own Prada bag, and that was it. I took a look in the mirror—the person facing me didn't resemble the crying, wounded woman I had been only a few hours ago. I went back to the BMW. The Man in Black wasn't going to let me go, it seemed. The screen of my smartphone displayed thirty-seven missed calls. I was shifting into Drive when he called again. This time, I decided to pick up.

"Fucking hell, Laura!" he cried, frantic. "Where are you? What the hell are you doing?"

He had never used such words when talking to me. And he had never shouted. I said nothing. What was there to say? I really had no idea.

"Goodbye, Massimo," I managed finally, when I felt another wave of tears flowing down my cheeks.

"My plane is setting off in twenty minutes. I know you're in Poland. I'll find you."

I wanted to hang up, but I lacked the strength to do it.

"Please, don't do this to me, baby girl."

There was despair in his voice. Pain and heartbreak. I needed to consciously push away the sympathy and the love that threatened to overcome me then. What helped me was the image of

Anna with her legs spread on his desk. I took a deep breath and clutched the steering wheel harder.

"If you wanted to keep fucking her, you shouldn't have brought me into your life. You cheated on me, and I can't forgive that. You'll never see me again. Me or your child. Don't look for us. You're not worthy to be a part of our lives. Goodbye, don Massimo."

I hung up, switched the phone off, left the car, and threw the device into a trash can by one of the entrances to the mall.

"This is the end," I said quietly to myself, wiping away the tears.

I went to the bank, feeling like a thief. All the scenes from gangster movies I'd ever watched flashed before my eyes.

The only things I didn't have were a gun, a balaclava, and a prepared line like, *Hands in the air! This is a robbery!* I had full right to use that money, but I couldn't help feeling like I was stealing from the Man in Black. There was no other choice.

If not for the fact that I was pregnant, I wouldn't have done it. I walked over to one of the counters and told the clerk how much cash I needed. The woman behind the counter made a weird expression and asked me to wait, before vanishing behind a door.

I took a seat on a couch nearby and waited.

"Good morning," a man said, obstructing my view. "My name is Łukasz Taba, and I am the director of this bank. Please follow me."

Calm and composed, I did as he told me, and sat in a chair in his office.

"You're asking for a large sum of money. Can I see your ID?"

About an hour later, the whole amount was heaped before me on the desktop. I stuffed it all into a bag I had bought for that purpose, said goodbye to the bank manager, and headed to the exit. In the car, I tossed the bag in the passenger seat and locked the doors. I couldn't believe how much money I had with me. *Fuck*, I thought, *do I need that much? Have I overdone it?* Dozens of thoughts flew through my mind, including the one telling me to go back and return everything at once. I glanced at my watch and felt shivers running down my spine. I could picture Massimo getting closer by the minute. It was time to go.

"Domenico texted me," Olga said when I entered the apartment. "Sent me a message on Facebook."

"I don't want to hear it. I spoke to Massimo and told him everything I wanted him to hear. Now, this is your new phone," I said, tossing her the box with the device inside. "No more talking about the Sicilians. Are we clear? I don't want anything to do with them. And remember: you can't log in to any social media, your email, or anything like that. They're on their way already. We need to go."

"Laura, listen to me, for fuck's sake! Domenico texted me that Massimo didn't cheat on you!"

"What was he *supposed* to write?!" I screamed at the top of my lungs. "He's going to tell us whatever we want to hear now. Anything just to keep me in line. You stay if you want, but I'm telling you—they're going to be here in three hours. I'm not going to listen to this bullshit. I know what I saw."

Olga clenched her teeth and grabbed two suitcases. "The car is ready. Come on."

I changed back into the sweat suit. Then we packed our bags into Olga's VW Touareg and went on our way.

"Someone's following us," Olga said suddenly, stealing glances of the rearview mirror.

I discreetly looked back and noticed a black Passat with tinted windows.

"How long has it been there?"

"Since we left home. At first, I thought it was a coincidence, but he's definitely following us."

"We need to change seats," I said coldly, looking around and trying to find a good spot to stop the car. "Turn right here. There's going to be a mall there. Take us into the parking garage."

"Fucking hell, Laura, you told me they were driving to the airport, not landing already."

"I think those are Karol's men. Remember his wife, Monika? The car has Polish plates. It can only be them."

We drove to the first level of the garage and stopped at the first unoccupied spot, before swapping seats without getting out. My driving skills had come in handy a lot of times during these last few months. I was grateful to my dad for teaching me how to perfect that particular skill set. I was grateful for all the courses he had sent me and my brother to.

"All right, bitch, buckle up," I said with a grin. "If you're right, it might be a bumpy ride."

I launched the car into motion, rapidly turning toward the exit. The Passat accelerated with a screech of the wheels, but was immediately blocked by a car reversing from a parking spot. I joined the traffic and sped toward the main street. I broke all the rules there were, and zoomed through Mokotów. The car wasn't powerful enough to lose our tail by speed alone, but I knew the area pretty well. That was my main asset. In the rearview mirror I could see the black sedan gaining on us. Traffic was thick, fortunately, and I could use that to my advantage.

"Aren't you afraid?" Olga asked, clutching the handle on the ceiling.

"No time for that. Besides, if they catch us, they won't hurt us. This is more of a race than an escape."

I kept my eyes on the road, searching for one specific street. I didn't remember its name, but I knew there was a spot there where we could hide.

"There it is!" I exclaimed, turning the car abruptly.

The lumbering Touareg nearly broke in half, but it managed to stay in one piece in the end. We drove through an archway leading to a yard behind an old tenement house where my gay hairdresser used to live. The yard was surrounded by tall buildings on all sides and had parking spaces where we could wait until the Passat lost us. I halted the car and killed the engine.

"We have to wait a while," I said, shrugging. "They're going to pass us by, but they'll be back, searching all the small streets. You have some time for a smoke now, if you like."

We stepped out, and Olga lit a cigarette.

"Have you called István?" I asked.

"Yes, when you were changing. He was crazy happy. He's preparing a bedroom for us in his apartment overseeing the Danube. He's not exactly young, you know," she said, shooting a glance my way. "To be perfectly honest, he's my dad's age. But he doesn't look it."

I shook my head.

"You're one perverted bitch, you know that?"

"Can't help it! I just like older men. Besides, you'll get it when you see him. He's gorgeous. Hungarians are pretty guys. He's got long black hair, bushy eyebrows, wide shoulders, and perfect lips. He knows how to cook, knows his way around cars, and drives a motorbike. A sexy daddy. And he's got this enormous tattoo on his back. And another enormous thing, if you catch my drift." She grinned.

I shook my head. "Jesus, shit-for-brains, keep it in your pants," I said, getting in the car. "Smoke your cig, while I call my mom. I need to sell her some bullshit. You know, why I got a new number."

I wasn't ready to lie to my mom again, so instead of calling her, I tried occupying my mind with something else.

Copying all the numbers from the piece of paper to my new phone took me about an hour. Meanwhile, Olga entertained herself with skipping from one radio station to another, searching for all the newest pop hits. She was perky and animated, completely at ease. Unlike me. Olga was behaving as if nothing had happened, and the fact that we were on the run from the Sicilian Mafia had seemingly not bothered her at all.

"All right, it's been enough time. They must have left by now. I'll drive until we're out of town. We'll switch later."

This time nobody followed us. As soon as we left Warsaw, we changed seats. Ten minutes into our trip, I was finally ready to confront my mother. She picked up quickly.

"Hi, Mom!" I chirped, managing to sound cheerful.

"What is this number you're calling me from, dear?"

"Oh, you know, I changed phones after my contract expired. I had all kinds of people calling. I don't know who gave them my number. So I said enough and changed it. You know how they can be . . . trying to talk you into buying more stuff you don't need."

"How are you, then? How's Sicily? It's dreadful here in Poland. Cold and rainy."

I know, I thought, *I can see that.*

The conversation continued for some time with us talking about nothing in particular. I had to tell her that the Man in Black might drop by, trying to find me.

"Mom, I have to tell you something. I left Massimo," I said out of the blue, changing the subject. "He cheated on me. He wasn't the man for me. I moved to work in another hotel to keep away from him. I'm doing a lot better now. There's more free time, and I feel good with myself."

My mother went quiet then. I needed to keep talking.

"So, anyway, the hotel is the same brand, just on the opposite side of the island. The director's decided to move me there, and I have to say it was a pretty good decision," I prattled on. "It's bigger, and the money's better. I'm learning Italian. I've been thinking of inviting Olga." At this moment, I winked at my friend, and she laughed silently. "Everything is perfect. I got a new apartment. It's a lot prettier than the old one. Maybe a bit too large—"

"Darling," my mother cut in, not convinced. "If you're happy and you know what you're doing, I won't try to talk you out of anything. You've never been able to keep in place for too long, so I'm not surprised you've moved on again. But remember that if anything bad happens, you always have a home right here with us."

"I know, Mommy. Thank you. Just don't give my number to anyone, please. It's important. I don't want people to start calling me again."

"Are you sure you're only talking about telemarketers?"

"Yeah, them, but also my ex-boyfriends and generally all the people I don't want to talk to. But listen, Mom, I have to go now. I'm having a meeting, so bye! Love you!"

"I love you, too. Call me as often as you'd like."

I put my phone down and crossed my legs, taking a look outside the window.

It was a rainy and cold day. Back on Sicily it probably was pleasantly warm and sunny.

"You think your mom fell for it?" Olga asked, before adding, "She's not that stupid, you know."

"What the fuck was I supposed to tell her, then? *Hi, Mom, I'm going to be honest with you. I was kidnapped three months ago, because this one guy kept dreaming about me, and then I fell in love with him, but don't worry—it's only Stockholm syndrome. Anyway, he's the boss of the local Mafia and he kills people for a living, and we're going to have a baby and we're actually married now. We were having a good time spending the money he made by selling drugs and guns, but then he cheated on me and now I'm running from the mob and going to hide in Hungary.*"

Olga couldn't keep it in anymore and snorted with laughter. She had to slow down to keep the car from swerving off the road. It took her a long while to calm down a bit. She wiped away tears and said, "Yeah, that's so improbable, it's dumb. I can see your mom's face. She'd think you'd lost it. You should really tell her the truth. She won't believe it anyway."

Olga's lightheartedness was getting on my nerves. At the same time, it was a welcome break from thinking about my own ill luck and sadness.

"We need to get some gas," she said at one moment and took a ramp off the highway.

"Wait a minute. I'll give you some cash," I said, reaching for the bag filled with money.

We were already outside of Poland, so the thick wads of euro bills would come in handy.

Olga peeked into the bag and grimaced.

"Is that how a million looks? I thought there was going to be more of it."

I zipped the bag shut and sent her a disapproving look.

"How much was I supposed to take? You think it's too little? I was thinking of going back to work after having the baby. The money was only supposed to last us until I gave birth. I don't want to live at Massimo's expense. At least not like we did on Sicily—pretending to be aristocrats."

"That's because you're stupid, Laura. You're not thinking about the advantages. Look at it this way: he got you pregnant without your consent or even your knowledge." I shook my head. "All right, you knew then," she said, "even though you really didn't, but fuck that. So he got you pregnant. He took your ex away from you, made you marry him, and then cheated on you. I'd have taken everything from the dumb fuck. As punishment, not out of greed."

"You know what? Just go get that gas. You're talking out of your ass. We can't use my card anymore. Massimo will track the transaction or at least find out where we're going. So let's keep our heads straight. There's no more cash, and that's that."

The rest of the way passed without incident. After some ten hours or so, we reached our destination. István lived in a beautiful historic building near the center of Budapest, on the western side of the river.

"Olga, how nice to see you!" he called, coming down a flight of stairs toward the car. "How long has it been since you've graced Hungary with your presence?"

"Not that long, István. Only five years," Olga replied with a smile, smacking the older man on the butt as he embraced her. "All right, enough of that," she said, pushing him away.

"This is my sister, Laura."

István bowed to me, planting a kiss on my palm.

"My beloved is back because of your trouble. I thank you, Laura, and wish you all the best—maybe not immediately."

Olga had been right when she said István didn't look his age. He was very sensual and handsome, with dusky skin and features I had often seen on Russians before. His eyes were cool, and he moved with a studied nonchalance. He was a strong, confident man who liked when things were going his way. But the most striking thing about him was that he just seemed to be . . . a good man. I couldn't explain it. There was something about him that made me trust him.

"A rather peculiar way of seeing things, but thank you," I said with a smile.

István took another glance at Olga and called out. A young, stunningly handsome man appeared on the stairs.

"This is Atilla. My son," the older Hungarian said. "You remember him, Olga?"

We both froze, dumbfounded, ogling the young man standing in front of us now. He liked working out—that much was apparent. His bulging muscles flexing under a thin, tight-fitting shirt made looking away quite difficult. His skin was tanned, his eyes green, and his teeth snow-white and perfectly straight. When he smiled, little dimples showed on his cheeks. He was adorable, and cute, and utterly breathtaking.

"I'm having a heart attack," I muttered in Polish with a dumb grin stuck to my face.

My friend stood hypnotized, unable to say a word.

"Hey there, I'm Atilla," the young man said. "May I take your bags? They look heavy."

"Can you take me instead?" Olga asked, still in Polish, finally managing to find her voice.

Meanwhile, Atilla grabbed our things and skipped upstairs, vanishing inside the building. We stood there, drooling, for a little while.

"Need I remind you you're pregnant and heartbroken?" Olga asked with a smirk.

"And you're still madly in love with Domenico, aren't you?" I retorted. "Besides, this one is a lot younger than us, isn't he?"

"I guess so. When I last saw him, he was still a kid. He must have been fifteen back then, so now he's about twenty." She nodded, satisfied with her calculations. "He was kind of pretty as a teenager, but damn, this is just ridiculous. And we're about to live under one roof . . ." She moaned quietly.

After taking our last bag, István returned to us, took the keys to Olga's car, and drove it down a ramp to an underground garage. Olga, Atilla, and I walked inside through the main entrance.

The house was beautiful. A grand old staircase greeted us from a wide hall, leading to a massive living room. It took up the entire ground floor.

The space was classical, with wooden furniture and floors as well as a stonework fireplace. It was all warm, discreet colors that made it seem cozy despite its size. There were animal skins on the floor, lots of knickknacks, and no plants at all. This house had been decorated by men, and it showed.

"It's late, but would you like a drink?" Atilla asked, uncorking a carafe and pouring something into a glass.

He sipped and sent me a questioning look with those big green eyes of his. It reminded me of Massimo—the same manly stare, the same quick movement on the tongue across the lips.

"I can't. I'm pregnant," I said, certain that the child would act as an efficient deterrent.

"Oh, that's wonderful. How far along?" he asked, genuinely interested. "I'll order you tea and some dinner. What would you like? We have a housekeeper. Her name is Bori. You can call her by dialing zero on any phone around the property. She's a great cook, and she's been with us for fifteen years."

I wasn't hungry, just tired. Exhausted, even. The last twenty-four hours had been hard.

"I'm sorry, but I'm on my last legs. I'd like to sleep, if that's okay."

Atilla put down his glass and took my hand before leading me upstairs. I was a bit taken aback by his directness, but his touch wasn't unpleasant, so I didn't resist. He took me to the second floor and opened one of the rooms for me.

"This will be your bedroom," he said, flicking the light on. "I'll take care of you. Everything is going to be okay, Laura . . ."

He trailed off, looked me in the eyes and planted a delicate kiss on my cheek. Pulling away, he traced a finger across it. I shivered, feeling uneasy. As if I was somehow cheating on Massimo. I took a step back, retreating deeper into the room.

"Thank you. Good night," I whispered and closed the door.

◇◇◇◇◇◇◇◇◇◇

The next day, as I woke up, my hand instinctively reached over the bed, trying to find my husband.

"Massimo . . ." I breathed, feeling my eyes tear up. My mom had told me you can't cry when you're pregnant, or the child will be whiny, but I didn't care much for her superstitions. I stayed in bed, crying, rolling from side to side. The pain I was in started surfacing only when I'd dealt with the exhaustion. It was slowly dawning on me that this was real. That it had all happened. My despair was overwhelming. My stomach knotted. I didn't want to live alone. Not without him. How could I, without his touch, his smell? I loved him so much, it hurt. I covered my head with a pillow and wailed like a wounded animal. There was nothing I needed more than to just disappear.

"Tears are like good friends," I heard a voice say behind me.

"Olga told me what happened. Remember, sometimes its easier to get something off your chest when speaking to someone you don't know."

I lifted the pillow from my face and looked at Atilla, who was sitting on the edge of the bed holding a cup of tea. Wearing only sweatpants. He was so adorable, so concerned and caring.

"I heard a noise, so I decided to pay you a visit. I can leave, if you want. But if you'd like me to stay, I can just sit here with you for a while." I watched him in silence, and he smiled, sipping his tea. "My mother always told me: 'There will be others.' You're pregnant, and that may complicate things a bit, but remember that everything happens for a reason. You might think that I'm being cruel, but I believe you know that I'm right."

I wiped away the moisture from my cheeks and pulled myself higher up the bed, resting my back against the wall. I took Atilla's cup and sipped.

"You drink your tea just as I like it. With milk," I said.

"Nope. I just sipped the tea Olga prepared for you. It's nearly two already. You've been asleep for more than twelve hours. My dad grew worried. He booked you a visit at his buddy's clinic. He's a gynecologist. I'll take you to him when you're ready."

"Thank you, Atilla. You'll make someone a very happy woman someday."

The young Hungarian turned and sent me a curious look.

"I sincerely doubt that," he replied with a slight smile. "I'm one hundred percent, certified gay." My eyes widened, and I must have made the craziest expression, as Atilla burst out in uncontrolled laughter.

"Jesus, what a loss to the women of the world!" I groaned.

"Isn't it?" He grinned. "I once tried girls, but being bi isn't me. I'm just not interested in vaginas. You women are beautiful, and you have better taste in footwear, but I simply like men more. Large, burly, and muscular—"

"Okay, okay, I get it," I cut him off.

Atilla got up and swayed his hips for me. "But you can always watch. I don't mind." Then he added, "Now, come on, Laura. We're leaving."

I washed myself, put on some clothes, and went downstairs. Olga was standing by the kitchen counter, wrapped in István's arms. They didn't even notice my arrival. She was coquettish, stretching slowly and inclining her head, exposing her neck, while he bit his lips in silence.

"Good morning," I said, putting the empty cup into the sink.

They didn't seem fazed at all, instead greeting me without taking eyes off each other.

"What are you doing?" I asked Olga in Polish, grabbing a sweet roll from the counter.

István smiled, hearing our native tongue, and left us alone.

"What do you mean? We were talking."

"Telepathically? Without words?"

"What the fuck is your problem, Laura?" she barked, irritated, and took a seat on the counter.

"You were in love a few days ago. Forgot about that?"

"Our lives looked completely different a few days ago. I can't be with Domenico anymore. Not when you're not with Massimo. So what? Am I to cry after the guy for the rest of my life and live in celibacy, thinking about all the good times we had?"

I dropped my head and took a deep breath.

"I'm sorry," I said, trying to hold back tears.

"Oh, darling," she purred, hugging me. "Don't apologize. It's not your fault. Massimo fucked up our lives." She wiped away my tears and continued, "I'm just not going to wallow in pain forever. I'd like to forget it as soon as possible, and that's my advice for you, too."

Atilla arrived at that point, and we stopped talking.

He was wearing melange-gray oversized sweatpants and a beige T-shirt with a deep, stretched-out neckline. On his feet were black Air Max sneakers, and he clutched a black leather jacket.

He pushed a pair of shades up his nose and smiled at us brightly, displaying his perfect teeth. "Ready?"

"You got to be kidding. I'm not leaving like this!" Olga cried and ran straight upstairs. "Give me five minutes."

I, on the other hand, didn't intend to change clothes. I felt good in my Emus, skinny jeans, and loosely knitted, oversized sweater. I put on my favorite smoky aviators and glanced at my watch.

My belly flashed with pain. I clutched at it with one hand, leaning over the kitchen counter with the other.

"What's happening, Laura?" Atilla asked with a worried expression, stepping closer and holding me up by the elbow.

"Nothing," I replied faintly. "As soon as I think about Massimo, I feel this strange pain. It's like the child misses its father." I raised my eyes and looked at the young man. "I know it's stupid."

"I wouldn't be so sure. I had my wisdom teeth pulled out some time ago. The sore spots mended quickly, but I felt pain for months after the teeth had been extracted. It's called phantom pain. So, you know, everything's possible."

I squatted by the counter and let out a short laugh. "Right, same story here."

"I'm back!" Olga announced, running down the stairs.

Fall in Hungary was a lot more beautiful than in Poland. And warmer, too. It was nearly November, but the temperature outside was a balmy fifty-three degrees Fahrenheit. We drove through the historical center of Budapest, delighting in the rich variety of architectural styles. Atilla was driving slowly and surely. His blue Audi A5 cruised gracefully along the crowded streets of the Hungarian capital.

We reached our destination in thirty minutes. Atilla stepped out and opened the doors for us before leading us to the private clinic of his father's friend. We entered. The young receptionist straightened out, seeing the young Hungarian, and flashed her best smile, responding eagerly to his questions. A moment later, we were in my new gynecologist's office.

"Is everything all right?" Olga called out, jumping to her feet as soon as I left the examination room.

"Not really. They've run some tests, and I'll get the results tomorrow. The doctor told me to lie down, don't do anything tiring, and avoid nervous situations. Fuck me, Olga—I'll go crazy just lying around."

"Don't you worry about anything," Atilla chimed in. "Now come. I'll buy you a *lángos.* It's a local specialty. Then we'll go home. We'll all lie around together. It's going to be fine." He wrapped his arm around me.

Olga grabbed my hand.

"Fine. We'll lie down, then. We're all pregnant with you," she said with a laugh, planted a kiss on my forehead, and led me back to the car.

They got me an unbelievably greasy but delicious cheese-and-garlic flat bread, and then we went back home, where I changed into a sweat suit and got into bed. A moment later, the door opened, and István entered my room.

"I spoke with my friend, the doctor," he said, taking a seat in an armchair by the bed. "I hope you won't hold it against me, but I'm worried about you. I know it's a high-risk pregnancy, and I'll do my best for you to feel as comfortable as possible here. So don't worry about a thing. I'll install Polish TV today. That laptop by the bed has access to the Internet, and it's yours. If you need anything—books, newspapers, anything—just say a word and I'll get it for you."

I looked at him with a grateful smile.

"Why are you doing all this for me? You barely know me. Besides, I've shown up out of the blue, on the run from the Sicilian mob, pregnant . . . I'm going to be nothing but trouble for you."

"Oh, it's simple. I love your friend, and she loves you."

His hand stroked my arm briefly, and then he got up and left, passing Olga on his way.

"Surprise visit!" my friend exclaimed, skipping into the room and putting a mug of cocoa on the nightstand by the bed.

"You didn't tell me what the doctor said."

"Well, the most important thing is that the baby already looks like a human being. It weighs about as much as a spoonful of sugar. It knows when I'm happy—the hormones my body produces make it happy, too. Too bad it's the same when I'm pissed. So according to the doctor I should be happy as a clam all the time. What else . . . It's got little feet and hands. Like a little human, but only a few inches long. As it's a high-risk pregnancy, the doctor will come here every day and run tests, like an ultrasonogram. I should probably stay at the hospital, but since István is his friend, I can stay here." I paused, remembering something. "By the way, do you know he loves you? He said as much a minute ago."

Olga lay down by my feet, hiding her face in her hands.

"Jesus . . . I know, but I just don't care. I love Domenico.

István is sexy, sure. He's caring, good, and handsome, and has a gorgeous dick . . ." She trailed off, biting her lip. "But there's no chemistry between us. Not like there used to be. I remember when I first met him. It was July. I went on vacation to Lake Balaton. You were with that guy who owned a restaurant then. Paweł, I think. And he was your whole world, remember?

"Anyway, I rented an apartment in Siófok. I went out one night, going from club to club, and I couldn't find a place I really liked. So I bought a bottle of rosé and a pack of cigarettes and just sat on the curb, still dressed like a fucking diva, and lounged around, watching people. I must have looked like a hooker—that's why he noticed me. Or maybe I was just too sober and still looked like a million dollars.

"Anyhow, he was walking by with his friends and turned around to have a better look at me as they were passing me by. And our eyes met. We stared at each other for a long time, like some crazy couple, and István walked straight into a guy. I didn't get up even when he disappeared into the crowd. A couple of minutes later, he was back, standing right in front of me. First, I saw his expensive biker boots, then the tattered jeans with that enormous bulge in the crotch—that giant dick of his . . ." Her face went all dreamy again, before she continued, "Then I lifted my eyes and took in his muscular body and his hypnotic stare. He took the cigarette out of my mouth, sat right next to me, and smoked it himself. Then he took a swig of my wine, got right back up, and left. I was fucking shocked. *What the hell was that supposed to be?* I thought, but I stayed put. Five minutes later, he was back. He sat down on the curb, placed a bottle of his own wine on the ground, and pulled out a pocketknife.

"He opened the bottle and said: 'If you're going to remember

Hungary by its wines, you have to start drinking better ones. But I'm going to make sure the wine won't be the only thing you remember.' And just like that, I was his. We talked through the night, sitting on that curb, then we had breakfast and went to the beach. And you won't believe me, but we did nothing more. The next day we met for dinner at a place he picked, and we talked and talked for hours. In the end I thanked him for the two wonderful nights and just ran."

"Wait . . . what?" I asked, surprised.

"Why did you do that?"

"He was perfect. Too perfect. And I was young," Olga replied with a sadness I rarely heard from her. "I didn't trust myself. I couldn't control my feelings, and I just got scared that I'd . . . fall in love. But don't worry. István didn't give up so easily." She raised her hand, stemming my questions. "I left the restaurant and headed off toward my apartment. It was just a few blocks away. When I reached the door, I felt someone's hand on my shoulder. I got turned around, pushed against the wall, and then I felt lips on my lips. It was the greatest kiss in my life. When he pulled away, he said: 'You forgot to say goodbye.' And he turned around and was about to walk away. What was I supposed to do? I ran after him, straight into his arms. That's more or less how we spent the next week. In each other's arms. Then we drove to Budapest and it turned out he was rich, divorced, and had a son. It was all too much for me, so I ran again. He told me he understood, but he wouldn't forget me or ever accept that I wasn't his anymore. He called me, visited me in Warsaw a couple times . . ."

I stared at my friend, enchanted by the way she was telling her story. There was so much emotion in her voice. So much passion.

"Why didn't you tell me this before? This is so sweet." I smiled at her, maybe a bit ironically, and she immediately retaliated by smacking me on the head with a pillow.

"That's why, bitch. You were going to make fun of me. Talking about feelings and shit is not my style. But I can tell you all about how I spent a week with his dick in my mouth. I guarantee it's an even better story."

CHAPTER *six*

I spent the next hours, days, and weeks in bed. Olga and Atilla kept me company. István joined in at times. We played games, read books, watched TV, and just hung out, getting used to one another. A bit like siblings. My test results came in and were getting better by the day. I grew calmer, too. I can't say I was happy—there was no day that I didn't think about Massimo, but at least I could live without him. I called my mom, switching numbers each time. Thank God my phone had caller ID blocking, so she didn't know I was changing them all the time. And she would never call me first. She always waited for me to do it.

Fall came and went. It was December. My mood was declining steadily—I grew too large for my clothes, even though my belly was still smaller than I'd anticipated. Olga was fighting with herself while István was fighting with her reluctance. One day, the conversation that couldn't be avoided finally came.

"It's time for us to go back to Poland, Laura. Either way, we need to move out of here," Olga said, sitting by the kitchen counter one morning, as I was having breakfast.

"The kid is okay now, you're feeling well, nobody is following us or looking for us. It's been nearly two months. Let's go back."

I was glad she'd proposed that. We both missed Poland—our parents and friends. Hungary was gorgeous, but we were only ever going to remain guests. We couldn't overstay our welcome.

"You're right. Did you tell István?"

"Yeah. We talked through the night. He understands. I have made him realize we weren't going to be together forever, no matter what. I think he's accepted that."

Atilla appeared in the kitchen and gave me his now-customary great hug and a smooch on the forehead.

"How's my favorite mommy doing?" he asked.

The fact that he was gay made it easier for me to get closer to him. He might have been one of the most handsome men I had ever known, but I treated him like a brother.

"I'm feeling well enough to tell you that we're leaving," I said, reciprocating his embrace.

He jumped back, his face suddenly filled with anger, and he rounded the counter, slamming his hands onto it and shouting, "You can't just leave now! You can't leave me here alone! Besides, you can't change doctors again. What if you start feeling worse in Poland? Who's going to take care of you then? I won't allow it! You're not going anywhere."

He slammed his hands on the counter again and pinned me with a furious glare. His reaction left me short for words. This abrupt change that had transformed a cute boy into a totalitarian lunatic unwilling to part with his possessions shocked me.

"Stop acting like a prick, Atilla!" Olga barked, getting up. "Don't you yell at us. There's nothing worse than a handsome man acting like a total douchebag. We're not leaving you. We're going back to our country. You can come and visit. It's not like we're from Canada. We can see each other every week if you'd like that. Besides, there are a lot of beautiful boys for you in Warsaw."

I pushed myself to my feet and walked over to him, cuddling against his muscular torso.

"Now, now, Godzilla, don't get so angry," I said placatingly. "You can come with us if you'd like. But we have to go home."

I patted him on the back and went upstairs. Just like I predicted, I didn't have to wait for long until my new gay brother stormed into my room. He slammed the door behind him, stomped across the room, grabbed me by the throat with a muscular arm, and shoved me into the wall. I felt the familiar tickling sensation in my stomach. Only Massimo had ever treated me like that. Atilla's tongue pushed its way into my mouth, and his body stuck to mine. I closed my eyes, feeling like I had gone back in time. Our tongues danced around each other as his strong, large hands gently cupped my face. His soft lips clung to mine, hot, passionate, and wild.

"Atilla," I whispered, shocked, pulling my head back, "what are you doing? You said—"

"You really believed I was gay?" he asked, his tongue tracing a line down my neck. "I'm as straight as it gets, Laura. I've wanted you since I first saw you. I adore your smell. I love watching you when you sleep. When you wake up. I love the way you cross your legs when you brush your teeth, or when you bite your lip, reading books, or when you are deep in thought." He sighed. "Oh, God, how I want you."

I was so shocked, his words didn't reach me at first. I didn't understand. And his tongue, inching its way across my skin, wasn't making anything easier.

"But I'm pregnant," I said, "and married to a mafioso. Don't you understand?" I pushed him away. "I've treated you like a brother, kid. And you pretended to be gay so you could what? Sneak up to me one night and fuck me? Jesus, that's twisted." With rising fury, I stepped to the door and opened it. "Get the fuck out!" He didn't react. I screamed, "Get the fuck out of here, Atilla!"

Olga, ever the loyal pit bull, appeared out of nowhere and stopped in the doorway.

"What's going on? Why are you shouting?"

"No reason. Pack your things now. We're leaving."

Unable to hide her concern, Olga shot a glance at me, then at Atilla. Having received no other explanation, she turned around and left for her room.

Two hours later, we were ready to leave. Olga spent a long time saying goodbye to István, who didn't look happy with our departure at all. I don't know how she thanked him for being such a gracious host, but when they left his room, he had a wholly satisfied expression. I kissed him on the cheeks, and he embraced me in a fatherly gesture, keeping me in his arms for a long time. I liked him. He made me feel calm and safe. And, unlike his son, he wasn't harboring any ill intentions.

"Thank you," I said, finally pulling away.

"Call me when you get there."

After our falling-out, Atilla left the house and didn't return. I felt bad, but at the same time I was so unbearably angry with him that my distress balanced out. All in all, his absence might have been for the best.

The road to Poland was long. Too long. With our sudden departure, we hadn't worked out where to stay. It dawned on us halfway.

"I got an idea. Guess what it is," Olga said.

"I think we had the same one at the same time. You were thinking we couldn't stay at your place, weren't you?"

"Sure, but I figured that out days ago. I have another idea now."

I sent her a searching look.

"So I've been thinking about this for some time now, and I decided it won't do us any good to be constantly on the run. He'll find you whether you want it or not. Besides, darling, there are ways to get things between you in order, you know. And fucking up your entire life only because Massimo is a bastard gets you nowhere. You've had time to rest and recuperate now. I'm not telling you to call him now, but let's just stop worrying about them finding us. We'll be in Poland, not Sicily. He's pretty powerless here. In Poland, he's just another pimped-up Italian hunk, not a mob boss everyone tries to please."

I listened in silence, wondering where this was going. I was slowly beginning to accept that she was right. I had acted like a totally egoistic idiot. My escape had nothing to do with Olga, and she had every right to be fed up with this whole situation.

"You are right," I acceded. "But I don't want to go back to my flat. We'll stay at the hotel I used to work for. It's downtown. We'll look for something more appropriate then. We have the money—it's only a matter of picking a spot. I'd like to live in Wilanów. Not the new projects, though. A bit farther away. It's calm there. Quiet. Close to the center, and the clinic is just a stone's throw away. Paweł Ome will hook me up with a good gynecologist and work his magic so I don't die of pain during childbirth."

"I can see you've already planned all this."

"Yes. Absolutely. But only, like, a minute ago." I shrugged.

It was late evening when we reached Warsaw. Before we

arrived, I had called Natalie, a colleague I used to work with, and asked her to book me a room under her name. I didn't want to run anymore, but I wasn't going to make it any easier for my husband to find me by booking it under my own. The closer we got to our destination, the more tired we were getting. I had taken over the driving all the way back at the border and immediately started speeding, in desperate need of a good night's sleep and wanting to get home as soon as possible.

The ring road around Warsaw was empty, and I exceeded the speed limit. An instant later, I noticed the twinkling lights of a police patrol car in the rearview mirror. They pulled us over.

"Shit. It's the police," I said.

Olga turned to look through the window, completely unfazed. "How fast were you going?"

"I don't know, really, but fast."

"That's all right. We'll spin some sob story, and they'll let us go."

We tried and failed. After fifteen minutes of trying to explain my pregnancy, the long road behind us, and the foul mood we were both in, the officers gave us a hefty fine and slapped some penalty points on my account. That in itself wasn't anything I felt particularly bad about, but they did write down my name and check it in the database.

Massimo would get his hands on that information, for sure. He'd know where I was. Maybe I was getting paranoid, but I had to assume he had access to police databases. When we finally reached the hotel, I paid for a week up front and we went to sleep.

I found a place for us three days later. It wasn't located where I wanted, but the place was so gorgeous, I just had to rent it. The owner wanted us to sign a contract, but I couldn't have that.

I paid for six months in advance and offered a large security deposit to boot. He was happy with that arrangement.

The flat was situated close to Martin's, my ex's, apartment, but I knew he'd probably give me a wide berth if we ever saw each other again.

So we moved in, Olga and me, and after long weeks, we had our own place. It was a great spot. Too large for the two of us, but that wasn't a problem. A massive living room with an adjacent kitchen took up nearly half of the total space. Then there were three bedrooms and a large closet, two bathrooms and a little lavatory. We wouldn't organize any parties or anything, but better to be safe than sorry. The extra space might come in handy.

It was Tuesday. We were sitting on the long couch in the living room, staring dumbly at the TV.

"I need to go to my parents' for a while," Olga said. "A day or two, tops. I'll also drop by your folks'. Tell them that you're doing super okay. I'm going to leave in the morning. Mom called me earlier today. I've got to go."

"Sure thing," I replied. "I'll just keep doing what I've been doing for the last couple of weeks. Lying around, watching movies."

Olga left the next morning. I was instantly overcome by loneliness. I grabbed my laptop and scanned through cinema lineups. There were so many movies I wanted to watch, I bought two tickets for two separate screenings—one after another. I spent about five hours at the cinema. After all, what difference did it make if I stayed in bed at home or in a seat at the cinema?

When my movie marathon ended, I caught a cab and returned to Wilanów. I turned the key in the door to my apartment and heard the TV chattering from the inside. Was Olga back already? I went in and headed toward the sound. It was dark. The gloom was illuminated only by the faint glow of the TV. My eyes wandered, finally focusing on the screen. I froze. This was some kind of nightmare. The screen was divided into two halves—the first depicted the CCTV recording from Massimo's study where he was fucking Anna, and the second was showing some sort of meeting taking place in the garden back at the mansion. I collapsed on the couch, trying not to faint. Someone paused the recording. The film stopped. I took a deep breath. He was here. I closed my eyes.

"Massimo?"

"If you take a close look at what's happening on the left side, you will notice a birthmark on my brother's buttock. I do not have a birthmark there." His voice resonated in the room. "If, however, you look at the right side of the screen, you will see that at the same time I was sitting in the garden, entertaining my guests from Milan."

I was so close to bursting out in tears.

I could hear his voice, smell his scent . . . I did not listen to his words, though.

"Now please fucking tell me what the hell you were doing for the last two months!" Massimo bellowed when I didn't react. "If you want to leave me, you say it! You don't get to run and hide! You treated me like your worst enemy, not your husband. And to make matters worse, you apparently decided that I was a complete idiot. Do you think I would have cheated on you with someone I despise?"

The lights came on and don Massimo stood up from the armchair and walked up to me. I raised my head and looked him in the eyes. He was the most beautiful man on Earth. In his black pants and dark turtleneck, he looked breathtaking. He stood still and pierced me with his ice-cold eyes. I had not felt the chill of his stare for such a long time. I made myself avert my eyes. The sight of him caused me physical pain. Instead, I looked at the TV. Massimo pressed Play again. Everything he had told me was true. It all became clear. He rewound the tape, and I saw him getting up from the table and walking to his study, where his brother was making love to Anna. I was going to throw up. I had not felt this bad in my entire life. I fucked up. I had made a mistake, and it had cost us both dearly. My mouth didn't want to open. What could I say? Was there anything that could make things better?

"Adriano left," Massimo said after a while. "And he took Anna with him. I think she's happy with him. The truce between our families has been officially established, and I'm sure now that you'll be safe." He sat back down in the armchair. "Now. Pack your things. We're going back to Sicily."

"I can't leave Olga."

"She's with Domenico. He was at her parents' place. They'll be here in an hour."

"I don't have anything I'd like to take with me."

"Then get up and come with me," he said coolly, deftly pushing himself up.

He was angry. Furious, to be precise. He had never been this cold to me before. I didn't want to stoke the flames of his fury, so I just did as he asked.

The trip to the airport took us fifteen minutes. Fifteen long, exhausting minutes. I took a seat on the jet. Massimo offered me a pill and a glass of water.

"Take it," he said. His voice was impassive.

"No. I'll manage without it."

"You have endangered my child enough. Do not test me any more."

I swallowed the pill and went to the bedroom cabin, where I

grabbed a heavy woolen blanket, covered myself, and closed my eyes. All the tension I had been holding inside me was dissipating. I was calm and happy. He hadn't cheated on me. I hadn't felt this good since my honeymoon. We had to talk, but if he needed time, I was going to give him as much as he needed. What mattered was that he was mine again.

When I opened my eyes, it was morning. I was in my bed on Sicily. I smiled and reached across the bed, but my husband wasn't there. I got up and threw on my bathrobe before going to Olga's room. I was just about to grab the doorknob when I remembered she might not be alone. As quietly as I could, I peeked inside. She was in bed, with a laptop on her thighs.

"Hey," I greeted her, closing the door behind me and slipping into her bed. "Massimo is so pissed off, he doesn't even talk to me. He only orders me around. It's getting on my nerves."

"Can you blame him, though? He didn't do a thing, and you accused him of cheating and took away the thing he loved the most. Forgive me when I say that he's simply in the right here. I'd have killed you already if I were in his place." She slammed the laptop shut. "I told you he didn't do it, but you didn't listen. Maybe that will teach you a lesson. You should sort those things out with conversation instead of running away from your problems."

"I'll take my penance with grace," I groaned, covering my face with a pillow. "How's Domenico?"

Olga smiled and closed her eyes. She muttered something under her breath and then said, "He came for me yesterday when I was at my parents' place. Imagine my surprise when I took their dog out for a walk and he just showed up. Leaning against Massimo's black Ferrari, aloof, serious and stylish as always. Jesus, he was so beautiful . . . I wanted to jump into his arms, but my dog ran away."

I snorted with laughter.

"What?! What do you mean?"

"Yeah, the fucking mutt just ran off, and instead of going for my man I sprinted after the dog, because he's Mom's favorite thing in the world. The evil little shit took off, and I gave fucking chase."

"What about Domenico?"

"And Domenico stayed in place, watching on. There was a bright side to that whole shitshow. I focused on the dog instead of the urge to suck Domenico off by my mom's house. I've been living without sex for nearly two months! How long can a human being . . ."

"What about István?" I cut in. "Back in Budapest, you two didn't . . . You know."

Olga shook her head, clearly proud of herself.

"We did nothing. I slept next to him, hugged him, but we didn't have sex. So anyway, I caught that goddamned mutt, led it back home, said goodbye to my parents, and a moment later I was with Domenico. He opened the car door for me, and before I got in, he pushed me against the side of the Ferrari and kissed me. And that kiss . . . Man, it was like he wanted to devour me. We kissed like teenagers do. Like he was fucking me with that tongue."

"All right, enough! I get it," I hissed, grimacing.

"And then he fucked me on the road. With his cock this time. There wasn't any space in that weird car, so we had to leave it. We were so fucking horny, we didn't even notice it was freezing cold. It was a first for him. I nearly froze my ass off. I mean, I've pulled my pants down in freezing winter conditions once or twice, but not for that long. But one time wasn't enough, so we stopped two or three more times, and we were late for the plane. I mean,

I know it's a private jet, but there are schedules and stuff, right? Anyway, I think I caught a cold."

"So did we fly together or not?" I asked. Ten minutes after I took the pill, I blacked out.

"Yeah. Me, you, Domenico, Massimo, and the security guys."

"Did Massimo tell you anything during the flight?" I wanted to know.

I glanced at the clock by the bed.

"No. He didn't sit with us. He just stared at you sleeping for the whole time. Looked like he was praying to you. I popped by for a while, but he didn't want to talk to me. Then he carried you out of the jet and put you in his car. Back home, he took you to bed, changed your clothes, and ogled you some more. I wanted to help him out, but he didn't let me. Then Domenico took me to the bedroom, and here we are."

"This is going to be a difficult couple of days." I sighed. "Okay. I need to go to the clinic. I'll call the doctor and book a visit. Be back in a sec."

I went to grab my phone and dialed the clinic. As usual, the name Torricelli opened every door. The range of options open to me was significantly wider than for any regular Sicilian. I put on a loose gray woolen tunic, my favorite black Givenchy boots, and a black leather jacket. There wasn't such a thing as proper winter on Sicily, but it wasn't exactly warm, either. When I returned to Olga's room, she was ready to go.

"How about breakfast on the beach?" she asked cheerfully. "I know a great place in Giardini Naxos. I was there with Domenico when you and Massimo were on your honeymoon. They have a delicious ham omelet and some local cheeses."

"Great. I need to be at the clinic in two hours, so we have some time."

We crossed the house, seeing no one on our way. I left Olga on the driveway and went around the building to fetch my Bentley. I opened the little wall cabinet where the keys to the cars used to be, only to realize there were none. The garage was filled with cars, though.

"What the fuck?" I muttered to myself, backtracking. There was a security guard sitting by the garden. I headed his way to ask what was going on.

"Hey there," I called out. "I'm going to the clinic. Where are the car keys?"

"You may not leave the property. Don Torricelli's orders. The doctor will come see you in the mansion. If you need anything, just let me know. I'll order it for you."

"You got to be kidding!" I said. "Where's Massimo and my bodyguard, Paolo?"

"Don Torricelli left with Mario and Domenico. They will return tomorrow. I will be your guard for today."

"Fucking shit," I hissed, sending the man a venomous look. "Home sweet home . . ."

I passed Olga on my way back. She was patiently waiting for me by the door.

"We won't be going anywhere after all. We're grounded. We can't leave. They took away the car keys, the gate is shut, the quay is empty, and the fucking wall around this damned mansion is too tall to jump over."

"Chill out, Laura. You'll have plenty of time to be pissed later. Let's go order some breakfast." Olga shrugged and wrapped her arms around me. "That omelet wasn't that good anyway."

Two hours later, the doctor came in. He told me everything was okay and took a blood sample to run some tests before leaving. Soon after, we got bored. That's when I came up with the genius idea to call a hairdresser and a beautician. The whole team was ready and waiting in an hour.

There's nothing better than a manicure, a pedicure, and a new hairdo when you're in a temper. We had our nails done, and then freshened up our hair. Before that last part, I googled the potential repercussions of dyeing your hair when pregnant. Just to be on the safe side. My gran used to tell me a kid might be born a ginger if you did that. As it turned out, dyeing your hair did nothing to the child. You only needed to tell your hairdresser that you're pregnant, so he used specialized products. Four hours into our makeover, we looked drop-dead gorgeous. I smelled of vanilla and Olga of cherries. It didn't make any particular sense to get so gussied up that day—our men were only returning tomorrow, after all—but any reason to get rigged out was good enough.

After all this, we had dinner in the dining room. The weather outside was a bit too glum to eat outside. Normally, there are just a few rainy days in December on Sicily. Today was one of them. Olga downed a bottle of wine and got wasted. She went to sleep early.

I wasn't tired at all. I switched on the TV and went to the dressing room, where I started rummaging through Massimo's clothes. I wanted to feel his smell. I dug through most of the things, but they all smelled clean and fresh. Finally, I found a leather jacket. It smelled like the Man in Black's skin. I took it from the hanger and plopped down on the fuzzy carpet, hugging the thing to my chest. My eyes watered as soon as I imagined how Massimo must have felt. Crazy with fear and despair. I had treated him like a piece of garbage when he'd called me. I couldn't hold back the tears any longer.

"I'm sorry," I whispered in Polish as a fat tear rolled down my cheek.

"I know that word." I heard a voice from behind me.

I raised my head and saw him standing right next to me. He wore a black suit, and his ice-cold eyes were drilling holes in me.

"I'm so angry with you, baby girl. Nobody has ever made me this furious. I want you to know that I had to get rid of all the people tasked with your safety. Flying around Europe, looking for you, I also lost a lucrative business deal and that damaged my authority among the families." Massimo walked over to the wardrobe and took off his jacket, throwing it over a hanger. "I'm tired now. I'm going to take a shower, and then I'll go to sleep."

He had never been this indifferent with me before. I was losing him! We were growing distant. A moment later, I heard the sound of water cascading to the floor. I decided to take a risk. I took all my clothes off and followed my husband to the bathroom. He was naked in the shower, and scalding-hot water was raining on his godly body. He looked exactly like he had when I first saw him in all his glory—leaning against the wall, allowing the water to flow freely down his shoulders. I snuck behind him and pressed myself to his back. Instinctively, my hands grasped in search of his manhood. Before they reached their destination, Massimo clasped his fingers around my wrists and spun to face me.

"No," he said coldly, with utter confidence.

I stepped back, letting my rear touch the glass. How could he push me away like that?

"I want to go back to Poland," I snapped, offended, and turned away to leave him. "Let me know when you stop sulking."

My provocation brought out the animal in him. He grabbed my arm and slammed me into the wall. His eyes were taking in the sight of my naked body, and his hands trailed paths across my skin.

"Your belly has grown," he smiled, kneeling before me. "My son is getting bigger."

"It's a girl, Massimo, but yes—she's big. Three and a half inches."

He put his forehead to my stomach and froze, ignoring the hot water running down his back. His arms wrapped themselves around my body, and his hands clamped around my buttocks, fingers digging into my skin.

"You have no idea how much pain you've caused me, Laura."

"Let's talk about it, Massimo. Please."

"Not now. Now, I'm going to punish you for running."

"Not too severely, though." Massimo froze, sending me a quizzical look. "The child was in danger at one point. It's a high-risk pregnancy," I said quietly, stroking his hair. "We can't . . ."

He didn't let me finish. He launched himself upward, clenching his fists and his jaw.

His chest was heaving. The water running down his body might have started to boil on him—that's how hot his fury was. He took a step back and roared before spinning on his heels and storming toward the door.

I scolded myself for my stupidity. I shouldn't have said anything about my health problems. I stayed in the bathroom, face hidden in my hands, still cursing myself, when I heard Massimo yell something in Italian. I grabbed a towel and ran back to the wardrobe. The Man in Black was just leaving, wearing nothing but gray sweatpants and sneakers. He tossed me the cell phone he had been holding in his hand and sent me a murderous look. I wanted to stop him, but he slipped away and stomped downstairs. I grabbed his shirt and my panties and ran after him.

He didn't look back, striding down the hall and hitting the walls with his fists, still rambling in Italian. He went through the door leading to the basement, slamming it shut behind him. I had never been there before. Somehow, I never gathered the courage to check out what was hiding on the bottom floor. My imagination was too vivid, and my brain offered only images I really didn't want to think about, such as bodies crammed into freezers, or torture chambers with people tied to chairs, awaiting their turn with the don's enforcers. The thought of going down those stairs made my heart race. It didn't stop me. I needed to follow Massimo.

I grabbed the handle and quietly slipped through the door, carefully planting my feet on the steps leading deeper underground. There were sounds coming from inside. Sounds of violence—screams, moans, and the dull thuds of bodies being hit. *God, save me*, I thought, unable to stop thinking about all the macabre things that must have been playing out farther down the corridor.

The stairs ended abruptly. I took a few deep breaths before peeking around the corner. My jaw dropped. Nobody was torturing anyone. It was a gym. There was a boxing bag hanging from the ceiling, a punching bag next to it, then some pull-up bars, a wrestling mannequin, and dozens of other types of equipment of unknown purpose. I scanned the room with my eyes. At some point the walls made a sharp turn so that the room formed the shape of the letter "L." Quietly, I took a few steps closer to look what was around the corner.

Inside, there was something like an octagonal cage. Behind the bars, there was Massimo and one of our security guards. They were swinging haymakers at each other. Well, at least Massimo was. The other man was desperately trying to defend himself. The difference in weight between the two was significant, but that didn't make it any more difficult for the Man in Black to completely dominate the fight with the larger man. When his opponent raised his arms, capitulating, another man entered the cage, and Massimo repeated the whole process.

I had had no idea he was such a consummate fighter. I had thought he had men to do his dirty work. I was wrong. Massimo's body was extremely limber and agile. He was indefatigable. I knew that much, but I hadn't thought it was because of pit fighting. He kicked out, his leg raised above his head, and efficiently used the walls of the cage to dominate his opponent. It was pretty sexy. I didn't even care that Massimo was just trying to blow off steam—it was turning me on.

When he finished another sparring partner, the Man in Black roared like an animal and finally collapsed to the floor, leaning against the bars. One of the men offered him a bottle of water before all three of them headed to the exit. They had to pass me on their way. I didn't care if they saw me. I was the boss's wife. As they walked by me, each nodded in respect before taking the stairs up. I took a deep breath and walked to Massimo. He raised his eyes at the sound of my steps. He didn't seem particularly surprised to see me. It didn't faze him at all.

Having learned my lesson back in our bathroom, I decided to play it smarter this time. I opened the wire mesh door and passed through, slowly unbuttoning the shirt I had on. When I was just about three feet away from my husband, I pulled it apart, presenting my full breasts and the red lace panties. Massimo's eyes grew dark, and he bit his lip. He took a last swig from his bottle and tossed it away nonchalantly. Without saying a word, I stopped very close to him, so that his head was level with my bosom. I tore my panties down, letting them fall to his sweaty stomach.

His scent was overpowering. Steaming sweat mixed with his

shower gel . . . It was the sexiest mélange in the world. I breathed it in. I had to make the first move now. Or, to be precise, a whole series of movements. Massimo wasn't budging.

I squatted and hooked my fingers over the rim of his sweatpants, keeping my eyes on his face, searching for a sign of approval. His face remained emotionless.

"Please . . ." I whispered, my eyes tearing up.

His hips lifted from the ground, allowing me to pull his pants off. I threw them behind me, and Massimo's slightly spreading legs displayed his monumental erection for me to see.

That in itself wouldn't be anything weird, but for the fact that he had been fighting three men for at least twenty minutes, and a few moments before that, he'd been ready to kill.

I stood above him, my feet planted on both sides of his sweaty body. I reached out with a hand, sliding two fingers into Massimo's mouth. When they were adequately moist, I dropped my arm to spread his saliva across my pussy. Before my hand reached its target, Massimo grabbed me by the wrist and pulled himself up, greedily pressing his mouth over my clitoris. I moaned in ecstasy, moving my hips closer to him, taking hold of the wire mesh wall behind his head. He licked me, his tongue penetrating deep, and his hands clasped around my ass. I didn't want to come. I didn't need an orgasm now. All I wanted was to be close to him. What I hoped for was that with him inside me I'd feel complete again. And that, maybe, he'd forgive me.

I grabbed Massimo by the hair and pushed away his head, pressing it against the wall of the cage. Slowly, I lowered myself over him, and when our eyes met on the same level, I felt the tip of his erect manhood entering my wet hole. The Man in Black inhaled sharply, keeping his eyes fixed on me. He was burning with lust. I could feel it. I slid even lower, impaling myself on him. He didn't like it when I had the upper hand, but since he hadn't allowed me to finish what I had been saying, I realized he didn't know how to act with a woman in my state.

My thighs clamped around his naked hips, and I pressed myself to his wet, hot body. There was only one thing in my head: I needed to feel him inside me. I bit his lower lip and sucked on it. Massimo delicately took my buttocks in his hands, moving me gently up and down on his shaft. His movements were getting faster and stronger by the second. The whole time, his eyes were searching for instruction in mine.

"I'm sorry," I said quietly as my knees landed on the ground and my hands gripped the cage behind him.

My hips picked up the pace. His eyes suddenly flared with panic. He wrapped his arms around my back and rolled us over, pinning me to the ground. He hovered above me, propped on his elbows, as his nose gently touched my lips.

"It is me who should apologize," he replied, sliding inside me again.

His movements were careful and delicate. I nearly forgot how brutal and unforgiving he could be when he wanted. His rhythmically undulating body was leading me straight to overwhelming bliss. I knew he didn't need to make things any more exciting. I didn't, either. All he wanted was to feel me. Suddenly, he stopped midstroke, touching his forehead to mine and squeezing his eyes shut.

"I love you so much . . ." he breathed. "When you ran, you tore out my heart and took it with you."

His words took my breath away. I felt tears running down my cheeks. My wonderful husband had opened up to me. His punishment for me was his sincerity. His lips were kissing each tear streaking down my face.

"I'll die without you," he said as his cock resumed its motion inside me.

I didn't want to come. Not now. I didn't want an orgasm after hearing those words. I only wanted him to sate himself on what I had taken away from him for those long weeks.

"Not here," he rasped, picking me up from the floor and taking me into his arms.

Completely naked, he crossed the room, then another. He grabbed a towel from a rack on his way. He put me down for a moment, wrapped his hips with it, and picked me up again, carrying me upstairs. We crossed the hall soundlessly, passing room after room. Finally, we entered the library. Massimo placed me on the carpet next to the fireplace, in which embers of a fire were still gently glowing.

"That first night, when you wanted to escape from me, I put you right here. I was sure I wouldn't make it." He pulled the towel from his hips and started to slowly push his manhood inside me. "When your bathrobe revealed what was beneath it, the only thing I wanted was to be inside you." His enormous cock dived to the very bottom, and I moaned, throwing my head back. "I wanted you so much that day that later, killing that man, I was still thinking about fucking you."

His body was moving faster now. I could feel the tension growing inside me, too. "When you went unconscious and I changed your clothes . . ."

"Liar," I interrupted him, catching my breath. I remember him telling me Maria had changed my clothes.

"I slid my fingers inside you. You were so wet. And even though you were unconscious, you moaned in ecstasy when you felt them."

"You're a pervert," I whispered.

He silenced me with a kiss. His tongue fucked the inside of my mouth. Then he pushed away and looked at me. His hand cupped my face, and he came with a loud moan, flooding me with so much hot jizz that I thought I'd overflow with it. He finished and collapsed down on me, cuddling against my neck.

We spent the next minute immobile. I felt his heart slowing down again.

"Grab the towel, honey," he ordered, pushing himself up. "Wrap it around my hips when I get up." I did as he told me. I didn't expect to meet anyone on our way, but it would be for the better. Only I had the right to see his naked butt.

We crossed the entire house and climbed upstairs, going back to the shower. He tore the towel off and pulled the shirt off me before turning the shower on and leading me straight under the stream of hot water.

In twenty minutes, we were in bed. Our standard position—me cuddling into his torso—had changed to him talking to my belly. Massimo held his head on my thighs, his chin propped on my pubis, while his hand stroked my bulging belly.

"What are you two talking about?" I asked absentmindedly, changing channels on the TV.

"I'm telling my son about all the extraordinary things that he's going to see here. About the people he's going to have to avoid and those he can safely ignore."

"It's going to be a girl, Massimo. And the only person you two should beware is me." The Man in Black raised his eyes to look at me. "Now, I'd like to finish what I tried to tell you earlier." He opened his mouth to protest, but I lifted my hand to shut him up. "Don't interrupt me. You know that this pregnancy isn't easy for my body because of my heart disorder. The events of that night when I ran didn't help. The doctor in Hungary said . . ."

"Where?" he asked, astonished. "You've been in Hungary this whole time?"

"What? You thought I'd stay in Warsaw, in our apartment, and just wait for you to come for me?" I asked with a smirk. "Never mind, though. I had some difficulties and overcame them. I stayed in bed for a few weeks, didn't leave or do anything. I just lay in bed. And since I wasn't thinking about sex at all back then, I hadn't asked the doctor if it was safe for me to have it."

"I'm angry with you," Massimmo growled, rolling to his side and lying next to me.

That was too much for me.

"What was I supposed to do then?" I sat up and grabbed a pillow. "You're mad I left, and that's okay. But if you saw what I saw, you'd probably have killed someone in my place. Besides, I can't really ignore the fact that you brought this skank to our house! And that evil twin of yours to boot. That guy can't seem to keep his hands to himself. So stop pissing me off, Massimo, accept my apology, and show some goddamn humility!"

He turned, watching me for a moment, confused. For a woman to talk back to the head of the family was probably unheard-of. I finished and felt a pinprick of pain in my belly. On instinct, I put my hands to my abdomen, grimacing slightly.

"What's going on, babe?" Massimo jumped to his feet, touching my stomach. "I'm calling the doctor."

I followed him with my eyes as he scurried around the room in search of a phone. He was stark naked, and his hair was ruffled. The sight of him was like a drug for me—it made me happy and satisfied. At the same time, it made me realize just how afraid he must have been when I had left.

"You smashed your phone on the wall about an hour ago.

Don't worry, Massimo. It's all right. It's just a stitch. Probably something I ate." The Man in Black stopped midstride and shot me a look. "You're paranoid, Massimo," I was saying, "and you're going to have a heart attack if you don't relax. I'm going to give birth in months, and if you don't lay off a little, I'm afraid you won't live to see that beautiful day. And our child will be half-orphaned." I raised my eyebrows and smiled, reaching for a bottle of water perched on the nightstand.

He wrested it out of my hand at once.

"Don't drink that. It's been open for three days," he said, throwing it to the trash can. "I'll order you some milk."

He reached for the landline phone, said a few words in Italian through the receiver, and hung up, his eyes wandering back to me. I paused, dumbfounded. His paranoia was getting out of hand. It was going to become a nuisance.

"I'm pregnant, Massimo. I'm not dying."

The Man in Black fell to his knees and laid his head on my thighs again.

"I'm just going crazy with fear, is all. I'm afraid something is going to happen to you or the child. I wish it was born already so I wouldn't . . ."

". . . go crazy?" I finished for him. "Stop worrying, darling. Be happy that I'm yours and yours alone for now. In a few months, I'll have my hands full with raising our beautiful daughter."

He raised his eyes and shot me a strange look. There was something completely new in his stare.

"Are you suggesting you might not have time for me?" he asked with outrage.

"Just think about it, baby. I'll be a mother to a little child, and children need all the attention. Our child will be entirely dependent on me. So yeah, I won't have as much time for you. It's only natural."

"The child will get a nanny," Massimo said and got up, before opening the door. "If I'm in the mood to fuck your brains out, no one—not even our child—will stand in my way."

I drank the milk he offered me and suddenly realized how late it was. I couldn't keep my eyes open. Massimo sat in bed with his laptop, working. I rolled to the side, put my leg on his, and cuddled against his shoulder. I fell asleep.

CHAPTER
seven

I woke up in the morning and reached over the bed, as usual. Surprisingly, Massimo was there. He was still sitting in the same exact position, laptop open on his thighs. He was sleeping. He's going to have one hell of a neck ache, I thought, intending to take the computer away. His eyes opened, and he smiled.

"Hey there, babe," I said softly.

"How's your back?"

"Not so bad that I couldn't eat my beautiful wife's pussy."

He lowered the laptop to the floor and started to pull away the covers, but the movement was too much. He hissed in pain and collapsed to the pillow.

"Roll over. I'll give you a massage," I said, slipping out from beneath the covers.

I sat astride him, on his naked buttocks, and kneaded his muscular back.

"That midnight sparring was a bit too punishing, don't you think?"

"Sometimes I need to blow off some steam, and the cage is best for that. Besides, MMA is the most efficient martial art. It blends elements of many different styles." He turned his head to the side. "Harder."

My hands rubbed him with more strength, and he sighed with satisfaction.

"I like that cage," I said, leaning to his ear. "I can see many potential uses for it."

Massimo smiled and jerked, rolling to the side and wrapping his arms around my waist. Then he did something, flexing and rolling so abruptly that I didn't even notice. A second later, he was on top of me, his body pinning me to the mattress.

"You see, my dear—that was MMA. And you probably like it so much exactly because it has so many uses in bed. You might be surprised, but the biggest MMA events in Europe are in Poland." He smooched me on the top of my nose and went to the bathroom. Fifteen minutes later, he was back, wrapped in a towel. He picked up a new cell phone and strolled out to the terrace.

"Don't think I don't know what's happening in my own country," I retorted. "I've heard about those things. They're on the TV all the time, though I've never seen one live."

Years back, Olga had been seeing a guy that used to train MMA. She decided it would be cool if we could go on double dates, so she hooked me up with a guy named Damian. A really hot one—a large man with a clean-shaven head. He looked like a gladiator. He had those large blue eyes, a crooked, broken nose, and large, full lips that could do miracles in bed.

We had a great time together. He was a great guy, all in all. A good man and surprisingly smart. The stereotypical fighter is a dumb troglodyte, but Damian had been super intelligent. A lot smarter and better educated than me.

Sadly, a couple of months into our relationship, he was offered a contract in Spain and left. He had tried convincing me to come with him, but my work had been my priority back then. He called me a couple of times and wrote me some emails, but I never replied. Long-distance relationships never end well.

Massimo's voice woke me from my pensiveness.

"What are you thinking?" he asked.

I decided to keep the truth to myself.

"Just that I'd like to see one of those fight nights."

Massimo returned from the terrace. Squinting slightly, he said, "That's actually a pretty great coincidence. There's one in a few days. It's going to be in Gdańsk. We can go, if you'd like to see it. We can visit your brother, too."

My eyes flared with glee and I grinned. I had missed Kuba. Our last meeting hadn't been what I expected, but I still wanted to jump up and down with delight at the prospect of seeing him again. The Man in Black observed me, amused, as I jumped to my feet and launched myself into his arms, showering his face with kisses.

"Pregnant women shouldn't jump," he said matter-of-factly and carried me to the wardrobe. "Let's have something to eat, shall we?"

He laid me down on the thick carpet and reached out to grab a pair of sweatpants from the shelf.

"Take me, don Massimo. Take me right here," I said, crossing my arms above my head and spreading my legs wide.

Massimo froze and slowly—very slowly—turned to face me as if he wasn't certain he'd heard me right. He put the pants back in their place and stepped closer to me. So close that our feet touched. His eyes dropped and fixed on my pussy. He bit his lip. Without a word, he grabbed his thick cock and started to slowly stroke it. In an instant, it grew rock-hard. I might have helped him a little—first, I stuck a finger in my mouth, and then played with my clit. Finally, he went down on his knees and grabbed my nipple with his lips, biting it gently and sucking.

"Harder," I whispered, running my hand through his hair.

His tongue circled around my nipple while his fingers fondled my tender clit. I couldn't wait until he slid his cock inside me. I had missed it so much, especially the feeling of it exploding with cum. I struck out with my hips, signaling my readiness, but he ignored it. Instead, he pulled himself up and his lips touched mine. He took my face in his hands and assaulted me with his tongue, biting my lip and kissing me so passionately that I could barely catch my breath.

"This is as hard as I'll go, baby girl," he said, pulling away.

I knew this was because of the baby. I also knew he was right, but my entire body yearned for a good fuck. I accepted his caring attitude without protest, sating myself with the gentle and delicate sex he offered me that morning.

Later, I went downstairs, only to witness Domenico licking chocolate off Olga's foot. Massimo's phone had chimed as soon as he had brought me to orgasm, and he had to pick it up, so I just put on some clothes and went to fetch some breakfast.

"Having fun?" I asked, stopping in the doorway and observing their childish play.

They didn't even acknowledge my presence, only continued their frolicking.

"Get a room!" I called out and walked over to the table. "Besides, Domenico, I didn't think you were such a stud. Haven't you been picking my clothes and shoes for the first two months of my stay here?"

The young Italian licked Olga's foot clean and wiped his mouth with a napkin before sending me a puzzled look.

"Not entirely true," he said, shrugging. "You might be disappointed, but most of those things were picked by Massimo. I only arranged that stuff into styles. Massimo knows what he likes. And he really does listen when you mention that something has caught your eye. Like those Givenchy boots. So I didn't do all that much, really."

"Oh, quit it with the modesty," Olga cut in, grabbing him by the scruff of his shirt. "You pick things for me, too, when you paint me."

"To be precise, I tend to undress you for the paintings more often than not," he replied and kissed her lustfully.

"I'm about to throw up here," I said, raising my arms. "I'm warning you. I'm pregnant, and I puke all the time, so watch out. And don't blame me."

Massimo appeared in the dining room and took a seat at the table. His phone started ringing once more. He picked it up and left again.

Domenico listened in, frowning, before returning to his coffee.

"What's going on?" I asked. "People keep calling him."

"Business," he said, avoiding my eyes.

"Don't lie." I slammed my mug on the table.

Domenico shot me a glance and narrowed his eyes.

"I can't tell you the truth, so stop asking." Domenico hid behind a newspaper, and I looked at Olga.

"Great. Go and sulk somewhere else," I said in Polish. "Sometimes they're too much for me."

"Oh, you know . . ." Olga muttered, picking at her pancake. "You really want to know what's going on? Why? Why do we need to know, Laura? As long as we can live this idyllic life, I don't care. I'm happy."

"It's done," Massimo announced, returning to the room and sitting at the table. He reached for the coffee. "We're going to Poland in a few days. We'll see the fights, I'll do some business with Karol, and you'll see your brother."

Olga rolled her eyes. Domenico didn't miss that.

"Aren't you happy?" he asked, sipping on his coffee.

"As a clam," she grumbled, sending me a cloudy look.

Kuba, my beloved brother, was a collector. Fully aware of his own handsomeness, he utilized his natural talents to the maximum, fucking every girl that allowed it. Especially my friends. Unfortunately, Olga had been one of his . . . trophies. We must have been around seventeen when he had put it in his head that he had to have her. I preferred to think it had only been that one time, but something was telling me it might have been a whole series. If not for the distance between them, they'd keep booty-calling each other. Thank God two hundred forty-eight miles had made it all but impossible. That had been before our Sicilian adventure, of course.

I realized the atmosphere was getting heavy, and Domenico was watching us closely, so I decided to change the subject.

"What are we going to do today? Are you two going to leave again and make us stay in this prison? Or can we count on your attentions today?" I asked ironically, flashing a fake grin at Massimo.

"If you were good girls and didn't keep running away, the gate would still be open and you'd still have your Bentley waiting on the driveway." The Man in Black turned to face me and propped an elbow on the table. "Were you a good girl, Laura?"

I considered the question for a while and decided to take a risk:

"Of course I was." I sent him my sweetest smile. "Both me and your daughter."

I stroked my belly with affection, knowing it might have a chance of melting the ice in his eyes.

He stared at me, keeping still. I didn't know what to think.

"Perfect," he said finally. "Santa Claus is going to visit today," he added, and his eyes flared like a little boy's.

"Get ready. We have to leave before noon."

"Right!" Olga exclaimed. "It's December sixth! Saint Nicholas Day!" She planted a quick kiss on Domenico's lips and ran off.

I sat with the men for a little while longer, sipping tea, before getting up and heading toward my bedroom.

There was no way to know what we'd be doing, and quickly I got lost in the sea of outfits I could choose from. They made me wonder. I thought about all the long months I had spent here, losing track of time. I had arrived on the island in August, and it was December now. The year was going to end in a couple of weeks.

My thoughts flew back to my parents. We had always spent Christmas together. I had always been the one to buy them presents, and that special holiday had always made me giddy with excitement. The phone rang, violently pulling me out of my reverie. I dropped the clothes and sped to pick up the receiver. Massimo was sitting on the bed, holding my iPhone. I reached out a hand to take it from him, but he muted the device and put it back on the nightstand.

"It's your mom," he said with a smile. "And I know why she's calling."

I stiffened, momentarily speechless, and frowned at the Man in Black, expecting an explanation.

"Give me my phone, please," I said, taking a step closer.

Massimo shot out with his arms and toppled me to the bed, showering me with kisses. I could always call Mom back later. My man was more important right now.

"She's calling to thank you," he was saying between kisses. "For the handbag. And your dad's new telescope."

I pushed away, staring at him quizzically.

"Excuse me?"

Massimo kept kissing my face. His supple lips delicately caressed my cheeks, eyes, nose, and ears.

"I like giving gifts," I said. "Especially to my family."

"I didn't want you to be sad just because you aren't spending Christmas with your family. I got your brother a ticket for a Manchester United game, too."

His tongue slid through my lips, but without a reaction on my side, it withdrew. Massimo raised his head a bit to see me better. I was prone, stunned by his words. The last couple of weeks had made me forget about the coming holidays and the presents I should buy, but how the hell had Massimo known this was so important to me?

"Massimo," I said, crawling out from under my husband. He sighed and rolled over. "How do you know what Christmas looks like in my family? And how did you know what they wanted?"

He rolled his eyes before closing them with a theatrical sigh.

"I was hoping you'd be happy for once."

"I am. Thank you. Now answer me."

"I had my people check your accounts. Your spendings." He grimaced, as if predicting what would come next.

"You did what?" I cried.

"Jesus Christ, here we go again."

"Is there even one part of my life you didn't meddle with?"

"Please, Laura. It's only money."

"No! It's a lot more to me. It's *my* money." I was fuming by then. "Why do you have to control everything? Couldn't you just ask?"

"It would ruin the surprise," he replied, staring at the ceiling.

My phone rang again. I snatched it from the nightstand. It was my mom again. Before I managed to answer the call, Massimo said, "The bag is from the last Fendi collection. In beige. You have one like it, only yellow." He shrugged.

"Hi, Mom," I chirped happily, keeping my eyes trained on my husband.

"Darling, the gifts are gorgeous, but that bag must have cost you a fortune. Have you lost your mind?"

Now I was going to have to explain myself. I imagined kicking Massimo in the stomach.

"My wages are in euro now, and besides, the discounts here are a lot better than in Poland."

If that was what I came up with, I might as well have just told her the truth. What discounts? It was the beginning of December! Kicking myself for my stupidity, I collapsed on the bed and waited.

"Discounts? Now?" I heard from the speaker. *Bravo, Laura*, I scolded myself quietly. The phone slipped from my fingers, and before it fell to the bed, the Man in Black snatched it from the air, flashed a wide grin, and said hello to my mom. I felt as if someone had slammed me in the head. The room started to whirl around me, and my fear turned into full-blown panic. I had told Mom that I left Massimo after he had cheated on me, and now he'd taken my phone and was chatting away with her like nothing had ever happened.

"Jesus fucking Christ," I moaned, but then, suddenly, Massimo gave the phone back to me.

"You watch your language, Laura Biel!" Mother cried.

I stiffened.

"Sorry. It just slipped my tongue," I mumbled, waiting for the inevitable decapitating attack.

"Your Massimo is a very nice man. I think he really likes you."

My jaw dropped. If it hadn't been attached to my head, it would have rolled downstairs.

"Excuse me?" I asked with disbelief.

"He just explained everything to me. You should have learned languages. You would have understood what he was saying."

That's when Dad chimed in, barely audible in the background.

"Christ almighty, I have to do everything myself." Mom sighed. "I need to go, darling. Your father can't assemble the telescope on his own. He's going to break it if I don't lend him a hand. I love you, sweetie. Thank you for the wonderful surprise. Bye!"

"Love you too. Bye!" I said, ending the call.

I put the phone down and stared at my husband, who was grinning widely, satisfied with his plan coming to fruition.

"What did you tell her?"

"That I gave you a raise, so you came back to work at my hotel." His muscular arms wrapped around me tightly.

"I also told her about the mix-up that made you think I cheated on you. But don't worry—I lied to her. You might have sounded a bit more absentminded in my story than you usually are. She laughed and told me it was typical." He rolled us both over so we lay on our sides, facing each other. His leg was wrapped around my hips. "By the way, I didn't know you were so jealous by nature. Anyway, your mom knows we're still together."

"Thank you," I whispered, kissing him.

"Thank you for kidnapping me."

The Man in Black swung his leg over my hips and sat astride me.

"I will take you now," he breathed, pulling down my sweatpants. "You know why?"

I writhed beneath him, throwing off all my clothes.

"Why?" I asked, pulling at his pants.

"Because I can." His tongue brutally assaulted my lips, and his hands cupped my head.

I marveled at his muscular, toned body. Then my eyes wandered down, and I took a look at myself, pulling away Massimo's shirt, which I was wearing. I sighed at the sight of my belly. I looked like I'd swallowed a small balloon. I was so happy with the thought that this was his child inside me, but I hated the way it was changing my body. My eyes lifted again, and I met Massimo's stare. He knelt by me.

"What's going on?" he asked, sitting me up and placing me on his knees.

I cuddled against his torso, inhaling the beautiful scent of his skin and his cologne.

"I'm growing fat," I sobbed. "Another month and I won't fit into any of my clothes."

"You're being silly now," he said, laughing and kissing my head. "You can get fatter than me and I won't have anything against it, because it means that my son is growing large and strong. Now stop worrying about this nonsense and get ready. We need to be where I'm taking you in an hour."

"Where are we going?"

"Somewhere you haven't visited yet. Dress casual."

Massimo put on a pair of worn blue jeans, a black long-sleeved T-shirt, and black military boots. *Wow,* I thought, looking at him. This was a new look. The Man in Black ran a hand through his hair and left, giving me a kiss. I got up and went to the dressing room again. Dress casual, he'd said. "Casual" means something different for everyone, but since I knew we weren't going to any official meeting, I could get creative. I grabbed a hanger and pulled off a black Kenzo T-shirt with a tiger motif. It wasn't hot outside, but it wasn't cold, either, so I decided to show off my toned legs. I settled on dark gray One Teaspoon shorts. I topped off my look with Burberry thigh-high boots and long socks. I moved my things to a Boy Chanel bag and went downstairs.

Olga was waiting by the door. She was explaining something to Domenico animatedly. When Massimo joined us, we all headed to the line of parked cars. Everyone had their own vehicle here. Massimo opened the door to a BMW i8 for me. It was another of those sci-fi machines pretending to be ordinary cars. Domenico led Olga to the Bentley.

"How many cars do you actually have?" I asked as he gunned the engine.

"To be honest, I don't know. I sold some, but I also got a few new ones. Besides, they're not mine. They're ours now. I don't remember getting a prenup. All that I own is yours." He kissed my hand.

Ours, I thought. *A pity only one of us is allowed to drive them all.* I either get a tank with a cockpit like a jet's and millions of useless controls, or I get that other ox of a car.

CHAPTER
eight

We took a turn off the highway and rolled down a dirt road wholly inimical to the low suspension of the BMW. The car jerked and jumped on each bump. I expected it to come apart at any moment. I scanned our surroundings. We were in the middle of nowhere, it seemed. A stony desert only speckled with single shabby plants suggested that Massimo's surprise wasn't one of those overly luxurious ones. If this whole ride had happened a few months before, I would have thought the brothers were taking us somewhere remote to shoot us. Nobody would have found us here. Suddenly, the road made a turn and I noticed a great stone wall with a massive gate in the middle. Massimo picked up his cell phone and dialed a number. The gate ponderously started to open.

We drove down an asphalt road on the other side of the wall. Palms lined the route, forming a green tunnel. I had no idea where we were, but I knew that asking wouldn't get me anywhere. That's what surprises are all about. Finally, the car stopped by a beautiful, two-story building made out of the same stone the main mansion had been built of. Most buildings on the island had that same, slightly soiled look.

We left the BMW and an elderly man appeared through the door, greeting the brothers warmly. He must have been at least sixty. The man kissed Massimo on the cheeks, patted his face with a gnarly hand, and said a few words in Italian. The Man in Black offered me a hand.

"Don Matteo, please meet my wife, Laura."

The elderly man kissed me on both cheeks and smiled brightly.

"I'm happy you're finally here," he said in broken English. "Your boy spent a long time looking for you."

All of a sudden, the air was pierced by loud bangs, like gunshots. I huddled to Massimo's side, shooting nervous glances around, trying to find the source of the noise. There was nothing but wilderness surrounding us.

"Don't be scared, babe," Massimo said, wrapping an arm around my shoulders. "Nobody is going to die today. I'm going to teach you how to shoot."

He led me across the beautiful house, and all the way I was trying to get to grips with what he said. Shoot? I'm pregnant and he wants to teach me how to shoot? He doesn't even allow me to carry my own bag, and suddenly I'm supposed to handle a gun? We passed the house and exited through the back door. I froze.

"Holy fuck, it's just like in the movies!" Olga exclaimed, stopping at my side and grabbing my hand.

Massimo and Domenico burst out laughing.

"Where have our brave and fearless Slavic girls gone?"

"We left them home," I retorted, turning their way. "What are we doing here?"

"We want to teach you how to handle guns." The Man in

Black embraced me. "I think you'll need it. And even if you don't, it's pretty relaxing. You'll see."

Another gunshot reverberated across the yard, making me jump up. I hid in Massimo's arms.

"I don't want to," I whispered. "I'm scared."

Massimo took my face in his hands and kissed me delicately.

"My love, it's usually scary to try new things. Don't worry. I've consulted with your doctor. Shooting guns is as dangerous for you as playing chess. Come."

Fifteen minutes later, having calmed down a bit, I was standing with protective earmuffs, watching Massimo lifting a gun. Don Matteo stood by, holding me by the shoulder, as if he was afraid I might need the support.

Massimo settled on slightly spread legs and loaded the 9mm Glock.

He wasn't wearing earmuffs, and instead of protective glasses he had his Porsche aviators on. He looked so manly, gorgeous, breathtaking, and sexy, I was ready to kneel straight down and suck him off. Suddenly, his casual outfit made sense. It all came together as he took the gun. He wasn't scary anymore. It was turning me on, taking away my ability to think clearly. Dangerous, imperious, violent, and wholly mine. I had butterflies in my stomach. I was horny. *How easy it is for him to make me pine*, I thought. He didn't have to do anything, and my legs were shaking.

The Man in Black nodded at the elderly man, took a deep breath, and sent all seventeen bullets flying so fast that the individual shots sounded like one long blast. He placed the gun on the counter and pressed a button, making the target zoom toward him. As it stopped, Massimo allowed himself a smile and raised his eyebrows.

"All shots on target. Headshots," he said with a boyish expression. "Practice makes perfect."

My stomach cramped. The joke was just too macabre for me.

"But the bull's-eye is in the middle of the torso, isn't it? So you didn't get points," I said, grabbing the piece of paper. Massimo smiled at that and pulled away one of my earmuffs.

"But I killed the enemy." He planted a kiss on my cheek. "Now your turn. Come on. I'll be unprofessional, and I'll stay right behind you, but I want you to feel safe." He led me to the shooting spot and briefly explained how the gun worked, what to push to free the magazine, how to reload it and switch from continuous fire to single shots. When I loaded the firearm and did everything he told me to, Massimo stepped back, pressing with his torso against my back.

"Watch the target. Align the gunpoint with the back sight. Now take a deep breath and pull the trigger as you exhale. Slowly but surely. Don't jerk your finger. Just one fluid motion. You can do it."

It's just like chess. Just like chess, I repeated to myself, trying to convince my brain to stop being scared. I felt Massimo plant his leg securely behind and put his hands on my hips.

I inhaled, and did as he told me. It was a fraction of a second. The recoil and the blast. Or the other way around. I couldn't really tell. The force of the bullet swung my hands up. I didn't expect that. The power I had in my hands was enormous. I could kill. I began to shake, and my eyes welled with tears.

Massimo took away my gun and put it on the counter. I turned to him and panicked.

"Chess?!" I shouted. "I fucking hate chess, then!"

The Man in Black embraced me then, stroking my hair. I could feel his torso shaking with the laughter he was doing all in his power to stifle. I lifted my head and saw the amusement mixed in with a dose of worry in his eyes.

"Everything all right, honey? Why are you crying?"

I pouted and hid my head in his armpit, ashamed.

"I got scared."

"Of what? I'm here."

"This is just such a responsibility. The knowledge that I could kill someone with that changes everything. The power . . . I got scared of it all."

Massimo nodded, and I think I saw pride in his eyes.

"You're so wise, baby girl," he whispered, kissing me softly. "Now. Back to the lesson."

The next shots were easier. After I unloaded a few clips, they stopped having any effect at all. I felt like an expert already.

Some time later, don Matteo left us and returned with a new toy.

"You'll like this one." Massimo grabbed the machine gun that the man had brought. "This is an M4. An assault rifle. Pretty nice weapon. It's light and doesn't have a recoil as hard as the Glock. And that's because you prop it against your shoulder."

"A nice weapon," I repeated uncertainly. "Let's try it out."

Shooting the M4 really was easier, even though it was a lot heavier than the previous gun.

An hour of shooting exhausted me. Don Matteo invited us to the terrace adjacent to the shooting range. We were served lunch—*frutti di mare*, pasta, meats, antipasti, and a whole range of desserts. It was crazy. I gobbled up everything the waiters put in front of me as if I hadn't eaten for a week.

Massimo sipped wine, nibbling on olives, hugging me once in a while.

"I love it when you have an appetite," he whispered to my ear. "Means my son is growing."

"Daughter," I corrected with my mouth full.

"It's going to be a girl. But if we want to be sure, we can sort this out during our next visit to the clinic."

His eyes flared, and his hand touched my belly.

"I don't want to know. I want a surprise. Besides, I know it's a boy."

"Girl."

"Gonna be pretty funny if it's twins," Olga said, pouring wine for everyone. "That would be awesome. Laura, her husband the mob boss, and two crying brats. Domenico," she said, turning to her boyfriend. "That's when we move out."

"Thank God it's only a single baby." I shrugged and continued stuffing myself.

After lunch, I lay down on a swinging couch with Olga. The three men were discussing something back at the table, and I thanked God for what just a couple of months back I had cursed him for.

"Do you believe in destiny?" I asked Olga.

"I was just thinking the same thing. How incredible it is that just a few months ago life was so normal, so ordered, and so ordinary. And now we're here, under the Sicilian sun. Our men are mobsters, pimps, and murderers."

She sat up, nearly falling off the swinging couch. "Fucking hell . . . It's all just so fucked up. They're bad men, and we love them for who they are. Are we bad, too?"

I frowned. Wasn't she right, though?

"But we don't love them for the evil they do. We only love them for the good parts. How can you love someone for killing someone else? Besides, we all do evil shit, just on a different scale. Let's take me, for example. Remember how in fifth grade I kicked Rafał in the face? That blond boy that kept poking you with a pin? It wasn't good at all, and you still love me."

"Jesus." Olga rolled her eyes.

The sound of chairs being moved made us turn back to the table. Domenico and Massimo were putting something over their heads, cheerful like kids.

"Shit, each time I see that smile, I'm scared of what it'll lead to," Olga said, pulling me toward them.

"Come watch a movie, ladies." Don Matteo pointed us to the entrance to the house.

We stopped, confused, our eyes darting from him to our men.

"What's this on your head?" Olga asked, patting Domenico on the little box strapped to his forehead.

"A camera. I'll have a second one on the gun. We'll show you exactly why you can feel safe with the two of us."

They high-fived each other and headed toward something that looked like a stone labyrinth.

"Ladies?" don Matteo repeated. We sat in deep armchairs, and he drew the curtains, bathing the room in complete darkness. Then he switched on two enormous screens, and we saw the view from Massimo's and Domenico's cameras.

"I will explain now. The young sirs will practice storming a building. Same training as special forces," he informed us in his imperfect English. "It tests quickness of reaction, judgment under pressure, reflex, and shooting technique. They were always better than most professional soldiers I have trained, but they hadn't visited me in a while, so we'll see."

I was dumbstruck. The same man who trained the military also trained the Mafia.

At some point something moved on-screen. Domenico and Massimo were passing through doors, expertly shooting at mannequins imitating terrorists.

"The hypocrisy," Olga said in Polish. "Killing baddies while being the bad guys themselves."

Hypocritical or not, their training routine was sexy as hell, and the focused expression on Massimo's face was turning me on in a way I hadn't felt before. The two men were sneaking through rooms, shooting and covering each other. They looked like boys playing war. The main difference was that their guns were real. It was over in a couple of minutes. They fooled around, shouting, laughing, and making funny faces to the cameras, waving their guns around like rappers on American TV.

"Idiots," Olga muttered, getting up.

Having said our goodbyes to don Matteo, we took the cars and drove back home. The sci-fi BMW silently raced down the highway to the accompaniment of the least manly song in the world—"Strani Amori" by Laura Pausini. Massimo was goofing around, singing along with the song. He acted and looked like a normal guy today—an ordinary, passionate thirty-year-old who likes to have fun. He didn't resemble the authoritative, totalitarian asshole obsessing over my safety and throwing tantrums whenever anyone stands in his way.

We passed the off-ramp that Domenico and Olga's Bentley took, and zoomed past them. I sent Massimo a searching look but didn't say anything. I didn't have to. He knew what I wanted to ask. His lips stretched in a smile as he stepped on the accelerator.

We drove another thirty-one miles until the signs directed us to Messina. For a long time, Massimo drove through the labyrinth of narrow streets, before finally stopping by a monumental wall made of elaborately arranged stones.

He produced a small remote from a pocket, and a great wooden gate opened for us. I sent him another quizzical look, but he only raised his brows, grinning and driving up the ramp.

The car stopped by a breathtakingly beautiful two-story house. He stepped out.

"Come," he said, offering me a hand.

I was still silent, expecting an explanation. Massimo offered none. Instead, he turned the key in the lock and led me inside. Holy crap... I was out of breath. A massive, cavernous living room was dominated by the most beautiful Christmas tree I had ever seen. It was gold and red. The fireplace crackled with fire, and a white fur carpet lay next to it. There were sofas and armchairs in various hues of brown and beige, a long wooden coffee table, and a large flat-screen TV. Adjoining the room was a massive dining room with a monumental oak table, shiny candle holders, and chairs upholstered with burgundy cloth. The whole space was warm, subtle, and luxurious.

"What is this, Massimo?" I spun on my heel and shot him an amazed look.

"This is my gift for you."

"The Christmas tree?"

"No, honey. The house. I bought it because I wanted it to remind you of me and our child. I want you to have only good memories of this place. This is going to be your place on Earth. I never want you to run away from me again. And if you ever need some time alone, this place will be waiting for you." He stepped closer to me and cupped my face in his hands. "If you want to move out of the mansion, we can live here together. There isn't going to be as much staff, but we'll be here together—just you, me, and our son."

"Daughter!"

"This place is private and entirely safe. Happy holidays, my love."

His lips touched mine, and his teeth gently bit into my lower lip. He grabbed my ass and lifted me from the ground. I wrapped my legs around his hips and returned his kiss. He caressed my lips, and his hands wandered all over my body as he carried me to the huge table in the dining room. He laid me on the tabletop and pulled his T-shirt off with a fluid motion. I couldn't stop grinning as he took my shorts off.

"What about the boots?" I asked as the shorts and my lace panties flew across the room, landing on the floor somewhere.

"You can keep those on."

He motioned to me to raise my arms, and a moment later I was splayed before him, wearing only the long, mid-thigh-high socks and black boots. Massimo placed his strong hands on my hips and lifted me, pushing me deeper onto the table. Surprising. I thought he'd rather want to pull me closer and slide his manhood inside me. His eyes, flaring with lust and half-closed, drilled holes in me. I spread my legs wide, propping my feet on the table and crossed my arms above my head. The Man in Black moaned.

"I love that," he whispered, unbuttoning his jeans. His gaze didn't leave my wet pussy for even a moment.

"I know."

He stood at the base of the table, naked, stroking the insides of my thighs.

"This house has another great feature," he said and took a few steps toward the wall, pressing a button on a panel by the fireplace. "Silence" by Delerium reverberated throughout the whole space. "The sound system," he said with a smile, before pushing his tongue into my moist hole.

I had been waiting for this moment since he first shot his gun back at the shooting range. My body writhed under his touch as his tongue assaulted me. It was violent, and full of lust, as it played with my clit. Slowly, he slid two fingers into my pussy and started to stroke. Lazily, he moved them in and out. Another moment, and I would come. I'd been at the very edge of ecstasy since he had taken his pants off, but I didn't want to climax so fast.

"I know you're about to come," Massimo said, slipping a finger into my ass.

That was it. I came immediately. My body arched, tense and shaking. The Man in Black didn't stop. His movements only quickened.

"Again, babe." Another finger in my back passage.

"Oh, God!" I cried out, surprised with the intensity of the sensation.

His tongue fondled my pulsating clit, picking up the pace. Another orgasm came a dozen seconds later. And then another, and one more. They came and went in waves of exhausting ecstasy. Images of Massimo were flashing through my mind—with his gun, focused and strong, then laughing and carefree. I opened my eyes and looked at him. His eyes were full of animalistic lust. I came so hard then. My fingers clenched around his hair, and when the last orgasm flooded like a wave through my whole body, I felt cramps all around. They were paralyzing. I collapsed back to the tabletop with a crash.

"Good girl," Massimo breathed, biting his lip. Then he grabbed my ankles and savagely pulled me to the very edge of the table.

The music, reminding me of prayers, undulated in the air, and I loved my husband more than ever.

Without taking his eyes off me, he grabbed his erect manhood and slowly, gently slid it inside me, keeping watch of my reaction.

"Harder," I whispered, nearly inaudibly.

"Don't provoke me, babe. You know I can't." I missed the old, violent Massimo. It was the only thing I really hated about my pregnancy—that he couldn't fuck me as I liked the most. I could see he wasn't fully satisfied, either, but the good of the baby was more important than good fucking.

The Man in Black moaned softly and dropped his head, sliding the entire length of his cock inside me. Shortly, his hips started swaying rhythmically. Back and forth. He made love to me. It was a paradox that this man could be the epitome of gentleness and care. He reacted to each breath coming out of my lungs, each movement of my head. With the fingers of his right hand, he caressed my nipples, squeezing harder once every moment. The thumb of his left hand circled my throbbing clitoris. The mix of pain and the ecstasy that was bubbling inside me, threatening to explode again, were making me feel completely weightless.

"Hit me," I pleaded when another song started. His hips stopped. "Hit me, don Massimo!" I cried when he didn't react.

His eyes flared with fury and his hand shot out, clasping around my throat. I let out a scream filled with lust and desire, throwing back my head. He was this close to fucking me like an animal, but I knew he wouldn't. For a second, he considered my words before finally pulling me off the table and standing me down by the wall, leaning me against it.

"Like a whore?" he hissed, pushing his dick back in as I leaned my forehead on the cold stone.

"Please." I felt the delirious bliss coming to me again. He grabbed my hair with one hand and my throat with the other.

It didn't matter that his movement inside me was slow and

gentle. The violence of what he did with his hands was making me red hot with lust. He strangled me, but very skillfully. I could barely keep my arousal at bay. At one point, he took his hand away from my throat only to painfully punish my swollen nipples. His teeth bit into my ear, then my neck and shoulder, but I couldn't do anything to retaliate.

When he felt he was getting close, he let go of me and turned me around.

"Sit down," he said, pointing me to a low stool. Then he grabbed my chin between index finger and thumb, opening my mouth. "All the way, girl."

Without warning, he pushed his cock into my mouth and started fucking it brutally, flooding my throat with a great wave of cum just a minute later. I choked, trying to rip his hands off me, but he didn't stop until he was done. Finally, his hips stopped pushing, but his dick was still resting on my lower lip.

"Swallow," he ordered, gazing at me coldly.

I did as he told me. Only then did he let me go, pushing me toward the couch.

"I love you!" I called out with a wide grin as he turned to the wall to lower the volume down a bit.

"You know most whores aren't as kinky as you?" he asked, lying next to me and covering the both of us with a soft blanket.

"They should look for another job." I shrugged, licking his nipple. "I'm going to the doctor tomorrow. I hope he'll allow us to do as we like in bed."

Massimo wrapped his arm around me.

"Me too. I don't know how long I'll be able to cope with your provocations."

"It's not my fault I like it a bit rough."

The Man in Black turned his face to me, looking me in the eyes. "A bit? I nearly choked you, woman!"

He sighed loudly and lay on his back.

"Honestly, sometimes I'm afraid of how you make me feel."

"Then imagine how scared I am of who I'm becoming with you."

CHAPTER *nine*

"Good morning." His warm voice cradled me before I opened my eyes.

I purred and pushed my face into his torso, inhaling the barely detectable scent of his cologne.

"My neck hurts," I said, my eyes still shut.

"Probably it's because we spent the night on the couch." My eyes snapped open, and for an instant I felt panic. Only upon seeing the gigantic Christmas tree did I recall where we were and what we had done the night before.

"Don't know about you, but in Poland we only decorate the tree on Christmas Eve. Maybe a day before that if the kids can't wait. But December sixth?" I yawned.

"If it pleases you, we can keep it for the whole year. And besides, what was I supposed to do? Wrap the whole house like a present?"

"For starters, you didn't have to buy it."

"Oh, please." He rolled to his back and pushed me under his arm. "It's an investment. Besides, I'm not sure if the mansion in

Taormina is the best place for the baby. I'd like to keep you here, only for me. There's always too many people over there."

"But Olga is there, too." I looked at him, propping myself on an elbow. "What am I to do here all by myself?"

Massimo sat up and leaned back, facing me.

"You'll have the baby and me as well. Is that not enough?"

I saw sorrow in his eyes. He was genuinely sad. I had never seen him like that. I quickly cupped his face in my hands and touched his brow with mine.

"Darling, but you're always out." I rubbed my temples nervously, looking for a solution. "I got it. When the baby is born, we'll try living in the mansion first. If it turns out you were right, we'll move here. If not, we'll stay there. And in that case, this place will be my private retreat. And a place for all kinds of debauchery, when I'll be able to fuck and drink to my heart's content again."

I slipped out from under the blanket and danced a wild happy dance of a sex-addicted alcoholic. Massimo watched me with amusement before taking me into his arms and carrying me across the house.

"In that case, let's stamp our mark everywhere around the house so it only reminds you of all the decadent things we do together!"

When we returned to the mansion in Taormina, I jumped out of the car and ran straight to the dining room. Food, food! It was the only thing I could think about. Our new house might have been gorgeous, but the fridge back there was empty.

"Pancakes!" I called out, barging into the room and noticing Olga sitting by the big table.

She glanced at me and closed the laptop she had been using.

"I remember the good old times when you used to puke at

the thought of food. And now? Your ass is getting fatter by the minute."

"Belly, not ass," I corrected, heaping my plate with food. "Besides, my ass is so small, it could use some fattening up."

Olga smiled and poured me a cup of tea, added some milk, and threw in two teaspoons of sugar.

"I got a Rolex," she said, waving her hand in my face. "Pink gold, mother of pearl, and diamonds. What did you get?"

"A house," I mumbled with my mouth full.

Olga's eyes bulged, and she swallowed loudly.

"You got . . . what?" she asked, shocked.

"A fucking house. You deaf all of a sudden?"

"Fucking hell, I got a watch, you got a house. There's no such thing as justice."

"Get pregnant with a mobster, marry the guy, and then live with a bossy asshole hiding a gun under his pillow. You'll get a castle."

We both chuckled at that, high-fiving each other.

"What's so funny?" Massimo asked, entering the room and taking a seat.

He was wearing a black suit and a black shirt, which meant he was going to a funeral, or just working today.

"Where are you going?" I asked, putting the fork down. "I need to see the doctor at one."

"That's where I'm going," he replied, helping himself to some eggs.

"In that grave digger's outfit?" Olga asked.

The Man in Black sent her a dispassionate look and poured himself a cup of coffee.

"Domenico is upstairs jacking off. Why don't you go and help him out?" he asked, keeping a neutral expression.

Olga snorted and leaned back in her chair, crossing her arms. "He came like a hundred times in the past two hours. I doubt he's even able to walk right now. But it's nice you worry for your brother, Massimo."

She flashed him one of her favorite fake-venomous smiles.

"All right, let's focus on me," I said, interrupting the squabble. "Who's going to the clinic with me?"

"I am," they both said, sending each other hostile glares.

"Great," I said happily. "Then we're all going together." Olga took a sip of coffee and got up.

"I was just kidding. I only wanted to piss Massimo off. I've missed you," she said and planted a kiss on my forehead, before leaving.

"You both act like kids," I grumbled, helping myself to another portion of Nutella pancakes.

◇◇◇◇◇◇◇◇◇◇◇

We were both on pins and needles, waiting for the doctor's opinion at the clinic. Though, judging by the doctor's expression, he was even more nervous. That wasn't surprising—the Man in Black himself had shown up in his office. Massimo wanted to make sure the doctor wouldn't tell me the baby's sex. When the examination started and the gynecologist pulled a condom over the ultrasonogram head, my husband nearly blew a gasket. I couldn't hide my amusement. My husband bravely stood by through the whole procedure, trying to keep his eyes on the screen, but shooting glances at my face once in a while.

Dr. Ventura sat at his desk, holding the USG images and test results.

"I called the Hungarian doctor that had taken care of Mrs. Torricelli," he said. "He sent me the documentation and added his own remarks. He did a perfectly good job taking care of you, although there were some critical points." He paused and took a sip of water. "What matters is that the latest test results are perfect. You are doing great, and the baby is developing like it should. It is big and healthy. Your heart is coping with the additional load. There are no reasons to worry at all."

"Dr. Ventura." Massimo knitted his brows and crossed his arms.

"Yes, don Massimo?" the doctor stammered.

"Why has the life of my child been endangered?"

"Well . . ." The doctor grabbed the documents lying on the desk and leafed through the pages nervously. "The Hungarian doctor informed me that your wife was under a lot of pressure. And it lasted longer than a day or two. Her heart couldn't keep pace. Her body . . . rebelled. To keep it simple, it started treating the fetus as a threat leaching its vitality."

"But everything is okay now, right?" I asked, caressing Massimo's hand but keeping my eyes trained on the doctor.

"Yes. It is absolutely okay."

"What about sex?" The Man in Black pinned Dr. Ventura with his icy stare.

I think the poor man would tell him whatever he wanted to hear now.

"If you're asking if there are any contraindications, then no."

"And what about more . . . intense sexual activities?" I asked, dropping my eyes.

I lifted my head and saw the doctor's eyes darting between me and Massimo. God, if we were going to keep beating around the bush with this, we'd never learn anything and my husband would keep fucking me like a lazy koala for the next six months. I took a deep breath.

"Let me rephrase it, Doctor. We like rough sex. Can we have rough sex?"

Ventura's face blushed and he leafed through some more papers, as if looking for an answer there. He might be a gynecologist and probably had conversations like this a couple of times a day, but never with the boss of the local mob.

"You can have sex however you like."

Massimo rose gracefully and led me to the door. I didn't even have time to say goodbye. We practically ran out to the street, where he pushed me against the closest wall.

"I want to fuck you . . . right now!" he breathed, his face inches from my own. "I'll pound you so hard, you'll feel just how much I've missed it. Come with me." He pulled me by the hand, leading me to the car. He pushed me inside and teleported to the other side. Before I managed to buckle up, the vehicle was already racing toward the highway.

We passed our turn, continuing on to Messina. I knew where he was taking me, and I couldn't hide my joy at the thought of getting fucked in the privacy of our new house. No people around, no security, no Olga or Domenico. Only the two of us.

"I have one more surprise for you," Massimo said, opening the wooden gate with the remote.

He glanced at me, waiting for it to finish opening. A sly smirk stretched his lips, and his hands clenched on the steering wheel. When the gate finally swung open, he stepped on the accelerator. The BMW's tires screeched, and we drove all the way to the entrance door.

Massimo jumped out of the car, opened the door for me like the gallant knight he was, and then unceremoniously threw me over his shoulder.

He turned the key in the lock with me still in his arms, carried me inside, and kicked the door shut. Then he climbed the wide stairs leading to the second floor.

"I'm going to wash you first," he announced, putting me down on the floor of the beautiful, classy bathroom.

"I can't stand another man's smell on you."

I snorted with laughter. I didn't think the rubber condom or the USG machine smelled of anything.

"He's just a doctor."

"He's a man," he barked. "Raise your arms." He pulled my cashmere sweater off, and then undressed me completely. All the clothes flew to the ground. "This is mine!" he growled, as his eyes took in the sight of my naked body.

"Only yours," I confirmed as he pushed me into the shower.

"You have three minutes." He turned his back on me and left without another word.

That was surprising. I had thought he'd fuck me in the shower or at least play around with soap a bit. It was disappointing. I squeezed out some shower gel and rubbed it over my skin.

"Time's up," Massimo called, returning to the bathroom.

I thought that was supposed to be a metaphor. I quickly rinsed away the soap.

"Ready!" I spread my arms, displaying my nakedness.

Massimo stepped closer, pulling off his shirt, and breathed in my scent.

"Much better," he said and took me into his arms again.

He carried me to the bedroom, which was pleasantly dark, even though it was the middle of the day.

What I liked most about the Mediterranean was that all the houses had powered roller blinds installed, making it very easy to blanket their interior in pleasant gloom. I liked darkness. Martin used to tell me it was depressing—one of my worst qualities. He had hated it.

A massive bed dominated the room. Supported by four thick columns, it was crowned with a black canopy. At its foot was a small bench padded with dark gray satin, matching the width of the mattress. On both sides of the bed stood night tables with richly engraved fronts, and a similar, though larger cabinet took up a corner of the room. Lit candles gave out a faint glow from its top. The furniture was dark, bulky, and very stylish.

Massimo laid me down on the mattress, quickly dumping a few dozen pillows that had been scattered all over the bed to the floor.

"Surprise," he said with a smirk, reaching behind one of the columns, revealing a chain ending in a soft cuff for the wrist.

Scenes from our visit to his hotel from a few months back flashed before my eyes. I recalled him tying me to the bed and making me watch Veronica the hooker sucking him off.

"Oh, no you don't!" I launched myself up, eliciting a completely dumbstruck expression on Massimo's face.

"Don't tease me, baby girl," he hissed, grabbing my ankle.

"You still owe me thirty-two minutes. I'll have them now."

He dropped my leg and sent me a quizzical look.

"Don't you remember anymore?" I narrowed my eyes, taking a step back. "You promised me an hour on our wedding night. I only used about half of my time. I still have thirty-two minutes left. Lie down," I said confidently, pointing to the spot where I had been sprawled just a minute ago.

Massimo's eyes were blazing with lust, and his jaw worked steadily. He bit his lower lip and did as I told him. He lay down in the middle of the expansive mattress and lifted his arms. That took me by surprise. I didn't expect him to show this degree of submissiveness, but I wasn't going to wait until he changed his mind. The shackles tightened over his wrists.

"There are small latches on the sides of the cuffs," he said, turning his head to look at one of the devices. "You need to press them with two fingers to make them open. Try it out now."

I followed his instruction. It might come in handy in another fifteen minutes. The mechanism was simple enough for me to work it, but at the same time, it made it completely impossible for the person tied to the bed to free themselves on their own.

"Very smart," I said, clasping the manacle over his wrist again.

"Thank you. I invented them myself."

"Do you know how to free yourself?"

The Man in Black froze, a momentary expression of unease marring his face.

"There is no way to free yourself. I didn't expect to be tied down myself."

For a while I pondered if he was telling the truth, but another look into his fearful eyes made everything obvious. He really was at my mercy. That was good. At the same time, it was frightening. I knew what I wanted to do with him, and Massimo wasn't going to allow it. He'd want to retaliate when I freed him.

"Is there anything you wouldn't like me to do?" I asked, slowly pulling off his pants and silently praying that he hadn't figured out what I was going to do.

For a moment, the Man in Black considered my question, finally concluding that there wasn't anything that popped into mind. He shook his head.

"Wonderful." His boxers flew to the floor, and I leaned over his body.

My fingers wrapped themselves around his manhood, gently stroking. Massimo moaned quietly and leaned his head over the pillows, closing his eyes. I liked it when he allowed himself to relax. What I was about to do would require a certain level of . . . looseness. I felt his cock hardening in my hand and heard his breathing quicken.

Without letting go of him with my eyes, my tongue traced a little circle around the hole on its tip. The Man in Black inhaled loudly and held his breath for as long as my tongue stayed in contact with his prick. It was red hot. I could tell just how much he wanted me right now by the taste.

I wouldn't want to rush anything, though. There were still thirty minutes to take advantage of, and I fully intended to squeeze every last bit of pleasure from the time left. My lips straddled the head of Massimo's penis, and I slowly pushed my head down, sliding it into my mouth. I wanted to feel each inch. Massimo's hips rose, as if he wanted to reach the back of my throat faster, but my hands held him down.

I continued the slow, agonizing caress as he muttered something unintelligible. When finally his cock reached the end of the road, pushing against the back wall of my throat, the Man in Black let out a deep moan and tensed. The chains grew taut, rattling. I lifted my head and repeated the torture. Massimo wriggled, trying to provoke me to pick up the pace, but I was only slowing down. I pushed myself up, propped on my arms, and bit his nipple, delighting in the hiss that came out of his mouth. I kissed his torso, caressed his arms, rubbing his throbbing cock with my pussy. It must have been exhausting for him. I could imagine his blackening eyes beneath his closed eyelids. My tongue trailed up his neck, reaching his clamped lips. Little by little, I pushed my finger into his mouth, opening it.

"Massimo?" I asked in a whisper. "How much do you trust me?"

The Man in Black's eyes snapped open, as he fixed me with a stare filled with lust.

"With all my heart. Now take it in your mouth."

I laughed derisively and let my tongue moisten his parched lips. He tried catching it with his teeth, but I was faster.

"You want me to suck you off?" My right hand gripped his cock while the left clasped around his jaw. "Ask nicely," I ordered through clenched teeth.

"Don't push it," he growled, his teeth snapping and missing my lips again.

"Have it your way, don Massimo. This is going to be the best blow job you've ever had."

I let go of his penis and started to leisurely lower myself until my head hovered above his rock-hard cock. I took it in my mouth, my lips clamping tightly around its head, and I sucked. I had never given anyone a blow job with such swiftness. The Man in Black's chest heaved as he muttered under his breath, pulling at his chains.

"Relax, darling," I said, licking my index finger and pushing it between his buttocks.

Massimo's body grew rigid, and his breathing stopped.

My hand didn't even manage to touch the spot I was aiming for, when his powerful hands grabbed me and rolled me over to my back. I was too surprised to react. His eyes were drilling holes in me, filled with fury. He hovered above me wordlessly, pinning me to the mattress, his breath heavy and his brow gleaming with sweat.

"Didn't you like it?" I asked sweetly, making an innocent expression.

Massimo kept silent, and his hands were tightening around my arms.

I closed my eyes, unable to watch his sudden anger, and felt him closing the manacles over my wrists. The mattress buckled, and the bed creaked a little. I opened my eyes, realizing I was alone. I could hear the sound of water running in the shower. *Great,* I thought, *he left before I could finish. Did I overdo it?* I didn't want to hurt him. My aim had been to prove something to him, albeit in an unconventional way. I had once read about male anatomy and learned that some experiments may prove very pleasurable to men. As enjoyable as for women, or even more so. It turned out the manliest man on Earth didn't enjoy those kinds of things. Most men would, in his place.

"I won't allow you to take control anymore," Massimo said, breaking my train of thought.

He was standing in the door, water trickling down his skin. His chest was still heaving.

"How did you free yourself?" I asked, changing the subject. "And why did you go to the shower?"

He flashed a sly smile at me and took a few steps closer, stopping only when his cock was nearly touching my face.

"I won't explain myself to you. Not now, when I intend to fuck you so hard they'll hear your screams all the way back in Poland." He took my head in his hands and shoved his prick in my mouth. "Now suck it hard," he said, thrusting with his hips. "And I didn't take a shower. I was trying to cool down."

His girth was making me gag. The fat prick was reaching so deep, it was what felt like inches from my stomach. For a moment, he slowed down, caressing my cheeks with his fingers, but then he thrust even harder. I was his whore.

Suddenly, Massimo's cell rang. He glanced at the screen and rejected the call. The smartphone vibrated again a couple of seconds later. This time, he picked it up, growled something in Italian, and accepted the call. His hips didn't stop.

"It's Mario. I need to take this. Keep sucking," he gasped out, untying one of my hands so I could grab the base of his penis.

He knew perfectly well that that was as titillating for me as it was for him. I loved to play with him when he was on the phone. My hand gripped him tightly, and I slid his prick deeper into my throat.

"Oh, Jesus," he breathed, inhaling deeply and putting the phone to his ear.

He didn't say much, preferring to listen, trying to slow down his breathing. His knees started to shake, and his whole body beaded with sweat. With his free hand, he leaned against one of the columns. I knew he was close. A minute into his call, which was more of a monologue on Mario's part, Massimo barked something in Italian through clenched teeth and tossed the phone away.

He grabbed me, rolled me over, untied my other hand, and pulled me to the edge of the bed. Then he tied me up again, but now I was lying on my belly.

"You're lucky I don't have as much time as I wanted," he said, lifting my hips so my butt was sticking out and my face pressed into the pillows. "We need to wrap this up."

He placed me in a position that suited him and reached for something from the nightstand, before spreading my legs even wider.

"Now you relax," he breathed into my ear, leaning over me, and bit into the back of my neck.

Then he slid down and his tongue pushed itself into my pussy, so hungry for his touch. I moaned in ecstasy and opened myself up for him. Soon, I was on the verge of orgasm, but at that moment Massimo stopped, pulled away, and knelt behind me. His hand delicately stroked my buttock. His other arm shot out, grabbed my hair, and jerked my head back brutally. I squealed, feeling his hand smacking my ass. His grip tightened and his hand slapped me again. My skin prickled, and the spot pulsated with pain.

"I said relax."

Massimo's hard shaft rammed into me, and I nearly fainted. I didn't realize how much I had missed my imperious lover until now. He let my hair go and grabbed my hips, thrusting faster and even more violently.

"Yes!" I cried, stunned with the intensity of the sensation. Massimo was breathing loudly, and his fingers dug into my skin. Suddenly, one hand left its place and reached for something lying next to his leg.

I heard a faint sound of vibration and tried turning my head to look, but my head was pinned to the pillow.

"Open your mouth," Massimo ordered. I obeyed and he slipped something rubbery into it.

It was slightly thicker than a finger. An instant later, he pulled it out and rubbed delicately at my anus. I quickly caught his intention and relaxed, though it wasn't easy with the constant thrusting of his hips.

The small vibrator went into my ass, and immediately a wave of bliss washed over me. I cried out. The rhythmic movement and the vibration were bringing me inexorably closer to an overwhelming orgasm. I couldn't wait!

Holding the plug inside me, Massimo slapped me on the butt again, and came. I felt him explode inside me and promptly joined him in ecstasy, silently thanking God we were the only people in the building. Our loud screams ripped the silence apart, accompanied by the slapping sound of hips crashing against buttocks. We orgasmed together, long and hard, until I felt my body going limp. I spread my knees and collapsed to the mattress, feeling Massimo following in my steps. He propped his body on his elbows so he didn't crush me under his weight.

With a fluid motion, he freed my wrists and rolled over, wrapping my waist with his leg and lying down next to me. His hand brushed away the hair from my face, and he kissed me.

"Can you pull it out now?" I asked, feeling my butt still vibrating with the device inside. Massimo laughed and took out the magic thing. I moaned, feeling it leave my body and hearing it go silent.

"How are you feeling?" he asked.

I couldn't think, let alone talk, but both the child and I were feeling wonderful.

"Great."

"I love fucking you, baby girl."

"I've missed you so much, don Massimo."

I took a shower and jumped back to bed, wrapped in a soft bathrobe. Massimo appeared in the room, too, wearing only a towel around his hips. He passed me a mug of cold cocoa.

"Two months ago this would have been champagne." I sighed with disappointment, taking the cup.

The Man in Black shrugged, pulled at the towel covering his midsection, and started to dry his hair with it.

Oh, sweet baby Jesus, he's so beautiful, I thought, nearly choking on my cocoa. It was just unfair and plain scary how perfect this man was. Nearly four months had passed, and I still couldn't get enough of him.

"We need to get back," he said coldly. "I should be in Palermo tonight."

I sat up, took another sip, and pouted.

"Don't look at me like that, baby. I need to go to work. There's a problem with one of the hotels. But I have an idea," he added, sitting next to me. "The gala in Poland starts in a few days, so maybe you take the jet and go right away. See your parents, you know. I'll join you as soon as possible."

Hearing the word "parents" made me perk up, but then I glanced at my bulging belly. "Mom would see that I've gained weight."

"You'll take Olga with you. I'll need Domenico here. The jet is yours. You can go whenever you'd like."

I was confused, sad, and—ironically—a little happy, too.

"What's going on, Massimo?"

He shot me a strange look and stood up. His face showed no emotion.

"Nothing you need to concern yourself with, baby girl." He led a finger along my lips. "I need to work, is all. Now. Get dressed." We returned to the mansion, and Massimo kissed me passionately, before disappearing into his study. I was left alone, standing with my back to the wall, staring at the door handle. There were dozens of conflicting thoughts flashing through my mind, and my eyes welled with tears. *What's happening to me?* I thought. *He left a minute ago, and I'm already missing him so much!* I placed my hand on the handle, pressing it gently and opening the door a fraction.

The Man in Black was standing by the window, facing Domenico, looking at something the younger man held in his hands. My eyes focused on the thing, and I froze. Was this an engagement ring? Was Domenico planning to propose to Olga? Or maybe it was something else they had been keeping secret from me? Staggered with the new information—or rather, the lack of it—I decided to leave the two men alone and go to my room.

I sat on the terrace and wrapped myself in a blanket, watching the setting sun. It wasn't actually that cold, but I just liked to feel the blanket on me. I didn't want to go back to Poland. It was freezing there this time of year. I didn't want to go without *him*, and most important, I didn't want to face my mother. On the one hand, seeing my parents would be great, but on the other hand—it would only lead to a confrontation, and I had no need for that.

Sipping on a cup of tea, I started planning. First things first—dress so my belly didn't show. Too much pasta and pizza—that would be my explanation for my weight gain.

Fortunately enough, I wasn't throwing up anymore. Faking stomach problems would undoubtedly have made my mother suspicious. She was just too smart. But then it dawned on me—I had nothing to wear! I didn't own anything that would hide my pregnancy. Tired with all that thinking, I dropped my head, allowing it to rest between my folded knees.

"I'll never get pregnant," I heard a voice say.

It was Olga's. "What would I do without booze?"

Frightened by that thought, she took a seat next to me, extending her legs over the table.

"Speaking of booze, I need to have a drink," she said.

"No can do," I replied, putting my cup down. "We're leaving."

"Again? Fucking hell . . . Where to? And why? We've only just got back here," she moaned, raising her eyes to the sky.

"Poland, my dear. The motherland. We're going in the morning. How about that?"

She took a moment to mull it over, shooting glances to the sides, as if she was searching for something.

"In that case, I need a good pounding first." She nodded, decided.

"Who is going to do the pounding, though?" I asked, teasing. Domenico was with Mario and Massimo after all.

"What kind of question is that? My man, of course. I took a short nap, and Domenico left, but I'll find him in no time."

I rose, folded the blanket, and placed it on the backrest of the chair.

"I'm afraid that's not going to happen." I shrugged, pushing out my lower lip. "Business! I'm your only companion for tonight."

CHAPTER
ten

Olga went to her room to pack her bags, and I intended to do the same, but ended up going to take my third shower of the day. I wasn't feeling dirty or anything. I just felt like procrastinating a bit in the hot water.

Having turned on all the various water jets, I allowed the large bathroom to fill with hot steam. Then I connected my cell phone with a speaker on the dresser and played "Silence" by Delerium, before stepping into the shower and closing my eyes. The water cascading down my back and the music were relaxing. I propped my hands on the wall, allowing the hot stream to engulf my body, silencing the irritating thoughts.

"I missed you," I heard a voice right behind me.

I twitched, though I knew who it was, of course. My abrupt jolt wasn't a sign of fear, but a simple reaction to the unexpected sound.

"I decided our goodbye wasn't affectionate enough," Massimo said, grabbing my hips.

I didn't turn to face him, instead grabbing a horizontal bar lined with buttons controlling the water flow. I pressed one, making the nozzles in the wall spout powerful jets of water. The Man in Black clasped his hands on mine, as his lips made their way up my shoulders, then the neck, to finally my lips. His tongue pushed itself in, tangling with mine. Massimo was naked and wet. He was also ready for me. His knees buckled a bit, and then he shot out with his hips, impaling me on his enormous cock. I moaned, resting the back of my head on his muscular torso. His hands cupped my oversensitive breasts, kneading them lazily, as his hips started to slowly thrust. I could feel the lust growing in me. My body tensed and relaxed to the rhythm of Massimo's movements.

"You didn't think I came here just to rub against your butt, did you?" His teeth bit painfully into my ear.

"I hope not, don Torricelli."

He took me in his hands and carried me from the shower across the bathroom, putting me down by the tall mirror. His strong arms pushed me to the cold counter, and then, with an abrupt jerk, he pulled my head up so I saw his reflection.

"Look at me," he growled, pushing his cock inside me again.

His free hand landed on my hips for support, and he began pounding me. It was crazy fast. My eyes narrowed in ecstasy. I was slipping away.

"Open your eyes!" he roared.

They snapped wide open. I looked at him. There was madness in his eyes. He was controlling himself, but just barely. It turned me on even more. My fingers bit into the rim of the sink, trying to immobilize my body. My lips parted, and I moistened them with my tongue.

"Harder, don Massimo," I whispered.

Veins bulged all over the Man in Black's body, and his muscles flexed, presenting his immaculate physique in all its glory. Biting his lip, he kept his piercing gaze fixed on me.

"As you wish." The pace of his movements was deadly. It didn't even take a minute, and I felt the first wave of bliss rising in my underbelly. "Not yet, baby girl," he hissed.

His words worked exactly the opposite way they were supposed to. I came almost immediately, still fixing my gaze on Massimo's reflection. A moan ripped from my throat, quickly rising in cadence and turning into a scream. The Man in Black didn't slow down even for an instant. A couple of seconds later, I had another orgasm. My breath heaved in my breast, and waves of shivers were going down my spine.

"Kneel," my lover said as I collapsed on top of the sink.

I couldn't catch my breath, but did as I was told. Massimo's manhood entered my mouth, and his hands clasped around my head. He didn't fuck my throat this time, instead delicately sliding deeper, allowing me to control the pace. His taste told me he was close.

I sucked his cock hungrily, taking it deep.

Massimo's buttocks tensed, and his breath quickened. He pulled his penis out and came with a loud moan, spurting hot cum all over my wet breasts. His eyes kept fixed on me as he flooded his seed over me. I leaned back and stuck my chest out, letting out a moan as my hand fondled his heavy balls.

When he was finished, he leaned over the marble counter behind me.

"You'll be the death of me, baby girl," he gasped out.

I laughed, spreading the sticky white fluid across my tits and sending him a furtive look.

"You think it's easy?" I asked.

"As if nobody tried before you!" I repeated his words from

that first night, when I had tried shooting him with the gun's safety still on.

Massimo's lips spread in a sly grin, and his hands cupped my face.

"You're a good listener. It flatters me, but it's also a dangerous trait."

I pushed myself to my feet and faced him, clinging to his muscled torso.

"I hate our goodbyes, Massimo," I said, suddenly close to tears.

"That's why we won't say goodbye this time, baby. I'll be back before you know it." He wiped away the remains of his semen with a towel, softly kissing my lips. "Your plane takes off at noon. You'll be there in a couple hours. Sebastian will pick you up. The same guy who drove you around last time. You have Karol's number in your phone. If you need anything, call him. He'll take care of you until I join you."

I sent him a fearful look. Those instructions sounded ominous. As if I was in some kind of danger. Everything he was doing now was suspicious—the sudden trip and sending me away to Poland. It wasn't like him to allow me to stay away for that long.

"Don Massimo . . . what is really going on?" He didn't reply, focusing on wiping my breasts clean. "Goddamn it, Massimo!" I cried out, tearing the towel from his hands.

He let them drop limply to his sides as he focused his glare on my eyes.

"How many times do I have to tell you, Laura Torricelli? Nothing is happening." He took my face in his hands and kissed me. "I love you, baby girl. I'll join you in three days. I promise. Now stop being angry. My son doesn't like it." He stroked my belly and smiled.

"Daughter."

"I just hope she isn't a shrew like her mother."

Having said that, he jumped away, knowing I'd take a swing at him.

I followed him, stark naked, trying to smack him with the wet towel, but he was faster. When I chased him into the bedroom, Massimo grabbed me and threw me onto the bed, pinning me down.

"You complete me, my love. I wake up every morning and feel alive just because of you." His eyes were warm and loving as he looked at me. "I thank God every day for that day I nearly died and saw you in my dream." He pressed his lips to mine. "I need to go now. Call me if anything happens."

He tore away from me, got up, and went to the dressing room, returning a couple of minutes later in his standard black suit and shirt. He gave me another kiss and went downstairs.

I woke up early. It was only seven. I spent the next fifteen minutes in bed, watching TV, before going to the bathroom and taking my fourth shower in the last twenty-four hours. I had all the time in the world. I didn't have to look good with Massimo away, but I spent some time doing makeup and perfecting my coiffure.

Then it was time to pack my things. Daunted by the task, I sat on the rug in the dressing room. Of course, Maria could pack for me as usual, but this trip required a very precise choice of outfits. I rummaged through my things, digging out a pile of expensive clothes. Most of my favorite things wouldn't hide my belly. In fact, they would do the exact opposite. When I was on Sicily, I liked to show off my pregnancy, but in Poland I'd rather wear a tarpaulin than display my growing abdomen. It would have felt so good to be able to tell the entire world about the baby

I was going to have. I curled up in the heap of shirts, blouses, and dresses.

"Having a yard sale?" Olga asked, appearing in the door with a cup of coffee in her hand. "I'm taking it all!"

"Damn, Olga," I cried, perched on top of my heap of clothes. "I don't have anything to wear! I don't even have anything for the winter. There are no winters on Sicily!"

Olga placed her cup on the table with a decisive motion and let out a piercing cry.

"The horror!" she wailed. "We'll have to go shopping." She collapsed to her knees right next to me. "What shall we do?"

I sent her an angry gaze. How could she be making fun of me now? I really didn't need any more clothes!

"Oh, fuck off," I hissed, tossing the few things I had already picked into my suitcase. "At least I still have my shoes," I said, hugging a pair of my Givenchy boots. "You ready?"

"More than you are."

We had breakfast and then spent some more time packing my things. Before eleven, we were sitting in the car, driving to the airport. I took a pill before we stepped on deck of the private jet.

I took a seat and blacked out right before we took off. Every trip was teleportation with that simple trick.

◇◇◇◇◇◇◇◇◇◇

"Nice to see you again, madam," Sebastian greeted me, opening the door to his Mercedes for me.

"Right back at you." I flashed him a wide smile and took a seat in the limo. A while later we drove into the underground garage beneath my apartment. Another minute, and we were there.

"Why don't I go to my place?" Olga asked, reclining on the sofa. "I do have my own apartment."

I put the kettle on and took a peek in the fridge. Surprisingly, it was filled to bursting.

"Because Massimo wanted us to stay together. Besides, why would you want to be alone? Don't you like me no more?"

I reached for a jar of chocolate pudding and dipped a spoon in it. Olga walked over, stopping in the doorway and leaning against the wall.

"What're we going to do? I just feel disoriented and . . . alienated." She grimaced and then pouted.

"I know. Me too. Isn't it weird how much a few months can change? We'll go to our parents' tomorrow. I to mine, you to yours. We need to prepare them for the fact we won't be spending Christmas together."

The thought of going to see my parents made me feel nauseous. I did miss them, but the need to put on a show to keep them in the dark was too much for me.

"Look," Olga said, looking out the window. "Snow. Motherfucking snow."

We stood side by side, gaping at the wintry landscape outside as if it were something out of the ordinary. And I dreamed of returning to Sicily.

"Shopping," I muttered with my face glued to the window. "We need something to lift our spirits."

"About that," Olga said, turning to face me. "Domenico gave me a credit card. It's got my name on it." She raised her eyebrows and nodded her head. "I'm getting the impression that he tries to be like Massimo a lot. So the thing is, I'm not sure if he really feels this way or is just trying to copy his brother."

The scene I had witnessed in the study yesterday flashed through my mind. I wasn't decided if I should tell her, but finally settled on keeping it to myself. It wasn't any of my business, after all, and I didn't want to be the one to spoil the surprise.

"You're overthinking it. Let's down that tea and go get me some baggy clothes."

"You're overthinking it, too. Your belly is barely showing. Don't worry." She shook her head.

"I don't know." I put my hands over my belly and stroked the bulge. "Maybe you're right, but I know my mom. She'll know I'm pregnant. Trust me. Better safe than sorry."

An hour, a tea, half a dozen candy bars, and a jar of Nutella later, we parked my white BMW by the mall. In the meantime, we had changed into something more appropriate for the cold Polish winter. I picked my black Givenchy boots, leather leggings I barely squeezed myself into, a loose cream-colored tunic, and a gray fox-fur vest. Olga went with what she liked the best—shorts and thigh-high Stuart Weitzman boots, a loose sweater matching the shoes, and a leather jacket. Hooker style. Her signature outfit.

We wandered around shops and boutiques, spending heaps of cash and collecting dozens of heavy bags filled with winter clothes. It wasn't strictly necessary to have as much winter stuff as we bought, especially since it wouldn't be of any use back in Italy. In the end, to drown out the pangs of guilt, we agreed to leave all of it in Poland. We'd need the things in the future, probably. With that thought in mind, we spent some more of our men's cash. My cell rang as we left yet another store. I pulled it out and saw the number was unlisted. I smiled.

"Hey there, baby girl." That gorgeous British accent sounded over the phone. "How's shopping?"

"Perfect. Baggy clothes are my new favorite thing," I replied sarcastically. "How did you know where I was?" As soon as I asked, I realized what a stupid question that was.

"Your phone has a tracker built in, honey. Your watch, too. And your car," Massimo replied with a laugh. "And the red dress you just bought is beautiful. It's not baggy at all."

A shiver went down my spine as I nervously looked around. How did he know what I had bought? I was about to ask him, when I noticed two tall men lounging nearby.

"Why do I need security, don Massimo?" I asked. "I'm in Poland, and there's nothing dangerous here." I hesitated. "Right?"

"Of course not," he replied at once. "I just like to be sure my two most beloved people are safe."

"You're talking about me and Olga, I presume?" I laughed and sat down on a bench.

Massimo muttered something in Italian. I didn't catch it. "You and my son."

"Daughter!" I cut in.

"You are not allowed to wear that red dress until I see it with my own eyes." His voice was full of authority. I could picture his face as he said it. "Now go back to your shopping. Say hi to your parents from me."

I sighed, putting the phone back in my handbag. I sent Olga a glance. She put two fingers in her mouth, pretending to gag.

"I'm gonna puke," she grumbled, rolling her eyes.

"Now, now. Don't be jealous." I grimaced and got up, taking her hand. "We got company," I said, pointing at the security guards. "They're documenting all our purchases."

"Fucking hell," Olga swore. "He's even worse than your mom."

"That is a fact." I snorted with laughter. "Now come with me."

The next day, dressed in a baggy tunic that was tightish only around my breasts, a pair of leggings, and a coat, I headed out to my parents' place. I'd decided not to tell them I was coming. This was going to be a surprise. Olga hopped out on the way, by the apartment block her parents were living in. My parents' was the only place I had ever thought of as home. A long time ago, my brother and I had decided that we'd never live there, but we wouldn't sell the house, either. Kuba lived nearly three hundred miles away, and—as long as I had stayed in Warsaw—the distance between me and our folks was close to one hundred and fifty. It didn't change the fact that my happiest memories had always been the ones from our parents' house.

Mom had done a lot of work to make the garden look gorgeous, and the building itself had changed dramatically over the last couple of years. I couldn't imagine anyone else living there but us.

Now I was standing on the porch. I rang the doorbell. The door opened, and my dad appeared.

"Oh, my goodness! Hello there, darling," he said, beaming and pulling me inside. "What are you doing here? You look astonishing!"

I could see his eyes were watering, so I gave him a great hug.

"Surprise," I whispered, cuddling against his shoulder.

My breathtaking mother walked through the door, impeccably dressed and wearing full makeup.

"Dear child," she cried, spreading her arms wide.

I threw myself into her embrace and started crying, who knows why. Every time she reacted emotionally to my appearance, it made my eyes tear up.

"Mommy."

"Why are you crying, darling?" she asked, stroking my hair. "Has something happened? Why are you here?"

Pessimism was my mother's primary peculiarity. She loved

worrying about anything and everything, coming up with problems even if there were none.

"It's all right, I-I-I just got emotional," I stammered, sniffing.

"Now, now, darling, that's enough." She patted me on the back. "Tom, why don't you make us some tea?"

My ability to come up with creative lies was about to be tested. I told my parents about training in Budapest and how wonderful I was doing at work. I spun them a long and winding tale of entirely imaginary parties that I had supposedly thrown, and when they inevitably asked about learning Italian, I just said the three or four words I knew and changed the subject.

An hour and a half of monologuing, it was time to check out Dad's new telescope—the one he had really got from Massimo, though officially it had been a gift from me. I watched him bustling about the cardboard cylinder, assembling the device, muttering something to himself.

"This may take a while," Mom said, bringing out a bottle of red wine and two glasses.

"Shit," I cursed under my breath. I hadn't predicted that. I should have.

Mother poured the wine and raised her glass, waiting for me to follow. Panicking, I raised my glass and wet my lips in the dark beverage. It was unbearably good. I had missed the taste of wine. If I could, I would have downed the whole bottle.

Dad was still fumbling with the telescope, trying to aim it at something, while Mom poured herself more.

"Don't you like it?" she asked, seeing I wasn't drinking my wine. "It's your favorite Moldavian pinot noir."

"I . . . don't drink anymore," I spluttered. Her stare couldn't mean anything good. "You see, Mom, everyone drinks all the time in Italy." I quickly tried to put the lie together, frantically thinking of what to say. "And alcohol means carbs!" I said, finally, sending her a hesitant smile.

"Yes, I noticed you looked rather . . ." Mom paused, looking for a word. ". . . plump. Did you stop working out?"

No, I'm just fucking pregnant, I thought, keeping the smile plastered to my face.

"No time for exercise lately. All the time to eat, unfortunately. Especially at work. Pizza and pasta all the time, you know? I've been gaining weight for weeks now." I tried to mask the lie with more words, praying she bought it. "That's why I quit drinking. To cleanse my body." It wasn't going to be an easy sell. I had always loved wine and never refused it. I'd more likely stop eating than say no to a glass of good red.

Mother watched me closely for a long while, clearly suspicious, turning the glass in her fingers. Her narrowed eyes were telling me that she didn't believe a word of what I'd said. My beloved father saved me.

"There it is! Come and see, Laura." He called me to the telescope.

I jumped up and launched myself in his direction, quickly sticking an eye to the visor. There it was. My dad had found the moon. It looked beautiful magnified by the lens. I babbled, marveling at the beauty of the silver globe with more enthusiasm than I actually felt. Luckily, my dad had always been a bit of a geek. He started telling me all about astronomy with his characteristic zeal, and my mom left the room, bored. I pretended to listen, secretly planning how to avoid another confrontation. Dad's astronomy knowledge was so extensive, I had another hour at least.

Fighting sleepiness, I stayed with him, bored out of my mind. As my eyes started to close, Mother saved me from Dad.

"Dinner is served," she said, motioning us to the kitchen.

I'm going to go crazy if I don't leave tomorrow, I thought. Dad had to save me from Mom, then Mom had to rescue me from Dad, and I was quickly going to lose myself in all the lies I had to tell them. I couldn't remember having to exert my brain like that for a long time.

My head was throbbing with pain.

I sat at the table, eyeing all the delicacies mother had prepared, and I felt ravenous. I helped myself to a bit of everything, then started another round. I wasn't eating; I *devoured* dinner. Twenty minutes into the blowout feast, I raised my eyes, meeting my parents' shocked stares. *Fuck*. I'd have to leave today after all. Mother was chewing her food, her eyes darting from my empty plate to my face.

"What?" I asked with my mouth full. "My stomach got a bit larger. It's because of all that pasta, I tell you."

"I can see that." Mother shook her head disapprovingly.

I was going to stuff my face with another piece of apple pie, but decided against it. That would be too much for my old folks. Besides, I'd already planned to visit the kitchen around midnight, when nobody would disturb me or glare at me.

After dinner, we watched a movie together, and then I excused myself and went to my old room.

I could sleep downstairs in the living room, but that would mean I'd be right next to my parents' bedroom. That wouldn't be a good idea.

In the morning, when I woke up, I realized my mom and dad had gone out. I had an hour to myself. Bored, I watched some TV and finally decided to take a shower. I turned the water on and stepped in. With eyes closed, I recalled the last shower I had taken with Massimo. I missed him. My skin prickled, almost feeling his touch. With that vision in my head, I started touching myself, rubbing my clit and cupping my swollen breasts. I would come so fast . . . This was one of the best things about being pregnant—my body was so sensitive, reacting to touch in a way it never had.

I thought about how violent Massimo could be, picturing him causing me pain and delighting in that image. I could almost feel his hands on me. I spread my legs, rubbing my puffy clitoris a little harder and faster. Scenes shot through my mind like a movie. The Man in Black holding my hips and pounding me brutally, impaling me with his fat cock. I let out a muffled cry as the orgasm flooded my body. I exhaled, feeling the tension leaving me. It was exactly what I had needed.

I turned the water off and left the shower, stopping by the closet. My eyes scanned my surroundings and didn't find a single towel. I had to go back to my room and find a bathrobe.

"Great," I muttered, opening the door and heading back to my room.

I stopped in the doorway, suddenly realizing I wasn't alone. My mother's eyes were drilling holes in me. She was staring at my belly. I couldn't move, frozen to the spot. Mother didn't say a thing, only shook her head, as if trying to get rid of a nagging thought or wake up from a bad dream. Her eyes didn't flinch. Finally, she sat down, sighed, and looked me in the eyes. I felt vertigo, nearly fainting. My lungs started heaving, hard and fast, and I heard a high-pitched whine in my ears.

I managed to grab the bathrobe from the armchair and throw it over myself before I collapsed into the seat.

I closed my eyes, trying to calm my breath.

"Take it," Mom said, pushing a pill between my lips.

"Can't," I managed. "Check my bag."

I heard her digging through my things, finally finding a rattling little bottle filled with pills and offering me one of them. I put it under my tongue, waiting for it to start working. There was a burning sensation beneath my sternum, and the sound of my pounding heart drowned out all other noises. I wanted to die. It would be easier than confronting my mother.

"I'm calling an ambulance," she said, getting up.

"No. Don't." I opened my eyes and sent her a wide-eyed, scared stare. "It'll pass."

She sat on the floor, facing me and measuring my pulse. Meanwhile, I was silently praying to God to teleport me to Sicily. Minutes passed, and despite having my eyes closed again, I could feel her scolding gaze on me. I put my hand on my belly on instinct, took a deep breath, and faced her.

There was disappointment in her look, but also concern and sadness. How did it come to this? I had thought of everything—the story, the clothes.

"What are you doing home, Mom?" I asked.

"I wanted to spend the day with you, so I canceled all my meetings," she replied, getting to her feet and taking a seat in the other chair. "How are you feeling?"

I considered the answer for a moment. Physically, I felt okay, but mentally . . . that was another thing altogether. "I'm good now. I just got nervous for a minute."

I knew she wasn't replying because she didn't want to cause me any more stress, but it didn't change a thing. We had to have this conversation. "Fourth month," I whispered, avoiding her eyes. "And I know what you're going to say, so please don't."

"I don't know what to say." She lifted her arms, hiding her face in her hands. "All this is happening too quickly, Laura.

You've never been like this. First you go abroad, then that strange man appears . . . You keep all these secrets. And now, a child!"

She was right, of course. Whatever I said next, it wouldn't change anything.

"I love him, Mom," I said pitifully.

"But a child?!" she cried, jumping to her feet. "You don't have to have a baby with someone all at once only because you fell in love! Especially when you only met him . . ." She trailed off.

I dug through my bag and grabbed the first outfit that fell into my hands. I dressed myself while my mother was counting silently.

"Laura Biel! Goddamn it, how long did you know that man before you decided to have his baby, anyway?"

I balled my fists. The anger I felt was directed at myself.

"What difference does it make, Mom?"

"That's not how I raised you! How long?"

"We didn't plan it. It just happened. You think I'd be that stupid?" I grabbed my bag. "And if you need to know, I knew him for three weeks."

It only dawned on me how absurd the whole situation was when I said that. I was trying to make my mom understand something that even I thought made no sense.

My mother went pale and froze. I had hurt her. That much was obvious. I had known this would happen. There was no way I could tell her about my abduction, Massimo's strange vision, the Mafia, or all that Sicilian mess.

"And what if he gets bored with you?" my mother asked, raising her voice. "He'll dump you and the child. That's *not* how I raised you," she repeated. "A family needs three people to function properly. How could you be so irresponsible?" She was trying to control herself, but that was a losing battle. "Have you ever thought how hard it is to be a single mother? This isn't about you anymore!"

"We got married a week after I left Poland. No prenup," I growled at her. "So all his fucking money is mine now! I have so much money, I can use it as diapers for the kid! And Massimo loves me and the baby so much that he'd rather die than let us leave." I raised my hand, shutting her up before she interrupted me. "And trust me, I know. I already tried. Don't judge me, Mom, because you know next to nothing about my life and the situation I'm in!" I cried and sprinted down the stairs, leaving her.

On my way, I grabbed my coat from its hanger and quickly pulled on my boots. I stormed outside. It was snowing. Freezing wind gusted into my face. I took a deep breath and pressed the button on the car fob, tossed my bag to the back seat, and jumped in the car, slamming the door behind me. Tears streaked down my cheeks. I was furious with myself. I needed to scream. To throw up. To die. A moment later, I drove off, leaving town and turning onto a forest path.

A couple dozen yards into the trees, I stopped the BMW, got out, and howled. I kept screaming until I had no air left. Then I kicked the tire of the car, even though I had those exorbitantly expensive Givenchy boots on. I needed Massimo like never before.

After a long while, I calmed down and got back in the car. I dialed my husband's number. He picked up after three rings. Sniffling, I opened my mouth to say something. No sound came out of my mouth. As soon as he said the first word, I just broke down and started crying. Mixing English and Polish, I tried explaining to him what had happened, smacking the steering wheel, bawling, screeching, and making a lot of other weird noises. I heard Massimo saying something in Italian, and a moment later, a black VW Passat appeared in my rearview mirror. Two burly men jumped out. The same two I had seen at the mall. One of them ran to my door, opened it, and stared into the BMW, clearly looking for someone.

"The fuck are you looking at? Can't a woman have a moment alone?!" I cried out and slammed the door in his face.

The man put a cell phone to his ear and left, taking his partner with him.

"Honey." I heard the gentle, calm voice flowing from the car's speakers. "Wipe your nose and tell me again. In English. What happened?"

I related the whole story, finishing it with a hit of my head to the top of the steering wheel.

"I'm exhausted, Massimo. I keep hurting the people who love me. I'm so angry and so sad. And you're not here." I felt a sudden fury raising within me. My body started shaking. "You know what, don Massimo?" I growled, my voice filled with rage. "You've complicated my life. It's all your fault! Everything's gone to shit because of you! I'm going to hang up now, before I start crying again!"

I ended the call and turned the phone off. He had told me never to do that, but there was the Passat behind me, so Massimo knew everything anyway. He had his eyes on me. I turned the car around, passed the two guys in the black VW, and drove back.

I stopped only when I reached Olga's house, left the car, and called her through the intercom. She picked up, and I told her we were going back to Sicily, which seemed to cheer her up.

"What's up?" she asked, getting into the BMW.

"Don't even ask. I had an argument with Mom. She learned all about the baby and the wedding. And then I had another argument, this time with Massimo. 'Cause I was so pissed off by the first one." I burst out in tears again, falling into Olga's arms. "I just can't take it anymore!"

She looked terrified, and her mouth gaped open in shock.

"We're changing places," she said, unbuckling her belt and walking around the car to open the door on my side. "Get out. Now," she ordered, pulling me by the coat. "You're not going to drive in this condition."

We must have looked ridiculous. I was still screaming, tears streaking down my cheeks, hands clutching at the steering wheel. And then there was Olga, jerking at me, trying to force me out of the car. I didn't budge. Suddenly, she stretched her neck out and bit my hand.

"Aargh!" I yelped and let go of the steering wheel. That was all she needed. Olga hauled me out of the car.

"If you weren't pregnant, I would have beaten your brains out! Now get back in!"

We drove for a long while in total silence. Eventually, the fury inside me subsided and turned into confusion and a feeling of guilt.

"I'm sorry," I whispered, trying a smile. "Pregnancy's a bit like going crazy."

"At least in your case. Now tell me what happened at home."

I recounted the whole story and waited for a reaction.

"Fucking hell," she cursed, nodding. "Your mom's got a hell of a nut to crack now."

"She'll fucking disown me." I shrugged.

"Nah. She'll get over it," Olga paused, thinking, before adding: "It's not every day you learn that your kid's pregnant and got married behind your back. Besides, it's not so bad. She doesn't know Massimo is a mobster. And she doesn't know he regularly nearly gets you killed. So look at the positives." I stared at her, mouth agape, unable to believe what I was hearing. "All right, all right," she conceded finally, "I'm joking. Just stop worrying now, Laura. At least you got this behind you. Maybe you didn't tell her the way you wanted, but at least you don't have to lie anymore."

She was right, but did that change anything? The situation was a bit less muddled, but I still couldn't count on my mom ever calling me again. And we were both too stubborn to back down. I wasn't going to let it go, either.

Two hours later, we were back in the apartment. It was only two p.m., but I felt drained. Pregnancy, heart disorder, argument with Mom—it all made me want to go to sleep and not wake up until the next morning. Olga made me tea and said she was going out to break up with her Polish boyfriend. She had a lot of unfinished business she was supposed to deal with weeks ago. I nodded, waited until she left, turned on the TV, and dozed off.

CHAPTER *eleven*

"Why aren't you naked?" I heard a quiet whisper by my ear.

I opened my eyes. It was completely dark in the bedroom and the living room. The clock showed eleven. I rolled over, cuddling against my husband's torso.

"Because I didn't expect to wake up next to you. And I needed to smell you." I pinched the edge of his shirt that I had on, pulling it off and throwing it to the floor.

The Man in Black wrapped his arms around me and pressed me against his chest.

"It didn't sound like you missed me over the phone." He pulled away and looked at me. "And while we're at it, your phone has been switched off since yesterday."

Petrified, I raised my eyes and met his gaze. I had turned my phone off yesterday, and with all that had happened, I had simply forgotten to turn it back on. If he raked me over the coals now, he'd be in the right. Massimo's stare was surprisingly gentle, and his hand caressing my hair didn't signify trouble.

"What are you actually doing here?" I asked, knitting my brows. "You were supposed to come tomorrow. Did something happen?"

"My love," he whispered, kissing my forehead.

"I got scared when you called me. I was worried about you." He sighed and tightened his embrace. "I should have been here with you when your mom learned about the baby."

"I'm sorry for yelling at you. Sometimes I can't control myself." I rolled onto my back. "And she didn't only learn about the baby. I told her about our marriage, too. I told her the whole story."

Massimo gracefully rose to his feet and pressed a button on the remote. The lights switched on. He bit his lip, thinking, and his beautiful, muscular body tensed, only to relax an instant later. He looked out to the windows, puzzled. I could have watched him the whole night, but my rumbling stomach had other ideas.

"I need to deal with some things at work, Laura," Massimo said finally, disappearing into the bathroom, where he brushed his teeth, and then into the dressing room. He changed into his black suit. "Get ready for another trip. We're going to Gdańsk. Domenico and Olga are at her place. I'll be back before four."

I stayed in bed, my face a mask of bewilderment, thinking about what had just happened. What had made him change clothes in thirty seconds and leave without another word?

"You've only just arrived, Massimo! Don't you want to have breakfast with me?"

"I came yesterday evening, so I spent the whole night with you." He sat at the edge of the bed and placed a gentle kiss on my lips. "I'll get it done in no time. I'll be all yours then."

I crossed my arms and pouted.

"I'd like you to know that my needs have not been satisfied

lately," I complained. "And as my husband, it is your duty to sate all my desires. Besides, I'm angry, frustrated, sad, and hungry." The words poured from my mouth as I felt despair encroaching again.

Massimo's eyes darkened. He narrowed them, looking at me. I ignored that signal, and that proved to be my mistake. I only noticed him shrugging off his jacket and stretching his lips in a half smile. Then he was right next to me. His hands lifted me up and he carried me to the dining room, putting me down so I faced the large table. He was behind me.

"We'll do this like we did it in the past," he said matter-of-factly, pulling down my panties and pushing his knee between my legs.

He knelt and pushed me over the tabletop. His warm, moist tongue left a trail of saliva on my pussy. I moaned loudly as it started to trace circles around it. I lay down, my body sticking to the cold surface of the table. Massimo was hungrily licking my cunt, leading me quickly to the verge of ecstasy.

Then he straightened and slid two fingers into my snatch, preparing the way for his cock. As his right hand rubbed the inside of my hole, his left unbuckled his belt.

"Quick and hard," he breathed into my ear as his pants dropped to the floor. "And don't ever say . . ." His prick took the place of his fingers, and his hand shot out to grab my hair, pulling my head back. ". . . that I don't satisfy you." His hips slammed into me from behind and started pounding like a jackhammer. I cried out.

Massimo let go of my head. His fingers bit into the skin of my buttocks as he kept impaling me.

"You like provoking me, eh?" he hissed, allowing one hand to drop lower, rubbing against my clit.

His rock-hard prick was thrusting in and out so fast, I was sure the whole thing couldn't last long. The Man in Black leaned over me, pressing me into the table without interrupting. His left hand cupped my breast, and his chest lowered itself onto my back. His fingers squeezed my nipple, crushing it. It was too much to bear.

I came with a loud moan, splayed on the cold table, now slick with sweat. As Massimo felt me orgasming, my muscles contracting around his penis, he bit into my shoulder and joined me, flooding me with a great stream of cum.

"I love it," he gasped out as we were both trying to catch our breath, sticking to each other.

Then he pulled away and rolled me over to my back. He glanced at his cock, still hard, and slipped inside me with a grin. Half-conscious after the massive orgasm, I didn't have the strength to resist as he picked up the pace again.

"You were saying something about not being sated?" He lifted my limp legs and propped my feet on the edge of the table. "Let's go again, baby girl." His thumb touched my swollen, red clit.

For the next fifteen minutes he fucked me like a machine. I prayed he wasn't planning on round three. How was it even possible that a guy his age was able to fuck like a teenager? I couldn't wrap my head around it. Massimo pulled up his pants and smiled with satisfaction, observing my drained body. He closed the distance between us, took me in his arms and carried me to the couch, covering me with a blanket.

"As I was saying, I'll be back around four."

He kissed me on the lips, grabbed his black coat and left the apartment.

He fucked me good, I thought as the door closed. *Maybe even too good. I got more than I bargained for.* I'd think twice next time before provoking him.

◇◇◇◇◇◇◇◇◇◇

I didn't get up for another thirty minutes, watching the snow behind the window. Finally, I went to the shower. I did my hair and applied some makeup—a bit more and a bit more carefully than normally. My perfect Italian tan had disappeared, but—though paler—I still looked great. I was searching for something to wear in the dressing room when I heard a commotion.

"I'm hungry! Let's grab something to eat," Olga shouted from outside.

I peeked into the living room, but she wasn't there, so I walked to the kitchen. There she was, ass sticking out as she rummaged through my fridge.

"Candy, booze-free wine, juice." She listed the things she found, still digging through the contents of the refrigerator. "I'd love me some pasta now . . . or a steak." She took a step back. "Yes. That's it. A steak, a bunch of potatoes, a salad, and a beer. Move your ass or I'll starve to death."

I stayed in place, leaning against the wall, studying the madness in her eyes.

"You haven't eaten yet?"

"There were more important things than eating, for fuck's sake. Let's go. Domenico went to take care of something with the guys. We don't have much time."

The door swung open, and the young Italian barged in. I stared at him, perplexed. What was going on?

"Why aren't you ready yet?" he asked. I shook my head, leaving the two alone, and went to dress myself. I had everything prepared—all the things I was going to wear to look pretty for my husband. Black suede Casadei boots, a short gray Victoria Beckham dress, and a short black Chanel coat. I grabbed my bag and went back to the kitchen, where Domenico and Olga were occupying themselves with licking Nutella off each other's skin.

"You two are disgusting."

All three of us took the elevator to the garage and got into a black SUV. Domenico sat with a security guard, and Olga and I took seats in the back.

"Everything done?" I asked conspiratorially, forgetting that no one but us knew Polish.

"I did fuck all." She sighed. "Before I met with Adam, Domenico arrived, and that was that."

I frowned and shrugged.

"But I bet he figured out what I wanted to tell him anyway," she added.

The car stopped by a popular restaurant run by a well-known Polish chef. I was surprised that the Italians knew such places here in Warsaw.

We entered the building. All tables were taken. That was to be expected. It was the middle of the day. Domenico approached the manager and whispered something into his ear, pushing a little package in his hand. The man quickly led us to a small room separate from the main restaurant. We sat at a round table and leafed through the menu before ordering. The waiter brought us a plate of Polish delicacies as we waited for the main course.

As we sated our hunger on butter, bread, and salty pickles, Olga leaned over to me.

"I need to go to the bathroom," she said. We both excused ourselves and left for the main hall.

The restaurant had a minimalist décor—tasteful, with wooden accents and black-and-white portraits on the walls.

There were white calla lilies in tall vases along the walls. The speakers hummed with subtle music and the mouthwatering smell of food filled the entire place. I got hungry all over again.

Suddenly, Olga halted, staring at a man sitting at one of the tables.

"Holy motherfucking shit-balls," she swore, her grip on my hand tightening.

I followed her eyes.

The cause of her sudden immobility was evident. A handsome blond man was rising from his chair. Wide torso, perfectly fitting expensive jacket, luscious lips. It had to be said that Adam was one hell of a stud. He was rich, attractive, and intelligent. He caught Olga's eyes, pushed himself to his feet, and started heading our way.

His confident gait led him straight to us. He stopped too close, kissed Olga on the cheek, and then gave me a terse nod.

"I missed you," he murmured, his tongue flicking across his lips as he kept his eyes fixed on my friend.

His hands slid into his pockets and his entire body relaxed into a nonchalant posture as he spread his legs and lifted his chin. All rich men have that in common—a certain casualness, an aura of authority and unshakeable confidence. Those very characteristics were what we were both looking for in potential partners, and Adam had all three in abundance.

"Hi, Adam," Olga stammered, shooting nervous glances behind him. "I wanted to talk to you, but this isn't the time or place for that."

I was desperately trying to extricate myself from this uncomfortable spot, but Olga's fingers clamped around my wrist, begging me to stay.

"You never cared about either the time or place."

He lifted his brows in a suggestive expression and flashed Olga a charming smile.

"I'll call you later, okay?" Olga proposed, taking a step back and pulling me with her.

Losing her angelic sponsor wasn't going to be that easy. Adam shot out with both arms and pulled Olga into an embrace, brutally pushing his tongue into her mouth. Olga's hand released my wrist as she pushed her horny sugar daddy away. Without thinking twice, she took a swing at him and slapped him in the face with such force, the sound drowned out the music. The eyes of every guest fixed on the confrontation. I drew back a couple of steps, noticing Domenico striding our way with murder in his eyes.

"D-d-domenico . . ." I stuttered, before the Italian's balled fist reached Adam's face. The blond man toppled to the floor, but the Sicilian didn't stop there, instead pummeling him until a pair of security guards restrained him.

The manager was shouting shrilly, guests shot up from their chairs, and Domenico strained against the two bouncers, red with fury. The Italian's own security guards tried to intervene, but more restaurant doorkeepers crowded into the room. Suddenly, the doors swung open and a group of police officers barged in, promptly handcuffing Domenico. Meanwhile, Adam pushed himself up from the floor, growling threats and cussing like a sailor, and Olga wailed, tears streaking freely down her cheeks. *Will my life ever stop being a damned soap opera?* I thought. A moment later, both men left, and we stood there, in the middle of the restaurant, right in the spotlight of the other guests' gazes. Olga bowed sarcastically and stormed off, heading to our table. We hadn't even reached it when my phone vibrated in my handbag.

"Are you all right?" It was Massimo, of course.

"The police took Domenico."

"I know. Are you all right?" he repeated.

"Yeah."

"Go home and wait for me there," he said, hanging up.

"Good talk," I muttered, grabbing my coat and motioning for Olga to follow me to the exit.

We got into the SUV. By that time, Olga's crying had transformed into a raging fury.

"How could he humiliate me like that? The fucking idiot!" she yelled, pummeling the back of the driver's seat with her hands.

"Calm down," I said, buttoning up my coat.

"They both got what was coming to them. The blondie won't kiss random women anymore, and Domenico will finally learn that he's not God everywhere."

There was a long pause. "And I'm still fucking hungry!" Olga burst out finally.

I chuckled and directed the driver to take us to my favorite Chinese takeout.

◇◇◇◇◇◇◇◇◇◇

We sat down on the carpet, laying out boxes with food on the floor. I grabbed a bottle of wine from the fridge and offered my friend a glass. She downed it and nodded, signaling that she was up for a refill. Three glasses later, she tumbled onto her back and hid her face in her hands.

"What if something happens to him?" she asked, close to tears again.

"I think he might have broken Adam's nose."

"I don't fucking care about his goddamned nose! I'm worried about Domenico!"

"Maybe now you don't care, but I remember the times when you cared about a lot more than Adam's *nose*," I said after a while, slurping a forkful of noodles. Olga peeked at me from between her fingers, sending me a disapproving look. I thought I noticed a twinkle of amusement in her eyes.

"You're a despicable person."

"And you were supposed to be hungry. Eat up."

Olga downed the bottle of wine and grabbed another. I didn't want her to keep drinking alone, so I fetched my own beverage. I switched the fireplace on and settled down on the couch next to my friend. Covered with blankets, we watched TV in perfect silence. This is the greatest benefit of having a true friend: feeling comfortable with someone without having to talk.

It was past twelve, and Massimo still hadn't called. I shot a glance at Olga. She had blacked out, falling asleep with her makeup smeared over her face and her clothes still on. I decided to undress her, but as soon as I touched her, she growled and wrapped herself tighter in her blanket.

"I guess that means no," I muttered, planting a kiss on her forehead and going to the bathroom.

I took a shower and returned to the living room. She wouldn't want to be alone when she woke up. I apathetically surfed channels, staring at the screen without thinking about anything in particular. Maybe I should have called Massimo? Checked on him? No. If he wanted to talk, he'd have called me himself. I finally dozed off around two in the morning.

Half-conscious, I felt someone's strong hands carrying me to the bedroom. My eyes flicked open, and I saw my husband's face. He looked exhausted.

"What time is it?" I asked as he laid me down in bed.

"Five. Go back to sleep, honey."

"What about Domenico?" I shook my head, clearing it, hell-bent on learning the truth here and now.

The Man in Black plopped down on the edge of the mattress, pulled off his jacket, and started unbuttoning his shirt.

"He's been arrested, and it looks like he'll have to spend some time in detention." He dropped his head and sighed deeply. "I told him this isn't Sicily. And it wouldn't be a problem if he hit any other guy, but he just had to target your young Polish potentate. A damned national treasure." He lifted his eyes, shook his head, and glared at the wall. "Karol tells me he might not get out for a while."

"What do you mean?" I asked.

"Three months behind bars so he doesn't 'obstruct the case' or run abroad. We would have dealt with this if not for the fact that the guy he threw a punch at is one of the richest men in town. Besides, he broke the guy's nose, and that means a 'health impairment requiring more than seven days to heal.' That is an indictable offense here. He doesn't even have to sue. The prosecutor does that ex officio."

I stared at Massimo wide-eyed, fully awake now.

"Massimo," I whimpered, cuddling to his back. "What's going to happen now?"

He sat perfectly still, but I could feel his heart racing.

"Nothing. I'm meeting our lawyers tomorrow. We'll have to see that asshole in person. Maybe I shoot him and bury him in a forest. Who knows?"

I moved around him and sat in his lap, taking his face in my hands.

"This isn't funny," I said seriously.

"We're flying to Gdańsk tomorrow. I'm not needed here. We'll go see the fight night. I also have some meetings to attend. Then we go back home."

He sighed and touched his forehead to mine. "Karol will take care of everything. Don't worry, baby girl." He smooched me on the nose. "This isn't Domenico's first rodeo. With his character, you didn't think this was his first stay in jail, did you?" He smiled and laid me in bed, snuggling down beside me.

His tone surprised me. It was full of worry, soft and gentle.

"My little brother is a hot-blooded man, but you know that already. He's also very impressionable, though he doesn't look like it. There was this one time he fell in love with a manager of our club in Milan. To his misfortune, she had a husband. A gorilla of a man. Domenico wasn't too discreet, and the husband learned of the affair."

Massimo laughed and kissed me on the neck. "I could have reacted, told him to stop, but I didn't. He knew what he was getting into. When the inevitable confrontation finally came, Domenico had to give his all to survive. They fought for fifteen minutes, but he finally managed to shoot the guy in the knee."

"Ex-ex-excuse me?" I stammered in shock.

Massimo grinned. I was dumbstruck.

"He shot him. He knew he wouldn't win in a fistfight. The problem was that the man turned out to be the son of a police officer. So Domenico went to jail for a while, and I paid off the local authorities." He shrugged. "So you see, there's nothing to worry about, really. Domenico doesn't learn from his mistakes." He rolled to his back and gazed at the ceiling. His mirth dissipated.

"The real problem is that now he attacked someone really wealthy and really proud. Just like himself. So money won't buy anyone off this time. Adam won't change his version."

I heard a clamor from the living room, and we both pushed up with our elbows. Olga was standing in the doorway, looking terrified. Her eyes were wet with tears.

"How long were you listening?" I asked, getting up.

"If you're asking if I heard everything, yeah, I did. Goddamn it." She leaned back, touching her back to the wall, and slid down to the floor, hiding her face in her hands. "This is all my fault! How could I be so stupid?" She sobbed, wracked with shivers.

I leaned over her and took her in my arms.

"Oh, honey, it's not your fault. You did nothing wrong."

Olga started crying for real now. She sobbed loudly. It was breaking my heart.

"If anyone is at fault, it's my brother," Massimo said, taking a step closer. "And since you heard our conversation, you know it wasn't his first time." He grabbed Olga's shoulders and lifted her up. "If you want to see him tomorrow, come with me. But getting hysterical won't help. Especially at this time of night. I haven't slept for a long while. Go to sleep, you two. We'll talk more in the morning." He turned Olga around and pushed her out of the room.

"Good night."

I shot him an angry glance and followed my friend, leading her to the guest bedroom and giving her a sleeping pill. She dozed off almost immediately.

When I went back to bed, the Man in Black was already asleep. I don't know why that surprised me. After all, he had said he was exhausted. But I rarely had the opportunity to watch him sleep. He was naked, lying in the white linens. His face was beautiful and serene, his mouth slightly agape. He was breathing calmly. One of his arms was bent and tucked under his head, and the other outstretched across the bed, as though waiting for me to cuddle up to him.

My eyes trailed down his muscular torso and abdomen, to finally stop at the spot below.

"There you are . . ." I breathed, licking my lips. His gorgeous cock rested on his right thigh, stirring me to action.

"Don't even think about it," he said without opening his eyes. "Go to sleep."

I groaned, sighed, huffed and puffed a bit, and then did as I was told like a good girl.

◇◇◇◇◇◇◇◇◇◇

I woke up around noon to discover that Massimo was already gone. Not surprising in the least. I went to the kitchen, prepared myself a cup of tea with milk, and switched on the TV in the living room. After one o'clock, worried by how long Olga was sleeping, I went to take a peek through the door to her bedroom. I opened the door as quietly as I was able and . . . froze. Her bed was empty.

"The fuck?" I muttered to myself, running downstairs and grabbing my phone.

I dialed her number and waited, but she wasn't answering. I tried again, then two more times, before I changed my approach and called Massimo. He didn't tell me much—he couldn't talk and didn't have Olga around. Disoriented, I sat on the couch, rubbing at my temples. Where the hell had she gone? Why wasn't she picking up the phone?

My stomach grumbled, breaking my reverie. I glanced down at it, remembering that I was still, in fact, pregnant. Since my bouts of morning sickness had disappeared, I was prone to forgetting that. I turned up the TV, switching the channel to one with music, and went to the kitchen to help myself to some breakfast. I opened the fridge and glanced at my watch. It was nearly two p.m. *Great time for the first meal of the day*, I thought.

Rihanna and her "Don't Stop the Music" rocked me as I fried

eggs. Dancing around the kitchen, I prepared a meal for about five people and took it with me to the dining room.

As I passed the door, entering the large room, my heart skipped a beat. There was a person sitting on the couch. Olga was staring at me with unseeing eyes, keeping deathly quiet. One glance at her was enough. I turned down the TV volume and put my plate on the table.

"Why are you dressed like that?" I asked, eyeing her up and down.

The dress she was wearing would be fit for a Saturday night out rather than the middle of the day, and the sky-high heels she had on would look good in a porno. The black material of her attire emphasized the roundness of her breasts, and the dress was so short, it practically didn't cover her ass. Olga shrugged off her gray fur jacket and tossed it on the floor. She kicked off her high heels, pulled off her ripped pantyhose, and burst into tears.

"I-I-I had to," she stammered between sobs. "I had to."

My heart stopped as I watched her breakdown. I took a seat at her feet, on the rug, and wrapped my arms around Olga's knees.

"What did you do?"

Tears trickled down her fake eyelashes, smearing her dark makeup. She looked wretched.

"Do we have booze?"

"Are you serious?" I asked with a frown. She nodded. "I think we have a bottle of vodka in the freezer. I'll go take a look."

I went back to the kitchen and returned a moment later with a shot glass, a can of Diet Coke, and a bottle of Belvedere. I poured her a shot, which she downed in one gulp, not even thinking to chase it with the Diet Coke.

"Crap." It was my only comment. I poured her another shot.

She drank three in total, wiped the tears and snot away, and began telling me what had happened.

"I thought about this for a long while. I know Adam and I'm sure he won't back down." Olga took a sip from the can. "It's not about love. He doesn't love me. It's about his pride. His goddamned pride. Domenico hurt his pride. You know who he was sitting with at the restaurant?" I shook my head. "His friends, those rich assholes, are all club owners. Fucking wannabe gangsters. So you can imagine how much of a humiliation it was for him to get beaten up like that. All in front of his buddies. Domenico broke his nose and jaw. The motherfucker can barely see now." She nodded at me to pour her another shot. "Anyway, I went to his place to talk."

"You did what?!" I cried out, spilling the vodka.

"What was I supposed to do? Wait for the case to blow over? Fucking hell, Laura, our boys aren't invincible. Not here, anyway. Massimo said it himself. That it would be difficult to deal with this."

"What did you do?" I repeated my question, raising my voice.

"Shut the fuck up and listen." She downed another shot and shuddered. "I got up in the morning and waited for Massimo to leave. I went to my place and changed into this. Adam always liked expensive hookers. I drove to his place then. Knocked at his door. He wasn't even surprised to see me. He let me in and just went back to his living room. I followed him, sat in a chair, and handed him a piece of paper. I asked him to write that this wasn't an assault. That Domenico was only defending himself."

"What?!" I exclaimed, suddenly fighting not to laugh. "Are you kidding me?"

"That's what he said. I wanted him to write down that he'd make it all go away if I gave him what he wanted."

"And?"

"He called his lawyer and asked around. You know, what he should write to have a guy released from jail without any consequences. And he did. He wrote it down and signed it with his own name." She pulled out an envelope from her bag and flicked it to the table. "He was supposed to repeat it all to the police, and that was that. So he folded the paper, slid it into that envelope, and stuck it in my bag."

I darted a glance at the paper, wondering if I really wanted to hear the rest of the story. Olga took a deep breath and looked at me with sad eyes.

"What happened next?"

"He told me to wait and left the room. He was away for a couple of minutes. When he came back, he told me I was to go to the bathroom. That everything was prepared. He gave me five minutes. I did what he asked. I kept my bag with me the whole time. There were a leather outfit, high heels, and a whip there . . . I changed and went back in the living room . . . What can I say? I allowed him to fuck me like a dirty whore. And not only once. He fucked me for thirty minutes, until he grew bored. And then, when I was leaving, he fucking smiled at me and said that a whore will always be a whore."

To say that her story shocked me would be an understatement. I felt like I was in some kind of thriller movie. Only this was happening for real.

"Fuck me, Olga," I whispered, shaking my head. "What now? Are they going to let him go? Nobody will believe that this was a stroke of luck."

"I thought about that. Adam's lawyer will call them and demand money for sweeping this under the rug. Adam will probably want an official apology, and Massimo will terrorize Domenico to give it. It will all be over before we know it. And the best thing is . . . You know why the police got there so fast?" I shook my head. "They came to collect a fucking bribe from one of Adam's buddies. Can you believe it? That fuckhead boasted to me about his connections."

I hid my face in my hands and exhaled, shooting another look into Olga's clouded eyes.

"How are you feeling?"

"I've felt better," she replied, shrugging. "The worst thing was that before I went into that bathroom, Adam told me he didn't want to fuck a doll. He wanted me to pretend that I liked it. Wanted me to have a real orgasm. And he told me I was supposed to talk to him in English the whole time, since I've been talking in English with Domenico." My eyes widened. "So believe me when I say it isn't the easiest thing to fucking orgasm when all you can think of is how to kill the bastard, all the while focusing on speaking to him in a foreign tongue. So I just imagined him to be Domenico, and if not for the fact that I had to suffer through thirty minutes of fucking with that piece of garbage, it would have actually felt good. I would have been fully satisfied. Sated from a good fuck. But it was Adam. I came six fucking times. So yeah, I feel like shit. I've cheated on the first man I really love." She shook her head and added, "I'm going to take a shower. I still stink of that motherfucker."

I stayed still, mulling over what Olga had said. I didn't know what to think. On the one hand, I admired her for her stubbornness and sacrifice, while on the other I was angry at her for not allowing Massimo to take care of it. I wondered what I would have done in her place, finally concluding that probably yes, I would have done the same thing.

That made me forgive her the rashness of her decision.

I glanced at the plate of food I had cobbled up for myself. It was cold. Suddenly, I realized I wasn't hungry anymore. I was too restless. At the same time, I knew the baby was innocent in all this, and I really had to eat for its sake. I went to the kitchen, microwaved the leftovers from yesterday, and ate without leaving the counter.

When I finished, Olga was sitting on the couch again, wrapped in a bathrobe, staring numbly at the TV. The main door opened, and Massimo walked in, followed by Domenico. Olga immediately burst into tears and ran into his arms, sobbing.

"There, there," he said, carrying her across the room.

"I'm here. It's over. We're the Torricellis. It's not that easy to get rid of us." He sat on the couch, stroking Olga's hair.

I walked over to Massimo, wrapping my arm around his waist. He placed a gentle kiss on my brow and smiled.

"We're leaving in two hours. How is my son feeling?" He put his hand on my belly.

"It's a girl!" Olga called out across the room.

Massimo kissed my forehead again, took off his coat, and sat at the table, switching on his laptop. I walked over and hugged his back, keeping my eyes on Domenico and Olga. She stopped crying and soon started yelling at the poor man, pummeling him with her fists and swearing at him. He avoided the punches with a grin on his face, finally grabbing her by the arms and toppling her to the floor. They kissed. I averted my eyes, feeling like an intruder. A while later, Massimo said something in Italian to Domenico. The younger man got up, kissed Olga one more time, and they both disappeared upstairs. I went to the dressing room and started packing my things.

"What if he wants to have sex?" Olga asked, appearing in the doorway and sitting next to me. "You think men can feel those things? Will he notice?"

I gawked at her, folding a dress.

"I don't have the slightest idea, but maybe try to think of something. Diarrhea. Or headache? Period!"

"He won't fall for that." Olga furrowed her brows. "But some sweet talk and a bit of hugging might do the trick."

I pointed a finger at her, signaling understanding. When I still hadn't known how to tell Massimo about the baby, I tried the same thing and it worked. We were ready in an hour. The security guards took our luggage, and we went to the airport. I was feeling great and didn't take a pill before boarding the plane. A brief moment in that metal can quickly changed my mind. I reached for my bag to fish out the drug, but Massimo grabbed my wrist and led me to the sleeping cabin.

"The flight is only going to last thirty minutes. I'll keep you distracted," he said, pushing me to the mattress and pulling his shirt off.

CHAPTER *twelve*

The flight was indeed very short, and with Massimo's face between my legs, I didn't even notice the takeoff and landing. We touched down in Gdańsk, where the security personnel took our luggage and handed Massimo the keys to his black Ferrari. Some poor sod had had to drive this thing all the way to the north so Prince Charming could show off his toy in Tricity. I shook my head, getting in. One look at the interior told me that it, in fact, wasn't the same car.

"Did someone drive this from Warsaw?" I asked as the engine roared to life.

The Man in Black laughed and made the supercar take off, leaving everyone behind.

"This is a whole new car, babe. We have a Ferrari Italia back home, but it's no good in the winter. Rear-wheel drive, you see. This is a Ferrari FF. Four-wheel drive. A lot better for snowy conditions."

I felt stupid. How could I not tell two different cars apart? In the dark both of them looked similar, but still. I stared outside the window, scolding myself. Needing to leave Warsaw so quickly had left me no time to wonder about Domenico's instant release. I turned to my husband, placing a hand on his knee.

"How did you manage to get Domenico out so fast?"

"It wasn't me. That asshole got greedy. His lawyer called us, we settled on an amount, and the whole case went away."

"Oh," I said curtly, unwilling to dig deeper.

"But it's a bit strange," Massimo added, glancing at me. "The guy is so rich, I thought we wouldn't be able to settle. I even dug deeper into his business, but I didn't need to use what I found out."

"What do you mean?"

The Man in Black chuckled, taking a turn from the ring road.

"There isn't a single rich man on Earth that has come into his wealth doing strictly legal business. Adam is no exception. He has a lot more in common with me than you think."

"So Domenico would have gotten out anyway?" I asked, confused and anxious. Had Olga's sacrifice been for nothing?

"There are two things I really know my way around, baby girl: making money and blackmailing people."

The thought of what Olga had had to go through suddenly made me want to throw up. She had thought there was no other way, though, so she'd done what she had to out of strictly altruistic motives.

"We're here," Massimo said, stopping by the Sheraton in Sopot.

Buckling under the burden of my newly acquired knowledge, I followed him across the main hall and into the elevator.

Our apartment was spacious. It took up part of the top floor and had a sea view. It wasn't anything spectacular at this time of night. And it was snowing. I sat in an armchair on the snow-glazed veranda, staring outside, numb. Should I worry or ignore the whole situation? It was in the past now, fortunately.

"What are you thinking?" Massimo asked, standing behind me and massaging my back. "Something's on your mind. I can tell. It has to be important. You've been thinking about it for hours."

I shuffled my deck of lies, but came up with nothing.

"I'm thinking about Mom," I said finally, scowling at the thought of what had happened back at my parents' house.

The Man in Black went around the armchair and knelt facing me, spreading my legs slightly. He edged closer, and his lips hovered just a few inches from mine. His thumb stroked my chin as he watched me with half-closed eyes.

"Why is my wife lying to me?" His eyes darkened and he knitted his brows.

I sighed, capitulating.

"There are things I cannot and will not talk with you about." I held his face in my hands and planted a kiss on his lips. "Your daughter is hungry," I added, pulling away and hoping that the change of subject would distract him.

"I already ordered dinner. We'll eat here," he replied, putting his hands over my hips and gently pulling me toward him. "Now tell me. What's going on?"

Fuck! I swore in my mind, frustrated that he wouldn't just back off. *Damn his unending curiosity!* I decided to stay quiet. It wouldn't do me any good, but he wasn't going to force me to say anything. Was he? Massimo didn't move, keeping his eyes fixed on me. I could see the anger rising in them.

"If you won't talk, I'll guess," he hissed, jumping to his feet and turning to the window. "Is it about Olga?" Saying that, he spun back to me, and his furious glare burned holes in my eyes.

"I take that as a yes," he said, crossing his arms. "Would it make you feel better if I told you I already knew?"

I prayed that he was bluffing. But since he already knew, what difference did it make?

"What do you want me to say?" I asked, feigning indifference. "What did she do to you this time?" Another lie wouldn't hurt, I decided. I could always just pretend to know nothing, even if he saw through my deception.

Massimo chuckled, slid his hands into his pockets, and leaned against the window.

"To me? Nothing. But the sacrifice she made for my brother . . . that's a different story. A pity it was entirely uncalled-for," he replied, unable to keep the irony out of his voice. My eyes widened to the size of saucers. "Oh yes, love. I know what she did to make that piece of shit withdraw his charges. At first, I was angry at her. I'd told her I'd deal with this. But then I realized how far she's able to go for Domenico. And guess what?" He took a step closer and leaned above me, putting his hands on the armrests of my chair. "It is what I always look for in women. Especially those who are to join the family. It was impressive." He kissed me on the forehead and went to the door, hearing a knock.

I sat immobile, confused, pushing myself deeper into my seat, wondering if there would come a day—a single damned day—without these kinds of revelations.

The waiter rolled the cart into the room, served our food, and placed a wine cooler on the table. It only took him a minute to get everything ready. I got up and sat by the table, putting a linen napkin on my knees. Meanwhile, Massimo took off his jacket and unbuttoned the collar of his shirt. He kicked off his shoes and joined me for dinner. I wanted to say something—anything—but my mind was blank.

"I ordered goose—"

"That's what I'd have done," I cut in. Massimo's fork clattered on his plate. "If you love someone, you make sacrifices."

"Enough!" he barked, shooting up. "Don't even say that, Laura."

"Well, it did impress you, didn't it?" I asked. His eyes were fixed on me, and his face was a mask of disbelief.

"Yes. In Olga's case. She's normally a capricious loudmouth. I doubted her love for my brother. Now I don't."

"Oh, so if she screws around to save her man, that's good, but if I do it, that's bad."

He stormed around the table and grabbed me by the shoulders, lifting me to my feet.

"You are my wife. You are going to have my baby. I would kill the man and then myself if you made such a sacrifice." His hands held me in a viselike grip. My feet dangled in the air. I couldn't breathe. "Never even think about doing that. Fuck!" he cried out, letting me go and murmuring things in Italian, pacing the room.

Judging by his reaction, I probably shouldn't have said what I'd said. It changed nothing. If it was necessary, I would have done what Olga had done.

"How did you know?" I asked, taking my seat at the table and impaling a piece of delightfully soft meat with my fork.

Massimo halted and shot me a glance, surprised at my unexpected calmness.

"The recording." It was my turn to drop the fork.

"The what?" I turned to face my husband, who at this point was making his way to his chair.

"Eat your dinner. I'll explain everything later."

It didn't make sense to protest and sulk. I started to eat. I stuffed myself with the goose, potatoes, salad, beet puree that didn't taste or look like beet puree, dessert, and then some more dessert. I topped it off with a cup of tea.

Massimo watched me with a smile, sipping on his wine.

"Done," I said, propping my elbows on the table. "I'm listening."

"At first I was confused, because it looked as though Olga was having fun."

He paused, took a deep breath, and poured himself another glass of wine, before continuing.

"What I saw was her arriving at his apartment dressed very enticingly. And then I saw him fucking her for the next two hours, at least judging by the clock, before she left. That's it."

"So how can you be sure it was recorded yesterday?"

"Because of Adam's swollen face. And yesterday's newspaper on the table." Massimo spread his arms and shrugged.

"How did you get your hands on that recording in the first place?"

"It wasn't for me. It was supposed to be sent to Domenico. That bastard wanted to humiliate my little brother and destroy Olga's life. His lawyer passed the CD to the officers at the detention center, but those numbskulls mixed us up and gave it to me instead."

It all made sense. Both Massimo's and Olga's stories. Adam had been scheming from the get-go to disgrace his enemy and wreck his relationship. That he wanted her to orgasm with him and talk to him in English made a lot more sense now, too. The recording had to show that she liked it. He had left Olga's outfit in the bathroom so she had to leave for a short while and he'd have time to set up the camera. Besides, it made it look all the more natural. And, from what Massimo had said, the recording only started when Adam had signed the papers guaranteeing

Domenico's release. So the only thing it showed was a good, long fucking.

"How did you know Olga hadn't simply cheated on Domenico?"

"I didn't," he said, rising. "I bluffed. Your reaction made me certain. I tried talking to you back in the car, but you weren't entirely focused after our flight."

"What now?" I walked over to him and cuddled against his torso.

"Nothing. I destroyed the recording. Domenico is free, and we're going to see the fight tomorrow night." He smiled, pulling away a tad. "But if you're asking about tonight, I'm going to enjoy the company of my beautiful, pregnant wife."

◇◇◇◇◇◇◇◇◇◇◇

The next day I woke up at Massimo's side. His presence astonished me so much that I actually asked him if everything was all right, eliciting a bout of laughter. We went downstairs to grab some breakfast, which was another shock to me—we weren't eating in our room, and it didn't seem like Massimo was in a hurry. We went to the hotel restaurant, where we met Olga and Domenico. I hesitated. The Man in Black tightened his grip on my hand, leading me in their direction.

After thirty minutes together at one table, our family idyll came to an end.

"We have a meeting at noon," Massimo announced. "Then another one. We'll be back around four. Sebastian is around. Call reception and tell them you need a car." He kissed me on the head, patted Olga on the shoulder, and left.

Her expression at this tender gesture was priceless. It was a mix of terror, extreme anxiety, and a dollop of revulsion.

"The fuck is his game?" she asked, rubbing at the spot he had touched.

I avoided her stare, considering whether to tell her the truth, finally settling on keeping it to myself. Olga was too much like Massimo in some aspects—unrelenting, persistent, and extra curious.

"I'm talking to you, Laura," she hissed.

Oh, God, here we go again. This was going to be another day filled with too much information, curiosities, and situations I'd rather avoid.

"He—he—he knows," I stammered, shooting her a furtive glance. "He knows about Adam. But before you start screaming, it wasn't me who told him." Her face went red, and then paled.

"Breathe, Olga. I'll tell you everything."

She started to bang her forehead on the table, making all the cutlery clatter. I quickly slid a hand between her brow and the tabletop.

"Stop it, for fuck's sake. It's all right." I took a look around, lowering my voice to a whisper. "But you should know what your fucked-up ex was planning."

Olga raised her head and stopped dead, screwing her eyes shut. "Lay it on me. It won't get any worse." I told her everything that Massimo had told me the night before, explaining his strange gesture from a couple of minutes earlier. And it had to be said it had been one of a kind—the older of the Torricelli brothers had never been Olga's fan before. He respected her and knew I wouldn't be able to survive without her, but I was sure he was also irrationally jealous of her, which made it impossible for him to really start to like her. Those times were over now, after what she had done for Domenico. Massimo's view of my friend had changed.

"Good morning." I heard a voice behind me and noticed Olga's terrified stare at the same time.

"Are you shitting me?" she growled, scowling at my handsome brother. I sprang to my feet and fell into his arms, momentarily forgetting that he used to screw my best friend.

"Hey there, Sis," he said, embracing me. "Your husband woke me up, and one of his goons drove me over through the snowstorm." He took a seat next to me and shot a glance at Olga. "Hello to you, sweet cheeks. How's it hanging?" His hand traced a line up her thigh as his lips stretched into an ugly smile.

"Quit it right away!" I scolded him. His eyes dropped, stopping on my belly.

"Ho-ly shit," he said slowly. "Mom wasn't lying. I'm going to be an uncle. And you're going to be a mom. That's crazy!"

I followed his eyes. In the tight-fitting shirt I had on, my normally perfectly flat belly was bulging.

"I'm going to go to the gym," Olga said, leaving us at the table.

"Why are you lying?" my brother asked with a smirk. "Just tell the truth. You're going to suck someone off, like you always do."

Here they were, with their constant squabbling.

"You caught me," Olga retorted with a scowl. "Unfortunately for you, you're never again going to know how it feels."

Olga walked away, heading to the gym—which really was a bit suspicious—and Kuba focused entirely on me.

"So, baby, husband, a move to Sicily . . . Am I missing anything?" he asked, stirring his coffee. I frowned, rubbing my belly. "Oh, the Cosa Nostra. I nearly forgot the best part."

I lifted my eyes and sent him an alarmed look. He just smiled innocently in response. His wide torso shook with laughter, and he put his cup down, crossing his arms behind his head.

"Come on, Sis, it's not like your husband is a nobody. I googled him."

"Jesus Christ," I breathed, hiding my face in my hands. "Do our parents know?"

"Are you dumb? Of course not. Well, maybe they suspect something. I've been looking into the finances of one of Massimo's companies. I couldn't miss some . . . discrepancies."

"What?!" I couldn't keep my voice down. Some other guests were turning their heads our way. "You're working for him now?"

"I advise. But let's not talk about it. Tell me how you're feeling. And what happened at home."

We talked for a long while, moving to my apartment at some point. There were just so many subjects and so little time. And my charming brother turned out to be a very caring man.

"Want to grab lunch?" I asked when it started getting late.

"You mean dinner, yeah? Don't you need to fancy up first? I'll pick you up at seven. The gala starts at eight." My eyes widened.

"*You* will pick us up?"

"Massimo told me to take you with me. He'll join us after he finishes a meeting."

I felt sad. Not for the first time and definitely not the last. Another meeting and yet another case of another man taking me somewhere I should have gone with my husband. I wasn't really that interested in the fight. Not without Massimo. He had been the one to inspire me to dig into that subject in the first place.

Kuba left me, and I called Olga. She had ordered us a hairdresser and some makeup artists. I had another hour to take a bath and rummage through my bags to find something to wear in the evening. I sat over the suitcases and gutted them, tossing their contents to the floor. I had never been to a fight night, so I didn't really know what to wear. Should I pick an elegant evening dress or a pair of jeans? Suddenly, it dawned on me—black. It didn't really matter what I wore. If it was black, it would fit.

I grabbed a pair of Manolo Blahnik boots, tight-fitting black leather pants, and a loose Chanel shirt that did a perfect job of concealing my pregnancy. Satisfied with my choice, I took a shower, put on black lace underwear, and threw on a bathrobe.

The makeup artists and hairdresser were done with me by six. I walked up to the mirror and took a look at myself. I looked awesome. The hair extensions formed a thick, long French braid, while the smoky gray makeup perfectly complemented my outfit. I threw off my white bathrobe and reached for my shirt.

"Call me when your asshole brother shows up," Olga said, leaving the room. "And get dressed, woman. Stop showing off that fancy lingerie."

"I *am* getting dressed," I barked. "Besides, I'm pregnant, and that's not sexy."

Olga sent me a scornful look. "Your pregnancy is barely showing, you dimwit. You're still thinner than me, and I'm not even expecting a baby. Now get dressed and call me when you're ready."

I shut the door behind her and switched off the lights, before playing "Silence" by Delerium from my phone, plugging my earbuds in. I had time. There was no need to hurry. It was snowing outside, and the white blanket covered the entire pier. I observed the storm from the darkness of my room.

The song was on repeat, playing for the second time, when one of my earbuds slipped out. I heard that British accent of my husband.

"You're mine," Massimo breathed to my ears, trailing his arms up my sides and over my belly. "Don't let me interrupt you," he added, putting the little earphone back in.

The gorgeous vocals reverberated in my head, but I couldn't focus anymore. Suddenly, I felt a soft scarf covering my eyes. I put my hand on the window, leaning against it. I couldn't see or hear anything now. Entirely at his mercy. Staying behind me, Massimo took the phone from my hand and slid it between my breasts, hanging it from my bra. Then he spun me around and lifted my arms above my head, grabbing both my wrists with one of his hands. He bit softly into my lip, slowly exploring it with his tongue. I opened my mouth, waiting for him to push inside, but nothing of the sort happened. I felt his teeth on my chin, neck, collarbone, and then my nipple. Massimo teased it through the thin lace, licking and biting. I moaned, trying to free myself, but his grip on my wrists tightened. With his free hand, he trailed a line down the inside of my thighs, spreading my legs. The music kept playing, disorienting me further, as he played with my breasts, his fingers slipping under the bra.

Eventually, all I felt was Massimo's measured rubbing of my puffed-up clit. Suddenly, he pushed his tongue through the barrier of my lips, freeing my arms at the same time. The kiss was passionate, and I returned it, greedily pressing my face against his. My hands fell to his shoulders without breaking the dance of our tongues. I shifted them down over his skin, discovering that he had thrown his clothes off some time earlier. Massimo's own hands cupped my buttocks, and he lifted me in the air with no apparent difficulty, carrying me through the room.

"Massimo," I said, unable to hear my own voice. "I want . . ."

"I know what you want," he breathed into my ear, pulling one of the earphones out. "But you won't get it, so don't bother asking." He put the bud back in and laid me down on the soft mattress of our bed.

I felt him pulling my cell phone free from beneath my bra,

before his finger hooked around one shoulder strap to slide it off, and then the other, freeing my breasts. I shivered as his teeth bit into my nipple, his lips sucking and caressing, his fingers exquisitely irritating, turning, and kneading. The music was deafening, but somehow it also increased the sensation in my whole body a hundredfold. I was breathing and moaning louder than normal, but without even hearing my own voice, I couldn't care less. Massimo's lips explored my abdomen, finally reaching the lace of my revealing panties. I spread my legs. Playtime was over—this was his cue to step up his game. He did not. I felt his hot breath on my skin, but that was it. The mattress rebounded, and I felt him get up.

I felt an impulse telling me to rip off my blindfold and get rid of the earbuds, but instantly I decided against it. I would only regret it. Not because my husband would punish me in any way. No. I'd just ruin my surprise.

So I stayed put, disoriented and impatient, finally feeling his touch on my face as he turned my head to the side.

Before I could react, Massimo's magnificent manhood pushed its way into my mouth.

I sighed in delight, grabbing the shaft with my hand, sucking and licking in a sudden spell of frantic activity. He tasted perfect, and the smell of his skin made my breath catch in my throat. There was no way to tell if he was enjoying it until his hands landed on my head.

I liked it when he showed me what to do. When he fucked my mouth just as he liked it. When I could be sure my body was bringing him closer to ecstasy. After a while, the Man in Black made me lie completely flat on the mattress. Then I felt his knees on both sides of my temples, and his cock gently settling on my lips. I opened my mouth, obediently taking his prick in. Massimo's hips started pumping as his lips touched down on my belly, slowly crawling down my body to finally reach my pulsating snatch. His powerful arms pulled my thong off, leaving it around my ankles. I kicked it off, and those same arms grabbed my legs and brutally spread them apart. Choking on his thick erection, I cried out as his tongue greedily devoured my clit. I felt his fingers sliding inside me at the same time. Suddenly, he jerked his whole body, rolling us over so now I was on top. Without wasting time, I propped an elbow on his thigh and closed his cock in a tight grip. Fast and hard, I started to stroke it, feeling it getting even harder. Massimo wasn't far behind. He licked and sucked, increasing the pressure of his fingers, adding another one. He fucked me with his tongue, bringing me to the very edge of bliss. I adored that position. Sixty-nine allowed me to feel in control, at the same time plunging me into true depths of rapture.

I felt the familiar warm sensation in the bottom of my belly. My muscles contracted, my breathing quickened, and Massimo's movements increased in their intensity as he felt I was getting close.

"No!" I cried out, ripping the blindfold off and the earphones out. I felt the orgasm subsiding, and the Man in Black shot me a surprised look. He smiled. "I want to feel you," I breathed.

That wasn't something I had to say twice. Massimo threw me off himself, instantly pinning me down with his body and shoving his cock into my wet, hot, throbbing pussy.

"Fuck me hard, I beg you," I whispered, grabbing his hair and pulling his face to mine, joining us in a deep kiss.

He liked it. I could tell. Massimo loved violent sex. He adored it when I was vulgar and acted like a slut. He shot up into a kneeling position, grabbed my leg and threw it over his shoulder, turned me slightly to the side, and assaulted me with his prick with enormous force. His long cock reached the deepest parts of me, diving deeper than ever, and his hand slowly tightened around my throat. His index finger made its way into my mouth. I sucked it. Massimo's eyes widened, and with a wild roar, he started pounding me with animalistic abandon.

Just a few minutes in, I greeted the familiar sensation back. The orgasm was getting closer, about to explode. Snow was falling outside, the room was perfectly dark, and the only things I could hear were my own raspy breath and the muffled sounds of Delerium still playing from my earbuds. I came. It was intense and lasting. My nails bit into Massimo's thigh. And just when I thought it was over, I felt the Man in Black coming, too, collapsing over my body, his cock throbbing inside me. That provoked another epic wave of orgasm to wash over me.

For a long time, we stayed still, joined as a single entity, sweaty and heaving with exhaustion.

"I had my hair done," I said finally, as I regained my wits. "And makeup . . ."

"But you weren't sated." He planted a kiss on my forehead, still breathing heavily. "Besides, I'm sure you look wonderful. Now let's go. It's time," he added and quickly disappeared into the bathroom.

You damned hypocrite, I thought, getting up and finding out I was barely able to walk to the mirror. As soon as I saw my reflection, I got angry. If my makeup was still more or less unscathed, my hair was in total disarray. I grabbed my phone, praying that the hotel hairdresser had a free spot. He did. Five minutes later, he was braiding my hair again, shooting me amused glances.

In the meantime, Massimo had taken a shower and was now talking on the phone, pacing the room and barking what sounded like orders in Italian. I thanked the stylist, and my husband slapped a high-denomination bill into his hand without interrupting his conversation, before he slammed the door in the poor man's face, pushing him to out to the corridor.

CHAPTER *thirteen*

"Over here!" the girl at the side entrance to the hall called out, lifting her arm.

The snowstorm made her nearly impossible to see. She wore a sweat suit and a sports jacket, and there was an earbud in her ear, connected to a walkie-talkie she shouted into once in a while. I took a look around, trying to spot the end of the massive queue leading to the main entrance. At least we didn't have to wait outside with the rest of the people. Massimo grabbed my hand and led me to the door. Domenico, Olga, and my brother were following us through the snowstorm. Kuba's very presence seemed to irk the couple.

The girl by the side entrance deftly wrapped a VIP band around my wrist and pointed me in the right direction. We entered through a narrow corridor, which quickly opened up into a large room. Waiters stood by holding trays filled with champagne glasses. More bottles were arrayed in coolers waiting on the tables. There were various refreshments, finger food, main dishes, and desserts. For a moment I wondered whether we'd gone to the right party at all, but quickly someone passed me the fight roster for the night.

Olga strode in with confidence, grabbing two glasses of champagne at once and downing one of them on the spot.

"What you got there?" she asked, prying the papers from my hands. "Let's have a look at the hot studs, shall we?"

She put down her glass and leafed through the booklet, murmuring with satisfaction at the sight of some of the fighters. I turned to my husband, who was talking to Kuba and Domenico. I tried overhearing what they were whispering about, but it was too loud around us, and I didn't catch anything. That's when Olga's squeal distracted me. All heads turned in her direction. Olga was standing by one of the tables with the weirdest expression on her face, trying to pretend the loud exclamation from a moment before hadn't been her doing.

"What? I just got a bit excited at the quality of the fighters," she offered.

With a shrug, she walked over to me and pulled me away.

"Look at this!" She pointed a finger at the penultimate fight.

I stared at the page in disbelief. The picture showed Damian. My ex. I snatched the brochure from Olga's fingers and gaped at it. Whether I wanted it or not, we were going to see my ex-boyfriend fight tonight. Feeling Olga's penetrating gaze on me, I swallowed loudly and turned to her.

"Is that what you're so happy about, you bitch?" I asked sharply, slapping her with the booklet. "Did you know? Answer me!"

Olga took a quick step back, putting the table between us and taking a sip of champagne.

"I might have heard this or that," she said, grinning.

"Why didn't you tell me?" I narrowed my eyes and fixed her with a murderous glare.

"Because we'd never have come here." She closed the distance between us and put a hand on my shoulder. "Besides, Laura, there's got to be a thousand people here. No chance you two will meet."

I cocked my head and shot another glance at Damian's picture, this time focusing on the visual elements and the information below. There was a note about his previous achievements, records, and successes in international tournaments. I felt hot, involuntarily recalling some of the times we had had together. I wished I could say something bad about the man, but there was nothing. Our relationship had been great. That was a pity, of course—it would have been easier to dislike him now.

"You think he'll win?" I heard a voice by my ear. "His opponent's ground game is very good."

Ground game, you say? I thought. *I remember Damian's ground game was pretty good, too. At least when we were alone.* I shook my head, trying to shoo away the intrusive thoughts, and spun to face the Man in Black with a dumb smile plastered to my face.

"I think he'll win," I replied, giving him a quick kiss. "With either a guillotine or an arm bar. He's a grappler, so he'll look for solutions on the ground." I shrugged, keeping the smile on my lips.

Massimo's jaw dropped. He looked at me, dumbstruck.

"What did you say?" he asked, laughing nervously. "Should I know something?"

I kept him hanging for a moment, basking in my own wit.

"You should know I can read," I said finally, tapping the booklet and pointing to the fighter's bio. "This says he does that often."

"I say he tested it on you," Olga said in Polish, keeping her face impassive, but fixing me with an intense stare.

I ignored her, grabbing the glass of juice Massimo had placed on the table beside me. I sipped, feigning disinterest, though inside I couldn't stop thinking about the fighter I was about to watch in the octagon later that evening.

◇◇◇◇◇◇◇◇◇◇

A staff member appeared, inviting us to follow her. We did, trailing the woman through a wide corridor until we passed a large gate and entered the arena. I looked around, wide-eyed.

The interior of the building was enormous. High stands surrounded the whole thing, and at their feet there were hundreds of chairs grouped into sectors. The cage stood right in the middle. I felt a lump in my throat, and my hand tightened on Massimo's. The cage here was a lot larger than the one we had in the mansion, but it didn't change a thing. I recalled our own octagon, remembering all the things I wanted to use it for, and suddenly I wasn't sated anymore—I felt an overpowering need to have sex. A violent, rough fuck. This pregnancy and the storm of hormones it pumped into my brain would surely make me fuck Massimo to death one of these days.

My husband sent me an impassive look, though I was sure he was reading my mind. He smirked and bit his lip, as though telepathically connected to me. The woman from the staff was still standing right beside us, but it didn't disturb him one bit. He kissed me, his tongue penetrating deep into my mouth. I wrapped my arms around him, allowing the kiss to last.

We stayed like that for a long while until my brother rolled his eyes and prodded the woman to point us to our seats. They disappeared, leaving us alone.

When my sudden need for love and attention passed, we walked toward the cage.

We had seats in the first row. That didn't surprise me a bit. It would have if the Italians had booked any other spots, in fact. What did take me by surprise was that Olga sat next to me, and Domenico and Kuba sat by Massimo. They immediately started talking again. Business, probably. This wasn't a strictly social event, it seemed. I decided to leave them to their scheming.

The first two fights were long and utterly fascinating. The brutality and violence of MMA was exciting. Despite that the discipline had a set of strict rules, to me it sometimes seemed there weren't any. When the third fight ended, a fifteen-minute break was announced. I decided I'd spend it in the bathroom. I grabbed Olga and pulled her with me, stopping to briefly inform my husband where we were going. At first, Massimo wanted to accompany us, but the president of the MMA federation showed up out of the blue and saved us by stopping him with some more business. We were introduced and then could go wherever we pleased.

Seeing the color of our wristbands, the security guards showed us through the gate and all the doors behind it. Having passed a few of them, I suddenly realized we were lost.

"Where the hell are you taking me, Laura?" Olga asked, darting glances at our surroundings. "This doesn't look like the bathroom."

I looked around and frowned. I nodded furiously, agreeing. We were standing in the middle of a completely empty corridor. There wasn't anyone we could ask for directions. I grabbed the handle of the door we passed through just a second ago, and found out it was locked. In order to open it from this side, we needed a magnetic card.

"Come on," I ordered, leading my friend. "This corridor has to lead somewhere."

A couple of minutes of aimless wandering led us to the backstage area. There were dozens of people with headphones over their heads, running this way and that, shouting over one another. A man was sitting on the floor, staring into a monitor and eating a sandwich. Others were lounging around, smoking cigarettes. Fascinated, I slowed my pace, watching this seemingly chaotic tableau. We passed by a pair of men wearing identical T-shirts with the logo of the organizer. They looked like coaches. A couple of steps farther in, there were dressing rooms for the artists that had performed before the main show started as well as the ring girls.

The "Octagon Girls," as they were called here, were breathtaking—lithe, athletic, long-haired beauties. They were laughing, doing their makeup, using the break to catch their breath. They were a sight to behold. Their manager was bustling about them, hollering and cursing, but they just ignored her tantrum. *What a despicable bitch*, I thought, looking at the manager. *They should do something about her.*

"There it is!" Olga exclaimed suddenly, pointing to a door with the letters "WC" written on it.

"I'm going first. I had too much champagne!" When we were both finished, we decided to ask someone from the staff to point us back to the main hall. I looked around, searching for signs that would lead us to the main office. Someone there would surely know something. I spun on my heel and took a step forward, walking straight into an open door. A giant of a man with a bushy beard appeared around it. We both jumped back, startled. The door to the changing room swung shut, revealing a familiar face.

I froze.

"Holy shit," I whispered, completely dumbstruck. "That's . . ."

I broke off as Damian turned and noticed me for the first time.

"I don't believe it . . ." he said, shaking his head. "You're finally here."

He wrapped his arms around me and lifted me from the ground, squeezing me in a bear hug. Olga was completely stupefied, too. Instead of trying to pry me from his massive arms, she gaped at the scene.

Meanwhile, I could only pray that Massimo hadn't followed us.

"I wrote you so many times! I wanted to see you, and here you are." Damian shook his head, taking a deep breath. "You've changed . . . and that hair." His bandaged hands touched my face.

"Hi," I spluttered. "You look good." That was the only thing that came to my mind.

Had I just said that? Dear God, I thought that was only in my head! But, to be perfectly honest, he did look stunning. Olga giggled but was cut short as *her* ex-lover Kacper appeared in the doorway.

"Oh shit," she groaned. The four of us stood in the entrance to the dressing room, and I couldn't stop thinking whether I'd prefer to die on the spot or kill Olga instead. The awkward silence was broken by a young man with headphones on his head, who shouted, "Three minutes until we go live!"

"We have to go," Olga said, pulling me away.

Damian's friend placed his paw on the man's shoulder and led him back into the room.

"Good luck," I whispered as he disappeared behind the wall.

We ran, ignoring the office, which had been our target in the first place. Shocked by that encounter, we sprinted down the corridor, until somehow we arrived at the arena.

I leaned against the wall, trying to slow my breathing, and glared at Olga, who stopped beside me.

"'A thousand people,' eh? 'There's no chance we're going to meet him'?!"

She tried looking apologetic, but her attempt failed. Instead, she burst out in uncontrollable laughter.

"Damn, girl, he did look like a total stud, though, didn't he?" she said, licking her lips lusciously. "And Kacper? You saw how good he looked?"

"Jesus, we acted like idiots back there." I laughed, too.

I couldn't believe what had just happened. On the other hand, I had to agree with Olga. Both of them had looked gorgeous.

We took our seats, trying to avoid Massimo's disapproving stare.

"Where were you all this time? Security is looking for you," he hissed through clenched teeth.

"It's a big place. We got lost." I sent him an innocent look and smooched him on the cheek. "Your daughter needed to go to the ladies' room." I grabbed his hand, putting it on my belly.

That was quickly becoming my number one solution to Massimo's chimeric temper. As long as I kept bringing up the baby, he stayed calm, quickly forgetting his anger. It worked again this time. The fury in his gaze melted away, and his lips stretched into a shy smile.

I didn't really watch the next few fights. The only thing I could think of was my knotted stomach.

I was waiting for the penultimate match. When the announcer finally read Damian's name, I jumped in my seat. The lights went out, and the speakers blared with a song I knew: "O Fortuna" by Carmina Burana. A shiver went down my spine, and

I felt my abdominal muscles tensing. I remembered this song and all the times I had heard it.

From a corner of my eye, I looked at Massimo. He was watching the fighters' entrance, blissfully unaware of my internal struggle. I glanced at Olga, noticing her amused stare. She was wiggling her brows at me. I knew that look all too well. She read my mind and grinned at all the nasty things I was thinking. The lights flared, and Damian appeared in the entrance. He strode confidently toward the octagon, shrugging every few steps to loosen up tense muscles. Kacper and the rest of the coaches followed in his stead. They pulled his shirt off. I couldn't tear my eyes off him as he rounded the cage like a gladiator, lifting his arm in salute to the audience, and finally taking his place in one of the corners.

Olga's hand tightened on mine as I did my best to keep an impassive face at the sight of the mountain of muscle just a few feet away. The reflectors dimmed again, and another song played. Damian was warming up in his spot, waiting for his opponent to join him, and I wondered if his eyes were scanning the crowd in search of me. I hadn't had time to explain what I was doing here.

He didn't know I had a husband now and that I was expecting a baby.

One of the beautiful ring girls walked around the octagon with a raised Round 1 placard. The gong rang, and the fight was on. I was getting nervous, and it showed, as Massimo started to gently stroke my thigh. The two fighters started off with an exchange of blows, but soon Damian grabbed his opponent and slammed him to the ground. The audience cheered as he straddled the other man and started to pummel him with his fists at an incredible speed. An instant later, as the other guy's head bounced off the ground for what seemed the hundredth time, the referee threw himself over Damian, blocking his punches and ending the fight. Everyone jumped to their feet, applauding the winner, who climbed the rim of the cage and sat astride it, lifting his arms triumphantly.

Suddenly, Damian's eyes found me and stopped for a second. I felt paralyzed, returning his stare as he jumped down, ran across the octagon, exited it through the open gate, and crossed the distance between us, stopping right in front of me. Occupied with discussing the knockout, Massimo didn't even notice the massive fighter rushing over to us.

Damian stopped, his torso heaving, and I pressed myself deeper into my seat. That's when Massimo turned his head and jumped to his feet. Domenico and Kuba followed suit. The fighter's eyes darted from me to the Man in Black with visible confusion. After what seemed like hours, someone from security signaled him to return to the cage for the announcement of the winner. Damian raised his gloved hand to his lips, fixed me with a stare, and sent me a kiss before roaring and raising his arms in triumph again. People cheered deafeningly, and the mountain of muscle withdrew to the octagon. His eyes were fixed on me the whole time.

I was frozen, afraid to look to my right, feeling the burning gaze of my husband on me.

"Care to explain what just happened?" he snarled, sitting down.

"No," I said simply. "I'm tired. Can we go now?"

"No, we can't." He turned to Domenico and said something, making the younger man get up and leave for the exit.

I spun to Olga, looking for support, but the only thing I got was her idiotic expression as she tried to stifle laughter.

"Goddamn it, Olga!"

"What?" She couldn't hold back any longer and burst out in a guffaw. "It's not my fault we're sitting in the first row and that your ex tried to kiss you right next to your husband! By the way, this is going to end in one hell of a show!" She grinned even wider.

I glared at her, but her eyes were focused on something behind me.

"Your man is going to burn holes in me with his eyes. Do something."

I turned around, looking at Massimo. He was shaking with barely repressed fury. I could hear him swallow over the din of the audience. His jaws were working rhythmically, and his fists were balled so hard, his fingers went deathly white.

"You turn me on when you're angry." I attempted to placate him by placing a hand on his thigh. "But you can't impress me with that anymore. I'm not scared of you, so you might as well quit it." I raised my brows, nodding.

The Man in Black kept glaring at me for another second before leaning in.

"What if I bring you that left arm of his. Would that impress you?" His lips stretched into a confident smirk as I stiffened. "Just as I suspected, baby girl." He stroked my cheek. "Now, this is the last fight. Then it's time for the after-party. I hope you're not planning anything more of the sort." He turned away, leaned back in his chair, and followed Damian with his eyes as the man left the cage.

I rubbed at my temples, wondering whether he was being serious or if that was only meant to scare me. It wouldn't be prudent to test my husband's limits. I didn't look at Damian even for an instant.

I didn't watch the last fight, thinking only about what the

evening still had in store for me. Going to a party was the last thing I wanted, but I had no idea how to avoid it. That's when it dawned on me.

"Baby," I said to Massimo as we were walking to the exit after the show ended. "I'm not feeling too good."

The Man in Black halted, sending me an anxious look.

"What's going on?

"Oh, I'm sure it's nothing." I put my hand on my belly. "It's just a bit of vertigo. I'd like to lie down for a moment."

He nodded and grabbed my arm, leading me to the car.

We got inside. Domenico joined us a moment later, taking his seat by Olga with his characteristic casualness.

He started talking to Massimo. The Man in Black clearly didn't like what he was hearing, as he let out a rough shout, slamming his hand into the seat and making the whole limo shake. The young Italian didn't relent, evidently pushing Massimo to do something.

"All right. I have to go away for a while," he said when the car started. "Olga will go with you. Domenico already called a doctor."

"Why would you need a doctor all of a sudden?" Olga asked in Polish. "You feeling unwell? What's going on?"

"Jesus, I'm pretending." I rolled my eyes, knowing the Italians wouldn't understand. "I just don't want to go to the party and see Damian."

"I knew I recognized that guy from somewhere," Kuba chimed in with a grin. "Maybe it would be better if you didn't show up at that party after all."

"Thanks," I growled in response.

"English, please," Massimo said, keeping his eyes on his phone. "I should be back in an hour. Olga will stay with you until I return. If anything happens, call me." He sent my friend a look, and she nodded seriously.

What a farce. I sighed inwardly. And it was my doing again.

We drove all the way to the end of a narrow street bordering the part of town where all the clubs were. Massimo kissed me with a worried expression, and the three men left the car.

Olga sat back in her seat next to me. "Sebastian," she addressed the driver, "drive us to a McDonald's. I'm in the mood for some junk food."

"Yes," I agreed. "Me too."

I'm not sure how much we ate, but over the thirty minutes we spent in the restaurant, we ordered at least three times more than I was used to. The woman behind the counter seemed to admire my appetite, especially since my outfit completely hid my pregnancy.

The driver took us back to the hotel and opened the door for us. We crossed the lobby, waving at Massimo's security guard, who jumped to his feet at our sight. At the same exact time, we both said good night, and he sat right back down, returning to whatever he was doing on his laptop.

We stopped by the elevator and I pressed the button to call it, leaning my head against the wall and waiting. I was tired, stuffed, and sleepy.

The elevator door slid open, and I raised my eyes. Kacper stepped out, followed by Damian. As soon as he realized it was me, he pushed away his disoriented friend, who landed straight in Olga's arms. Then he pulled me inside.

The door slid shut, and the elevator started moving up.

"Hey there," he breathed in my face, propping his hands on both sides of my head.

"Hey yourself," I stammered, confused.

"I've been missing you." His hands moved to cup my face as he stuck his lips to mine, taking my breath away.

I waved my arms around, desperately trying to free myself from his iron grip. I stood no chance. I pushed, but he didn't let go.

His tongue slid between my lips.

I knew this feeling. In spite of the violence of that move, he was gentle and passionate. I fought with myself not to return the kiss. And then the door slid open again. I felt my assailant pull away, only to land with a thud on the floor. I spun and saw Massimo. He was holding the railing inside the elevator, savagely kicking the prone man. Then Damian launched himself upward and barged into Massimo, catapulting him outside the elevator. Terrified, I followed them. None of the men paid me any attention. They flung fists at each other, trying to kick each other, until they both toppled to the ground and wrestled. They rolled, throwing fists and kneeing each other in the gut. There was an obvious weight difference between the two, but the fight was very close.

I was furious and afraid in equal measure, but I couldn't intervene—in the heat of battle, they could hurt me or the baby.

That's when Domenico arrived to the rescue, shouting and leading a unit of security guards. They tore the two opponents apart. The Man in Black was raging, shouting, while Domenico stood right in front of him, immovable like a wall, calmly explaining something. A moment later, hotel security arrived, and guests started peeking their heads through opening doors.

The bodyguards released Damian, who shot me a furious glare and vanished into the elevator.

Domenico walked over and motioned me to my room, giving me a little shove in the back. I left the scene, followed by my husband.

"What the fuck was that?!" he roared, slamming the door shut behind him. "You told me you felt unwell!" He started pacing the room, wiping blood from his face. "I bailed on an important meeting, worried sick about you, while *you* . . ."

He paused, stopping right in my face. "My pregnant wife is making out with some motherfucker in the goddamned elevator!"

A deep roar tore from his throat, and he shot out his arm, smashing the wall with his fist. He kept hitting it until his hands started leaving bloody marks on the white surface.

"Who the fuck was that?!" He stormed back to me and gripped my chin in his hand. "Answer me!"

I was afraid. For the first time in months, I was really scared of this man. Suddenly, I remembered who he was. And how dangerous and unpredictable he could act. My heart raced, and my breathing quickened. A thin screech rang in my ears, and my vision swam. I caught the lapel of his black suit jacket and sank to the floor. Before I blacked out, I felt his hands grabbing me.

◇◇◇◇◇◇◇◇◇◇

I opened my eyes. Massimo was sitting in a chair next to the bed. It was bright outside the window. I could see it was still snowing.

"I'm sorry," the Man in Black whispered, kneeling by my side. "Olga told me everything."

"Are you all right?" I asked, taking in his swollen, purple cheek and the gash in his brow.

He nodded, taking the hand that hovered by his face. He pressed it to his lips and kissed it, avoiding my stare.

"He didn't know I was taken," I breathed, trying to push myself up. "I'm sorry, too. I don't know how this happened." I closed my eyes, collapsing to the pillow. "What were you doing in the hotel?"

As soon as I finished the last sentence, I realized it might have come out wrong. The Man in Black took his seat and observed me with hooded eyes.

"If I didn't know what really happened yesterday, I might have misunderstood the intention behind that question," he said, inhaling and running a hand through his hair. "I went to a club and met who I had to, but the only thing I could think about was you. So I drove back. You were not in your room, so I called the driver. You weren't taking my calls. He told me he dropped you off at the hotel after you had dinner.

"I left the room to meet you halfway. That's when I bumped into you two." His bruised hands balled into fists. "Why did you lie to me?"

I watched him, trying to come up with a good explanation, but found none. There was only the truth left.

"It was the only way you wouldn't make me go to the party," I said, shrugging. "And since I knew I could bump into him at that party, I didn't want to take any risks."

I pulled the bedcover over my head, but the Man in Black ripped it back off. "It was a mistake. Please don't kill him. Please." My eyes watered.

Massimo kept glaring at me, not even trying to hide his irritation.

"It's good the doctor stayed around." He caressed my cheek. "I might employ him full-time."

"Promise me!" I pressed on when he tried changing the subject.

"I promise," he replied, pushing to his feet. "Besides, I wouldn't do that anyway. He's Karol's man. A cousin." He shook his head in disappointment and left the room.

I stretched and glanced at my watch. It was nearly noon.

Massimo returned with his laptop and lay next to me, throwing a leg over mine.

"Did you sleep at all? You don't look too good," I said.

He shook his head, keeping his eyes on the monitor.

"Why?" I edged closer, wrapping an arm around him.

He rolled his eyes and sighed, irritated, putting the computer down.

"Maybe it had something to do with the fact that my pregnant wife blacked out and I was worried for her well-being." He sent me a look and added, "Or maybe because my wife kissed another man, and that made me so mad I won't be able to sleep until next weekend. Want me to go on?"

"You're so sexy when you get mad."

My hand slithered into his gray sweatpants. "I want to suck your cock." I felt his muscles tense.

He bit his lip.

"Please, don Massimo, please let me suck you off."

My fingers rubbed at his dick as I kissed his bruised shoulder.

"You nearly died a couple hours ago. What's with the sudden burst of energy?" he asked as I started pulling his pants down.

"I get good drugs," I replied, amused, yanking at the leg of the sweatpants. "You're not helping."

I pouted and knelt down, dropping my arms.

Massimo's hips lifted a bit, but his eyes didn't wander from his monitor. He was pointedly ignoring me. It didn't matter one bit. He was naked, and his thick cock was fully awake now, erect and spurring me to action. However Massimo tried to keep his expression impassive, he couldn't cheat nature.

I crept up his leg, preparing for oral assault, when Massimo murmured a few words in Italian and, unexpectedly, put down the laptop and twisted away, leaving the bed. I followed him with my eyes, openmouthed, locked in place. He grabbed his black shirt from the backrest of the chair and put it on, as I watched.

"I have a video call to make," he said, pulling a laptop stand to the bed.

He buttoned his shirt and took a comfortable position before adjusting the camera on the monitor to show only his head, his shoulders, and the top of his torso. His fingers hovered above a button for a moment before pressing it. A man's voice rang out from the speaker. All the time, I stayed on the bed, observing my husband's unusual provocation. Don Massimo, the head of the Sicilian Mafia, was spread out on the mattress, dressed only in his black shirt, doing business over the Internet with his erect dick out and ripe for the sucking.

The Man in Black snatched a file of papers from the nightstand and leafed through it, presenting them one by one to his interloper.

I crawled like a cat, my back arched, closing in on Massimo's crotch. He took a quick glance at my ass and cleared his throat before focusing on his call. Slowly, I edged closer to his feet and licked his toes, positioning myself so he could see my behind better. I stuck out my buttocks, passing just inches from his face. My mouth climbed higher and higher up the inner side of his calves, spreading my man's legs inch by inch. He couldn't see me now. The laptop obscured his view. I could do as I pleased with the entire lower half of his body.

Having finally reached his bulging erection, I hovered above his cock, blowing at it gently, signaling that I was there—ready to begin. His free hand gripped the sheets in anticipation of an attack that wasn't coming. I blew, tickling the tip of his penis with my tongue, and softly brushed my fingers along the skin around it. The Man in Black put the documents back on the nightstand and shifted the laptop a bit so that he could see me with the corner of his eye.

I leaned over his erect prick and looked Massimo in the eyes, freezing in complete stillness. I waited. He did nothing, getting impatient. Waiting. I withdrew a little, changing position. The camera could see only a small fraction of the room, so I lay down next to Massimo, careful not to enter its field of view.

I took his hand—the one still gripping the sheets—and slid it into my underwear. Massimo's eyes, still focused on the man on his screen, widened suddenly, as he felt how wet I was. I sank his fingers deeper, at first rubbing them against my clit, and then guiding them into my hole. I played with myself, using his hand, every once in a while taking it out and licking the fingers clean, before spilling the fingers back inside me.

Massimo's chest started rising and falling faster. His breathing became deeper and more strained. Finally, his hand started acting on its own, pushing itself harder and faster against my cunt. I rested my head on the pillow and closed my eyes, allowing the feeling of pleasure to overcome my whole body. I had to stifle a moan. It was only a matter of time until I started making noises. My hand landed on his wrist, pulling it away, making the ecstasy fade. For now.

The Man in Black didn't interrupt his call. He lifted his hand, rubbing his lips with a finger, pretending to consider something the other man said. Leaving the taste of my pussy on his lips, he flicked out his tongue briefly, and his dick grew so hard it nearly broke in half. The hand hovering over his mouth flew toward my head, grabbing my hair. It gently tugged at it, directing my head back to his crotch. He couldn't bear much more of this torment. I allowed him to guide me to the place I was planning to end up anyway. I opened my mouth. As the first inches of his manhood were pushing their way in, and as I recognized the scent of my imperious husband, I went crazy. I swallowed his entire long cock, grabbing the base tightly and stroking. My lips followed the movement of my hand. Massimo tightened his grip on my hair, trying to slow me down, but he stood no chance as long as he had to focus on two things simultaneously. I sucked him with full force, clamping my mouth on his delicate balls every so often.

His hips began to fidget, wriggling nervously. His entire body tensed, and his voice broke. I raised my eyes. Massimo was sweating profusely and his face was contorted in an expression of deep regret. Letting me play with him suddenly wasn't such a good idea. This conversation must have been very important indeed—otherwise, he would have ended the call a long time ago. I liked torturing him like that. It was turning me on better than almost anything else could. Massimo snatched the papers from the nightstand again and pretended to look at them. He was actually staring at me. His body was burning with passion. His eyes were dark and through parted lips he was greedily gasping for air. Then I felt it. The first drop, before a great wave of sperm flooded my throat. Massimo was still listening to the voice of the man speaking to him, desperately trying to look like someone reading through a stack of documents. He was shooting his seed into my mouth the whole time—a lot longer than usual. And in this particular case he didn't look especially happy to be doing so. When he was finished, his body relaxed, and he cleared his throat, locking his eyes back on the monitor. I pushed myself up, licked my lips, and went to the bathroom.

I took a shower and returned to the bedroom. Massimo was still talking. I went to the large window and stood there dry-ing my hair with a towel and watching the sea. I didn't manage to turn back and see if my husband had finally finished his call, when his hand pressed me against the glass.

"You are unbearable," he said, tearing my bathrobe off and slamming the towel to the floor. "I'm going to punish that little ass of yours for that." He lifted me into the air and carried me to the couch. "You like to test my limits? Okay. Kneel."

My breasts pressed into the back of the sofa, I spread my legs, feeling Massimo's knee prodding me. I grabbed the couch and waited for what was about to come. The Man in Black stayed behind me, rubbing my back entrance with a lubricated thumb.

"I like how you look in that position," he said, pushing me deeper onto the sofa. "Now relax." I did as he asked and felt his finger brutally push inside me. I cried out. "You're not listening to me, Laura," he said and added another finger. I wanted to jerk away, but he pinned me down, grabbing my wrists.

"We both know you'll like it. Just do as I say."

Massimo's lips touched the skin of my back, and I felt a shiver run down my spine. He released my hands and his fingers shifted over to my swollen clit, beginning their circular motion around it. I moaned, pressing a cheek into the backrest of the couch.

"You see," he said, increasing both the strength and the pace of his motion. "You wouldn't want me to stop now, would you?"

"Fuck me," I breathed.

"I can't hear you," he growled, as his fingers increased the pressure.

"Fuck me, don Massimo!"

"As you wish." With one expert movement, he replaced his fingers with his cock and launched into motion.

His hips slammed into my buttocks again and again, but his hand didn't leave its place on my clit even for a second.

It wouldn't take me long to come, especially since I had been close before, as I had been sucking him off. At one point, the thrusting stopped. Massimo grabbed my waist and rolled us over. Now I was sitting astride him, facing away. He spread my legs and sank his fingers into my wet hole.

I cried out loudly, not caring who might hear. Massimo's other hand clamped around my breast, pinching my sensitive nipple. I was on top, so I had the power. The rhythm was under my control. I propped my hands on the backrest on both sides of his head and started racing toward orgasm, picking up the pace with each second. My arms weren't strong enough to keep this up for long, and they started shaking just a couple of minutes into the exercise. The Man in Black placed his hands on my hips and impaled me on him with full force.

"Play with yourself," he breathed straight into my ear. As my fingers set off with their circular motion, I felt every muscle in my body tense, while my voice died down in the frantic heaving of my lungs. Massimo kept lifting and dropping me over his cock until I orgasmed—totally and overwhelmingly. As I came, I felt him spilling his seed inside me with a loud roar, additionally multiplying my ecstasy. We finished together in concert. Massimo placed me carefully on the couch, next to him.

We were trying to calm our breathing, lying on our sides, when the phone rang. Massimo inhaled deeply and took it. For a moment he only listened, finally bursting into laughter.

"Noises?" he asked in his fantastic British accent and listened some more. "In that case, I'd like to rent all the rooms bordering mine. Move the guests somewhere else and compensate them any way you see fit. Put it on my tab. Thank you." He hung up and hugged me tighter.

"Puritans," he chuckled. "In Italy, we would be an example to be followed, instead of a nuisance to complain about. Nobody tells *me* how loud I'm allowed to fuck my wife."

CHAPTER *fourteen*

We didn't have time to make use of the space Massimo had rented. At five p.m., after seeing off Kuba and grabbing a late lunch, we drove to the airport and set off to Sicily.

When we were home, it suddenly dawned on me that Christmas was just around the corner, in just a week. The staff was preparing the mansion, cleaning up and decorating. A tall Christmas tree appeared in the garden, flashing with hundreds of lights, and wreaths of holly replaced flowers inside the house. I needed only two things to feel the festive atmosphere: snow and my parents.

"We'll spend Christmas among family," Massimo said, placing his coffee cup on the table. "That's why I'd like to ask something of you. Make sure everything is just the way you like. I want Polish dishes to be present, too. I employed a Polish chef. He'll be here in three days."

Olga put down her newspaper and glanced at the Man in Black.

"What family are you talking about, exactly?" she asked as I was about to voice the same query. "The Mafia family?"

Massimo chuckled ironically and looked back at the monitor of his laptop. I rocked in my chair, stuffing pancakes into my mouth, and watched him. He was acting weird since we had returned from Poland—quiet, subdued, absorbed. He hadn't given in to a single provocation on my part and even was civil when speaking with Olga. Something must have happened, though I didn't have the slightest idea what.

In the afternoon, when Domenico and Massimo locked themselves in the library to discuss something, I grabbed my laptop and went outside to the terrace. I didn't notice Olga joining me with a bottle of wine and a glass of juice.

"What's up?" she asked, taking a seat next to me.

"The usual, it would seem." I nodded at the wine in her hand. "I wanted to check in with my parents. But I don't know how. On the one hand I know Mom was right, but she really shouldn't have said all those things." I switched the laptop on. "And it's not like she hasn't got a phone, right? She could have called."

"You're both too stubborn."

She took a sip of her alcohol and smacked her lips. "Shit, this is good. Domenico's choice for Christmas."

"Stop pissing me off," I growled, gulping down my juice. "Let's see what's happening on Facebook."

I spent nearly an hour looking through the profiles of my parents, my brother, and my friends. I checked on my work colleagues and replied to messages that had been sent weeks ago.

There had been a time where social media was my world. I used to be totally addicted to it. Now, I had other, more important and satisfying things to do. I had practically forgotten about social media.

I was just about to shut the laptop, when a friend's post stuck out. I opened the link and gasped.

"I'll kill him. I swear I will. Listen to this," I hissed, turning to Olga. "It's about Damian and some kind of accident."

Olga's eyes widened.

"'The night after the MMA event, where he won his fight, a young fighter from Warsaw suffered grievous injuries during a car crash. His life is not in danger, but multiple arm and leg fractures won't let him compete for months.'" I slammed the computer shut. "I fucking saw him leave the hotel on his own! I'm done with this!" I yelled and stormed through the terrace, past the bedroom and then down the corridor, straight to the library.

I barged in. It didn't matter that Massimo wasn't alone. I didn't care.

"What's wrong with you?!" I screamed, crossing the room in a fury. Mario intercepted me before I reached Massimo.

"Let me go! Goddamn it, Massimo, tell him to release me!"

The Man in Black said something to the men around the table, who were observing me with amused expressions. The three of us left the room. Mario put me down and closed the door, disappearing behind it.

Massimo leaned against the wall, crossing his arms.

"To what do I owe this particular tantrum?" he asked. His eyes flared with anger.

"Why is Damian in the hospital?"

"I don't know." He shrugged. "Maybe he felt bad?"

"You think I'm an idiot?" I growled. "His arms and legs are broken."

"I think it was an accident." A sly smile appeared on Massimo's lips.

"So you don't know what happened." I took a step closer and

slapped him so hard my hand throbbed with pain. "What about what you said after the fight? You said you wouldn't hurt him!"

Massimo's head slowly turned back to me. His eyes were burning with fury now.

"I promised I wouldn't *kill* him," he hissed through clenched teeth, as his arms shot out and grabbed my shoulders, pushing me onto a couch. "And besides, *dear*, we spoke after it happened. Moreover, not everything is as it seems."

I tried getting up, but he sat astride me and pinned me down.

"First of all, calm down or I'll have to call the doctor again. Now, listen to me."

"I'm not talking to you anymore," I replied, summoning all my calm. "Let me go."

The Man in Black watched me for a while before getting up.

I pushed myself to my feet, glared at him for a moment, and left, slamming the door behind me. I went to the bedroom, grabbed my bag and the keys to my new home, and stormed out of the house, heading toward the garage. All the car keys were in their place, luckily. I would have grinned if I weren't so totally pissed off. I snatched the keys to the Bentley and left the property.

I wasn't running. Massimo knew where I was—that much was evident. As soon as the Bentley passed the gate, a black security SUV started following me. What I needed now was simply some time alone, away from the Man in Black, in a place where I could brood in solitude.

The drive didn't take very long. In the meantime, I stopped at a gas station, where I bought a heap of sodas, chips, cookies, ice cream, and a whole lot of other junk food. I drove up to the door and left the car, lugging the heavy plastic bags. A man jumped out of the black SUV and quickly tore them out of my hands. I didn't have time to react. It would make no sense to try and overpower him or tell him to fuck off—he wouldn't listen. So I just followed him inside.

"We'll be outside if you need us," he said, placing the groceries on the kitchen counter and leaving.

I unpacked everything, armed myself with a spoon, a gallon of ice cream, a bag of chips, and a pack of cookies, and went to the living room, where I switched the fireplace on. Then I took my cell and dialed Olga. She picked up after a short while.

"Where the fuck are you right now, Laura?"

"My new house. I got pretty upset and didn't want to talk to Massimo."

"What about me?" she asked, annoyed. "You don't want to talk to me, either?"

"I'd like to be alone," I replied. "May I?"

She paused for a couple of seconds.

"Is everything okay? Are you feeling good?" she stammered finally.

"Yeah. I've got my pills, and everything's fine. The security guys are right outside, too. I'll be back tomorrow."

I ended the call and stared into the fire. Should I call Damian? Apologize? Was there even anything to say sorry for? After my anger abated, I analyzed the spat, and realized that I hadn't allowed Massimo to finish before I left. I didn't know everything about what had happened. Everything I thought was conjecture. That's me, though. I was too impulsive and driven by emotions. The only thing I had in my defense was that I was pregnant and couldn't fully control my behavior.

The next day I woke up around nine in the morning. I checked my phone, but Massimo hadn't called. I stayed in bed, thinking about what I had done yesterday, but any pangs of guilt quickly transformed into anger at his reaction. How could he ignore me now? With my bad heart and my pregnancy, he should have at least tried to check up on me! The security personnel were still waiting outside, and they had no idea if I was okay.

I went down to the kitchen and made myself a cup of tea. Without milk. I hadn't bought any. I unpacked the last of the chocolate cookies, and, as I was about to put one in my mouth, I noticed something near the ceiling. A red dot. I took a few steps closer.

"That's why you haven't called," I murmured, nodding.

There were cameras all over the house. I hadn't noticed them earlier, but they really were everywhere. Including the bathroom. The Man in Black had his eyes on me the whole time. He was probably watching me right now. I finished the cookies and went to the bedroom to gather my things, deciding to drive back home.

I drove back to the mansion and parked the car by the house. A BMW was in front of the main entrance. Its window was broken. Hesitantly, I stepped out of the Bentley and took a look around. There was nobody there. Including my security detail. A cold wave of fear washed over me. A few steps closer to the house, I noticed the door to the gym was open. Some kind of noise, a ruckus, was coming from downstairs. I took a couple of steps inside, keeping close to the wall, and stuck my head around the corner.

It was Domenico. He was half-naked, raging, smashing furniture into pieces. Massimo observed him, standing aside, flanked by several of his men. The younger of the brothers was clearly trying to get out of the room, but the others were standing in his way. Domenico was thrashing around, screaming at the top of his lungs, punching walls. I had never seen him like that before.

Even that day when he had nearly killed my security guards after someone tried pushing me and my car off the road hadn't been that bad.

I showed myself, but this only stoked the inferno of Domenico's blazing fury. Massimo sent me a quick look before rushing toward me.

"Go upstairs!" he ordered, pushing me to the stairs.

"What's going on?

"I gave you an order!" he roared in my face. I cringed, and my eyes watered.

I ran straight to Olga's bedroom and tensed in shock as soon as I crossed the threshold. The room was completely devastated. The bed was splintered, the cupboards toppled over, and the windows broken. I fished out my phone and dialed Olga with shaking hands. Her phone chimed from somewhere beneath the wreckage. I scanned the room again, making sure she wasn't there, and went to the library. As soon as I left the bedroom, one of the security guards appeared and escorted me.

"Why are you following me?" I asked after fifteen minutes, when it became clear the man wouldn't leave me alone.

"I'm not following you. I'm making sure you're okay, madam."

I frowned but kept silent.

A long while later, the door opened and Massimo entered. His hands were all scratched. He looked as if someone had dragged him out of bed by force.

He stopped in front of me. My eyes teared up. I couldn't help it. The Man in Black took a seat and pulled me into an embrace.

"Everything's fine. Don't cry."

I pulled away, tears streaking down my cheeks, and looked into his eyes.

"Everything's fine? Olga's room is completely wrecked,

Domenico looks like he lost his mind, and you're saying everything's fine?"

Massimo took a deep breath and got up, leaving me on the couch. He walked over to the fireplace and propped his hands against it.

"Domenico saw the recording." At first, I didn't understand. "He went mad; they started arguing. He didn't let Olga say anything, instead wrecking the place. She ran to my room. When I got there to calm him down, he was trying to shoot himself."

"What?" I exclaimed.

"He might not look like it, but my brother is a very sensitive man. An artist at heart. It's very hard for him to survive another betrayal."

"Oh my God . . . *that* recording," I whispered, hiding my head in my hands when it finally dawned on me what this was all about. "Where's Olga?"

"She left."

"What about the BMW in the driveway?"

"She tried taking it, but it made him even worse, and he tried stopping her. He broke the window. My men took him downstairs. It's soundproof. I locked him in there. Olga is safe. Don't worry about her. I'll take you to her as soon as things die down a little."

I shook my head, listening to his story. How could this happen?

"Can you explain all that once more?" I asked, wiping away the tears and focusing my entire attention on my husband.

"We received a parcel this morning. Olga was still asleep. Domenico always gets up at six, so he collected the package himself. He went to the study, played the recording, and went on a rampage. He ran to her room, she ran to mine, I ran downstairs, we fought a bit, and I took his gun."

He shook his head. "That's when Olga joined in, shouting that she did it for him. But then, Domenico had no idea what she was talking about, so he went even more mad. He followed her when she left. For a while they ran around the house. He threw things, breaking our stuff. She ran to the driveway, took the BMW, which I was planning to drive today. I wanted to collect my disobedient wife as soon as she woke up." He paused, sending me a disappointed look. "So when Olga wanted to leave, Domenico jumped on the hood and started pummeling the window. Then he kicked it and broke it. That's when I decided to step in. We dragged him to the basement. I gave Olga another car and sent her away to the hotel you stayed in when you first came to Sicily. I sent some men with her."

"Wait a minute," I broke in. "You said 'another betrayal.' When was the first one?" I asked, confused.

Massimo sat down again and stretched, pressing his back into the sofa.

"What an absolutely draining morning." He covered his eyes and yawned. "Let's grab some breakfast. We can talk there. I want you to eat something healthy. You can't keep bingeing ice cream, chips, and cookies forever. It isn't good for my son." He took my hand and led me to the dining room.

We sat at the massive table, laden with food, but the room felt empty. I couldn't remember having breakfast without Olga and Domenico.

"Will they make up?" I asked, nibbling on some bacon. Massimo raised his eyes and shrugged.

"If he starts listening and allows her to explain everything, I'd wager they will. But will she want him back after what he did?" He pushed his chair away from the table and looked at me. "No normal woman would take a man that keeps wrecking stuff, trying to kill her and himself."

"Oh, really?" I asked sarcastically. "And how about a man who kills people, shoots their hands through, or breaks their legs out of jealousy?"

"That's a completely different matter," he replied, shaking his head. "But since we're speaking of Domenico, he was in love once before. Olga isn't his first true love. Katya was.

"Several years ago we went to Spain on business. We stayed at a hotel owned by one of the local bosses. A day before we left, he invited us to his house, hosting us like kings. There was cocaine, alcohol, and women. One of those girls was Katya. She was gorgeous. A Ukrainian with golden hair. She was that Spanish guy's favorite, but he had a weird way of showing it. Namely, he treated her like shit. I don't know what was so special about her, but Domenico lost his head. At some point he couldn't hold it in anymore, and he asked her why she was letting the man treat her like that. She told him she didn't have anywhere to go. So Domenico, always the gallant knight, gave her his hand and said she could go with him, right then and there. He must have impressed her, but she finally decided against it, and we went back to Sicily. A couple weeks later, she called him and said that other guy wanted to kill her, was holding her against her will, and had knocked out her teeth. And she didn't have anyone else to call." Massimo sighed with a chuckle. "And my stupid brother got on a plane, went to the guy's place. Alone. The Spaniard let him in. He knew Domenico. As soon as he went inside, my little brother knocked out the guy's teeth with the handle of his gun, tied him up, and snapped a dozen humiliating photos of him."

"What do you mean 'humiliating'?" I interrupted.

"Darling," he replied with a laugh, putting a hand on my knee. "I'm struggling to put it into words." For a while he considered how to best put his meaning across. An amused smile flashed across his face. "Well, to be blunt, he put his dick in the man's mouth so it looked like the guy was sucking him off. And he said that if the Spaniard ever went after him, he'd hang one from each lamppost all across the country. Then he took Katya and flew back to Sicily. I went pretty mad, but I couldn't exactly do anything. Nothing happened for another few months. The Spaniard didn't want to do business with us anymore, but at least he didn't try to kill Domenico. But it all went downhill that summer. We were at a banquet in Paris. The Spaniards were there, too." He dropped his head and snorted with laughter, shaking his head disapprovingly. "Once a whore, always a whore. Domenico discovered her fucking her ex in the bathroom. He didn't go there entirely by accident, but that's not the point. The point is that she did what she did. Domenico broke into pieces then. He started doing drugs, drinking, fucking around. As if she'd give a shit. As if she'd know."

"Didn't she?"

"The Spaniard took her in again, and she was found dead a week later. Overdose." Massimo sighed. "So you see, baby girl, the situation is rather difficult and more complex than it appears."

"I need to speak with him." Massimo's eyes widened. "I'll explain it to him."

"Okay, but do not make me untie him."

"Excuse me? You tied him up?"

He nodded with a smile.

"You're sick. Come on." Walking down the stairs, I asked Massimo to stay on the ground floor. He agreed but stayed on the mezzanine to hear what was being said.

I entered the wrecked gym and looked around. Domenico was sitting in the middle of the room, tied to a metal chair. That nearly broke my heart. I walked over to him and took his face in my hands. He was calm now. Or exhausted. He raised his eyes, red with tears, but wasn't able to say anything.

"My God, Domenico, what have you done?" I whispered, stroking his cheeks. "If you just listen to me, all will be clear. But please, *listen* to what I say."

"She cheated on me!" he growled, and his eyes flashed with anger. I pulled away. "Another whore betrayed me!" he roared, thrashing on the chair. I jumped back, shocked. Domenico tried to break out of his ties, but Massimo was a master at tying people up. I knew that from experience.

"Fucking hell, Domenico!" I cried out, out of ideas. "You fucking egotistical bastard! You might be an idiot, but that doesn't mean everyone else has to be one!" I walked back to him and cupped his face in my hands. "Now listen to me for five minutes. Then I'll untie you."

He glared at me for a moment. When I was sure I could start speaking, he released another furious roar. The chair he was tied to toppled over, with Domenico still bound.

The Man in Black appeared and lifted his brother. He walked over to one of the cabinets still in one piece and returned with a roll of black duct tape. He plastered it over his brother's mouth.

"Now you keep quiet and she speaks. Then we'll all have lunch," he said coldly and took a seat astride a boxing bag Domenico had torn down.

I grabbed a chair and sat facing the young Italian. I started talking.

It took me twenty minutes to tell him all about Olga's sacrifice, Adam's scheme, and sending the parcel as revenge. Massimo confirmed my story, and we ripped the duct tape off Domenico's lips. The Man in Black untied him. The young Italian crumpled to the ground with a dull *thud* and started crying.

Massimo knelt by his side and picked him up, hugging his little brother. It was the most touching scene between the two I had ever witnessed. I decided to stay away. With each passing minute, I was feeling more and more like an intruder. I went upstairs and stopped halfway so they couldn't see me. For a long while, the two men stayed still, arms wrapped around each other. They spoke in Italian, and I didn't understand a word.

"Let's go see her," Domenico said, getting up. "I need to see her."

"Take a shower first," Massimo suggested.

"And I'll tell the doctor to dress those bruises and cuts. He's been waiting for an hour now. I thought we'd have to tranquilize you, to be honest," he said with a smile.

"I'm so sorry," Domenico sobbed, dropping his head. "She won't forgive me."

"She will," I said, walking upstairs. "She's seen worse."

◇◇◇◇◇◇◇◇◇◇

I stopped at the door to Olga's room and turned the key in the lock. Back in the car, I had decided to talk to her alone first, before Domenico made his own attempt. I crossed the threshold and the short corridor, reaching the living room. Olga was nowhere to be seen. I went deeper inside, finally finding her on the terrace with a bottle of vodka clutched in one hand.

"Is it any good?" I asked, taking a seat next to her.

"Tastes like shit," she replied, not looking at me.

"He's here. Downstairs."

"Fuck him. I want to go back to Poland," she growled, turned to face me, and put the booze down. "He fucking threw a vase at me."

She glared at me, as I fought to stifle my nervous giggling. I failed and burst out laughing.

"Shit, I'm sorry," I stammered, putting a hand over my mouth.

Olga sat still, confused, watching me with rising anger as I tried to compose myself.

"He tried to kill me!"

"With what? A vase?" I laughed uncontrollably again, raising my arms. "I'm sorry, but that's just hilarious!"

Her face slowly but surely lost its cross expression. After a while, she finally joined me in laughter.

"Fuck off," she managed, between spasms of cackling. "Attempted murder with a vase is still attempted murder."

"He wrecked the car, the gym, and the bedroom, and finally Massimo tied him up in the basement."

"Good for him." She crossed her arms. "He should leave him there to rot."

I put my hand on hers. "Hey, he was right to react that way." Olga narrowed her eyes, still looking at me. "You know yourself how that recording looked. What was he supposed to think? Maybe you two should talk it over. Right now."

I was about to call my husband when the two brothers barged into the room with a loud *bang* of the door swinging open and hitting the wall. I raised my arms, capitulating. Olga slid the terrace door shut with an equally loud noise, staying outside. Before I even started shouting at the two idiots, Massimo grabbed me, threw me over his shoulder, and carried me to the living room, making space for his brother. Domenico stormed across the room and went to his knees at Olga's feet.

"Let them talk it out," Massimo said, kissing me with a roguish smile.

I took a look outside and froze, dumbfounded. Domenico was kneeling down, holding a ring in his outstretched hands. He was proposing to my friend. Olga's face expressed total and complete surprise. She clasped her hands to her face, pressing her back into the sunbed. Domenico spoke to her. Seconds passed, but it felt like hours.

Then she did something I hadn't expected at all. She got up and crossed the room, saying nothing, disappearing into the corridor. I released my hold on Massimo and followed her.

I caught her in the elevator. We rode it to the ground floor.

"I'm leaving," Olga said, her eyes tearing up. "This is just too much. I'm out."

I hugged her and broke down crying. I couldn't make her stay. She had already done too much for me.

We got into the car and drove back to the mansion, where she quickly packed her things. An hour later, Massimo appeared in the doorway, announcing that the plane was waiting at the airport, ready to take her to Poland.

I cried all the way to the airport. What would the future hold for me now that I was completely alone?

Olga left.

CHAPTER *fifteen*

Two days until Christmas Eve. I cared very little for a holiday season spent without my family, friends, and—most important—Olga. Domenico vanished as soon as she left, and Massimo didn't seem to care at all. He worked, hosted various guests, and came up with the weirdest tasks for me to keep my mind off my loss. I accompanied Maria in picking decorations for the house and tested Christmas dishes with the new chef. Massimo had even sent me to Palermo to shop. None of that had made me happier without Olga. We made love every day and every night, as if that could bring me some solace. It didn't. Slowly, I started realizing my true circumstances—I was completely, totally, absolutely alone. When normal people marry, they usually only lose their freedom to have sex with anyone. In my case, the loss was a lot greater. I had lost my entire life.

I called Olga often, but she sounded numb, like a zombie. Maybe she was drunk. I tried chatting with Kuba, but he didn't have time for me. The only thing that kept my spirits up was the fact that my baby was developing correctly and was healthy. The ostensible idyll of my new life did not bring me true happiness. The day before Christmas Eve, I needed some time alone.

"I'm going to Messina for a day," I said to Massimo as we were having breakfast.

He put down his fork and faced me, trying to read my mind.

"When are you leaving?" he asked.

That took me by surprise. Conflicting feelings flitted through my mind—anger, confusion, and satisfaction. I had predicted he'd start a fight, ask too many questions, or simply look worried. Instead, my husband just accepted my choice.

"Right now," I grumbled, getting up.

"I'll ask Maria to pack you some food. I don't want my son to eat cookies and ice cream."

I sat behind my Bentley's steering wheel, watching the security guys load their SUV with tons of food for me. There was a lot of it. Too much by far.

An hour later I reached my house. The dour guards unpacked my stuff, leaving it in the kitchen, while I waited on the couch in the living room. I stared at the ceiling, the fireplace, the Christmas tree, with rising ire. I had to talk with someone. Anyone. I grabbed my laptop and switched it on, scanning my friend list, searching for someone I'd like to talk to. There was no one that came to my mind.

I was just about to slam the computer shut, when I had an idea. There was another person that I could, and should, talk to. I typed the name into the Facebook search bar. It popped up immediately. We were friends, it seemed. For a while, I tried remembering how that might have happened, but since nothing came to mind, I pressed the Message button. What should I write? And should I even contact the man? Was it only a subconscious need to provoke my husband or did I really want to talk to Damian? My finger slipped, sending a single random letter.

"Fuck," I muttered.

It took only a couple of seconds for the laptop to notify me that Damian was calling me. The app chimed repeatedly. Panicked, I frantically started clicking on everything, trying to close the window, but instead I accidentally accepted the call.

"Everything all right?" Damian asked, looking right at me.

I didn't respond, dumbstruck, gaping at him. Wasn't *I* supposed to be the one asking that question?

Despite all the bruises on his face, he still looked good. His thick lips were even thicker now, with the swelling. He was resting on a white pillow, watching me closely.

"Hey. Everything cool?" he repeated when I didn't reply.

"Hi there, warrior," I stammered. "How are you feeling?"

He smiled and shrugged.

"I'd feel better if I got it in a fight, but . . . you know." He sighed and averted his eyes.

"What happened?"

"I can't say." His eyes flicked back to look at me and his lips narrowed into a thin line.

"Damn it, Damian," I growled, annoyed. "What does that even mean? If my husband did that to you, I'd like to know!"

"Husband?" he cut in. "Massimo Torricelli is your husband?"

I nodded, and he paused, hesitating.

"What did you get yourself into, girl?"

He pushed himself up on the pillow. "Do you know what this man does for a living?"

"I do well enough." It was my time to interject. "And the last thing I need now is a sermon about morality. Especially from you. You're not a saint, either. Besides, it's already done. I'm married and expecting a baby. I tried telling you before the fight, but there was no time."

Damian's eyes grew wide, and his jaw dropped. Time passed, and I wondered if I should say something else, hang up, or just smack my head into the monitor. Finally, he spoke.

"You're going to have a baby?"

I nodded with a smile.

"Now it makes sense." I sent him a questioning look.

"If I knew all that, I'd never have done what I did. I'm not suicidal, you know," he replied to my unvoiced question. "What happened to me is my fault. No one else's."

I stared at him, waiting for an explanation.

"As soon as I went downstairs, Karol's men showed up and took me with them. They wanted to have a talk, you see. I went along, still having no idea who I threw punches at back at the hotel. So I challenged Massimo again. Karol was there. He got so angry, he called Massimo. Your husband accepted my suggestion to finish what we had started. We met in Karol's villa and fought outside, like stupid kids," Damian said, sighed and shook his head. "It was slippery with all the snow.

"I slipped and broke a leg and an arm. Very humiliating. Your husband just finished what I started and got my other leg and arm. But he didn't take my life, and I'm eternally grateful for that. I didn't know who I was fighting. When they told me, I thanked God for my luck. Normally, he would have shot me."

I sat back, mulling over Damian's words. What Massimo had told me days before—that not everything is as it seems—suddenly started making sense. I didn't know if I was more angry with Damian or Massimo. Or maybe I had no reason to be mad at all. Damian's voice brought me back to reality.

"How are you feeling?" he asked.

"Great, not counting the bit where my totalitarian husband tried to kill someone on my account."

We both laughed.

"I live on Sicily now. In Taormina. But I had to move out for a day or two. Catch my breath." I shrugged. "So I'm alone and wanted to talk to somebody."

"Care to show me around?" he asked, crossing his arms behind his head with a grin.

He was just too gorgeous to say no to. I grabbed the laptop and turned it around so he saw the house.

I passed through rooms, showing him the property, finally reaching the garden, where I sat in one of the big white sofa chairs. I put on my shades and uncorked a bottle of alcohol-free fizzy wine I had grabbed back in the kitchen.

"So that's that. My humble abode. Well, my humble retreat, where I go when I want to be alone, but—"

"Is that alcohol?" Damian growled, cutting me off as I lifted my glass. I laughed.

"This is one hundred percent alcohol-free. Tastes like the real thing, but that's it. No other effects, unfortunately. If Massimo saw me drinking, he'd lock me up in the basement."

"Aren't you sick of all that?" he asked hesitantly. "Wouldn't you like to return to your life? To Poland?"

I took a moment to consider his question. The last couple of days had been unpleasant. That was true. And I had entertained that very thought. But when I was asked to assess how I felt and what I wanted, I suddenly wasn't so sure anymore.

"It's not that simple. I'm the wife of a very powerful man. He wouldn't let me go. But I carry his child, too. And nobody normal would have me. I have too much going on."

"Maybe nobody normal, but a guy who gets his arms broken for you . . ." He trailed off, leaving an awkward silence between us. "I know this might be a surprise for you, but—"

"I love him," I cut him short before he said too much. "I'm madly in love with him. And that's my biggest problem. But let's talk about you. Or rather, what you're doing for Karol."

I fixed him with a stare, crossed my arms, and waited. Time passed, but Damian only fidgeted uneasily in his sheets.

"To be perfectly honest, I'm not doing much at the moment." He frowned. "You know how it is. I was young when he asked me to work as a bouncer at one of his clubs. I used to work out a lot. I was big and stupid, so I agreed. The money was okay, and there wasn't a lot of work. At some point it turned out I wasn't that stupid after all, so I got promoted. If I hadn't gotten the contract in Spain, I'd probably have known Massimo from a different perspective."

"Wait . . ." I lifted a hand. "When we were together, you were—"

"Yeah. A 'bad boy.'"

"Why didn't I ever notice?"

Damian laughed, accidentally hitting his cast-covered arm on his head.

"Ouch." He rubbed the hurting spot. "Oh, you know, babe. How would that sound? *Hi, I'm Damian, and I'm in a gang, but I'm a good guy at heart.*"

"Wait a minute," I interrupted, seeing Rocco and Marco—my identical twin bodyguards—sprint across the garden toward me. They shot nervous glances around, and I stared at them, raising an eyebrow and sipping on my wine. "Don't speak now," I warned Damian, turning the laptop around so the camera caught the two security guys' confusion. "See what I have to cope with?"

I asked in a whisper and switched to English. "What's going on, gentlemen? Are you lost?" My sarcasm elicited a snort of laughter from my ex.

"Madam, the cameras in the garden haven't been connected yet. Can you return inside?"

I sent them a disbelieving look and scoffed.

"Get me my husband," I ordered, pointing my chin at the phone Rocco was holding. He dropped his head. "Right now."

I took the offered smartphone. "Aren't you overreacting a bit, Massimo? The day is warm, and I need some time in the sun," I said before he managed to open his mouth. "Your son needs fresh air. Tell your goons to scram."

Silence was his only reply. For a long while he said nothing, but finally he spoke. "They won't be able to see you when you're in the garden. Maybe let Rocco stay around?"

I glanced at the monitor. The window showing the view from Damian's camera was minimized, but I was certain the bodyguard would report my conversation to Massimo.

"Darling," I said softly, knowing this was the best way to change his mind, "if I wanted company, I would have chosen yours. Trust me and let me be alone now. I'm feeling great, I'm okay, and I'm going to eat lunch in a minute. I can report in every hour if you'd like."

"I'm about to have a meeting. It may last until the evening." He paused and sighed after a while. "The security guards will check up on you every so often."

I nearly clapped my hands in glee.

"I love you," I whispered.

"I love you, too. See you tomorrow. Now give me Rocco."

I breathed out with relief and passed the phone to the man,

flashing him a wide smile. He responded with a grim stare and left, barking something into the receiver.

"I'm back," I said, opening the window with the conversation. "That's my life now. I'm under constant surveillance." Damian laughed and shook his head in disbelief.

We spent another hour or two talking about the good old times. He told me about his life in Spain and all the places he had visited during his career as a successful MMA fighter. He spoke about the people he met, training in Thailand, Brazil, and the USA. I listened intently, inwardly happy that I had sent him that random letter. On the one hand I felt sorry for him because of the injuries he had suffered on my account, but on the other I was glad we could have this talk.

"I got to go," he said as the microphone registered a noise in his room. "Sebastian is here with my food."

I smiled, looking at him with fondness.

"Will you promise me something?" Damian asked hesitantly.

"You know I hate questions like that. I don't know what you're asking for."

"Promise me you'll call me once in a while. I can't call you." He frowned and shook his head. "Karol will break the rest of my bones if I do. Or your husband will shoot me."

"I adore you, my warrior," I replied with a smile. "And yes, I can promise you that. Now, bon appétit."

Damian blew a kiss at the camera and ended the call.

I was getting a little nauseous after drinking all the fizzy wine. I hadn't eaten since morning. I went back into the house and spent fifteen minutes in the kitchen, preparing a hefty meal. Then I lugged it all to the garden. I sat at the table, nibbling on an olive, and sank into the depths of the Internet.

"Madam Torricelli." I jumped to my feet, clutching at my heart. "I'm sorry, I didn't want to scare you."

I lifted my eyes, shielding them from the sun with one hand, and saw a man. He edged closer, stepping into a spot of shade and flashing a friendly smile. His head was bald and angular, almost square-shaped. His chin was covered with a light stubble that surrounded his wide mouth. The man offered me a hand, fixing me with a stare of his green eyes.

"I am Nacho. Your gardener. Nice to meet you."

"Not an Italian name, is it?" I replied dumbly.

I shook his hand. His grip was strong.

"I'm Spanish." Nacho raised his brows, his smile widening as he stepped deeper into the shadow so I could see him clearly.

I nearly cried out aloud, seeing his body for the first time. It was entirely covered with colorful tattoos, forming something akin to a long-sleeved shirt on his skin. They began around the wrists and ended on the neck. It was evident the man was accustomed to physical labor. His body was perfectly toned, with not a gram of fat visible anywhere. He wasn't big or overly muscular, though, but wiry—like a footballer or an athlete. His tank top barely covered his shaven torso and his bright denim trousers were loose on his hips, revealing white underwear. If not for the tool belt, they would have slid even lower, uncovering an even more interesting spot. I gawped at him. I might have drooled a little. I slapped myself hard, though only in my mind, to shake myself out of my daze.

"Are you thirsty?" I asked, batting my eyelids, and immediately scolded myself for that blatant attempt at flirting. Thirsty! What a ridiculous question . . .

I shook my head, angry at myself. *The only person who's thirsty here is me,* I thought.

The man pulled a dark bandana from behind his belt and wiped his head with it, taking a seat on the chair next to mine.

"I could use a drink, thanks," he said, pouring himself a glass of water.

I was surprised by his openness. Normally, people working at the residence preferred to keep their distance.

"How long have you been working for my husband?" I asked, helping myself to another olive and pushing one of the plates his way.

"I'm fairly new. I will only take care of this house," he said, reaching for a piece of melon. "Don Torricelli wanted specific things in his garden. Will he be available today to talk about them?"

"I doubt that." I shrugged, sighing with resignation. "He works late usually. Besides, I kind of ran from him to here." I raised my wineglass in a sarcastic gesture. "Alcohol-free champagne?"

My words seemed to make the man happy. Or maybe that was just my imagination. Anyway, he relaxed and glanced at his watch, grabbing another piece of melon.

"No matter. We'll talk next time." He got up and started patting down his tool belt, searching for something. Without looking at me, he asked, "Why are you drinking alcohol-free wine?"

"I'm pregnant," I replied immediately. He nearly spat out his melon. His eyes widened in something that looked like panic. He quickly zipped up one of the pouches fastened to his belt, and his hands fell to his sides.

"Massimo Torricelli will have a child?" Nacho's behavior was unsettling, and his questions and direct manner were disquieting.

"Does this change anything?" I asked. "For the garden, I mean."

"For the garden, Laura? No. But it does for you. And for me, too. A bit. My sister is pregnant, too. This changes a lot. Yes. Have a nice afternoon." He took my hand and kissed it, before leaving with a glance at the entrance to the house.

A short while later, Rocco appeared in the doorway. He sent me a curious look, looked around, nodded, and disappeared.

What a strange man, I thought about the new gardener, returning to my meal and my Facebook. He was probably a junkie, or maybe his plants had some narcotic effects on him. Normal people don't behave like that. And they definitely don't talk nonsense.

CHAPTER
sixteen

I woke up at eleven a.m. on Christmas Eve. The sun shone through the window, bathing the bedroom in bright light. I chided myself for not closing the blinds. I crawled out of bed, oblivious to the time. Italians didn't celebrate Christmas Eve. Their holidays started a day later. Massimo had decided to change that tradition for my sake.

I went downstairs and was surprised to see a large box perched on the kitchen counter. I opened it and rummaged through. There was a red envelope inside with a short letter, saying, *The car will come for you at three in the afternoon.* I shook my head and returned to digging through the contents of the box.

The word "Chanel" written on the top side of the box confirmed what I was expecting to find at the bottom—a black satin-and-velvet jumpsuit and a pair of beautiful black round-toe stilettos. I clapped my hands, jumping up and down and hugging the new things to my chest. The jumpsuit had a wide neckline that kept the shoulders bare, while its wide sleeves were topped with an elastic belt that kept everything in its place. The top wasn't tight-fitting. On the contrary—it was very loose. The waistline itself was narrower. This allowed the pants to spill down the buttocks in a very sexy way without stretching over them, but beautifully accenting all the right curves at the same time. It was perfect! I snatched up my cell and dialed the hairdresser, booking him for one o'clock. I put the jumpsuit on a hanger, ate breakfast, and took a shower.

Fifteen minutes before the appointed hour, I was ready. Surprised, I discovered that the car was already waiting. I took my seat in the limousine and plucked my smartphone from my clutch bag, intending to call Mom, but what was I going to say to her? I'd have to apologize. Or keep quiet, waiting for her to begin. I stared into the screen, hesitating, finally tossing the thing back into my bag.

The car stopped at the driveway of the mansion, and I saw Massimo waiting for me at the door, leaning against the wall. The day was sunny but not as warm as yesterday. In fact, it was cold. The thermometer had shown fifty-one degrees Fahrenheit in the morning. Seeing the car, Massimo set out for the limo. He opened the door for me and offered me his hand. Overwhelmed with sudden emotion, I threw myself into his arms. With my face pressing into his sweater, I could feel him smile as he stroked my hair and kissed my neck.

"Merry Christmas, my love," he whispered, pulling away. "Now come, before you freeze to death."

I raised my eyes to look at him, and my legs buckled. He was so beautiful. Softly, slowly, I ran my fingers through his hair, pulling him into a passionate kiss. I was greedy, as though this were to be our last time.

"Let's skip dinner." I bit his lip and grabbed his crotch, completely unruffled by the fact that his cock was hard like a battle cannon. "How about a Christmas fuck, don Torricelli?"

The Man in Black groaned softly and made himself pull away from my embrace.

"I'd love that, but the guests are already waiting. Come," he said, straightening his pants around his erect prick and leading me down the hall into the house.

There were voices coming from the main dining room. Conversations, laughter, and the sounds of Polish carols. That was unexpected, but pleasing. Despite having invited his Italian family, my husband wanted me to feel the atmosphere of a Polish holiday. I tightened my grip on his hand and sent him a grateful look. He halted and spun on his heel right in front of the main door. Then he planted a gentle kiss on my forehead before revealing the room.

The first thing I saw was the massive Christmas tree rising from a mound of colorfully wrapped gifts. Then my eyes flew over to the long table laden with candles and decorations. Finally, I turned my head toward the sounds of the conversation. And froze.

"Merry Christmas, darling." Massimo hugged me tightly and kissed me on the top of my head.

I glanced at him, unable to believe what I saw, and then turned to the people inside the dining room. I kept darting glances from my husband to the festive tableau, and my eyes welled up with tears.

Seeing my reaction, my mother set out toward us and took me into her arms.

"I'm so sorry, darling," she whispered.

My voice stuck in my throat. I couldn't say a word, instead shaking with sobs. When Dad joined in the embrace, it only made it worse. I couldn't breathe! We stayed like that for a long time, and I felt my exquisite makeup streaking in dark smudges down my cheeks.

"Don't cry or the kid's going to end up a wimp." That was my brother. "Hey there, Sis," he said, pushing away our parents and wrapping one arm around my shoulders. There was a glass of wine in his other hand.

It was too much to bear.

"Let's get you cleaned up." Another familiar voice. Olga's.

I nodded numbly as everyone burst out in raucous laughter, delighted by my reaction. As we passed Massimo on our way to the bathroom, my hand brushed against his. I looked him in the eyes.

"Surprise," he said, winking.

I wiped my eyes, my cheeks, and pretty much my entire face, and sat on a chaise in the washroom, looking at my friend.

I needed to ask her a question, but wasn't sure how to phrase it. "What the hell are you all doing here?"

"Don't know about them, but I was kidnapped," Olga replied with a chuckle. "But seriously. He came for me to my parents' house, you know, asking, begging, crying and stuff.

"And when I told him to fuck off, he bribed my dad. It wasn't too hard to get him on his side. My dad is a simple English teacher. So the vision of me living in luxury until the end of my days did the trick. And him professing his undying love for me and a subtle hint at a free vacation on Sicily for my parents didn't hurt, either. But Domenico didn't end there. He persuaded my dad to take part in a scheme that would break through my wall of indifference."

"Jesus Christ, what did he do?"

"He rented a theater." I sent her a quizzical look. "A fucking theater. You know, with a stage and shit. A theater!" she repeated, raising her voice as if I was deaf. "At least he skipped the audience. So Dad took me there, right? And there was a choir and a fucking orchestra just waiting for my entrance!

"They played 'This I Love' by Guns N' Roses. And who was in the middle of that whole shitshow? You guessed it. Domenico—strong, beautiful, and dressed to kill." Her eyes sparkled as she continued, "And he fucking started to sing. That's another thing I didn't know he could do. He sang so unbelievably nicely, I just couldn't say no."

She stuck out her hand. There was a ring on one of her fingers. "I said yes."

I sat in perfect stillness, my eyes darting from the massive diamond to Olga's face. And to think Massimo had proposed to me in the bedroom. I had always dreamed of a spectacular proposal that would bring me to my knees. It took me a while to recover, but as soon as I did, I trapped Olga in a great hug.

"In all that scheming and planning, did he mention to your parents that he was a mobster?"

"Yeah, that was the opener." She chuckled. "He also added that he'd tried to kill me, demolished a whole house, and wrecked a really expensive car. But you know my dad. He's pretty flexible about stuff. Doesn't worry about dumb shit." She paused and then scoffed. "Are you kidding me? Dad thinks Domenico is an artist. An Italian gentleman."

"He's not wrong, though." I pushed myself to my feet and offered my friend a hand. "Cool stuff. Let's go back to the others."

We returned to the dining room, where my whole family was deep in conversation again. As soon as I appeared in the doorway, Mom stifled a yelp, and her eyes watered. I walked over to her and begged her not to start crying or I might follow suit. She calmed down, wrapped by Dad's arm, and wiped the tears away with a napkin.

Massimo nodded to the waiter and the dishes started arriving on the table. I was surprised by the chef's ingenious blend of traditional Polish dishes and Italian touches. The atmosphere grew more laid-back as more delicacies were served. Whether it was an effect of the great wine or if we'd simply needed some time to get comfortable in one another's company, I don't know.

At one point, Kuba, Dad, and Massimo went out to an adjacent room. The stench of cigar smoke reached us a few minutes later. Just like in the movies: a glass of something stronger and a puff of cigar after dinner. Olga led Mom away to show her the house. Meanwhile, I took Domenico's arm, stopping him before he joined the other men.

"Let's talk," I said seriously, directing him to the sofa, before asking in a deep voice, "Are you sure you want this, Domenico?"

"Aren't you a little hypocrite?" He fixed me with dead eyes and his lips stretched into a thin, grim line. "Need I remind you that you married my brother after knowing him for a month?"

"A month and a half," I growled in response, dropping my eyes. "But I didn't have a choice. Massimo kidnapped me, remember?"

"But he didn't make you marry him. He didn't make you get pregnant." I sent him a scornful look. "Well, okay, maybe the baby is his doing, but understand me—what am I supposed to wait for? I'm in love. I want Olga to be with me. I'm not losing anything. There's always the option to divorce later, but that's not the point. I know she's the one." His fists balled, and his eyes flared with anger. "And what she did for me proved that she feels the same way about me."

I nodded, agreeing to that, at least. To be honest, I was probably the last person who should be telling him what to do, and I realized that. I stretched out a hand, wanting to hug Domenico.

"You there!" I heard a voice and felt a hand on my shoulder. "He's my fiancé!"

Olga sat in Domenico's lap and kissed him passionately, ignoring the presence of my mom.

"Where are your parents?" I asked.

"They couldn't come. They stayed with Grandma." She shrugged.

We spent the rest of the evening by the fireplace, singing carols—me and my family the Polish ones and the Italians their own—and opening presents. Olga got a car. A beautiful red convertible Alfa Romeo Spider. Olga couldn't help remarking that this particular car would probably get wrecked after the first spat. I smacked her in the back of her head.

Anyway, I hadn't expected the presents from my husband to be cheap, but when I saw what he'd gotten my parents I was left speechless. The Russian sable-fur coat that Mom got stopped the blood flow to my brain. Hers, too, I think. Meanwhile, Dad discovered that he was now the owner of a sailboat parked at the Masurian Lake District in Poland. He nearly broke down crying. He had always dreamed of one. I sent Massimo a disapproving look, shaking my head a little.

"Isn't that a bit too much?" I whispered to his ear. "Nobody expected such expensive gifts. And we can't get you anything remotely this great in return."

The Man in Black smiled lightly and kissed me on the forehead, pressing me against his chest.

"Who else am I supposed to buy things for? Besides, I don't want you to return anything. Now. Open yours."

He prodded me toward the Christmas tree. I dug through the gifts, searching for one signed with my name.

I looked among the branches but found nothing. Finally, I plopped down on the floor and pouted. Massimo got up with an amused expression and reached to a branch above me. There was a black envelope hanging from it. He offered it to me and waited.

It was a bit surprising. Scary, even. I hated envelopes. Especially from him. They reminded me of the night when he had told me I couldn't leave. I turned the paper in my hands, searching for an answer in Massimo's eyes. He must have read my mind and shook his head briefly.

"You can open it. Don't be scared." A little half smile appeared in his lips.

I ripped the envelope open and pulled out a thin stack of documents. I scanned them with my eyes, but the writing was in Italian.

"What is it?" I knitted my brows.

"A company." He knelt beside me and took my hand.

"I wanted to give you some independence, but still allow you to do what you love. We're going to create a clothing brand for you." I was speechless. "You will have an atelier in Taormina. Emi will help you with picking the designers. You'll be able to . . ."

I didn't let him finish, instead throwing myself into his arms, toppling him to the ground. I fell onto him and shut him up with a long, fiery kiss. Massimo's hands found my ass and clamped around it. Even my mom clearing her throat loudly didn't disturb us. This was the greatest gift I had ever received. It was something I couldn't have expected—a job.

"I love you," I breathed when I finally pulled away.

"I know." He took me in his arms and got us both to our feet.

My parents watched us the whole time. They looked happy with what they saw. I thanked God everything was fine and that nothing unexpected had happened. I also knew that Christmas doesn't last forever. With my luck, something would happen soon. I didn't want to think about it. I was only glad my family had no idea they were spending their holiday in a Mafia-owned mansion guarded by dozens of armed goons. Or that my husband had shot a man on the driveway just a few months earlier.

"I also have a present." I took a step back so everybody saw me.

"It's difficult to give something to a man that already owns everything," I said in Polish and repeated it in English, gently stroking my belly. My husband's eyes widened and darkened. "I will give you something you wanted above all else."

My voice broke, and I took a deep breath. "I will give you a son." Massimo froze.

"It's a boy, darling. I know we weren't supposed to check, but . . ."

Massimo's strong arms picked me off the ground, and I squealed as I flew above my family, held by my husband. The Man in Black grinned triumphantly, putting me back on the ground and kissing me on the lips.

"I told you!" he cried out, high-fiving Domenico. "I told you I'll have an heir! Luca Torricelli!"

I sent him an angry glare then, but he didn't care, focusing on receiving congratulations. *An heir?* I thought. *Another mobster? Over my dead body!*

Some time later, when everyone had enough and couldn't stifle their yawns, I decided it was time to go to bed. Massimo placed my parents in a room located in the part of the house farthest from our own bedroom as well as any other spots that could allow them to glimpse his other, secretive side.

"Darling," I said, placing a hand on my husband's cheek, as we went in the dressing room to get rid of our formal outfits. "How did you do it?" He sent me a quizzical look. "My parents. How did they get here?"

Massimo's arms closed around me as he chuckled heartily.

"You remember when I had to deal with something when Domenico got arrested?" I nodded. "I met your parents then. I explained some of our current predicament and assured them of my feelings for you. I apologized for everything and took all the blame. I also promised Klara another wedding party for her daughter. I didn't tell them about what I do for a living, of course."

"You are the best husband in the world." I tried pushing my tongue between his lips, but Massimo clamped his mouth shut.

"I need to speak with Domenico," he said and kissed me on the forehead. "I'll be back before you finish showering."

I grimaced. I had hoped he'd join me, but my libido had to wait. Massimo kissed me again—this time on the cheek—and disappeared down the stairs. I stayed in place, rooted in place, and fumed silently, knowing that fuming in any other manner wouldn't do me any good. When the door closed, I shrieked and stamped my feet. Then I went to take a shower.

There wasn't any reason to hurry. I had to shave my legs, which I hated, and wash my hair, which I hated even more. The amount of hairspray I had on my head was staggering. I decided that my damaged hair needed a long, intensive regenerating treatment. I came up with all kinds of treatments, massaging various cosmetics into the skin of my head and my hair. All in all, the shower took me an hour, but I emerged clean, fresh, and with immaculately soft skin.

I went to the bedroom wrapped in Massimo's black bathrobe, my hair still dripping with water. I halted at the top of the stairs. My husband was occupied with tossing logs into the fireplace, sipping on an amber-colored liquor. Hearing me, he turned, eyeing me hungrily. For a moment, we just stood there, hypnotized by each other. His legs were slightly spread, his feet bare, and the white shirt he had on was buttoned only halfway up.

I took the belt of the bathrobe between two fingers and pulled it, untying the knot. Massimo bit his lip, straightening. I allowed the black fabric to slide down to the floor. When it did, I took a step toward my husband. He narrowed his eyes, and I could see the bulge in his crotch growing.

"Put the glass down," I said, stopping.

Obediently but slowly, the Man in Black did as I told him, bending over the coffee table and carefully putting the crystal glass down. I covered the distance between us, halting just a few inches short of the man I loved. Slowly, carefully, I started unbuttoning his shirt, unpinning the cufflinks, and finally taking the shirt off and caressing his bare skin. Massimo stood still, his lips slightly parted, as I kissed the scars on his shoulders, his chest, and his abdomen. The kisses formed a trail leading down, until I knelt facing him, my face level with his zipper. He swallowed loudly as I tugged at his belt. His hands hovered toward my face. I looked him in the eyes, fighting to unbuckle the belt and then unzip his pants. I was turning him on. Before the zipper slid fully down, Massimo's massive, erect cock slipped from his pants. His hands quickly moved to the back of my head and impaled my mouth on his bulging prick.

I resisted, which seemed to surprise him, but he released my head and allowed me to pull his pants all the way down.

"Why aren't you wearing any underwear?" I asked, feigning anger and rising from my knees.

He shrugged with an amused expression and grabbed the glass he had just set down. I turned and slowly walked to the sofa, sitting down and spreading my legs. Wide.

"Come over here," I commanded, pointing to the place on the floor between my legs.

The smile on Massimo's face took on a roguish quality. He

downed the liquor and went to his knees in front of me. I gripped a handful of his hair, balling my fist, and looked deep into his eyes, before I started pulling him in toward my wet snatch. His eyes flared with fire, and his parched lips parted. He fidgeted impatiently, but I punished him for making me take the shower alone. I trailed my thumb along his lips, sliding it inside his mouth. He gently jerked his head away. He wanted to dive in already, but I wouldn't let him.

Suddenly, he had enough. His arms shot out and clamped on my thighs, pulling me down the couch so that my clit was right in front of his mouth. Predicting an attack on my part, he grabbed me by the neck and pinned me to the sofa. With one fluid move, his tongue slid between my wet, glistening pussy lips, and his lips clamped greedily onto my clit. I cried out, digging my nails into the surface of the couch. Massimo latched on to my sweet spot with his mouth, sucking. I nearly came right then and there, before he began in earnest. He spread my labia further and again reached the most sensitive point, relishing the way my body squirmed and twisted in ecstasy. I tried looking at him, but the view turned me on so much I had to close my eyes and bite into the plush pillow under my head. The torture only intensified as his fingers joined in, as he pushed them inside me in one swift move. They started thrusting to the rhythm of his tongue. I moaned, writhed, and arched my back under his expert attentions, as his slender fingers impaled me harder. A wave of heat seethed inside me, and then a massive shiver went down my entire body. The orgasm came so abruptly, I didn't have time to take in a breath. I exploded, my hole tightening around his fingers, but it only made his movements faster. As soon as the first orgasm died down, another washed over me. After the third one,

I had to push Massimo away. I couldn't bear a second more of this exquisite agony.

The Man in Black pulled me a couple of inches toward himself, planting my feet on the ground before impaling me on his cock. He slid inside me without any friction at all—my snatch was so wet with his saliva his massive shaft could easily penetrate it. I was half-conscious by that time. Massimo's hips started their slow dance, picking up the pace by the minute. His still-wet fingers pinched my nipple.

"I need to feel you better," he breathed and pushed a thick pillow under my waist. My back arched. "That's perfect," he said, satisfied, and started fucking me so extremely fast and hard, I couldn't even cry out.

The dying embers of the previous orgasms were stoked into a roaring fire with the thrusting of his hips. My eyes snapped open, meeting my husband's wild stare. His lips were parted, and his jaw clenched. He was an animal. Beads of sweat glistened on his chest as his breath rasped. The sight, the smell, and the motion made it utterly impossible for me to fight the impulses of my body.

"Harder!" I cried, slapping his cheek with a swing of my arm. All muscles in my body tensed to their limit, spurred on by the massive wave of ecstasy washing over me again.

My strike made Massimo roar like a wild beast. He came inside me, exploding in my cunt. His hips weren't slowing down. He bellowed and shook until he was spent, collapsing on me and growing still.

Our chests heaved, trying to calm down our raspy breath. Massimo's sweaty torso pumped the air into his lungs, as I ran my fingers through his hair and kissed his face, my lips brushing against his rugged jaw. I was taking in the sight of his unblemished, perfect skin.

“Why don’t you have any tattoos?” I asked, rolling onto my back.

“I don’t like tattoos. Why would I scar my body with them?” He shot me a strange look. “And I’m a bit conservative when it comes to that. Tattoos are the domain of criminals. I wouldn’t want to be reminded of the perspective of going to jail each time I looked at myself in the mirror.”

“Why did you hire a gardener completely covered in tattoos, then?”

“Gardener?” Massimo cut in, the mirth momentarily disappearing from his eyes.

I frowned, confused by that sudden change.

“Nacho. Our bald, tattooed Spanish gardener at the new house. He asked for you yesterday.”

The Man in Black inhaled sharply and swallowed.

He sat up and gripped my shoulders, turning me toward himself.

“Tell me everything that happened. Don’t leave out any details,” he said calmly, but I felt a deep undercurrent of tension in his voice.

I was getting scared. I pulled away, shrugging his hands off, and got to my feet, starting to pace around the room.

“You tell me first. What’s going on?”

He stayed silent for a while, but his eyes followed my every step. He bit his lip.

“I haven’t hired a gardener yet,” he said somberly, getting up. “Now tell me everything about your meeting with that man.”

My legs buckled. What did he mean, he hadn’t hired a gardener? I had talked to the man myself! The nice, handsome, a bit quirky guy with tattoos. Completely harmless, right?

I sat on the couch, and Massimo knelt at my feet, listening as

I recounted yesterday's events. As soon as I finished, he grabbed his phone and dialed a number.

He spoke in Italian for a few minutes, shooting me nervous glances. Then, suddenly, he slammed the phone into a wall with such force that the device crashed into a thousand pieces.

"Fuck!" he cried in English. I cringed on the couch, afraid of his unexpected fury. He was fuming, shaking with anger. I got up and closed the distance between us.

"What's going on, Massimo?" I put my hands on his shoulders. He was breathing heavily but didn't reply. He was thinking, trying to figure out a way to tell me something without scaring me.

"The man you spoke to is Marcelo Nacho Matos. A member of the Spanish Mafia and a . . ." He paused, trying to find the right words. I wouldn't like what he was about to say. "Laura, my love. The man you met yesterday is an executioner."

"What do you mean?"

"A hit man." His jaws clenched. "I have no idea why he spoke to you. Why are you even . . ." He trailed off, and I shivered.

"Alive." I sighed. "That's what you wanted to say, didn't you? That you're surprised I'm still alive."

The Christmas spirit evaporated. I was sure Massimo was about to explode with the pent-up fury inside him. He passed me without another word and went to the dressing room.

A moment later, he returned, wearing a dark sweat suit. I took a seat on the couch, wrapped in a blanket, staring into the fire. Massimo walked over, sent me a gentle look, and sat next to me, setting me in his lap. I snuggled against his chest. His strong arms around me were making me feel safe.

"Why did he want to kill me?" I asked, squeezing my eyes shut.

"If he wanted to kill you, you would be dead. I think he might have wanted something else."

His arms tightened so hard I yelped in pain. "I'm sorry." He loosened the embrace. "I had a certain run-in with his people a couple months back . . ." He paused, considering something. "You will never again stay anywhere alone. I'm being serious, Laura. You will have a full security detail. No more trips to Messina without me. I should send you away somewhere . . ."

"You have to be kidding!" I cried out. "Your people won't be able to keep me safe. Nothing ever happened to me when I was with you. And each time you leave me, something bad happens. I'm not going anywhere!" I tried freeing myself from his embrace, but he kept his arms wrapped tightly around me.

My eyes watered. "What about my parents?"

The Man in Black inhaled loudly.

"We will take the *Titan* tomorrow. All of us. And when they return to Poland, Karol will protect them. I promise you I'll take care of them."

His tone was deadly serious. "They're safe. They're not hunting you. The Spaniards only wanted to hurt me. The only way to do that is through you." He turned my head and looked me straight in the eyes. "I promise you I'd rather lose all I have and sacrifice my own life than allow you or our son to be hurt."

That calmed me down a little. Domenico knocked on our door and said a few quiet words in Italian. Massimo left the room. I went to bed, plagued by waking nightmares featuring the sexy Spaniard. I couldn't understand how this nice man I had talked with in the garden could be a hired killer. His sparkling eyes were so full of life and so happy. I analyzed our meeting, recalling his movements and his words, but no conclusions came. *Why didn't he kill me?* I asked myself over and over again.

He could have done that at least a couple of times during our conversation. Why had he allowed me to see his face? Maybe he had thought I was stupid enough to keep it from my husband? Or maybe he wanted to kill me and he would have done that if not for something I hadn't noticed. Maybe his conscience? Or what if he just really liked me? Tired with brooding over all that, and of hearing noises that weren't there, I finally went to sleep.

I woke up on Christmas and found I was alone in bed. Nothing out of the ordinary. The sheets on Massimo's side were untouched, which could only mean that he hadn't slept in our bed. Or hadn't wanted to share his bed with me anymore.

I got ready for breakfast and headed downstairs, but didn't reach the bottom before the door opened and my husband entered the apartment. He looked completely drained. I halted, staring at him.

"I had to plan out the new security procedures and check the entire mansion," he muttered.

"Personally?"

"When it comes to your safety, I do everything myself." He walked past me and disappeared upstairs. "Give me thirty minutes. I'll join you at breakfast."

I went to the dining room, where all the guests were already gathered at the table. Everyone looked happy. They were talking agitatedly in at least three languages. When I entered, all attention turned to me. Mom started piling food on my plate, and Dad began telling the story of Mom's pregnancy with me. For the seventieth time. I had to listen to how she used to crave chocolate in the middle of the night, and how difficult it had been to get chocolate in communist Poland. So Dad had been doing all kinds of weird deals to get her the sweets she wanted, and as soon as she had taken the first bite, she threw up, saying that chocolate hadn't been what she had wanted in the first place. Dad told the story in Polish, so Olga—clamped to Domenico's arm—translated it in a whisper.

"May we talk in private?" Mom asked, leaving the table and walking to the opposite end of the large dining hall.

I got up and followed her, stopping at her side. She took out a cigarette and looked outside the tall window leading to the terrace.

"Who are those people?" She pointed to two security guards patrolling the path down to the beach and two more posted in the garden.

"Security," I replied.

"Why are there so many of them?"

"There's always that many," I lied, avoiding her eyes.

"Massimo is a bit paranoid. Besides, the property is huge, so there's not really *that* many." I stroked her back and retreated to the table, worried I'd have to answer more of her incessant questions.

Jesus Christ, I thought, taking a seat, *these two days will be the death of me.* I was seriously worried my parents would connect the dots and discover who Massimo really was.

Why had he invited them here? He could have cobbled up a Christmas party in Poland. It would have been better for my nerves, that was for sure. I silently prayed that he would finally join us, so we all could board the *Titan* and sail away. The weather wasn't exactly perfect, but I preferred to freeze my ass off on the yacht than sink into complete paranoia in the villa. To be honest, there wasn't much to complain about—back in Poland it was probably snowing. Compared to that, fifty-nine degrees Fahrenheit and a cloudless sky wasn't too bad.

"Dear guests," Massimo said, entering the dining room. "I have an announcement."

I felt so relieved I nearly collapsed in my chair. He was finally here and would take us all away to safety. I decided to translate from English.

"We'll attend a Christmas ball in Palermo."

"Goddamn it," I groaned, dropping my head.

My mother nearly fainted from shock. Dad gripped her shoulder nervously. Disoriented, I sent Massimo a wide-eyed stare, plastering a fake smile on my face.

"Weren't we supposed to go sailing?"

"Plans have changed." He smooched me on the tip of the nose.

Oh, how I dreamed of a calm and orderly life then.

I needed boredom! To sit on a sofa at home, eating and drinking wine. To watch a Christmas movie like *Home Alone* and just delight in sweet idleness.

"What's going on, darling?" Mother's high-pitched voice drilled through the awkward silence. "I have nothing to wear for such an occasion. Besides, it's all a bit unexpected."

"Welcome to my world." I spread my arms and shrugged with an ironic smile.

Massimo detected my mother's anxiety, which didn't really surprise me. He would have to be deaf and blind not to see her change of mood. Switching to fluent Russian, he started talking to her, flashing her a smile so adorable, it melted my heart. Klara Biel batted her eyelids at him, returning the smile, and I wondered what bullshit he was selling her. A moment later, she was grinning madly, her hand absently stroking my dad's shoulder.

"That's done, then," Massimo whispered to my ear. "Come with me."

He jumped to his feet and guided me out of the room, surprising everyone.

"We'll be right back, everyone!" I called out with a disoriented smile.

He led me through the enormous house so fast, I didn't even have the time to ask what was going on.

We passed the door to the library, where the Man in Black locked us in and latched on to me in a long, passionate kiss. His lips, teeth, and tongue pressed to me, greedily drinking me in.

"I need adrenaline," he breathed. "And since cocaine is out of the question . . ."

His hands slipped beneath my long skirt and grabbed my buttocks, lifting me in the air. He walked across the room and dropped me by the desk, bending me over it. Bewildered, I shot him a quick glance, feeling my heart picking up its pace. Massimo unbuckled his belt and then unzipped his pants. Hooking his thumbs over the rim of his trousers and his underwear, he quickly pulled them down, freeing his erect cock.

"Kneel," he growled, propping his arms on the edge of the desk. "Suck me off right now!" he commanded as my knees touched the floor.

Surprised and a little confused, I raised my eyes. His glare was dark and full of lust. I slowly wrapped my fingers around his penis and leisurely brought my lips closer to the tip. Massimo's own lips parted as his chest heaved. I heard him moan softly. I started stroking my hand from the base to the tip of his prick, keeping my eyes on my husband's face.

"How do you want me to do it, don Torricelli?" I asked seductively, which he ignored.

"Quick. Hard," he barked. His brow beaded with sweat, and his legs shook a little.

I gathered spit in my mouth and spat at the thick shaft, which grew harder in response. The Man in Black let out a throaty roar, and his hand slammed into the back of my head, impaling me on his throbbing, erect dick. I had been waiting for it. He slid all the way down my throat. I took it without a hint of gag reflex, which he rewarded by putting his other hand on my head and pressing harder. His hips swung forward, and quickly my sucking him off turned into his fucking my mouth. Another moan rose from his throat, and he spoke softly to me in Italian as I took my favorite part of him even deeper. I clasped my hands on his buttocks, nails digging into his skin. He loved it. In bed, my Man in Black didn't only like to cause pain—he liked it rough himself. Pain was an inherent part of our sexual life, stimulating us both the same way. I felt his penis ramming against the back of my throat, testing my limits. My teeth bit into the skin of his underbelly. I choked finally, trying to pull away, but his grip on my head only tightened. My eyes teared up, and I couldn't breathe. I dug my nails into Massimo's ass harder and deeper, leaving marks, and felt his hot seed flooding my throat. The hands on my head stopped pushing, but his throbbing cock was still stuck deep down my throat. I wanted to swallow it all, but I couldn't breathe. He withdrew a few inches, his hips undulating slowly, finally letting me inhale. Eventually, his movements stopped, as his hands landed on the edge of the desk again. Slowly, I pulled his still-hard cock out of my mouth and wiped the tears from my cheeks. My right hand shot out, grabbing his balls, and I licked him clean, all the time keeping my eyes on his.

Massimo's thumb stroked my face as I pulled up his boxers and pants. I zipped them up and buckled his belt, pushing myself to my feet, straightening his white shirt.

"Enough adrenaline for now?" I asked, raising an eyebrow and wiping away the dark smudges of makeup from beneath my eyes.

"For now," he breathed, kissing me on the forehead. Massimo didn't like the taste of his own sperm, which wasn't in itself anything to blink at, but I liked to defy him and test his limits. As his mouth pulled away, I cupped his chin with my hand and kissed him, my tongue penetrating deep into his mouth. He tensed but didn't push me away. He waited for me to finish, while I tried giving him a taste of himself.

"That was for my smudged makeup," I hissed, kissing him once again on the lips, which had stretched into an amused smile.

We got ourselves in order and spent the rest of the morning talking, strolling through the gardens and reminiscing about our (predominantly my) childhood. My parents told Massimo all about my weird quirks as a child. For example, that time I had eaten sand. The Man in Black replied that he owned a gravel pit, so we could drop by for some lunch.

During our walk, Mom still couldn't wrap her head around the fact that I was followed by four security guards at all times, but I simply ignored her questions, afraid I'd tell her too much. If not for the increased security measures, I would have all but forgotten my meeting with the "gardener" and the danger I was in. At least according to my husband. I couldn't make myself believe that the Spaniard posed a threat. The way he had looked at me had nothing aggressive or threatening in it. This time, I just didn't trust Massimo's suspicions.

CHAPTER *seventeen*

It was around three p.m. when three hairdressers and a whole team of stylists arrived at the mansion. Dad and Massimo both sighed with relief, disappearing for a nap, while Mom and Olga and I allowed the coiffeurs to do their magic. Mom told me what the Man in Black had said to her during breakfast. It turned out he had informed her that there were dozens of dresses bought for her for this specific occasion, waiting in her private dressing room. Either my man had lied to me or his power was really limitless. Was he able to predict the future now? We were supposed to sail on the Titan, but then that ball popped up at the last minute, and still Massimo had managed to prepare everything for that occasion. Weird. The longer I thought about it, the more logical it seemed that the trip had always been a ruse only designed to calm me down last night. I didn't want to stay angry with my husband, as there was a party waiting for us and I was about to play the trophy wife again. I forced myself to settle down.

I found Massimo in our dressing room, fighting with his bow

tie. I halted in the doorway, dressed only in my bathrobe, and watched him for a while. He was wearing gray pants and a white shirt. His hair was slicked back. Now he looked like a real Sicilian. He finished with the bow tie and turned to look at me. His piercing gaze observed my reflection in the mirror, and he softly bit his lip. With a quick whip of his arm, he snatched a blazer and threw it on. Then he straightened his sleeves, all the while fixing me with an intense stare.

"I picked a dress for you," he announced.

I inhaled his overpowering scent and felt my head swim. I couldn't stop thinking about all the ways in which I could manipulate him into staying with me here instead of going to the ball.

"Can't I go like this?" I asked, throwing off the bathrobe. Massimo's jaws clenched, and his pupils widened when he saw I was wearing his favorite red lace underwear. "I have a proposal for you." I reached out and unbuttoned his blazer. "You'll lay me down on the counter by the sink and lick me." I pulled the jacket off his shoulders and tossed it over the hanger, watching as his lips parted. "And when I come, you'll turn me around and, watching my reflection in the mirror, put your cock into my . . ."

I reached for his belt, but he grabbed my wrists and stopped me.

"Where?" he asked sharply. "Where will I put it?"

"My ass," I breathed, licking his chin and lip, slipping my tongue into his mouth.

He growled and took me in his arms, kissing me deeply. I felt his fingers enter me, rubbing the wetness all over my clit.

"I can't." The words were like a punch to the gut. He pulled away, passed me on his way out, and slapped my butt. "You won't need that underwear. Get dressed. We have thirty minutes." He licked the fingers he had pushed inside me just a moment before.

I knew what he was doing. This wasn't the first time he'd tried it. It was cruel. I balled my fists and shook with anger, silently cursing him, before I took a deep breath and walked over to the fabric dress cover he had prepared for me.

I unzipped it and discovered a breathtaking gown inside. A Polish brand. La Mania. It was bright, off-white with silver embroidery. Airy, as if made of spiderwebs. Delicate and very, very sexy. It was rather revealing, especially on the sides and the back, and fastened over the neck. In places, the dress was nearly fully translucent while in others it covered the skin with silvery floral motifs. A classic fit and flare, it stole my heart as soon as I saw it in its full glory. Now I knew what Massimo had meant, saying that I wouldn't need underwear. I couldn't wear a bra with that dress, and my G-string would have to be skin-colored and really scant. As I took the dress off the hanger, I discovered another cover, which housed a silvery-gray cloak. Tom Ford had introduced that trend in his 2012 collection, but I hadn't even dreamed of wearing something as gorgeous back then.

"The cars are waiting," Massimo said, entering the dressing room twenty minutes later. "My queen," he breathed, eyes widening at the sight of me dressed in that incredible ensemble. He took my hand and kissed it, watching me with visible delight.

I did look ravishing. The short bob on my head, which the hairdresser had freshened up, was perfectly shaped. The smoky gray makeup perfectly complemented the darker elements of my attire, and the short tips of my Manolo Blahnik heels topped off the entire raiment. I grabbed a minuscule Valentino clutch bag and turned to face my husband.

"Shall we?" I asked haughtily.

He grinned, presenting his perfect white teeth. Silently, he took my hand and led me toward the stairs.

"How long will the drive take?" I asked as we walked to the exit.

"We're going to the airport first. The flight itself will only take fifteen minutes."

The sound of the word "flight" made me tighten my grip on his hand. It was a reflex. His thumb stroked the top of my palm, and somehow I was sure he'd be able to distract me in the private jet. Even one filled with my family.

I found the rest of the crew by the main door. They were happy and a little tipsy. Everyone looked amazing. The men in their tuxedos looked like movie stars, but it was Olga who drew my attention the most. It might have been the first time she hadn't dressed in her signature style. Or maybe Domenico had picked her outfit? She was wearing a long, black, tight-fitting bandeau dress that served to emphasize her curves. Her shoulders were wrapped in a fur bolero.

"There you are," Mom said coolly. I spun to take a look at her.

My jaw dropped. I was speechless. There she was—my mom—wearing a one-shoulder nude dress. I stared at her in shock. But it was my husband who had bought that dress for her. I sent him a slightly reproachful look, but he only shrugged and smiled, showing everyone to their cars.

◇◇◇◇◇◇◇◇◇◇◇

"When your parents are around I feel like we're in high school again," Olga said quietly as we stepped out of the limo by a historical hotel in Palermo. "I have to be all prim and proper and never fucking swear. Goddamn it, everyone in the world understands when I swear in English!"

"They're returning to Poland tomorrow." I chuckled and grabbed her hand. "Believe me, I'm pretty fed up with the constant tension and fear that something will happen and they'll find out who Massimo really is."

"Oh, right. Forgot to ask you," she said, lowering her voice. "What's with the increased security around the house? Domenico wouldn't tell me."

"That. It's . . ." I began, but the Man in Black appeared out of the blue and put a hand on my shoulder.

"Ready?" he asked, looking at the throng of paparazzi crowding the main entrance.

I'd never be ready for something like this. I'd never feel comfortable with this much attention. I tightened my hand on Massimo's arm, and he covered my palm with his as the crowd started calling out. Reporters and photographers pushed through, trying to get to the very front and snap the best possible photo. Massimo stood still, exuding an aura of calm indifference, and I tried desperately not to blink in the flashing lights of the cameras.

"Signora Torricelli!" they were shouting.

I raised my head high and flashed them my most glamorous smile. A while later, don Torricelli nodded, and we entered the building.

"You're getting good at this," he said, kissing my hand and leading me through the main hall.

We took our seats at a table, and I was glad to discover we didn't have to sit with strangers this time. My smile faltered as I remembered we would soon be joined by the dour goons from the security team. I surveyed the monumental ballroom. It was cavernous, with the ceiling at least three levels above me. It was richly decorated, carved in fantastic shapes. The massive columns supporting the roof were joined with Byzantine arches. They were stunningly beautiful.

Candles were glowing from all around me, and the room itself was lined with large Christmas trees. The tableware was pure silver, and the buffets—of which there were at least a dozen—were laden with various delicacies. Waiters in white tuxedos were serving antipasti, and I couldn't help but wonder how I had become a part of this world. My mother didn't seem to be worried at all. She acted naturally, without a hint of discomfort, focusing the attention of most of the men in our part of the ballroom. Dad sat straight, beaming with pride, completely unfazed that Mom had been asked to dance at least five times since we had arrived.

"What is this party?" I leaned over to Massimo, gently stroking his thigh.

"A charity ball," he replied. "And stop teasing me." He moved my hand to his crotch. He had an erection.

"I'm not wearing any underwear," I whispered, adopting my most innocent smile as I noticed Mom was watching us.

Massimo's hand tightened around mine, crushing it, and his black eyes drilled holes in me.

"You're lying," he cleared his throat, raising his glass and nodding at Klara.

"Why don't you check for yourself? Slide your hand down my back." I raised my eyebrows and widened my smile.

My husband's hand touched the skin of my back and moved down. It slid beneath the fabric of my dress and froze. Back home, I had put on underwear only to discover it was too visible beneath the translucent dress, so I'd decided to skip it altogether.

Don Torricelli tensed, delicately caressing the spot where my back ended. He inhaled deeply and put both hands on the table. *Point for me*, I thought.

I dropped my hand, pretending to fiddle with my shoe, and slid it under my dress. My fingers found my wet pussy, playing with it for a short while, until I was sure they were covered in its juices. I rubbed my fingers together and then offered my hand to Massimo, leaning to his ear.

"Kiss me and taste it." I bit his earlobe.

He did as I commanded, softly brushing his lips against the wet spot on my hand. His pupils dilated, and his breathing quickened as he felt the scent and tasted it.

"You . . . do not . . . refuse me," I hissed, emphasizing each word and withdrawing my hand.

The Man in Black was burning with lust by then, but he took a quick glance at my parents, sipped his wine, and leaned back in his chair. His torso gradually stopped heaving, and he closed his mouth, stretching his lips into a semblance of a smile. I was impressed by his self-control and discipline. The only sign that he was struggling internally was his rock-hard cock bulging in his pants.

"Those Louboutin stilettos are gonna be the death of me," Olga said, plopping down in her chair three hours later. "Domenico can't dance. I'm not good at it, either, but still he keeps dragging me back to the dance floor. It's not *Dancing with the Stars*, for fuck's sake."

I sent her a commiserating look, knowing how she felt. I had been exhausted by Domenico's love for dancing after two songs at the Venice Film Festival. I glanced at Massimo, who was deep in conversation with Kuba. At least he was a great dancer. For the entire evening, my husband didn't leave my side. Whether it was my parents or my lack of underwear, he was glued to me the whole time.

◇◇◇◇◇◇◇◇◇◇

It was around one when Mom and Dad excused themselves and one of our men escorted them to their room. An elderly man joined us at our table. He greeted everyone politely, including my brother, and the men started talking.

"Back to square one," I muttered, glancing at Olga, who was still rubbing her feet.

"What did you expect?" She shrugged. "Let's go to bed."

It sounded like the best option, so I turned to Massimo and asked him if we could go now. He only glared at me, annoyed, and returned to his conversation.

"We're going," I said, getting up.

The Man in Black nodded absently at two guards who were waiting by the wall, and they came over, taking positions behind me. I shook my head and grimaced, before leaving.

The two goons knew the way better than I did and soon overtook me. I followed. A moment later, I realized something. I had left my phone in Massimo's jacket. My clutch was too small for it.

"I'm just going to grab my phone," I barked at the bodyguards, who halted and turned around. One of the men launched himself after me, but I waved him away. "I'll just be a minute!"

Back at the ballroom, I discovered that our table was already empty. I hovered by my chair for a while, scanning my surroundings until I noticed the waiter who had been serving our little group. I asked him if he knew where the men had gone, and he pointed me to a door on the opposite end of the hall. I thanked him and went there.

It was completely dark behind the large wooden door, the way lit only by small lamps affixed to the wall every couple of feet. I followed the corridor until I found another door. Someone was talking behind it. I didn't think twice. I grabbed the handle and opened it. The door led to a small room. A group of men were sitting by a table inside. The ones I was looking for were among them.

"Shit," I groaned, seeing Massimo bending over the table and snorting a long line of white powder. He rose, calmly placed the rolled-up bill on the tabletop, and sent me a cold stare. The others turned their heads, too.

"Are you lost, baby girl?" he hissed through clenched teeth. I felt nauseous.

Accompanied by bursts of laughter, I approached him, sticking out my hand.

"My phone," I barked. Massimo reached for his pocket and passed me the smartphone. "Fuck you, don Massimo," I spat, taking the device. The room went completely quiet. The men around the table were staring at the Man in Black expectantly.

"Out," he growled, pointing at the door. One of the security guards opened the door for me.

I glared at Massimo hatefully for a short while, clamping my jaw to keep from breaking down in tears. I spun on my heel, raised my head haughtily, and stormed out of the room, hearing don Torricelli say something in Italian, eliciting another fit of laughter.

I was fuming. He had to play macho with the other mobsters around, but why the hell did he have to take drugs? I ran across the ballroom, stifling a sob, and headed to the place where I had left Olga.

At some point, I must have taken a wrong turn.

"Goddamn it," I swore, stamping my feet like an angry child.

Sense of direction had never been my forte, but when I got mad it usually reached whole new lows.

I turned around, intending to go back, when I felt a sweetish taste in my mouth.

CHAPTER *eighteen*

My head hurt. It felt like a hangover, but I hadn't been hungover for months. I slowly opened my eyes. The room I was in was unpleasantly bright. Light was not what I needed now, with the migraine pounding in my skull. Had I blacked out again? I couldn't remember anything from last night. A moan left my throat as I rolled over and covered my head with the duvet. I tried wrapping myself tighter in the sheets, and in doing so I ran a hand down my side. I froze. Were those cotton boxers over my waist? I didn't own cotton underwear. My eyes snapped open, heedless of the pain in my head. I threw off the sheets and glanced at myself, panicked.

"What the fuck?" I muttered to myself.

"I don't know Polish," I heard a man's voice. My heart stopped. "But if you're feeling unwell, your pills are by the bed."

I felt my pulse raging and my breath quickening. I squeezed my eyes shut and took a deep breath, rolling over.

"Hi," Nacho said, smiling cheerfully. "Don't scream."

I tried breathing in, but my body tensed and my lungs locked up. I couldn't inhale. Couldn't breathe.

"Laura." The man sat on the edge of the bed, grabbing my hand. "I won't hurt you. Don't be afraid."

He offered me a pill.

"Open your mouth."

I stared at him, wide-eyed and mortified, hearing only the whine in my ears. He stuck his fingers in my mouth and pushed the pill under my tongue, stroking my hair. I jerked my head away.

"They told me you'd react badly." His voice was calm and cheery.

I closed my eyes, trying to relax. I don't know if I fell asleep or opened them just a few seconds later, but he was still there.

"Nacho," I whispered. "Will you kill me?"

"The name's Marcelo, but you can call me Nacho, yes. And no. I'm not going to do that." He checked my pulse. "Why would I rescue you only to kill you?"

"Where am I?"

"The most beautiful place on Earth," he said, still counting my heartbeats. "And you'll live." His eyes were sparkling. I wasn't scared anymore.

"Where's Massimo?" I asked.

He laughed and offered me a glass of water. I lifted my head, and he poured some into my mouth.

"Probably raging impotently back on Sicily." He grinned and stretched. "How are you feeling?" His question was . . . strange. Out of place. I took the glass from his hand and put it away.

"You're a killer, but I'm still alive."

"A very astute remark."

He lay on his side, propping himself up on an elbow and putting his other arm over me. "Now, to preempt your other questions. I've kidnapped you, but that's nothing new for you, is it? I don't mean you any harm. I'm only doing my job. If everything goes as planned, you should be back with your husband in a couple weeks," he explained with a more serious expression. His eyes didn't lose their merry glint. He rose and glanced at his watch. "Anything else?"

I gaped at him. Was this some kind of joke? The man in the white tank top, standing over me, had nothing in common with the ruthless killer Massimo had told me about. Nacho pulled up his loose jeans and smiled, sliding his feet into a pair of flip-flops.

"No questions? Good. I'm going for a swim."

"Wait," I called. "Where am I, and how long have I been here?"

"You disappeared two days ago. It is December twenty-seventh, and you are on the Canary Islands. Tenerife, to be precise." He put on a pair of shades and went to the door. "I am Marcelo Nacho Matos, son of Fernando Matos, who ordered me to bring you here. And, once again, you are perfectly safe. No one is going to kill you. We only need to clear up some issues with your husband, and you'll be back home before you know it."

He crossed to the door and sent me one last look before closing it. "If you get any funny ideas, remember you're on an island, a good way away from the continent. And the bracelet on your leg is a transmitter." I touched my ankle and felt a rubber-and-plastic band around it.

"So I know where you are at all times. And if you try to contact your family without my consent, I'll kill them."

The door closed, and he vanished.

I lay without moving, shocked. Thank God I was pregnant and married. The thought of my life going full circle was making me sick. I stared at the ceiling, trying to digest all that Nacho had told me. I was tired and wanted to cry. And to make matters worse, the very moment before I was kidnapped, my husband had treated me like garbage, and that did absolutely nothing to improve my mood. I rolled over, hugged a pillow, and quickly fell asleep.

◇◇◇◇◇◇◇◇◇◇

Hunger woke me up in the middle of the night. My stomach rumbled loudly. I couldn't stay hungry for long—I was pregnant. I got out of bed and switched the lamp on.

The room around me was modern, bright and simple, with white walls and wooden, fabric, and glass details. Looking for something to wear, I fumbled through the room, finally reaching a closet with sliding doors. I opened one wing and found myself standing in front of a small wardrobe. It was packed with sweatpants, flip-flops, shorts, T-shirts, some underwear, and swimsuits. I reached for a baggy hoodie and a pair of shorts. They were too small for me.

Warm wind gusted through the open window. I heard the monotonous whisper of the sea. The terrace overlooked the ocean. The water was black and calm. Surprised, I discovered the place of my imprisonment wasn't a house at all. It was an apartment block. A small garden with a Jacuzzi stretched below the terrace.

I went to the door and grabbed the knob. It was open. A nice change after my last abduction, when I had to wait for Domenico to arrive and let me out. I stepped out to the corridor. The crisp coolness of the glass floor invigorated me. There were stairs opposite my room. I descended to the lower floor, passing a pair of doors, and reached the kitchen.

"Fridge," I moaned, dashing ahead and opening the door to the land of treats aplenty.

With a smile, I scanned the contents of the refrigerator, looking at cheeses, yogurts, and lots of fruit, as well as Spanish meats and beverages. I rummaged through the groceries and tossed whatever I wanted to the counter, before reaching for some bread rolls.

"If you're hungry, I can heat you up some paella." Startled by the sound, I dropped a plate. It shattered on the floor. "Don't move."

Nacho knelt at my feet and started collecting the broken pieces, throwing them into the trash can. There were too many. He took me in his arms and carried me out of the kitchen, before returning and sweeping up the shattered fragments with a broom. I watched him, confused.

"I don't get it." I crossed my arms on my chest. "You care about me—that is evident. You worry about my well-being. Why kidnap me?"

He pushed himself to his feet and looked me in the eyes.

"You're pregnant. And your problem is that you married the wrong guy." I avoided his stare, but he pinched my chin between thumb and index finger and lifted it so I had to meet his gaze. "You did nothing wrong. You're innocent. And you're a pretty girl. What's not to understand?"

He sat on the counter, and suddenly I became uncomfortably aware of the fact that he wasn't wearing anything aside from his boxer shorts.

"You," he continued, "are a means to an end. You are not our target." He sighed and propped both hands on the counter, stretching. "If you were a man, we would have kept you in my dad's basement, tied to a chair. Naked. But you're a pregnant woman, so I thought I'd keep you here, cleaning up your mess. Besides . . . we don't want a war with Torricelli. We only want him to talk to us."

He jumped off the counter. "So. Paella?"

"This is too fucking weird," I muttered, sitting on a bar stool.

"Preaching to the choir. I would have preferred to run a kite-surfing school instead of shooting people in the head." He took all the things I had prepared for my midnight meal and put them back in the fridge, instead pulling out a large pan. "Seafood and rice, with saffron. Made it myself." He flashed that disarming smile of his again.

I watched him, taking in the colorful tattoos. They were everywhere: on his back, his arms, probably his butt, too. Only his legs were free of them.

"What does your woman say to all that?" I asked despite my better judgment.

Nacho placed the pan on the stove.

"Don't know. I'm single," he replied without looking at me. "But I have pretty high standards. I want my women intelligent, smart, pretty, fit, and preferably without an idea of who my father is. But it's a small island. And women on the continent are . . ."

He paused for a moment. "*Loco.* If you know what I mean."

I didn't, but nodded anyway. He looked gorgeous, scuttling about in the kitchen. I wasn't really listening.

Instead, I watched the man preparing my meal and concluded that I really didn't fear him. But maybe that was what he had planned. Maybe that's why he was acting all friendly. So that I relaxed and dropped my guard. My mind suggested many different scenarios, all ending in him attacking me in the end, until a plate full of delicious-smelling food appeared in front of me.

"Eat," Nacho said, sitting next to me and grabbing his fork.

The food was so delightful, I didn't even notice I'd eaten two full portions before feeling stuffed. I slipped off the bar stool, leaving the plate on the counter and thanking him for the meal.

"It's only eight in the evening. You're going back to sleep?" he asked as I plodded toward the stairs.

"Really?" I opened my eyes wider.

"We can watch some movies." He pointed at a couch in the living room.

I sent him a confused look, trying to figure out what my role in this was.

"You kidnapped me, Nacho, and you've threatened my relatives, and now you think you can just watch movies with me?" My voice might have been a bit too aggressive. I didn't wait for a response, turning away.

"Well, the last guy who did that to you will be the father of your child," Nacho muttered, keeping his eyes on his plate.

I froze and was about to retort with something, but he *was* right. I bit my tongue and went to my room. This was too strange. I snuggled into my bed and turned the TV on.

When I opened my eyes again, it was still dark. Upset that I might have slept through another day, I launched myself out of bed. My baby couldn't starve for so long. The flat white TV on the wall opposite the bed was showing seven thirty. Even in Poland at that hour it's brighter. I stumbled back to bed, covering myself, happy that it was only morning.

The next time I woke up, the room was bathed in the warm light of the sun. I stretched and kicked the duvet off.

"You're really pregnant?" A man's voice. I jumped up in alarm. "You're very thin."

I rolled over and saw Nacho, sipping something from a cup,

sitting in a sofa chair by the bed. I was beginning to think he slept there.

"Beginning of the second trimester. It's a boy," I replied, getting up. "Now, explain something to me."

I stepped closer to him, stopping at his feet. He eyed my stomach. "What did you want from me back in Messina? In the garden." I crossed my arms, waiting for an explanation.

"Same I wanted in Palermo. To kidnap you." He chuckled. "Those idiots Massimo calls bodyguards wouldn't notice me even if I sat on their ugly mugs. I just didn't know you were pregnant. And the tranquilizer I was about to use might have hurt you. Or, rather, your baby." He nodded at my belly. "But that's enough idle chitchat. Let's call Massimo. You'll tell him you're feeling great and you're safe. No more." He pushed himself to his feet, and dialed a number on his cell phone. As soon as the person on the other side picked up, Nacho fluidly switched to Italian. For a few seconds he talked in a calm, quiet voice, finally handing me the phone. I grabbed it and retreated to the opposite side of the room.

"Massimo?" I breathed.

"Are you all right?" His calm voice was just a cover. I knew he was crazy with worry. All the thousands of miles between us couldn't mask his anxiousness. I took a deep breath and shot my captor a defiant look. I took the risk.

"I'm on Tenerife in some kind of apartment block with a sea view!" I sputtered as fast as I could.

Nacho wrested the phone from my hand and hung up.

"He knows where you are," he growled. "But before my father allows it, your husband won't come here.

"You've risked a lot right now, Laura. I hope you're happy with yourself. Have a nice day." He spun on his heel and left, slamming the door.

I stood immobile for a whole few minutes, feeling a rising fury. My helplessness transformed into red rage, and such emotions rarely led to anything good. I grabbed the knob and rushed down the corridor, heading to the stairs.

I filled my lungs with air and started shouting before I even saw him.

"What the hell are you thinking? You think I'll just sit here and wait?!"

I took the steps down two at a time, looking down to keep myself from missing one and falling. "If you think I'll . . ." I trailed off. There was a young woman standing next to Nacho. She stared at me with a half-open mouth.

She snapped it shut and turned to him, speaking in Spanish. They talked for a short while, and I watched them, frozen in midstep on the stairs and wondering what was going on.

"Amelia, this is my girlfriend, Laura." Nacho wrapped his arm around me and pulled me toward him. "She came a couple days ago. That's why you couldn't reach me."

He kissed me on the forehead, and as I tried breaking free from his embrace, he added, "We're in the middle of a little spat. Could you give us a moment?"

His long, tattooed arms grabbed me and lifted me into the air. He carried me back upstairs.

"I'm Amelia!" The girl smiled radiantly and waved at me as Nacho lugged me away.

I tried jerking away, but he was too strong. We entered the first bedroom and he closed the door, putting me on the floor. As soon as my feet touched the ground, I took a huge swing, fully intending to smack him in the face. My hand didn't reach its target. Nacho dived, dodging my strike. It only made me angrier. I dashed toward him, waving my arms like a crazy hag, but he kept dodging. Eventually, we reached the end of the room. With a lightning-fast motion, he grabbed my wrists in one hand and pushed me against the wall. I couldn't move. It took him only a few seconds to reach for something in the cabinet we were standing next to. Before I knew it, I had a gun to my head.

"We both know you can't kill me," I hissed through clenched teeth, glaring at him with all the hatred I could muster.

"Sure," he said, uncocking the gun. "But are you willing to bet on it?"

I considered the circumstances, quickly admitting defeat. My arms relaxed. Nacho released me and put the gun back in its drawer.

"That is my sister down there. She doesn't know what I do." He took a few steps back. "I would like it to stay that way. She thinks I run one of Dad's companies and that you're my Polish girlfriend. We met a few months back at a party when I went to Warsaw on a business trip."

"Are you out of your mind?!" I cut in, and he took another step back. "I won't pretend anything! Especially being your girlfriend." I stormed off toward the door.

Nacho grabbed me and shoved me onto the bed, sitting astride my legs.

"And we slept together and that's why you're pregnant now," he continued, unfazed. "Our relationship is a bit of a necessity, but we do love each other very much. Get it now?"

I burst out in laughter, and he let go of my hands, confused. I crossed my arms, still laughing.

"Nope," I said, suddenly turning serious. "I'm not going to make it any easier for you."

The Spaniard lowered himself on his arms, as if he was going to kiss me. I stiffened, afraid and unable to run. His breath wafted past my parted lips, and a shiver went down my spine. I smelled the mint of the gum he was chewing and a fresh scent of cologne, or maybe shower gel. I swallowed loudly, staring at him hesitantly.

"As far as I know, your parents have no idea what your husband does for a living," he breathed, fixing me with his green eyes, his mouth stretching into a sly smile. "So we're in a similarly difficult situation. Yours may be a bit harder. So let's make a deal. I won't tell your folks your husband is a mobster, and you won't tell Amelia that her brother is a kidnapper and a murderer." He withdrew a fraction, paused, and then got up, offering me a hand.

"Deal?"

I sent him a resigned look, defeated. I shook his hand.

"Deal."

He pulled me up.

His eyes were gleaming with childish glee again as he straightened out his T-shirt.

"Great. Come, then, honeybuns. Amelia is going to want some breakfast." He grabbed my hand and guided me to the door. I tried yanking my arm free, but he tightened his viselike grip. "We're a couple now. Show me some love." We went downstairs, holding hands. Nacho kissed me right on the mouth as soon as his sister noticed our return. That riled me, but I had to keep up appearances. My parents couldn't learn the truth. That was too important to blow our cover right away. I offered the beautiful blue-eyed girl a hand.

She was sitting on one of the bar stools.

"Laura," I introduced myself with a friendly smile. "By the way, your brother is an asshole."

Amelia grinned and nodded, apparently agreeing. She looked just like Nacho when she smiled. The main difference was that she had a head full of hair and no visible tattoos. Her clear-cut, severe features gave her the appearance of someone uppity and stuffy, but the cheerful glint in her eyes belied that.

"My brother *is* an egotistical asshole, isn't he?" She got up and patted him on the back. "He's just like Father, but at least he can cook." She smooched him on the cheek.

They both looked so adorable together. Nothing like stereotypical Spaniards.

"Are you two Spanish?" I asked, a bit confused. "You don't look Spanish."

"Mom was Swedish. Apparently, her genes prevailed."

"And we're not from Spain. We're from the Canary Islands," Nacho corrected. "Now, what do my ladies want to eat?" he asked cheerfully, walking over to the fridge and gesturing for us to sit at the bar.

The siblings spoke in English so I didn't miss anything, even though they weren't talking about anything that might have concerned me. They spoke of Christmas and their friends, who were going to come visit for New Year's Eve. They were very laid-back, which did wonders for the tense atmosphere.

"Your Italian was very impressive, honey," I said at one point without hiding the sarcasm in my voice. "How many languages do you speak?"

"A few," Nacho replied, stirring something in the pan.

"Oh, come now, brother." Amelia turned to me. "Marcelo can speak Italian, English, German, French, and Russian."

"And Japanese, lately," Nacho added, rummaging through the fridge.

That was impressive, but I wasn't going to let that show, so I only nodded sagely and continued listening to their conversation.

Amelia had been right—her brother was a great cook. Ten minutes later, the kitchen counter was filled with food. We both dug in. I only noticed she was pregnant, too, when I saw how much she was eating and noticed her belly.

"How far along?" I nodded to her bump, and she put a hand on it in a gentle gesture.

"A month and a half to go," she replied, smiling radiantly. "His name is going to be Pablo."

I wanted to tell her about my own baby, but noticed Nacho who was shaking his head slightly.

"I hope he takes after his mom," he said, taking a bite of tomato. "His father is an utter dickhead. And a troglodyte. And he looks like an ass."

I snorted with laughter, but immediately reined myself in, apologizing to Amelia. "What? That's the truth. She fell in love with that stick-thin dork. Even worse, he's Italian. I still don't know why Father loves him so much."

I felt my muscles tensing. Spending time with the two siblings wasn't a chore. Far from it. I felt like I was on vacation. But Nacho's words reminded me why I was here. I put down my fork and eyed him.

"I like Italians. They're great people," I said.

Amelia nodded vigorously.

The man leaned over the counter, glaring at me.

"Oh no, dearest. You like Sicilians."

His smirk made me want to come up with a witty riposte.

"You're absolutely right. I *love* them," I retorted, sporting my own sly smirk.

Amelia darted looks at the both of us, finally breaking the awkward silence.

"Want to go for a swim?" she asked her brother, who nodded in response. Then she turned to me. "Shall we go to the beach, then? It's not too hot. We'll sunbathe and watch Marcelo surf."

"Surf?" I was surprised by that revelation.

"Of course. My brother is an international surfing champion. Didn't he tell you?" I shook my head. "Well, then he'll have the opportunity to show off a little. The waves are high, and the wind is perfect." She clapped her hands. "Great! We'll have dinner on the beach. I'll be here at three."

She kissed me on the cheek and then hugged her brother.

"Adios!" she called, disappearing through the door.

Nacho brooded over his plate, his knife clinking against the empty dish.

"We need to talk," I said over the annoying sound. "How long will I be here? You said we would have to wait for your dad, but you didn't tell me when he was going to return. Or why we had to wait in the first place." He didn't respond, but raised his eyes and fixed me with a somber stare. "Please, Marcelo." My eyes teared up, and I bit into my lower lip, trying to keep myself from crying.

"I don't know." He hid his face in his hands, sighing. "I don't have the slightest idea how long I'll have to keep you here. Father ordered me to kidnap you before Christmas, but you know how that ended." He nodded at my tummy. "He had to leave then, and unfortunately he's not the kind of man who tells others of his plans. I'm supposed to keep you here and keep you safe until he gets back. That's all I know."

I dropped my eyes, wringing my hands.

"Safe?" I asked, annoyed.

"You are the very person who's the greatest danger to me right now. And the only threat to you is Massimo coming here and taking me away."

"Your husband has a lot more enemies than he tells you about." He stood up and took the dishes to the washer.

That conversation was taking us nowhere. I returned to my

room, heading for the wardrobe, recalling Amelia's words. The choice of outfits became clear. The colorful T-shirts, flip-flops, hoodies and shorts that had replaced my collection of expensive clothes were the logical choice for a surfer. And Nacho was one. He had probably bought all that himself, picking what he liked best.

I sighed, deciding that it wouldn't do me any good to fight everything all over again. When I had last accepted the situation fate had thrown me into, life had become easier. I grabbed a pair of gray denim shorts, a rainbow-colored bikini, and a white T-shirt with a setting-sun motif, tossed the clothes onto the bed, and went into the bathroom.

I had discovered earlier that there was only one of those in the entire house and that I'd have to share it with that man. Nacho had done his best to ensure my relative comfort. My things were grouped on one side of the sink, while his occupied the other. There wasn't much, but it would be enough to satisfy my most basic needs. A facial cream, a body lotion, a toothbrush, and—this surprised me—my favorite perfume. I lifted the Lancôme Trésor Midnight Rose and glanced at my reflection in the mirror. How had he known?

I brushed my teeth and took a shower. Then I braided my hair and applied some cream to my face. It wouldn't make sense to do any makeup. For starters, I didn't have any cosmetics on hand, and besides, this was a place where I could potentially catch a tan.

A knock brought me back to reality. I threw on a bathrobe that hung by the mirror and walked over to open the door.

"We only have one bathroom," I said, looking at Nacho through the crack. "And only one bathrobe."

He grinned.

"Get a move on."

I closed the door again and returned to my preparations. I did not hurry. Then I walked over to the bed and dressed before taking the stairs down to the living room.

The TV was on. There was an open laptop on the coffee table. For a moment, I listened. The sound of water from the shower upstairs wasn't abating. I had time. I crept closer to the computer and switched it on. My fingers pattered on the tabletop, as if that could make the machine start up faster. The screen asked me to enter the password.

"Fucking shit!" I yelled, slamming the thing shut.

"Careful, it's delicate," I heard behind my back and swore inwardly. "I need something." I turned around and froze.

Nacho was standing before me, completely naked, dripping with water. I should have averted my eyes, but I couldn't. Instead, I swallowed loudly, feeling my throat going dry. With his right hand, Nacho was covering his penis. His left was propped against the glass partition. *I need something.* The words reverberated through my head.

What would happen now? Would he step closer, uncover his manhood, and ram it down my throat? Or maybe he'd fuck me on the kitchen counter, with me lying on my back and taking in the sight of his wonderful tattoos . . .

"You took my bathrobe," he said.

What? In my mind, I slapped myself with all my mental force for cheating on my husband. Even if I'd only imagined doing that. What can I say? I'm a healthy young woman with a raging libido. Being pregnant made me horny all the time, and I'd probably have fucked anyone right in that moment. I ignored what he had said, staring into his eyes. He chuckled and turned around, walking back upstairs. His butt cheeks were tattooed, too. I groaned softly despite my best efforts to keep myself in control, trying in vain to turn my head away.

"I heard that," Nacho called, disappearing upstairs.

I collapsed onto the soft cushions of the couch and buried my face in them. I hated that so many attractive men had so suddenly appeared in my life. Or was it my pregnancy? Maybe they weren't that attractive. How was it possible that the world had become populated by sexy, muscular men all of a sudden? I allowed myself a while to silently despair, before sitting up and grabbing the remote.

I kept switching channels mindlessly, when something dawned on me. My parents already knew what Massimo did for a living! Unless they had somehow missed my disappearance and the Man in Black's rage. I jumped to my feet. That would give me some kind of advantage and a chance to negotiate. I had started making a plan, when I heard steps on the stairs again. Fearing Nacho would still be naked, I kept my eyes fixed ahead. The Spaniard sat down next to me. He wore shorts and a zipped-up hoodie.

"Let's talk," I said. He dropped his head, hiding it in his hands.

"Really? Again? Is there anything we haven't discussed yet?" Two of his fingers spread, and he sent me an amused look.

"My parents already know who Massimo is. The truth must have gotten out when you kidnapped me." I got up from the couch, wagging a finger at him. "Now. Give me a good reason not to tell your sister that you're a hit man. The last one isn't that appealing all of a sudden."

Nacho only leaned back on the sofa, crossing his arms behind his head. "Nice try." He snorted, stifling a fit of laughter. "But I got better."

He snapped up the laptop from the coffee table. He entered the password so quickly, I had no chance of catching it.

"Let's call your mom." He turned the computer around, presenting me with the Facebook login page and leaning in so close I could smell his fantastic, fresh scent. "Log in and learn for yourself what your parents know. Will you take the risk?"

I wasn't sure if he was bluffing, but this was at least a chance to talk to my mom and tell her that I was okay. I typed in the password. Mom was offline.

"If what I know is true, before your husband sent them to the airport, he lied to them about why you couldn't see them off. Klara Biel going to the police would only make his life harder." He took the computer back and switched it off. "Anyway, great talk, but I got to go," he said with a wink. "Remember not to tell my sister too much about our life together."

"How much does she know already?"

"More or less everything, minus the pregnancy. I'm sure she won't notice. But if I'm the only one that doesn't see it, and she really does notice that microscopic belly, keep to what we've discussed. The kid wasn't planned, and as soon as you discovered you were pregnant, you came here. See you around," he finished and grabbed his surfboard from the terrace.

"Wait. How will you explain my sudden disappearance when I finally leave here?" I asked, smirking.

He halted midstep and put on a pair of rainbow-rimmed shades.

"I'll tell her you miscarried."

He grabbed a duffel bag and left.

I stayed on the couch, propping my chin on its backrest, considering the strangeness of my new circumstances. Nacho had an answer to all my questions. His plan was flawless. I wondered how long he had been planning the whole operation. Probably a long time. That made me think of the reason I was really here, in his house. I rolled over to my back, sighing deeply.

What was Massimo doing right now? He had probably killed half of the security personnel for losing me again. That thought would have made my heart race a while ago, but there wasn't anything left in the world that would surprise, scare, or startle me anymore. How many times can a person be kidnapped? How many more strange men would I meet in my life?

I stroked my belly. It was enormous, at least to my eyes.

"Luca," I whispered. "Daddy is going to take us back home in no time. For now, we're on vacation."

At that moment, I heard knocking on the door. Then someone turned a key in the lock. Amelia entered the apartment. "Why do I even knock? I have the keys. Where are your things? Come on!"

"I don't have anything." I grimaced. "I came here . . . Without giving it much thought." I shrugged.

"Okay, come with me, then." She took my hand and led me out.

"There are sunglasses in the car. We'll buy you everything when we get there."

CHAPTER *nineteen*

We left the apartment and walked to the glass-walled elevator that took us to the ground floor. It was dominated by a cavernous main hall, its walls glass just like the elevator's. We passed the receptionist's desk and waited on the pavement in front of the building. A young valet drove a white BMW M6 right to the entrance, stepped out, and waited with the door open until Amelia took the driver's seat. The cherry leather inside was a perfect complement for the bright paint job.

"I hate this car," Amelia said, accelerating. "It's so ostentatious. Though there are many gaudier rides here on Costa Adeje. Including my brother's." She giggled, glancing my way.

Costa Adeje? Where the hell was that? I kept looking out the window as we drove along a picturesque promenade. Amelia continued talking about her family and how they had lost their mother in a car accident. I learned that Amelia was twenty-five and that Marcelo was ten years older. I also learned that she didn't really know what her father did for a living. At least not entirely. And she knew nothing about her brother's real job.

Amelia was very open and talkative. Besides, she must have really thought I was Nacho's great love. She was doing her best to tell me as much about her family as she could in the short time we had during the ride. She was giddy with excitement when she spoke of her father's return from the continent and spending New Year's Eve among friends and family. Which made me realize that she knew when her old man was coming back. And that meant Nacho had lied to me. I nodded politely, never interrupting—hoping I'd catch some more interesting tidbits about the Spanish Mafia.

"We're here," she said finally, parking by a hotel. "I live here when Flavio leaves." I looked at her, raising my brows. "My husband went abroad with my dad, and I like staying close to Marcelo." She started walking toward the entrance. "It's a bit bare over at the beach, so I told the staff to bring us two sunbeds and a couple other things. We'll look like tourists or groupies, but I don't care. I'm not going to let my spine break from fidgeting on the sand, trying to make the baby comfy."

We passed through the hotel, then a garden, another promenade, and finally we reached the beach. The strangest part of the view was that the ocean was calmly undulating along the majority of the coast, but there was a couple-hundred-foot-long section of the beach where the waves were two stories high. A few dozen people were in the water, floating on their surfboards and waiting for the perfect wave. There was something magical in this sight—the sun on the one side, the snowy slopes of the Teide volcano on the other. Small groups of people were clustered on the beach, drinking wine, laughing, and smoking pot. At least I thought that was it—I detested the reek of marijuana.

It wasn't hard to make out the spot prepared for us. Two large, soft sunbeds were standing a little to the side. There was a massive closed sunshade by them, a basket of food, a blanket, and a waiter. Or a bodyguard. I couldn't tell. At least he had the decency to stay a couple of steps back, sitting in a small folding chair. He wasn't wearing an official outfit like the guys back on Sicily, but light linen pants and an unbuttoned shirt. He waved at us, but didn't move from his place, staring into the ocean. Or at us. He wore sunglasses, and I didn't see his eyes.

"Oh, good," Amelia said with a sigh, taking off her clothes and lying down on a sunbed in her bikini.

"Aren't you supposed to avoid the sun when you're pregnant?" I asked, pulling down my shorts.

"Nah, you just have to keep the belly in shade." She covered herself with a thin shawl and sent me a look over her shades. "Pregnancy isn't that bad. Worst-case scenario, I'll get some blemishes. What's with the weird band?" she asked in turn, pointing to my ankle, cuffed with the tracking device.

"It's a long, boring story." I waved a hand at her, reclining on my own sunbed. I shot her a glance and cursed inwardly. Amelia was gaping at me. She noticed.

"Are you pregnant, too?"

I said nothing.

"Is it Marcelo's?"

I stuck a finger in my mouth, biting my nail.

"That's why I'm here," I groaned and closed my eyes, thanking God for the sunglasses on my nose. "I got knocked up back in Poland. When I told him, he kidnapped me and took me here. To care for me and the baby."

I thought I was going to throw up. The lie was too close to the truth. I grabbed a bottle of water.

Amelia was sitting with her mouth open, shocked. An instant later, her lips stretched into a wonderful smile.

"That's marvelous!" she exclaimed. "Our babies are going to be the same age! How far along are you? Four months?" I nodded, not even listening. "Oh, that's so much Marcelo's style! He was always so responsible and caring! When we were kids, he used to . . ."

I had stopped paying her any mind by that time, instead listening to the crashing waves, looking out to the sea and desperately trying to keep my eyes from watering. I missed Massimo. I wanted him to hug me, fuck me, and keep me in his arms forever. I only felt safe with him. There was no one else I wanted to share the happiness of having a baby with. Pretending to be someone else's woman was vile. It disgusted me. What angered me even more was that I was lying to someone sweet and innocent like Amelia for no other reason than to keep someone else's loathsome secrets.

"Here's Marcelo!" she called out, pointing to someone on the water. I followed her finger and saw a man standing on a surfboard. "The one in that horrid teal wet suit." She shivered.

It was abominable, but at least it made him visible. Most other surfers wore gray long-sleeved wet suits. Nacho had his chest bare and those colorful wet suit pants. He zoomed along a wave, reaching out with a hand to keep his balance. His knees were bent as he adjusted his position on the small board, completely unfazed with the gigantic wave breaking over his head.

Everyone looked on in admiration, clapping and cheering, as he suddenly turned and swung into the air, holding his surfboard above him in one hand.

"Wow. I want to learn how to do that," I breathed, stunned by the display.

"The waves are too big today. Besides, I don't think Marcelo would allow you to surf in your state. But you could always try paddleboarding. Even I do that sometimes. Even though I hate salt water."

I turned to the ocean, watching the tattooed, hairless man walking our way with the surfboard under his arm. He looked breathtaking in those tight-fitting pants, his skin dripping with water. If not for the fact that he was a kidnapper and a murderer and I had a husband and was pregnant, I'd have fallen in love with him in that moment.

"Hey there!" He dropped the surfboard and walked over to me. I knew what he was about to do and managed to shake off my stupor and turn my head to the side, so his lips landed on my cheek. He smirked, leaning to my ear. "Nice try," he whispered and turned to his sister.

"Congratulations! You're going to be a dad!" She gave him a great hug. His eyes darted to me. I shrugged.

"I told you it was obvious, but you didn't believe me." I sighed and took a sip of water.

"I'm so happy we're going to have kids the same age," she prattled on, showering him with kisses. "We should throw a party when Dad's back! Or announce it on New Year's Eve! I'm going to get it done! There's not much time, but we'll manage. I'm so happy!"

She fished her phone out of her bag and took a couple of steps away, calling someone.

"Should I tell her or will you?" I took my glasses off and rolled over on the sunbed. "You know what? It's your problem. I won't get involved. And anyway, how can you hurt your sister like that?" He looked at me with a puzzled expression. "Oh yes, you're hurting her. Do you have any idea how she'll feel when I . . .

miscarry? And disappear? She's already treating me like family. You're heartless."

"I kill people for money," he said in a cold, calm manner, right into my ear. "I do not have a heart, Laura." I snapped my head back, looking him in the eyes. His gaze was unsettling. Ice-cold. Now I knew the man kneeling by me on the sand was just what Massimo had said he was. A cold, ruthless, cruel man. "Take some time to sunbathe. I'll go for a swim and we'll go home. You won't see Amelia again."

He grabbed his surfboard and left me alone, jogging toward the sea.

Amelia showed up again. I suggested she hold off her plans for a bit longer, explaining that I had a heart condition, my pregnancy was high-risk, and I could lose the baby at any time. She seemed very worried and a bit upset, but understood why I didn't want to announce anything just yet. I wasn't doing Nacho's work for him. I only wanted to save Amelia the heartbreak. She really did seem like an honest and good person.

Nacho spent another two hours surfing. When the sun was starting to set, he planted his board by our sunbeds and dried off with a towel.

"Shall we have dinner together?" Amelia asked, looking at her brother.

"We're already engaged," he replied. I was getting dressed and Amelia sat wrapped in her thin blanket, watching her sibling with a disappointed expression. It wasn't my fault that she felt this way—it was the Spaniard who should feel guilty. He ignored her pouting and tossed me a hoodie.

"Put it on. It might be cold in the car." We said our goodbyes and walked Amelia to her apartment before going to the parking lot by the beach. Nacho packed the surfboard onto one of his friends' cars and grabbed me by the wrist, pulling me with him along the promenade.

"Aren't you taking it home?"

"I take you or the board. Come," he barked, opening the door to his car.

"What is that?" I asked, gaping at the strangest car I had ever seen.

"A sixty-nine Corvette Stingray." He was annoyed—I could hear that. I got inside the beautiful, black car. It was shiny, very rare, and had tires with white writing. Amelia had been right when she said her brother's car was even more ostentatious than her own. He gunned the engine, which let out a mighty roar. I felt vibrations throughout my entire body. I couldn't help but smile, and the Spaniard noticed.

"The Sicilian probably drives some faggy Ferrari, eh?" He raised his brows, smirking, and stepped on the accelerator.

The colossal V8 rumbled as we drove along the promenade. The sun had set, and I would have felt genuinely happy, if not for the fact that I was in a country I knew nothing about, with a man I didn't like at all. I glanced at Nacho, whose head was bobbing to the rhythm of "I Want to Live in Ibiza" by Diego Miranda. The song flowed gently, and he patted the steering wheel with his fingers, singing under his breath. Here was my captor. A kidnapper and a murderer. Vibing to a song that seemed further away from what I'd consider his style than pretty much anything else. But what was the weirdest was that I just couldn't feel afraid of this man. Even when he tried acting tough or scary, my entire subconscious laughed at him.

◇◇◇◇◇◇◇◇◇◇

We entered the apartment, and Nacho tossed his bag to the floor by the door before grabbing a towel and walking out to the terrace. I didn't really know what to do with myself, so I just sat by the kitchen bar and nibbled on some grapes. Amelia had been eating throughout our stay on the beach, and I had accompanied her. I had no room left for dinner.

"You lied to me. Why?" I said finally, as I recalled what his sister had told me in the car.

Nacho returned to the room, leaned against the counter, practically lying on it, and smiled.

"Which lie are you talking about?"

"Are there so many?" I left the grapes alone.

"Pretty much all of it. The situation made lying a necessity."

"Amelia told me when your father will return. It seems kind of strange that you don't know. Aren't you supposed to work for him?" He grinned. "Why did you lie to me, Marcelo?"

"You know what? I think I like it better when you call me Nacho." He turned to the fridge and opened it. "You'll be free in two days, yes. Probably."

"Probably?"

"There's always the possibility that the volcano will explode and your Sicilian prince won't come." He grabbed a bottle of beer. "Or I kill him and you stay with me forever."

Dumbstruck by his words, I didn't say anything for a long time. Nacho stayed silent, too, sipping on his beer and watching me closely.

"Good night," I managed finally.

"You didn't say no!" he called after me as I walked to the stairs. "Good night!"

I shut the bedroom door and leaned my back against it, blocking the way in. My heart was pounding, and my hands had this strange tingling sensation. What was happening to me? I hid my face in my hands, trying to calm down. I wanted to cry, but my eyes wouldn't tear up. After what seemed like minutes of inaction, I gathered up the courage to leave my room again and go to the shower. I endured the steady stream of cold water until my body stopped acting up. Only then did I properly wash myself and apply lotion. I did all that in a hurry, afraid I'd run into Nacho at some point, but thankfully managed to avoid him. I got into bed, cuddled up to a pillow, and stayed still for a long time, thinking about my husband and all the wonderful moments we had spent together. I wanted to dream about him. Better yet, I wanted him to be there when I woke up.

Steps. I woke to the sound of steps in the bedroom. I was afraid to open my eyes, though my mind was telling me it was Nacho, creeping to my bed. I had rolled down the blinds before going to sleep, and the room was completely dark. The floorboards creaked softly once more, and I stiffened, waiting for the Spaniard's next move. After his admission from last evening, I could only imagine what he wanted from me. Half-awake, I frantically tried coming up with ways to deal with what would inevitably happen in a moment. All the muscles in my body tensed, as I heard Nacho's breathing in the dead silence. He was close. Immobile, as if waiting for something. Then I heard sounds of a struggle.

Terrified, I jumped out of bed, scrambling away from the source of the sound, reaching for the lamp. I flicked the switch, but it didn't work. My heart was racing. I crawled behind the bed and kept on crawling until I hit the wall. The sounds of fighting weren't dying down. Was I about to die? My hand slid across the wall, searching for the wardrobe door. I huddled inside the small dressing room, beneath the rows of hangers, pulling my legs to my chest. I was so afraid. The worst thing was, I had no idea what was happening. My forehead rested on my knees as my body started rocking back and forth. Suddenly, the sounds abated. I saw the pale beam of a flashlight and felt nauseous.

"Laura!" Nacho's cry finally made my eyes water. "Laura!"

I tried responding, but didn't manage to make a sound. My throat was too tight for that. That's when the door slid open and a pair of arms picked me up. I huddled against Nacho's neck, breathing in his fresh scent as my body began to tremble.

"Your heart pills. You need them?" he asked, sitting me down on the bed.

I shook my head and ran my eyes across the room, illuminated with the flashlight. It was wrecked. The lamp had been broken and thrown to the floor, the candles scattered, the rug ripped, the curtains torn. And there was a body on the floor. My head swam. I turned my head and threw up. I was dying. After a moment, the convulsions stopped, and I collapsed on the bed, lifeless.

Nacho grabbed a blanket and wrapped me in it, taking my wrist and checking my pulse. Then he carried me downstairs and switched on the lights.

"It's all right now." His strong arms were wrapped around me, giving me at least the semblance of safety.

"He's . . . dead," I stammered, sobbing. "Dead."

Nacho's hands stroked my hair and I felt his lips on my head as we rocked on the couch.

"He was about to kill you," he whispered. "I'm not sure if there's more of them. The alarm's been cut. I need to take you away from here. You'll go to Amelia. Tell her we had a fight. I'll come get you when I know what's going on." He rose, lifting me and placing me on the kitchen counter. "Father's security staff has her apartment under constant surveillance. Nobody will look for you there. Hey, I told you I'm here to keep you safe. Be back in a sec."

I wanted to stop him, but couldn't speak. I was too drained to ask him to stay. It felt like I was still asleep and everything that had just happened had been a nightmare. I rolled to my side, laying my head on the cold counter. Tears streaked down my cheeks. They cleared my head and calmed my breathing.

Nacho returned after a while, dressed in a dark sweat suit. Before he zipped up his hoodie, I noticed the harness with two guns beneath it. I didn't move or make a sound, even when he tried asking me things.

"You're in shock, Laura, but it will pass." He let out a cry of helplessness. "You can't go to my sister in that condition. Come with me." He took me in his arms again, wrapping me tightly in the same blanket, and carried me outside the apartment, slamming the door shut behind us.

As he took the elevator to the garage, he placed me on the floor. He unzipped his hoodie, took out his guns, and cocked one. The route was clear. Nacho took me in his arms, carried me to the car, and buckled me in. The engine roared and the Corvette shot out of the garage.

I don't know how long we drove. I remember hearing the Spaniard talking on the phone several times, but I didn't know Spanish, just like I didn't know Italian. I had no idea what he was saying. I felt him checking my pulse every once in a while, flicking my hair from my forehead to check if I was still alive. I think I must have looked like I had died—completely numb and staring ahead without blinking.

"Come to me," he said when we stopped, taking me in his arms again and starting to walk.

At first I could only see the sand. Then the ocean. Finally, a small house on the beach. He walked up the three steps to the veranda and entered the building. I closed my eyes, feeling the touch of a soft mattress under my back. And then Nacho's arm wrapping itself around me. I fell asleep.

"Make love to me." The sound of his voice was an invitation. "Make love to me, Laura."

The colorful, tattooed hands explored my naked body as the first rays of the sun illuminated the room. Through half-closed eyelids, I saw slender fingers tightening on my naked breasts. I moaned and spread my legs as he slid between them. Our lips met for the first time, and his soft, delicate mouth brushed against mine. He didn't use his tongue. He wrapped his lips over mine, delighting in the taste of me. That was slow torture, but also turned me on, making my underbelly buzz with excitement. I needed to let loose, defuse the tension inside me. His hips rubbed against my thigh, and I felt his hard, ready manhood. Our fingers entwined and tightened. I slid my tongue into his mouth, and he returned the kiss. He was subtle, gentle, and sensitive. I lifted my hips slightly. He didn't wait for another sign. I felt him entering my wet pussy. I cried out, but my voice was stifled by his kiss. His body tensed. His face hovered above my neck, biting, licking, kissing, as he leisurely moved inside me . . . *Nacho* . . .

"Either you're having a bad dream or a very good one." I heard his warm voice and opened my eyes.

He was lying next to me, half-awake, with that charming smile on his face. His eyes closed and he rolled onto his back, taking his hand away.

"So. A good one or bad?"

I didn't respond.

"A good one, I'd wager. Me or Massimo?" he asked, opening one green eye.

He watched me, gauging my reaction.

"You," I breathed. He hesitated, taken aback.

"Was I good?" he asked, allowing a grin to form on his lips.

"Gentle," I whispered, rolling to my back. "Very gentle." I stretched. It was quiet for a while. I closed my eyes, slowly shrugging off the dream. Suddenly, the pleasant images vanished, replaced by a recollection of last night's events. It felt as if someone had punched me in the gut. My breath stuck in my throat. There had been a dead man in my bedroom. I swallowed. When I opened my eyes, I saw Nacho hovering above me.

"Everything all right?" he asked, taking my wrist again.

"How did you know that man wanted to kill me?"

I stared into his eyes as he counted the passing seconds.

"Maybe because I found him by your bed with a syringe of something that would cause you to die of a massive heart attack? They were going to make it look natural."

He released my hand and brushed the hair off my forehead. "Did you know that man?"

"How did you see anything in the darkness? And what were you doing in my room?" I asked.

"That numbskull went to my room first. Amateur." Nacho shook his head. "So when he left and I was still alive, I knew it was about you. I got my night-vision goggles and went after him. Did you recognize him?"

"I don't remember," I replied. He reached for his phone and showed me a photo of the dead body. I nearly fainted.

"I-i-it's Rocco," I stammered, covering my mouth with a hand. "Massimo's bodyguard. Is my husband trying to kill me?" My eyes watered.

I couldn't believe that. I wouldn't.

"While I'd love that to be the case, I don't think so. Someone bribed him. I'll get to the bottom of this." He got out of bed and stretched, went to the window, and opened it, letting in a waft of fresh ocean air. "If you'd died, it would have meant all-out war. I believe the people who ordered Rocco to kill you were my father's enemies."

I jumped to my feet and faced him, suddenly buzzing with anger.

"I thought you said nobody could get here without your father's say-so!" I hissed. "You were supposed to know everything that happened here. You know nothing!" I balled my fists and spun on my heels, storming out of the room and outside the house.

I sat on the steps leading to the beach and cried.

Despaired, more like.

I wailed like a wounded animal, slammed my fists on the wooden boards until the pain was too much.

And then, Nacho appeared. He wore a wet suit and had his surfboard under his arm. He passed by me and went straight toward the water. I piped down, staring at his back as he plunged into the waves.

The audacity!

As soon as a conversation had gone the wrong way, he'd just run. Or maybe there was something that he didn't want me to know.

I went back inside and made myself a cup of tea, sitting by the table and scanning the room with weary eyes.

It was a large, open space—a dining room with a kitchen annex plus a living room with a massive fireplace and a large flat-screen TV above it. The décor was minimalist, but the earthy colors made it feel comfortable, homelike. A surfboard was propped against the wall by the door. Another one stood in the corner of the dining room. I looked around and discovered there were more of them. Hanging from the walls or lined up on a rack.

Some of them—the older ones—had been transformed into furniture. There were colorful rugs on the floor, giving the space some much-needed life, and the large, soft sofas looked very inviting. The windows on three walls overlooked the ocean. The house was also surrounded by a wide terrace.

I got up and went to the kitchen, opening the fridge.

It was full.

Had Nacho planned everything?

I helped myself to cold cuts, cheese, eggs, and some other things, preparing a hearty breakfast. When it was ready, I ate and then went in search of the bathroom. It was right next to the bedroom where we had slept. I took a shower and wrapped myself in a towel before going to check out the wardrobe by the bed. The contents were neatly arranged. I grabbed one of Nacho's colorful T-shirts and put it on before going back to the bathroom. I needed to brush my teeth, but there was only a single toothbrush on the counter. I looked everywhere, but had to admit defeat.

"There's only one." I turned around and saw Nacho, dripping with water, standing in the doorway with only his boxers on. They were white. And wet. And completely translucent. He stepped closer as I turned back to the sink, stepping right behind me.

"We'll have to share," he said cheerfully, and the intense look of his green eyes in the mirror finally made it possible for me to tear my own stare away from his crotch.

I turned the tap on and started brushing my teeth, avoiding his gaze.

"Like a married couple," he added, amused. I raised my eyes and saw him enter the shower cubicle. Naked.

The toothbrush fell out of my gaping mouth and hit the stone surface of the counter. A trickle of minty foam dribbled down my chin. I fixed my eyes on the black granite of the sink and rinsed my mouth. My mind was working frantically, trying to come up with an elegant way to extricate myself from this absurd situation. I put the toothbrush back in its place and went straight to the door. My hand was already on the doorknob when the sound of running water died down.

"Do you know why you're running from me?" he asked, and I heard the tapping of his feet on the floor. "You're afraid." I snorted and turned his way. He was right there, just a few inches away.

"Of you?" I smirked, looking him straight in the eyes as he wrapped his hips with a towel. I was silently thanking God that he'd covered his dick.

"Of yourself." He raised his brows and leaned closer to me. "You don't trust yourself, so you prefer to avoid things that feel more and more enticing."

I took a step back, but he followed. With each inch I retreated, my panic was growing. A couple more steps and I'd hit the door. My back touched the wooden surface. I was trapped. The two of us stood immobile, looking at each other as our breathing quickened.

"I'm pregnant," I said dumbly. He shrugged.

Nacho's arms landed on the wall on both sides of my head. His face drew closer to mine. The gaze of his sunny green eyes pierced me to my core, making me shiver.

The uncomfortable silence was broken by the sound of the ringing phone. I shifted slightly, making way for Nacho to leave and pick it up. He went outside and sat in a sofa chair by the door and accepted the call, putting on a pair of surfing shorts.

"Tomorrow," he growled, his jovial manner replaced with a grim frown as he tossed the cell phone away. "The Sicilians will come tomorrow." He paused for a long while before reaching out with a hand, palm held upward. "Pass me the yogurt." I obliged, and he took the bowl of white stuff.

I plopped down on a chair, stunned. Inside, I felt giddy excitement. *I'll see Massimo tomorrow! He'll take me in his arms and carry me away from here!* I exploded with glee, jumped to my feet, hugged Nacho briefly, and started to run around like a maniac. The Spaniard shook his head, pouring the yogurt over a bowl of cereal. I zoomed through the door and sprinted outside to the cool sand, jumping around like crazy and finally collapsing to the ground and staring into the cloudless sky.

He'll come for me and make all this go away. But would that be so easy? I sat up and looked at the house, watching Nacho as he ate his breakfast, leaning against the door frame, with nothing but his surfing shorts on. His posture was relaxed, and he slowly chewed his food, keeping his eyes on me. Would I be able to just . . . go back to normal now? After meeting this child in a man's body?

We stared at each other, unable to peel our eyes away. My belly grumbled. I put both hands to it, stroking, calming the baby down. This was the first time my son had done that. I stood up, patted the sand off my skin, and went back to the veranda.

"Care for a swim?" Nacho smiled, putting his bowl down. "I'll teach you how to paddleboard. Amelia told me you wanted to try it." He placed his hands on my shoulders and squeezed. "You're perfectly safe. Don't worry. Nothing is going to hurt you two."

He had never mentioned the baby when referring to me before. I looked him in the eyes. He nodded slowly, with a smile on his face.

"I don't have a swimsuit." I shrugged apologetically.

"That's not a problem. There's nobody around."

I shook my head, scowling.

"You can paddleboard in your everyday clothes. Or a wet suit. I'll go grab you one. Besides, I've already seen you naked!" he called out, disappearing in the house.

I froze, rooted to the spot, suddenly disconcerted, and wondered when. When had he seen me naked? I stepped inside, rubbing at my temples, thinking.

"The first night," he said, reading my mind. "What? I didn't know you weren't wearing any underwear!" He hung the wet suit on the backrest of the chair next to mine. "You have a sweet pussy," he added with a smile, leaning over me briefly, before walking into the kitchen.

"This isn't funny." I shot up, pointing a finger at him. "Not funny at all, Marcelo."

He placed a pile of dishes in the sink and turned to face me, crossing his arms.

"Who said it was supposed to be funny?" He narrowed his eyes, paused, and then closed the distance between us in one great leap. He wrapped his arms around me before I could react. "I couldn't look away. You were unconscious, but you were so wet."

His green eyes scanned my face. He brushed his lips against the tip of my nose. "You were asleep after what I gave you, but I made you come. I fucked you until morning. You're very tight," he said, pushing me back until I touched the fridge. "I put it inside you slowly. Softly. That's why I was like that in your dream." He rubbed his crotch on my hip.

I listened, saying nothing, feeling a rising wave of petrifying fear. It was staggering, what he said. I froze, unable to move a muscle. My eyes watered. I had cheated on my husband. Not consciously, of course, but the fact remained. I wasn't pure anymore. And his son had been . . . defiled. Massimo would die if he discovered that.

Another wave of fear washed over me. And another, and even more, until I felt weak, about to faint. Nacho must have noticed my expression, because he released me and took a step back.

"I'm a pretty good liar, eh?" He grinned. I swore I was going to kill him then. He didn't manage to duck this time, as my open palm swung through the air and slammed into his cheek. His head jerked back.

"You are," I growled, snatching the wet suit from the chair and stomping off to the bathroom.

I put on a sleeveless shirt and the tight-fitting wet suit over it. I couldn't believe how easy it had been for him to string me along. I swore under my breath, hitting things at random.

Still shaking my head in disbelief, I stopped by the mirror and unzipped the wet suit, freeing the upper half of my body. In my fury, I had sweated through my shirt already. I styled my hair into two French braids and smeared some cream over my face. *What a dick*, I thought, snorting.

Nacho was spreading some paste over two surfboards on the veranda. He had his gaudy teal wet suit on. The sight of his little butt made me seriously consider giving him a humongous kick in the ass. By way of punishment.

"Don't even think of it," he said as I raised my leg, making me halt midswing. "Start waxing."

I knelt beside him, took a small puck of wax, and started repeating his movements.

"Why are we doing this?" I asked.

"So you don't fall off. I don't have surfing shoes for you, and we don't want to take any risks." He paused, turning my way. "But you can swim, can't you?"

I screwed up my face. He laughed.

"I've trained to become a lifeguard," I announced, raising my head proudly.

"The only person here that needs guarding is you," he retorted and propped the board up. "That's enough. Ready for your lesson?"

He grabbed both boards and headed toward the coast.

"There are a few things you need to remember," he said when we reached the water.

There wasn't much theory, as the activity we were about to embark on wasn't too complicated.

The ocean was calm, but Nacho explained that waves could come without warning and vanish equally unexpectedly. Just like the wind. The water around the Canary Islands was predictable enough, and I was sure I'd quickly tame it. Unlike Nacho himself.

Anyway, after a couple of accidental falls into the salty ocean, I finally got the hang of paddleboarding. My eyes stung and I felt like throwing up after gulping down a mouthful of water, but I was proud of myself and felt happy. Nacho didn't rush me, paddling right next to me, and I watched the play of his muscles under his skin.

"Bend your knees and try not to position your board parallel to the waves." He just managed to say that when an unexpected wave washed over the side of my board and I landed in the water again.

This time, I panicked. I fell in pretty deep and lost my bearings. Which way was up? I tried swimming, but another wave rolled over me and I spun.

Suddenly, I felt a pair of strong hands slide around my chest and pull me toward the surface. I coughed as Nacho threw me over my board.

"You all right?" he asked with real worry in his voice, and I nodded faintly. "We're going back to the beach."

"No, no. Let's stay," I managed between coughs. "I like it, and I've wanted to try it for a long time."

I crawled over the board and sat astride it, looking at the Spaniard as he floated next to me with uncertainty in his eyes. The sun was shining warmly, and the beautiful sight of the long, black-sand beaches made me feel so carefree.

"Please." I made the cutest face I could muster, but it didn't seem to work. "You owe me for that vile lie!"

I got up and smacked him with the paddle.

Nacho laughed and jumped on his own board, pulling away.

"Are you sure it was a lie?" he asked when he was far enough that I couldn't reach him with my paddle. "You have a small scar on you right butt cheek. Looks like a burn. How did you get it?"

I wobbled on my board, nearly falling off again. How the hell did he know about that? I definitely hadn't shown it to him, and I only wore those cotton boxers all the time. He didn't have anything else in his drawer. I started paddling furiously, trying to catch up to Nacho, but he quickly escaped me. We played like that for some time, happy like children, chasing each other, until I felt just how exerting this sport really was. I decided to swim back to the beach.

I unbuckled the board from my ankle and left it in the water as I stepped out of the sea. I unzipped the wet suit and pulled it halfway down, and when I reached the veranda I got rid of it altogether, hanging it on a peg on the wall.

Nacho followed me, lugging both boards. He stopped by the house, leaning them against the railing. He lifted his head, and I saw his smirk vanish from his face, replaced with an expression I hadn't seen yet. I took a look around, wondering what shocked him so much, finally looking down and realizing my mistake. I'd had only that white sleeveless shirt under the wet suit. When it got wet, it became completely translucent.

"Start running," Nacho said coldly, his wild green eyes fixed on my erect nipples.

I took a step back and he followed me at a run. I rounded a corner and started running. His hand clamped around my wrist as he pulled me to him. Then his tongue slipped past my lips before I could react. He released my hand and instead put his hands on my cheeks, kissing me deeply and passionately. Why wasn't I trying to defend myself? I didn't want to. I couldn't. Maybe I just wanted it as much as he did. My hands dangled along my sides, and I found that my tongue returned the kiss, as did my lips. Seconds passed, and I didn't retreat, standing with my head raised, allowing myself to be kissed and feeling a wave of lust rising inside me. That finally sobered me up. I clenched my teeth. Nacho stopped, our foreheads touching. He screwed his eyes shut.

"I'm sorry. I couldn't help myself," he breathed, his voice drowned out by a gust of wind.

"I can see that," I replied, exasperated. "Let me go."

He took his hands away, and I turned my back on him, heading to the door. My knees were shaking, and the pangs of guilt that appeared immediately took my breath away. What was I doing? I was alone with a murderer in the middle of nowhere, cheating on my loving husband, who was probably mad with worry by now.

I took my clothes off in the bedroom, closing the door first, and putting on a pair of boxers and a shirt I found in the closet. Then I got into bed, covering myself with the sheets, head included. I felt the salty water trickling from my hair to my face.

The sound of the doorknob being turned made my breath catch. I listened.

"Everything all right?" Nacho asked, staying in the doorway.

I murmured something in assent and heard the door close again. I fell asleep.

It was sunset when I woke up again. I wrapped myself in a blanket and left the room. The house was empty, but I thought I could hear quiet sounds of a guitar playing outside. I passed the threshold and saw Nacho, standing by a grill, sipping a beer. He was wearing loose, torn denim trousers. They kept slipping off his butt, displaying the white Calvin Klein boxers underneath. A small bonfire was dancing next to him, and a Bluetooth speaker was playing "I See Fire" by Ed Sheeran.

"I was just about to wake you up," the Spaniard said, putting down the bottle. "I made dinner."

I wasn't sure if I wanted to talk to him right now, but my growling stomach told me I had no other choice. I took a seat on a sofa chair nearby and pulled up my knees, covering myself with my blanket.

Nacho moved a small table and another chair so that we sat facing each other. I looked around and nodded. This was beginning to look like a proper romantic dinner. There was bread seared over the fire, olives, tomatoes, and pickled onions. The table was illuminated by candles. Nacho placed a plate before me, and grabbed another for himself.

"Bon appétit," he said.

The smell of grilled fish, squid, and other delicacies brought out the demon in me. I cared nothing for *savoir vivre* and devoured my dinner, tearing myself great chunks of the delicious bread and following each bite with olives.

"This is my private retreat," Nacho said, glancing about. "This is where I go when I want to escape the world. I'd live here if I could." He paused. "With someone . . ."

I lifted my eyes and observed as the Spaniard's eyes changed under my scrutiny.

"He'd never know," Nacho added. His smiled had vanished as he leaned back in his chair. "It's only you and me."

I raised a hand to cut him off.

"I'm not interested," I said, which was a lie, but I managed to sound convincing, I think. "I love Massimo. He's the love of my life and nobody will ever replace him. I can't wait for Luca to be born. Massimo will kill you all if you try to take me away from him." I nodded vigorously, but it only seemed to amuse him.

"Tell me, where is he now?" He raised his brows, waiting for an answer. With none forthcoming, he continued, "I'll tell you where your beloved husband is. He's off making money. Because, you see, what Massimo Torricelli loves the most is *money*. Not you, you poor, naive girl. He came up with that ridiculous vision and embroiled you in his fucked-up life out of sheer egoism. Were you ever kidnapped before you met him?" He leaned in closer and waited for a reaction. "I thought not," he said, hearing nothing in reply. "What's more, he couldn't even properly care for what he took responsibility for. But if you'd like, I can dispel your doubts."

He narrowed his eyes. "The decision is yours. I can show you materials that will show your husband in a different light. You are not going to lie to yourself any longer. Your life with him is one big lie. I can show it all to you. If you just ask."

"Listening to you makes me want to throw up," I growled and got up. "You don't have anything that would make me love Massimo any less."

I spun around and stormed off, heading to the door. Before

I went inside, I turned my head and called out, scowling, "And you're not better than him! You've kidnapped me, blackmailed me, and now you think that what? I'll fall in love with you?"

He watched me for a long while, saying nothing, but then his expression changed abruptly, and that familiar smile crept across his face. He clasped his hands behind his head.

"Me? No. I just wanted to fuck you."

He wiggled his eyebrows.

I stretched out a hand and gave him the finger, passing through the door.

"You're a fucking bastard," I told him in Polish. "A piece of trash."

I muttered some more obscenities and finally calmed down enough to take a shower and go to my bedroom, locking the door behind me.

CHAPTER
twenty

The next day, we ate breakfast and headed back to town. Nacho took dozens of calls but didn't speak to me at all, not counting the bark of "Let's go" when he was ready to leave. We drove into the underground garage of the apartment block, and I recalled the night I was attacked.

"What about Rocco?" I asked, staying in the car.

"You didn't think I just left him there, did you?"

He slammed the door and went to the elevator.

I felt sick as he was turning the key in the lock and passing the threshold. It was getting difficult to breathe, and I couldn't follow him inside. Nacho snapped his head back and saw me standing in the doorway. He grabbed my arm.

"The house is safe. My people cleaned up." He pulled me inside.

"I need to change. Then we'll go to my father. I advise you to change clothes, too." He disappeared upstairs.

I followed him, but slowly, taking the steps one at a time, afraid of what I'd see on the upper floor. Nacho wouldn't be so cruel as to leave a dead body in my room. Would he?

I grabbed the handle, feeling my stomach cramp. The door opened a fraction, and I peeked inside. Everything was in perfect order, and the strangled Sicilian was gone. I went to the closet and rummaged through it to find something more appropriate. After almost a week, I was about to see my beloved. I wanted to look dignified, like the wife of don Torricelli instead of a tattooed surfer's girlfriend. It wasn't easy. My choices were shorts or . . . shorts. Eventually, I managed to fish out something less gaudy. It was a pair of faded gray jeans and a white long-sleeved shirt. I also pulled on a pair of loafers and styled—though that wasn't saying much—my hair. There was some mascara in the bathroom. I was also happy to see that my skin had gained some color in the sun, as there was no foundation to see anywhere.

"Let's go. Get your ass moving!" I heard from downstairs.

I took a last glance at the room, checking if I had left anything. I know—that was totally irrational. I hadn't brought anything, because this wasn't a vacation. I had been kidnapped. I went to the lower floor and froze on the penultimate step. In the middle of the living room stood Nacho. In a suit. His tanned skin and clean-shaven head looked perfect with the white shirt and black suit jacket. He kept one hand in his pocket and the other by his ear, holding a phone. He turned to me and looked me up and down. That outfit looked strange on him, but it was a nice change, and—it had to be said—it made that arrogant prick look handsome as hell.

"You look nice," he said, trying to keep himself from smiling. He failed.

"Well, right back at you," I replied, returning the smile.

"Let's go already. I need you out of my life," he said, forcing himself to adopt a more impassive expression.

I crumpled my face. I knew he was just pretending, but those words still reverberated in my head, ruining my mood.

He didn't think that, but he wanted me to think that it was just business for him.

Something dawned on me then—I had grown to like this man. Despite all his flaws, mainly the most jarring one—that he was a murderer—I did like him.

On the one hand, I was glad Massimo would take me away, but on the other I couldn't bear the thought that I'd never see Nacho again. If I was to overlook one little detail—that he had kidnapped me—I was losing a friend. A man that impressed me and who I had very much in common with. A man that could make me smile or rage in fury, but most important, a man I liked to spend time with. It had only been a week, but I had grown close to him. That happens when you spend all your time with someone.

The Corvette sped down the highway and I thanked God the Spaniard had closed the roof. Otherwise, my hair would have already been in complete disarray. We climber higher and higher up the slope of the mountain, and the road became narrower and more curvy. Suddenly, the car stopped.

"Come on, I'll show you something," Nacho said, stepping out of the car. He grabbed my hand and led me to the edge. "Los Gigantes," he said. "The name of the town comes from those tall cliffs. They're almost two thousand feet high in some places. When you swim up to them, you really see how enormous they are."

I watched and listened, enchanted.

"There are whales and dolphins in those waters. I also wanted to show you the volcano. Teide. But—"

"I'll miss you," I whispered, cutting in. He froze. "It's just so unfair that I met you in those circumstances. We could have been friends," I said without any regrets. He pulled in closer. I felt his heart racing.

"You could stay," he breathed.

He lifted my chin, making me look at him. I closed my eyes.

"Look at me, baby girl." His words ripped me apart. That was what Massimo used to call me. My eyes welled up with tears that streaked down my cheeks. I pushed my hand into Nacho's pocket and pulled out his sunglasses. I put them on, hiding behind the mirrored lenses, and went back to the car, saying nothing more.

The house of Fernando Matos was a fortress. It was perched on a rock, overlooking the ocean. Unconquered. There was an expansive garden hidden behind a tall wall. It was more a park than a garden, though. Colorful, squawking parrots sat on tree branches, and there was a lake filled with fish. I had no idea how large the whole thing was, but if I had thought the mansion in Taormina was big, now I knew better.

Nacho parked the car by the entrance, passing several armed men stationed along the driveway. I stepped out hesitantly, unsure of how I should behave, before walking up to the Spaniard. Two goons appeared in the door. They took positions behind me. Nacho told them something in an irritated voice, and then started shouting. The two men dropped their heads but didn't relent. Nacho grabbed my elbow and pulled me toward the monumental mansion.

"What's going on?" I asked, disoriented.

"They want to take you. My work is finished."

He was serious. And angry. "I won't let them take you away from me." My stomach cramped. "I'll take you to my father personally."

We walked into the mansion and across an enormous hall,

which ended in a great door. The room behind it was massive, too, with tall windows overlooking the ocean. Nothing obstructed the view. This part of the fortress floated in the air, situated on an overhang of the cliff. The view was breathtaking and terrifying at the same time. I didn't even notice the rest of the room until I heard a voice behind me. It was heavily accented.

"So it's you!"

I spun on my heel and saw an older, long-haired man standing by Nacho. He looked a lot more Spanish, or Canarian, as the locals liked to be referred to, than Nacho. His skin was dark, and so were his eyes. The man was elderly, but it was apparent that years back he had been very handsome. He wore cream-colored pants and a shirt of the same hue.

"Fernando Matos," he said, placing a kiss on the back of my palm. "Laura Torricelli, the woman who tamed the beast. Please, have a seat."

He gestured me to an armchair, taking a seat in another one. Nacho nervously poured himself a glass of some colorless beverage from a carafe on the desktop, before taking off his jacket, unveiling the harness and two guns. He downed the glass and poured another one. He then sat on the couch and started turning the glass between his fingers.

"I'm very grateful for your hospitality, sir, but I'd like to go home now," I said in a calm and cultured voice. "Nacho has been a wonderful host, but if you're finished with your games, I would like to—"

"I heard you were loudmouthed," Fernando interrupted me, pushing himself back to his feet. "Unfortunately, my dear, your husband didn't grace us with his presence. I heard his plane didn't take off." He spread his arms and turned to his son. "Leave us, Marcelo."

Nacho got up and downed his drink, placing the glass on the desktop, grabbed his jacket, and left the cavernous room obediently. He didn't look at me. I was alone and afraid. The man facing me now was an enigma. The one that had left had at least given me an illusion of safety.

"Your husband treated me like a nobody!" the old man roared when the door closed. He propped his arms on both sides of my shoulders. "And one of you is going to pay for that!"

Suddenly, the door to the room opened again, but I wasn't able to turn my head. I was rooted to the spot, terrified. Fernando left my field of view and greeted somebody. Their conversation was in Spanish. I only understood one word. "Torricelli." Then the voices died down and I heard the *clank* of the lock. I was alone. I sighed with relief.

"You stupid bitch!"

A large, meaty hand landed on my head, grabbing my hair and pulling me to my feet before thrusting me onto the floor.

I fell and hit my head on the edge of the coffee table. Blood streaked down my face. I touched my temple and raised my eyes.

A man the age of Nacho was standing above me. His glare was full of disgust. With a strangely stiff hand he patted down his hair, before taking a step toward me. I kicked out with my legs, trying to scamper away, but didn't manage to escape his own powerful kick.

His foot pistoned into my side.

I wrapped my hands around my belly, desperately trying to protect my baby from the maniac attacking me. My head swam, and my ears rang, but I knew I couldn't black out. What had I done to this man? I was clueless.

"Get up, bitch!" he roared, taking a seat in the armchair.

I swallowed, pushing myself up on shaky hands, but did as he commanded. The man gestured me to the other chair.

"Remember me?" he asked when I sat down.

I wiped the blood from my face.

"No," I muttered.

"So maybe you remember Nostro?" I raised my eyes, frowning. "A club in Rome. Several months ago. It doesn't surprise me that you don't. Like all other whores, you were hammered."

A bleary image of that night flashed through my mind.

"Remember that, bitch?!" He launched himself to his feet and slammed a fist into my face. He raised his one hand in front of my eyes, holding me by the hair with the other. "Your bastard of a man shot my hands through!" His palms had identical, circular scars on them.

That's why I remembered. The Nostro, late evening. I had finished my pole dance, and one of the men there thought I was a hooker. He grabbed me, and then Massimo . . . I covered my mouth with both hands. Massimo had shot his hands through.

"The right hand will never be fully functional again. And the left is completely useless." The man looked at his hands for a while, turning them around. "Humiliated because of a whore!" he snapped. "I've been thinking what I'd do to you for a long time. But I decided to off that motherfucker instead. Your husband."

He punched me again and I felt my lip bursting. Blood seeped down my chin. *He's going to kill me!* I huddled in the armchair.

"At first, I sent that idiot Anna to kill you, but even though she's a very good driver, she wasn't able to ram you off the road." The man leaned over me.

"I didn't want to drag Mr. Matos into this. I wanted to deal with you myself, but that bitch fell for one of the damned

Torricellis." He slammed a hand into the backrest of my chair and I squeezed my eyes shut in terror. "Luckily, before that I managed to set her brother against Massimo. She told him Massimo had killed her unborn child. I met Emilio myself and told him your beloved husband had a little too much to drink one time and boasted of making Anna abort her baby. That made things appropriately tense."

He paced the room with a satisfied smirk on his face, speaking as if it were any funny story you could tell your friends over a dinner table. "Then it got even better. They tried killing each other. Unfortunately, Massimo got lucky again. But at least he got rid of Emilio for me, and this allowed Matos to take over part of Naples."

The man paused, pouring himself a glass of the same colorless beverage Nacho had had, though his hands were stiff and it took him some time.

My head hurt, but at least the blood had congealed and wasn't streaking down my face anymore. I felt my lip swelling, but all I could think of was my baby.

"What are you going to do to me?" I asked, trying to sound fearless.

The man rose from his seat slowly, strolled toward me, and unexpectedly shot out with his arm, punching me again in the same spot. My mouth burst in a cascade of blood. I cried out in pain.

"Don't interrupt me, you bitch!" he roared, wiping his hand on my shirt, before taking a seat again. "You can scream all you want here. The room is soundproof. If I shot you, nobody would hear it."

A triumphant smile appeared on his face. He basked in his victory for a while, before continuing, "I watched Massimo and finally realized nothing would hurt him more than losing you. And that's good, because you're the reason I can barely hold a glass of water on my own." He raised his right, stiff hand. "I had to learn to use my hand. But my condition is so bad, I can't do a lot of things without help. I had to order a special gun. But, as you see, my hands are still good for some things," he said, laughing morbidly. "Before I kill you, I intend to cause you so much pain, you're going to puke out that little bastard you're carrying."

The ringing in my ears intensified. I prayed for the strength to survive this. The spot beneath my sternum cramped painfully. I couldn't think clearly with all that pain and fear.

"And since your husband decided not to come, afraid for his own life, I'll record our night together for him." He stroked my leg, and I jerked back.

"And then I'll send him that brat of yours packed in a nice box." He nodded at my abdomen, smiling horribly.

"By the way, I didn't think Marcelo would find his task so easy. We tried kidnapping you before, but Massimo kept you safe each time. My people caused fights in his clubs and hotels, trying to get his attention off you and bait him out. I turned most other families against him, but he just kept you under guard all the time."

He raised a finger and paused. His disdainful tone was maddening.

"That's when I thought of Marcelo. He's the best there is. Ruthless and completely obedient to his father's will. And he had no idea! That spoiled, tattooed little fuck! He just did as he was ordered."

"Massimo will find you, you piece of shit!" I growled.

"I sincerely doubt that," he replied with a slight smile.

"He will focus his fury on Marcelo. He was the one who

kidnapped you. Torricelli will come for him first. And then for the old man. Meanwhile, I'll become the head of the Matos family as the old fart's son-in-law." I started to giggle hysterically. I couldn't help myself. The man threw his glass at the wall, where it shattered into pieces. "What's so funny, bitch?!"

"You're an ass." I recalled Nacho's description of Amelia's husband. "Flavio. Now I remember. How could I not?" His hand shot out again, slamming into my face. The swelling grew. I couldn't see with one eye now.

Flavio's phone rang in his pocket. He pulled it out and took the call, listening for a while before hanging up and pushing the device back into his pocket.

"The situation has grown a bit more complicated," he growled. "It seems your husband is here."

My heart skipped a beat. Tears rolled down my face. I closed my eyes. *He's here. He's going to save me.* I smiled, but Flavio didn't notice. He was looking for something in the desk.

Then I heard a loud crash at the door. Massimo barged into the room, followed by Domenico and a dozen men. *Oh, God.* Here he was. My beautiful, powerful husband. I burst into tears. The Man in Black looked at me, and I saw an infinite depth of fury in his eyes. He was just a few feet away, and his pain-filled black eyes were trained on my bloody face. With a wild roar, he reached for his gun and aimed it at Flavio. In that very moment, two pairs of secret doors opened and a few dozen men stormed into the room. Nacho was among them. He froze, seeing the state I was in.

The last person to enter was Fernando Matos.

"Massimo Torricelli," he said calmly. The two groups were aiming guns at each other. "How nice to see you've accepted my invitation."

I felt someone's eyes on me. I looked around frantically. With guns held in both hands, Nacho stared at me, his eyes full of pain and despair. I knew he felt it was all his fault. That's when one of Matos's men put a gun to my head.

"Put your guns down," Fernando said. "Or he splatters her brains over the wall."

Massimo growled to his men. They lowered their weapons. The others followed—everyone aside from the man behind me.

All security guards and retainers left the room, commanded by Fernando Matos. Nacho headed toward me, trying to keep an impassive face. He patted the man behind me on the shoulder and they swapped places.

"Laura," he whispered as the gun touched my temple. "I'm sorry."

Tears streaked down my face, and my throat constricted. Massimo and Domenico faced Flavio and Fernando, and I wondered if this was my last day on Earth.

The four men talked, rooted to their respective spots. It looked like they arrived at some kind of an agreement. Then I heard my husband's calm voice. "Come to me, Laura."

Having understood the entire conversation, Nacho lowered his gun. Barely able to walk, I staggered to Massimo. When the Spaniard jumped to help me, Massimo's jaw clenched.

"Don't you touch her, you bastard," he growled, sending Marcelo a withering stare. Nacho released me and took a step back.

Before I reached the Man in Black, I heard a commotion. Out of the corner of my eye, I saw Flavio pull out a gun, aim it at Fernando Matos, and shoot the man dead. Another shot reverberated through the room at that same moment. I saw Flavio crumple to the floor and then felt my husband pull me behind himself, reaching out a hand and aiming his own gun at Nacho.

Nacho, who had just shot his future brother-in-law, after the man had killed his father.

I stayed behind Massimo, feeling the adrenaline in my veins subside, and my knees weaken. I was safe now. I was saved, and I didn't have to fight anymore. I slid to the ground. Massimo spun toward me and took me in his arms, leaving Domenico and Nacho to themselves.

Then I heard one last shot. I felt something hitting me, and then a wave of heat spilling all across my body. I couldn't breathe. Massimo's face was becoming blurry. My muscles all weakened, and I slid the rest of the way to the floor. My husband's face screwed up in a grimace of terror. He was saying something, but I couldn't hear him.

His lips were moving, and he lifted a bloodied hand to his face. My eyelids grew so heavy . . . I was drained. Exhausted. Blissful. Did my husband kiss me? Was he shouting now? The silence around me became complete. And nothing remained. I closed my eyes . . .

◇◇◇◇◇◇◇◇◇◇

"Massimo!" Domenico's voice brought me violently back to reality. "They can't wait any longer." His voice was calm and measured, but it felt like a scream.

I turned from the window behind which a group of doctors were looking at me expectantly.

"Save them both!" I hissed through clenched teeth, shaking with fury and fighting not to cry. "Both, or I kill every last one of you."

My bloody hands reached for my belt to grab my gun, but my brother stopped me.

"Brother," he whispered, tears rolling down his cheeks. "This has been going on for too long. They can't save both Laura and the child. We don't have any more time . . ."

I raised a hand, silencing him, and dropped to my knees, hiding my face in my hands.

Would I be able to raise my son without her? Would I be able to live without her myself? My child . . . a part of me. My heir and successor. Millions of thoughts flitted through my mind, but none of them brought any measure of solace.

I lifted my eyes and took a deep breath.

"Save . . ."

ACKNOWLEDGMENTS

As always, I would like to thank my parents. Mom, Dad—you are my inspiration, my love and my whole world. I love you so much and I can't imagine a life without you! Thank you for always being proud of me, even when I doubted.

I would like to thank the man who proved to me that age is just a number, that being an adult is a state of mind, and not a date on your ID. Maciej Buzała, darling, there are no words that would express my gratitude for your patience, care, and involvement. Those months were the hardest time of my life. Without you, I'd have given up. I love you, kid! Thank you for being there for me! Ania Szuber and Michał Czajka—thanks for making me look so great on the cover. Your photo is awesome and your talents unparalleled! And you're cheaper than a plastic surgeon.

But most of all, I'd like to thank you, dear reader. Whoever you are. I can only change the world because of you. I hope you liked the second book better than the first, and that you're already waiting for the third! Because the third one is going to be . . . incredible!